ENTER TH
EDGAR RICE BURROUGHS
UNIVERSE
™

A century before the term "crossover" became a buzzword in popular culture, Edgar Rice Burroughs created the first expansive, fully cohesive literary universe. Coexisting in this vast cosmos was a pantheon of immortal heroes and heroines—Tarzan of the Apes®, Jane Porter®, John Carter®, Dejah Thoris®, Carson Napier™, and David Innes™ being only the best known among them. In Burroughs' 80-plus novels, their epic adventures transported them to the strange and exotic worlds of Barsoom®, Amtor™, Pellucidar®, Caspak™, and Va-nah™, as well as the lost civilizations of Earth and even realms Beyond the Farthest Star™. Now the Edgar Rice Burroughs Universe expands in an all-new series of canonical novels written by today's talented authors!

KORAK™
AT THE EARTH'S CORE™

EDGAR RICE BURROUGHS UNIVERSE™

The Edgar Rice Burroughs Universe is the interconnected and cohesive literary cosmos created by the Master of Adventure and continued in new canonical works authorized by Edgar Rice Burroughs, Inc., the corporation based in Tarzana, California, that was founded by Burroughs in 1923. Unravel the mysteries and explore the wonders of the Edgar Rice Burroughs Universe alongside the pantheon of heroes and heroines that inhabit it in both classic tales of adventure penned by Burroughs and brand-new epics from today's talented authors.

TARZAN® SERIES

Tarzan of the Apes
The Return of Tarzan
The Beasts of Tarzan
The Son of Tarzan
Tarzan and the Jewels of Opar
Jungle Tales of Tarzan
Tarzan the Untamed
Tarzan the Terrible
Tarzan and the Golden Lion
Tarzan and the Ant Men
Tarzan, Lord of the Jungle
Tarzan and the Lost Empire
Tarzan at the Earth's Core
Tarzan the Invincible
Tarzan Triumphant
Tarzan and the City of Gold
Tarzan and the Lion Man
Tarzan and the Leopard Men
Tarzan's Quest
Tarzan and the Forbidden City
Tarzan the Magnificent
Tarzan and "The Foreign Legion"
Tarzan and the Madman
Tarzan and the Castaways
Tarzan and the Tarzan Twins
Tarzan: The Lost Adventure (with Joe R. Lansdale)

BARSOOM® SERIES

A Princess of Mars
The Gods of Mars
The Warlord of Mars
Thuvia, Maid of Mars
The Chessmen of Mars
The Master Mind of Mars
A Fighting Man of Mars
Swords of Mars
Synthetic Men of Mars
Llana of Gathol
John Carter of Mars

PELLUCIDAR® SERIES

At the Earth's Core
Pellucidar
Tanar of Pellucidar
Tarzan at the Earth's Core
Back to the Stone Age
Land of Terror
Savage Pellucidar

AMTOR™ SERIES

Pirates of Venus
Lost on Venus
Carson of Venus
Escape on Venus
The Wizard of Venus

ERBUNIVERSE.COM

ERB UNIVERSE™

The Dead Moon Super-Arc

by Win Scott Eckert

Korak at the Earth's Core

Pellucidar: Land of Awful Shadow

Tarzan Unleashed

Swords of Eternity Super-Arc

Carson of Venus: The Edge of All Worlds
by Matt Betts

Tarzan: Battle for Pellucidar
by Win Scott Eckert

John Carter of Mars: Gods of the Forgotten
by Geary Gravel

Victory Harben: Fires of Halos
by Christopher Paul Carey

Other ERB Universe Books

*A Princess of Mars:
Shadow of the Assassins*
by Ann Tonsor Zeddies

Mahars of Pellucidar
by John Eric Holmes

Red Axe of Pellucidar
by John Eric Holmes

Tarzan and the Forest of Stone
by Jeffrey J. Mariotte

Tarzan and the Dark Heart of Time
by Philip José Farmer

Tarzan and the Valley of Gold
by Fritz Leiber

*Cosmic Epics: Seminal Works
of Edgar Rice Burroughs*

*Savage Epics: Seminal Works
of Edgar Rice Burroughs*

EDGAR RICE BURROUGHS UNIVERSE™

KORAK™
AT THE EARTH'S CORE™

WIN SCOTT ECKERT

Includes the bonus novella

PELLUCIDAR®
DAWN OF THE DEATHSLAYER™

BY
CHRISTOPHER PAUL CAREY

EDGAR RICE BURROUGHS, INC.
Publishers
TARZANA   CALIFORNIA

KORAK AT THE EARTH'S CORE
© 2024 Edgar Rice Burroughs, Inc.

PELLUCIDAR: DAWN OF THE DEATHSLAYER
© 2024 Edgar Rice Burroughs, Inc.

Cover art by E. M. Gist © 2024 Edgar Rice Burroughs, Inc.
Map by Mike Wolfer © 2024 Edgar Rice Burroughs, Inc.

Trademarks Edgar Rice Burroughs®, Edgar Rice Burroughs Universe™, Enter the Edgar
Rice Burroughs Universe™, ERB Universe™, Korak™, Korak the Killer™, Tarzan®,
Tarzan of the Apes®, Lord of the Jungle®, Lord of the Apes™, King of the Apes™,
Tarzan and Jane®, John Clayton™, Lord Greystoke™, Tarzan Yell®; The Tarzan Twins™,
Jane Porter®, Jane Clayton™, Lady Greystoke™, Kala™, Kerchak™, Kavuru™,
Meriem™, Jad-bal-ja™, Nkima™, La of Opar™, Opar™, Gryf™, Mangani™,
Mugambi™, Terkoz™, John Carter®, Dejah Thoris®, Barsoom®, Jasoom™, Pellucidar®,
At the Earth's Core™, Land of Awful Shadow™, David Innes™, Abner Perry™,
Darva the Shadow™, Deathslayer™, Dian the Beautiful™, Jason Gridley™, Mahars™,
Carson of Venus®, Amtor™, The Land That Time Forgot®, Caspak™, Va-nah™,
Beyond the Farthest Star™, Victory Harben™, The Mucker™, and The Custers™
owned by Edgar Rice Burroughs, Inc. Associated logos (including the Doodad symbol;
Edgar Rice Burroughs Universe logo; Enter the Edgar Rice Burroughs Universe logo;
ERB, Inc., solar system colophon; and Korak logo), characters, names, and the distinctive
likenesses thereof are trademarks or registered trademarks of Edgar Rice Burroughs, Inc.

ERB Universe Creative Director: Christopher Paul Carey

Special thanks to Jason Scott Aiken, Steven K. Dowd, Win Scott Eckert,
E. M. Gist, Geary Gravel, the Kunstles (Amy, John, Rowan, and James),
Chuck "Kreegah" Loridans, Janet Mann, Demos Sachlas, James Sullos,
Jess Terrell, Cathy Wilbanks, Charlotte Wilbanks, Mike Wolfer, and
Bill Wormstedt for their valuable assistance in producing this book.

First paperback edition

Published by Edgar Rice Burroughs, Inc.
Tarzana, California
EdgarRiceBurroughs.com

ISBN-13: 978-1-945462-62-7

- 9 8 7 6 5 4 3 2 1 -

With sincere thanks to Edgar Rice Burroughs, Inc. for allowing this return trip to Pellucidar—and to ERB himself for creating these wonderful worlds and characters

I am indebted to John Eric Holmes for the characters and situations he created in his two Pellucidar novels, and to his son, Christopher West Holmes, for his kind encouragement to expand upon them

I am also deeply grateful to Mercedes Lackey for her creation of Mok the Sagoth, Dek, son of Kolk, and especially Mirina the bird-woman, "The One Who Fell" from the Dead World

This is for Lisa—without your support, encouragement, and love, nothing else is possible

CONTENTS

FOREWORD
A Mysterious Visitor

I T WAS AT AN OPEN HOUSE held at Edgar Rice Burroughs' old office in Tarzana, California, that I met *him* face to face.

I had been alone in Mr. Burroughs' back office, quietly perusing the incredible collection of that great man's literary achievements, as well as art prints and other items of deep interest to lifelong Burroughs readers and fans. I carefully thumbed through a first edition of *Tarzan at the Earth's Core*, taking in the thickness of the paper as the pages flipped past my thumb, the dark text against the slightly yellowed background upon which it was printed, and the wonderful sweet-woodsy scent—the bibliosmia—that filled the alcove in which I sat comfortably in a leather club chair.

I was lost in a ruminant frame of mind, musing upon worlds and times now lost to us—although we would always be able to travel to them by revisiting Mr. Burroughs' wondrous books. Finally, sighing and putting aside my retrospective mood, I returned the book to its proper place on the shelf and made my way to the next room, intent on rejoining my friends and the festivities at the front of the building.

As I passed the rear entrance that gave into the back alley, I saw a shadow flutter outside, for the door had been left ajar to allow guests ingress and egress.

Warily, and probably foolishly, I stepped outside to check and ensure that the lurker was not intent on nefarious activity, but no one was there. Perplexed, for I was sure I had seen something, I turned to reenter the office, and found myself staring directly at a tall, black-haired, muscular man of imposing demeanor.

His magnetism was undeniable, and I knew I was standing face to face with Tarzan of the Apes.

The ape-man handed me a thick envelope and said, "This is a follow-up to your last novel." Of a sudden, someone from the festivities called to me and I turned my head for the briefest of moments. When I turned back, the Lord of the Jungle had gone, as silently as Usha the wind.

After the party had concluded, and we had straightened up the office in the wake of the guests' departure, I confided what had happened to my hosts. To their credit, they did not snort in disbelief, for their offices had of late been the site of other most interesting visitations and peculiar communications.

With the blessing of my hosts—the overseers of Mr. Burroughs' legacy at Edgar Rice Burroughs, Inc.—I converted the detailed notes from the package to novel format, and the resulting book you now hold in your hands. According to Tarzan's wishes, and due to the length of the remaining manuscript, it is anticipated that two more books will encompass what the company has chosen to call the "Dead Moon Super-Arc," which may be considered to be a somewhat fantastical nomenclature, but in the end is entirely accurate, as it involves the epic adventures of Korak, Meriem, their daughter Suzanne and her mate Lordan, their son Rahnak and the Waziri warrior princess Kyrianji, as well as Emperor David Innes and his daughter Dav-An, and Wolff Hines . . . not to mention a certain Lord of the Jungle and his devoted mate, Jane.

I do confess that upon completion of the narrative, I was left with a sense of wistfulness, for the events described had occurred a little more than fifty years in the past. Knowing that the Lord of the Jungle had returned eventually to the outer crust, I could not help but wonder what adventures he and Jane and other members of the Clayton family might have experienced in, for instance, the last thirty or forty years.

Or, for that matter, within the last ten years?

For all of Tarzan's skills, and for all of Korak's wiliness, Meriem's spunk, and Jane's steadfastness, how could they avoid detection in the modern world? A world in which satellites track our every movement, where cameras mounted on businesses and hospitals, and hotels and private homes, and freeways and traffic intersections, record every move we make . . . A world in which facial recognition, biometric scans, and DNA analysis, are the norm . . . How were the Greystokes supposed to function in this world?

Or did they count Pellucidar as their permanent abode, and had Tarzan and the others only made brief sojourns to the outer world in order to convey their exploits to me, and to perhaps briefly address other pressing matters?

One might wonder why I stated that these thoughts put me in a blue funk. Like any human driven by curiosity and a sense of wonder, I wanted to *know*. I knew the ape-man still lived, but I wanted to know of his latest adventures and circumstances. I can only hope that one day we *shall* know.

And yet now I draw myself from such speculations, for at least I do know *this* whole adventure, while for the moment you must content yourself with only the first part. Rest assured, parts two and three are well in hand, and will be in *your* hands sooner rather than later.

WIN SCOTT ECKERT
In the mountains of Colorado
September 2023

PELLUCIDAR

HIME

AMIOCAP

KORSAR AZ

TANDAR

ZURTS

THE TERRIBLE MOUNTAINS

SUVI

KALI

LURAL AZ

AMOZ

THOTRA

KAZRA

LIDI PLAINS

LAND OF AWFUL SHADOW

SARI

GREENWICH

ANOROC IS.

PHUTRA

THURIA

LUANA IS.

HOOJA'S IS.

ISLE OF TREES

UNFRIENDLY IS.

SOJAR AZ

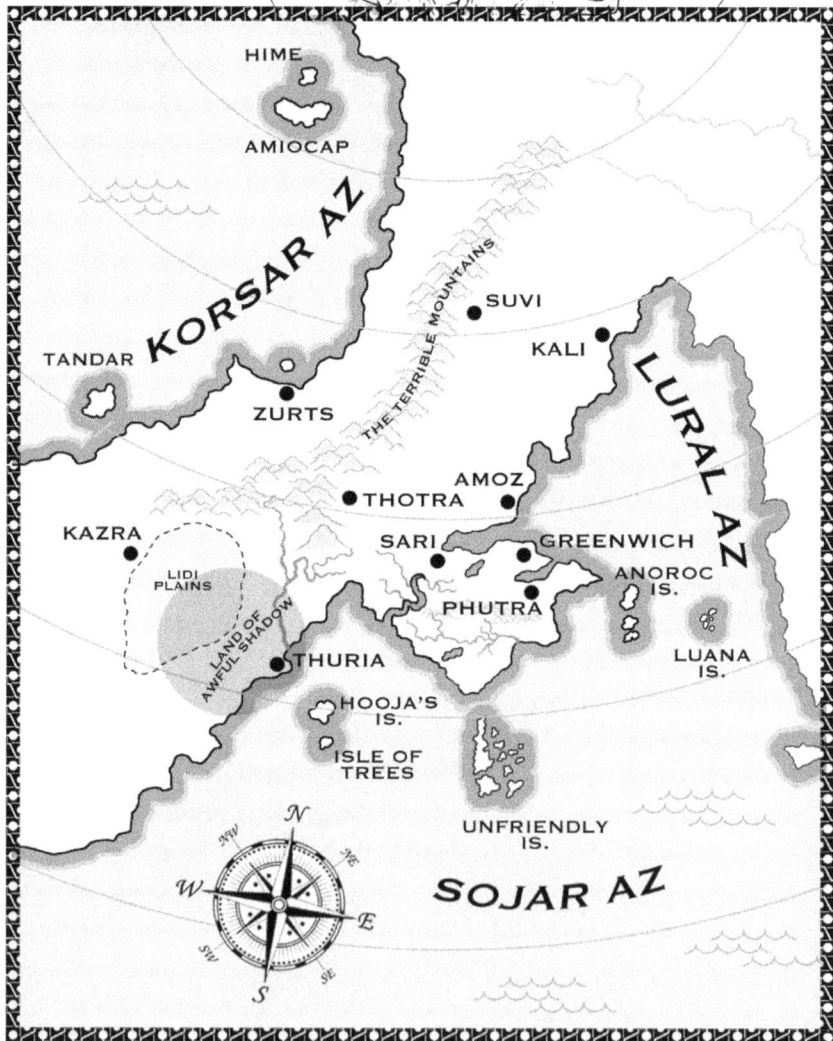

DETAIL OF PELLUCIDAR AS DESCRIBED BY DAVID INNES AND KORAK VIA
GRIDLEY WAVE TRANSMISSIONS RECEIVED AT THE OFFICES OF EDGAR RICE
BURROUGHS, INC., IN TARZANA, CALIFORNIA.

1

THE HORIBS ATTACK!

KORAK THE KILLER, Akut, and von Horst braced themselves against the onrushing horde of Gorobors, ten in all, astride which were twelve armed Horibs, the terrible snake-men of the inner world.

Korak, under the blinding rays of Pellucidar's eternal central orb, leaped from the back of Old White—von Horst's faithful woolly mammoth—and crashed upon one of the opposing riders, tumbling them both to the sunbaked earth. Korak hammered a punishing roundhouse punch to the thing's snout, his fist, bronzed by years under the African sun, crunching the bone beneath the Horib's scaly skin. Its yellow eyes, black pupils vertically slitted, slid upward in its bony sockets. Before the snake-man could recover its wits, Korak's steel hunting knife quested for and found the fleshy gap between its thick neck and lightly scaled cranium; the ape-man savagely thrust the blade inward and upward, piercing its windpipe and an artery. Snake blood jetted from the Horib's throat as Korak, grimacing with effort, twisted the knife further upward into the beast's skull and speared its brain, dealing a final death strike.

Korak tossed the carcass aside and evinced a weird, silent "cry," raising his arms and head to the heavens—his signature upon a kill. There was no time for further victory ritual, as the eleven remaining Horibs, momentarily shocked still at their comrade's swift defeat and death, recovered their collective wits and closed in for battle, circling the three defenders

1

on their huge Gorobor mounts, in the manner of the horse-riding Indigenous peoples of North America.

Abner Perry, were he present, would have expounded the facts that Gorobors were related to the tetrapodic anomodont reptiles of the Late Permian and Triassic, otherwise known as Pareiasaurus, with bony triangle-shaped skulls containing multiple rows of teeth, and were of a mass and dimension capable of carrying one or more humanoid-sized Horibs, and that they were among the swiftest creatures in all of the inner world of Pellucidar, rendering the possibility of escape on foot well-nigh impossible.

A battle of eleven against three constituted, perhaps, long odds. Korak, Akut, and von Horst sized up the situation, and then each acted, their deeds taking a tenth of the time of that consumed in the telling.

Akut, still astride loyal Old White, launched himself at the closest circling Horib. The latter was garbed in a simple sleeveless tunic belted at the waist and reaching almost to the knees of the rather shapeless legs. Grabbing the Horib's lance in one paw, Akut tore away the creature's leather belt with the other and whipped the tunic over the snake-man's horned head, blinding him. Akut's strong Mangani jaws clamped about the other's throat, huge fangs sinking deep into the snakelike flesh. The Horib's neck crunched. For added good measure, Akut thrust the lance repeatedly into his opponent's torso, ensuring to his satisfaction that no spark of life remained in the snake-man. The Mangani, astride the late Horib's mount, swung the creature's corpse about him in several revolutions and let it fly, knocking an adjacent snake-man from his Gorobor.

Von Horst—Frederich Wilhelm Eric von Mendeldorf und von Horst, leader of the nearby village of Lo-har—leaped from the back of Old White upon the dislodged Horib and ran him through with his spear. He was loath to leave the side of his loyal mammoth, but judged that in this case the best defense would be a strong, rapid assault. The blond-maned German looked up from his kill, assessing the next front in their battle, and observed Korak running—fleeing!—up through an adjacent narrow canyon.

Korak the Killer, for his part, was cursing himself soundly for leaving his Enfield rifle on the O-220 when they had briefly disembarked at Lo-har. He sprinted up the rocky canyon, long spear held firmly in his hand, the eternal central sun of the hollow inner world glinting off his well-muscled, sculpted physique and bronzed hide, covered only by a simple leopard-skin loincloth, and casting subtle brown highlights in his tousled head of black hair. A leather quiver filled with arrows hung from his back, and in his left hand he carried a bow. From a belt at his waist hung a leather sheath in which was secured a steel hunting knife, a gift from his father.

The bow and arrows and the spear were from von Horst and his people, provided to Korak after the vacuum airship had inexplicably stranded him and Akut at Lo-har; they had been landed in the small village for a matter of only minutes—or at least what seemed a matter of only minutes in timeless Pellucidar—before Akut had raised the alarm and Korak had turned to see the O-220 speeding away in a southerly direction.

Now, in the canyon, Korak scrambled nimbly over rocky terrain. The soil was red clay, with rust-colored rock formations thrusting from the uneven ground at weird angles. The three—Korak, Akut, and von Horst—had been turned aside from the vertical declivity at the far end of the canyon, as they had been making their way from Lo-har to the coast of the Lural Az. They had been forced to trace a long, winding downward path around the ravine, eventually turning back in the direction toward the sea that was their ultimate destination, and thereafter making the mouth of the canyon—where they had been confronted by the dozen ravening Horibs.

Korak scrambled upward, the margins of the canyon narrowing on either side of him, until at the far end a sheer cliff face halted his progress. The ape-man's gray eyes surveyed the surface of the rock, descrying no viable handholds in the granite face for at least twenty feet above him.

He turned, scanning the descending chasm up which he had just raced. There was no sight of pursuit from the remaining Horibs, nor any sign of Akut or von Horst. He feared the worst, that the insidious snake-men had bested his Mangani friend and mentor, Akut, and their newfound ally, von Horst. But, if his companions had been defeated, surely the remaining Horibs would have pursued him up the narrow canyon by now.

Korak sprinted back toward the mouth of the gorge, as swiftly as his strong legs would carry him.

Von Horst yanked another Horib from his seat upon his Gorobor, the snake-man pulled down by his own lance when he foolishly failed to release it from his grasp. The Horibs were less imposing when faced on the ground, deprived of the advantage provided by their speedy mounts. The snake-men's legs were shapeless and wobbly, supported by three-toed feet. They were better formed from the waist up, with arm musculature almost matching that of humans, and five-fingered hands, but it was obvious they were at their best when astride their Gorobors. Or at least so it seemed to von Horst, who, being a *gilak*, as the humans of the inner world called themselves, admittedly knew little about the mysterious snake-men.

Just as the downed Horib regained his feet, von Horst swept his spear low and horizontally, taking the creature down at the ankles. He stabbed it in the gut and stomped on the thing's neck, eliciting a sharp crack and a final hissing exhalation as the creature breathed its last.

Von Horst saw Akut clinging to a Horib's back, fangs ripping at scaly skin and clawed fingers tearing at and plucking out the snake-man's eyeballs, and ripping the horns out of its skull by the roots. The Horib, blinded, roared in pain, and Akut dispatched it by tossing it under the squat, thundering legs of an onrushing orange-and-green-striped Gorobor.

Akut and Von Horst dove out of the way of the speeding

anomodont and they both crouched, backs up against a huge boulder.

Von Horst confronted Korak's mentor. "Your friend has deserted us!" The German spoke in Akut's Mangani language, for he had picked up the lingo in various past encounters with the imposing Sagoths of Pellucidar, who also spoke in the tongue of the great apes. "Is this the way of the son of the great Tarzan of the Apes?"

Akut growled menacingly in response. Horib blood stained his otherwise white fangs. Then: "More *slizaks* come. We fight later."

Von Horst knew the great ape was correct; there were at least seven opponents left, by his count, and they were regrouping for a coordinated attack. Von Horst and Akut took defensive stances and prepared to make a stand, the German's spear raised in defiance at the battle to come. Now that the snake-men had reformed their ranks, the defenders' guerrilla-style attacks would prove much less effective, and they would likely be overwhelmed by the uneven numbers.

The Horibs placed their mounts in a semicircle around the boulder, cutting off the possibility of escape from either side. The lead snake-man, charging on his Gorobor, stabbed at Akut with his lance as he rode by, but, having observed the Mangani's previous tactics, avoided allowing the great ape to grab the weapon and disarm him. The Horibs continued this pattern of charge and retreat, charge and retreat, inflicting cut after cut. Von Horst's spear, expertly cast, removed another reptile-man from the field of battle, but now the two defenders, without any weapons other than their hands and fingers and teeth, began to succumb to the relentless pattern of cut and retreat. Both were bleeding and weakened from multiple wounds.

"I say again," von Horst breathed, "where is Korak?"

Korak the Killer emerged at the mouth of the canyon, taking in the dire scene before him.

A flash of rage swept over him, and he saw red, shaking his self-control. Hot sweat dripped from his forehead, and his heart pounded uncontrollably. Nothing—absolutely *nothing*—would come between him and saving his friends. He once again regretted the absence of his Enfield rifle, and then his head swam. He thought he had shaken it off, and then believed he felt the comforting weight of the rifle in his hands: a short magazine Lee–Enfield Mk III, issued to British troops, of which he had been one, during World War I. It was said the rifle could be fired quickly enough that some German troops, encountering fire from the Tommies equipped with this model, reported coming under machine-gun fire. It had served John "Jack" Clayton—Korak the Killer—quite reliably over the decades, saving his life more than once.

Now, the Enfield was doing its bloody job, decimating the Horibs, rapidly firing at and slaughtering the hideous snake-men.

Chameleon-like, the Horibs shimmered before his eyes and morphed. Korak now blasted away at enemy German soldiers, fighting on the front of the Meuse-Argonne offensive in the twilight months of the Great War. He looked behind him and saw his mangled biplane, a Royal Aircraft Factory S.E.5 (Scout Experimental 5), an RAF fighter that was fast, maneuverable, and tough, able to endure high-speed attack dives. Well, that was a tough break; his aircraft was a total loss. He had originally trained in the Royal Naval Air Service, and then was appointed to a renowned British squadron when the combined Royal Air Force was formed in April 1918, but for the Argonne operation he had been attached to an American unit, carrying out bombing raids behind the front lines against German concentrations, going on strafing runs to obliterate machine gun nests, and conducting aerial reconnaissance to observe enemy movements.

Now, his plane wrecked, with no way to return to his unit, he had joined the First Army on the ground, the ranks of the Allies fighting to take the Argonne front, foot by foot, mile by mile, battling as best as he was able to with his Enfield and his wits and his bare hands if necessary.

The days and nights and weeks had blurred into one, a mixture of blood, and mud, and blown off limbs, and exhaustion, and the cries and screams of men—boys, really. The American approach of open warfare reigned, breaking the three-year stalemate characterized by the French and British trench warfare tactics, and to Korak's mind this was the better method, meeting the enemy bayonet to bayonet, knife to knife, hand to hand if needed. It was brutal, mean, and vicious, and the years he had been lost in the African jungles, wandering with Akut, had well prepared him for it.

On one occasion, Lieutenant Clayton, his superiors having recognized a certain ferociousness in his approach, had been sent to take out a particularly troublesome defensive machine-gun nest. Machine guns opening fire on advancing infantry had had a disastrous effect on soldiers who got bogged down in the mud or caught up in thickets of barbed wire, making them easy targets. Bombardments had failed to eliminate the threat, and in recognition of Clayton's talents for stealth, forest craft, and all-around ruthlessness, he was sent on a one-man mission, a gamble that he might succeed where the bombardiers had failed. And if the lieutenant didn't return, well, it was the loss of only one man, after all.

Korak had reached the nest by traveling from tree to tree in the dense Argonne Forest, and peered down on the nest in question from high in the branches above. The nest was dug into the dirt, bounded by and hardened with sandbags, behind which ten German troops took shelter and alternated manning the hot weapon.

Although he would have preferred to put a stop to the hot lead churning up the bodies of his comrades immediately, the quiet approach was more prudent.

Korak had targeted the resting soldiers who were crouched at one end of the protected enclosure of the nest. He slipped in, and, with his left hand clasped about the unfortunate's mouth, with his right thrust his knife between the man's ribs. The lieutenant dragged the man into the trees, his comrades none the wiser, as the shrieking noise of the machine gun drowned out everything around them and dulled their senses. Korak made sure the man was dead, and then repeated the gruesome process, either stabbing the enemy soldiers in the heart or slitting their throats before they even knew what was happening to them.

There were four German soldiers remaining, crewing the water-cooled Maschinengewehr 08. They had finally noticed something was amiss when the crew of four was mysteriously reduced to three. One of them drew his pistol as Korak approached, only to receive an expertly thrown commando knife in the throat. The man in the gunnery position, realizing his peril, stopped firing and came at Korak with his knife drawn, while his comrade dropped his binoculars and struggled to free his Luger from its holster.

Korak grasped the gunner's wrist and snapped it, causing the latter to drop the knife. As the man writhed in pain, Korak took the man by the head and snapped his neck. The last remaining enemy soldier, failing to free his pistol, which had snagged in his gun belt, repeatedly clubbed Korak on the head with his binoculars, knocking him solidly out.

When Korak had come to, he was tied to a tree. His head pounded mercilessly. The German soldier stood over the lieutenant. He smiled, said, "Awake now, eh?" and punched the ape-man viciously in the mouth.

Korak spat out blood and smiled back, as if to say, "Do your worst."

The German, his lips still twisted in a sneer, said, "You will not be smiling after a while, my friend. I am of the Landsknechte; therefore, your fate is sealed." The man withdrew a *kriegsmesser*, a "war knife," a curved weapon about a foot and a half in length, from a sheath strapped to his forearm.

"That's not standard issue," Korak said in German, his tone dry and calm.

"Indeed not, my friend. I told you, I am Landsknechte. My family have been warriors for centuries." He held the kriegsmesser two-handed. "This is our weapon of choice."

The blade flashed, expertly wielded by the German, and Korak bled from a sharp cut on the cheek, just under his left eye.

"You missed," the lieutenant said.

The German chuckled. "Oh no, my friend, not at all. We are just getting started, yes?"

"Don't you have better things to do?" Korak asked. "After all, there is a war on."

The other man laughed out loud. "Hadn't you heard? No, of course not, you were unconscious for almost a day. I do hope you are not concussed. Well, I do not have anything better to do. Armistice has been declared! At eleven o'clock this morning, we shall all lay down our arms and go home.

"But first, my friend, for killing my comrades, and my cousin, you will die at 10:59."

For the next fifteen minutes, the German used his booted feet, his fists, and his "war knife" to particular ill effect upon the son of Tarzan. Korak's lips were swollen, his nose smashed and bloodied, and his eyes bruised, and his vision blurred. His fingertips were blistered from the flame of the German's lighter. His body was covered in innumerable cuts of varying depths, some oozing blood, others bleeding profusely. He would bleed out soon if not treated.

"You are tough, my friend. Others who have been kissed by my war knife have either passed out by now, or have begged for the mercy of a killing blow."

Korak uttered a rude oath in the Mangani language. Unseen by the German, his nimble fingers worked at the knotted rope binding his wrists behind the bole of the tree.

"What was that?" the German taunted. "Some kind of debased grunting is coming from your ruined mouth."

The man looked up, cocked his head.

They both heard it: the sound, several yards away, of heavy

boots clomping though the thick trees and dense underbrush. And voices, soldiers speaking English in a distinctly recognizable American accent.

"Well, my friend," the German whispered, "this is it for you." He raised the war knife, ready to plunge it into Korak's chest.

The ape-man's left arm shot forward, grasping the other's knife hand by the wrist, halting the point of the kriegsmesser a half inch from his breast. He squeezed, and the German gritted his teeth.

"Don't cry out," the lieutenant warned, "or those soldiers will be on you in less than a minute."

The German grimaced and attempted a final thrust, only to be held fast by the ape-man's implacable thews, hardened by years battling the endless perils of life in the jungle. He was always ready to kill—or be killed.

Korak tightened his grip further, and the other man's wrist bones gave a satisfying crunch. The German cried out, involuntarily. The nearby soldiers' voices raised, indistinctly, and the tromping of their boots grew louder.

The German had dropped the war knife in the dirt. He looked frantically behind him, in the direction of the approaching American voices, grabbed the knife with his good hand, and managed to sheath it.

He put his face close to the lieutenant's, showering the ape-man with stinking breath and spittle. "Don't ever forget, this is the face of the man who bested you, Hans Kriegmesser. My face and voice will always haunt you."

Kriegmesser took off into the forest.

Korak's field of vision shimmered again in undulating, disorienting waves, and once again he was in Pellucidar, armed with his Enfield rifle, blasting away at the attacking Horibs.

The ape-man mentally shook himself out of it. This is not real, he told himself. My Enfield is gone. There is no shooting.

After the Great War, Tarzan and Jane had made sure Korak had had the best doctors. Childhood trauma and attachment issues, the physicians had said. But he was the only one who could heal himself. And he had—he had not experienced a traumatic flashback such as this in some four decades.

Less than a second had passed. He was at the mouth of the canyon in Pellucidar.

The terrible Horibs still threatened his friends.

The ape-man commandeered a stray Gorobor, left at loose ends after the death of its master, turned the beast, and headed back up the canyon. He looked behind and observed with satisfaction that five of the remaining six Horibs raced in pursuit, astride their mounts. The last Horib stayed on guard over von Horst and Akut, and Korak felt there was little danger to his companions from one snake-man—at least little danger compared to the dire straits in which they had found themselves moments ago.

Korak urged his mount on to greater and greater speeds, and soon the cliff wall bounding the far end of the gorge came into view. Behind, he heard a terrible hissing-whooping, presumably a victory cry of the pursuing snake-men, for to where could their quarry escape? It was a dead end.

The ape-man stood up upon the Gorobor's backside, which fortunately was fairly flat, or rather, flat enough for his flexible feet and toes, so accustomed to jungle branches, to balance and maintain a sure-footed stance. He quickly glanced back again and was reassured that his Gorobor was keeping a steady lead ahead of their pursuers. Facing front again, he saw the sheer cliff face coming closer and closer as they raced for it at the tetropod's top speed.

2
HIJACKED

CAPTAIN HEINRICH HINES, commander of the airship O-220, did his best to look his captor in the eyes, but he was constrained by the wrong end of the automatic shoved against the side of his neck.

"Alex, what is this all about?"

"Shut up, old man," Alexandra Ryadinsky replied. "And make sure your son follows my orders, or I'll paint the walls of the bridge with your brains.

"Wolff," she said, addressing the young blond officer at the helm, "retract the cables and prepare to lift off. Keep it quiet. Hands away from the intercom. Just do your job and your dad gets to keep his brains."

Wolff Hines, newly installed as the helmsman of the O-220, glanced back at his father.

"Don't do it, son," Hines ordered.

Ryadinsky shoved the barrel of her gun deeper into the older man's neck, and he winced in pain.

"I'm sorry, Dad," Wolff said. "She's leaving me no choice."

"Smart boy," Alex said. "Get moving, and keep it smooth. I want us in the air before anyone realizes what's happening. Got it?"

"Got it, Alex," Wolff replied, and made to comply with her orders. Automatic clamps released at the ends of the docking cables, and the magnificent airship slowly began to rise. Wolff maintained stability and controlled the airship's ascent carefully, and slowly, so that none aboard felt a difference in attitude or elevation.

"What's next?" he asked.

"Don't do it, Wolff," Hines said, and in response Ryadinsky pistol-whipped him across the back of the skull. The captain slumped back in his chair, unconscious.

"Do it, Wolff," she ordered. "Nice and steady. He's just knocked out; he'll be all right. Slowly turn the ship as we rise and set course for Thuria."

"Thuria!" the young man exclaimed. "But that's where we were headed for anyway."

"What's your point? Keep your mouth shut and do it."

Wolff Hines complied, and glancing out the port side of the bridge's wide, curved pane of transparent Harbenite, he saw Korak and Akut on the ground, racing after the departing dirigible, followed closely by von Horst and some of his Lo-harian tribesmen.

The young man turned his eyes away with regret and activated forward-thrust propellers, piloting the dirigible away from Lo-har at top speed.

Wolff Hines was perplexed, for Alex and her group of fellow hijackers had ordered the O-220's course be set for Thuria, at the verge of the Land of Awful Shadow—and this already had been the airship's ultimate destination, save for a brief planned stop at Sari to drop off Dav-An Innes, daughter of David Innes and Dian the Beautiful.

Their mission to Thuria was a dual one: deliver a large tribe of Mangani to a new settlement on the very edge of the Land of Awful Shadow, situated just adjacent to Thuria, and, even more urgently, hunt for Korak's daughter, Suzanne Clayton, who was recently reported missing in the area.

Suzanne had been leading the charge to relocate as many of Africa's great apes—the Mangani—to Pellucidar as possible, given their homeland jungle and forest habitats were being wiped out by encroaching "modern civilization." The verge of the Land of Awful Shadow, and the territory of the tribe of Thuria, had been selected to help the Mangani acclimate to the inner world, given that the great apes could easily go back and forth between the perpetual daylight cast by Pellucidar's central orb and the perpetual shadow cast by the small pendent world hanging stationary one mile above the surface—the Dead World—thus simulating the outer world's day and night, and easing their transition.

In fact, the name "Thuria" in the common tongue of Pellucidar translated roughly to "verge" or "transition" in English. The people of Thuria were the only natives in all of Pellucidar who were accustomed to darkness as well as daylight, although, unlike inhabitants of the outer crust, they were not at the mercy of a rising and setting sun; all they had to do, to experience light or dark, was to walk back and forth across the verge.

Although the Thurians were well adapted to their land and its idiosyncrasies, other denizens of Pellucidar attached legend and myth to the area. As Wolff understood it, the Land of Awful Shadow was situated beneath the so-called Dead World, which hung in an unerring geosynchronous orbit between Pellucidar's eternal sun and the land below it. Abner Perry had once called it a "moon" of Pellucidar, or a tiny planet within a planet.

Because this land was always in the Dead World's shadow, it had developed different flora and fauna from that found in other parts of the inner world. For instance, the *lidi*, known in the outer world as the diplodocus, were herbivores once found nowhere else but the Lidi Plains in the dark country. Now they were used as beasts of burden throughout the Federated Kingdoms of Pellucidar. At up to a hundred feet long, with small heads at the end of long necks some forty feet above the ground, the lidi's movements upon their robust legs appeared sluggish, but they were so massive that they were able to cover long distances relatively quickly, carrying both gilaks and supplies.

Suzanne Clayton's mission was not a solo effort, by any means. Along with the coordinating and supporting efforts of her parents and grandparents, and the crews of the airships O-220 and *Favonia*, she had recruited allied Sagoths to assist the Mangani in their transition to life within the hollow Earth. Tarzan had always suspected an ancient relationship between the great apes of the outer crust and the gorilla-people of Pellucidar, for both spoke dialects of the Mangani language and could easily understand one another. Of course, the Sagoths also spoke the common Pellucidarian tongue (which must have had regional variants given Pellucidar's vast size), as well as the sign language used to communicate with the Mahars.

A Sagoth named Tar-gash had willingly migrated with his tribes to Thuria, to settle there with the Mangani and help them acclimate, and hopefully thrive in their new home. A second Sagoth also joined in the effort. This was Mok, who had been raised among an isolated tribe of Sagoths, and later, upon being orphaned and then discovered by David Innes and Abner Perry, had been taken in by Golk, son of Goork, the king of Thuria. Having been raised alongside gilak tribesmen and apart from any others of his kind, Mok had not known that many Sagoths were indeed intelligent and good-hearted; not all were beholden to the dreaded Mahars.*

This was a true mission of mercy, Wolff thought. What was Alex up to? Why would she want to interfere in that?

He heard his father, Captain Hines, stirring in the captain's chair behind him. At least Alex had allowed the ship's medic to treat his wound and monitor for signs of a concussion. But he was tied securely to the seat. Wolff vowed that Alex would get her due.

Captain Hines spoke, his voice weak. "What's this all about,

---

* Mercedes Lackey's short story "The Fallen: A Tale of Pellucidar" introduces Mok the Sagoth, as well Dek, son of Kolk, and Dek's mate Mirina. See page 275 of this book for where to read this story online for free.

Alex? I know your parents. I've known you since you were a little girl. What is happening here? What happened to you?"

"What happened to me?" she said. "You just don't get it. My parents and I, my whole family, have been playing the long game. The really, really long game. And it's all coming to fruition now."

"Your parents," the captain replied, "have been dear friends of ours for quite a while. Are you saying they are not who we all thought they were?"

Alex only smirked. She was attractive in a tough way, tall and blonde. The smirk did not enhance her looks.

"So," Hines continued, "it was all a sham. The Ryadinsky family emigrating to America before the Russian Revolution . . ."

"Of course," Alex said. "We only came to the U.S. after the war in Europe. And we're not Russian—or Jewish."

"We embraced you," Hines said, sadness evident in his voice.

"That was your mistake, old man."

Wolff decided to try to alter the trajectory of the discussion. "Alex, since you won't explain yourself, clearly, can you at least reassure us that our passengers and supercargo are safe?"

"Well now," she said. "I was waiting for this one. Don't you worry your gorgeous little blond head, Wolff. Your precious princess Dav-An is safe and sound. Just as long as you keep on doing what I tell you, we won't harm a single hair on her head."

"She's not my precious princess—"

"Come off it. You never gave me a second thought, but she waltzes into your life and it's bye-bye Alex."

"For God's sake, Alex, what are you talking about? You're like a sister to me."

Alex gave a nasty little laugh. "Yeah, I guess you did always feel that way. Too late now."

Wolff sighed. "So, what about the rest of the crew and the passengers?"

"The crew are all safe, under guard and confined to their bunk rooms. The Mangani are all gathered in the hangar bay, along with your precious airship's most excellent Waziri security force—who were all caught entirely off guard and are completely disarmed. You should hire better mercenaries next time, guys. We control the whole ship. The radio operator has been confined and the Gridley Wave radio apparatus has been smashed. My people have taken over key positions shipwide, while I've held you both hostage here on the bridge. Face it, you don't have a chance.

"Just keep doing what I say, and you'll all be fine—even your little princess Dav-An."

3

L.A. CONFIDENTIAL

THE SUN HAD LONG SET upon downtown Los Angeles when Meriem Clayton stepped into the taxi on Grand Avenue, gave the cabbie an address in Santa Monica, and told him to step on it.

"There's an extra twenty in it for you if you make it in thirty minutes." Her accent was exotic, a mixture of French, Arabian, and British English.

The cabbie took one look at her in the rearview mirror and, heeding her resolute expression and the grim set of her jaw, hit the gas. "You got it, lady!"

Meriem was a petite fury, madder than hell at her husband, Korak, and didn't care who knew it. He was supposed to have come to pick her up in California aboard the O-220 so they could travel together to Pellucidar. Meriem, a celebrated opera singer, was in Los Angeles on a "farewell tour" with the New York City Opera company; in fact, it was her last performance, as she planned to retire both from singing and from public life.

And Korak had missed it.

Somehow, she had gotten through the opera, Puccini's *Tosca*, despite her overwhelming worry at the news that her daughter, Suzanne, had gone missing. She had had no choice but to go on with her last performance; no lie would have held against the media scrutiny that would have been engendered over the famous opera diva missing her final show. She couldn't exactly say she was off to rescue her daughter Suzanne, who had been officially listed as missing and

18

presumed killed in action in World War II, almost thirty years prior.

Korak had not been there to support her. Her dark eyes blazed with anger as she thought about how he had abandoned her. He had decided to skip picking up Meriem when David Innes, using the Gridley Wave, had informed them both of their daughter Suzanne's disappearance. Korak, instead of coming from Africa to California as planned to pick up Meriem after her crowning performance, the conclusion of a remarkable singing career, had departed from Africa straight for Pellucidar with a full load of Mangani and other endangered animals.

Meriem brushed her black hair from her eyes as it blew about in the wind from the taxi's half-open rear window. Her hair was cut in the current "blunt bangs" style: fashionable, and easy to care for. The five-foot-five spitfire cared about her appearance, but she didn't want something elaborate that she'd have to put a lot of time and effort into maintaining. She shook her head; damn it all, of course she was worried sick about Suzanne. But she couldn't see how picking her up in the O-220, as long planned, would add any significant time to the overall trip. She knew the dirigible's capabilities well enough, and had a deep trust in Captain Hines that he would push it to the limit to get to the inner world in record time.

Now the whole initiative, the entire plan, years in the making, was in jeopardy, being changed on the fly. Rather than her planting with certain media organizations the news of her and Korak's—that is, Jack Clayton's—demise in a Pacific Ocean light plane crash off the California coast, a few days hence, she'd have to initiate the plan sooner, due to Korak's premature departure. She didn't like last-minute changes in plans, particularly a subterfuge as crucial as this one: namely, faking their deaths and creating new lives under different names and identities.

Even back in 1944, Tarzan's wartime compatriots in the

Far East had thought it odd that he hadn't visibly aged, and that he could perform in active service at his age. Tarzan had navigated successfully around that situation. Staying alive had been more important than convincing them of the truth of the stories he had conveyed to them, of the African witch doctor who had granted him perpetual youth—though the cost had been ingesting a sickening brew that had made him violently ill for a month—and of the Kavuru tribe who had independently come up with a life-extension elixir. She and Korak, and her children Suzanne and Jackie, and Jane, and her sister-in-law Charlotte, and even little Nkima, were all beneficiaries of those longevity pills, for an American doctor friend of Tarzan had succeeded in artificially synthesizing and reproducing the elixir from inorganic compounds, thus eliminating the gruesome manner in which the Kavuru tribespeople had created the mixture—by the wanton murder of young girls for the purpose of extracting certain glands to be used in the process.

Tarzan had sometimes expressed that it might have been better if they had never discovered the secret of longevity, and that death was a part of life and the law of the jungle. Overpopulation, famine, and misery would be the result if the secret got out.

Too, Tarzan was a Trickster and could not resist cheating Old Man Time himself. When placed in the position he had been, should he have been expected to turn it down? It was unavoidable that he would remain young, from the witch doctor treatment in which he had initially disbelieved. Should he watch while his immediate family grew old and died, while he lived on? Of course not, not when an ethical manner of concocting the Kavuru pills existed.

Perhaps, when denizens of Earth established meaningful relations with scientists on Barsoom or Amtor, where life spans were significantly longer than those of Earthlings, secrets of longevity would be shared and sweeping change would engulf the world of Tarzan's birth.

But that was not for the ape-man to decide one way or another.

If people had been taking note of Tarzan's unnaturally youthful appearance back in 1944, Meriem mused, imagine the situation several decades later. In Meriem's opinion, they had all let it go on too long and should have disappeared years before. But what was done was done, a situation in which the cliché "better late than never" was more applicable than it ever had been.

What if unscrupulous individuals decided the Greystokes did have the secret to eternal youth? Tarzan, and the rest of them, would be hounded to the ends of the earth. One of them certainly would end up being captured. The women would be targeted, Jane and Charlotte and Meriem herself, and held hostage, with the price being Tarzan and Korak handing over the formula. In fact, such an incident had already happened. As far back as 1918, an eccentric American billionaire, James D. Stonecraft, had gotten wind of the story of Tarzan's African witch doctor brew, and had hired big game hunters to bring in the biggest game of all—Lord Greystoke. Stonecraft had wanted the secret of immortality, but like so many who crossed the ape-man, all he had found was death.*

If it had happened then, it could happen again, here and now. Arranging records and creating paper trails of false deaths was the only solution. Even now, certain parties had started to get a little too close to the family and their secrets. And secrets were harder to maintain now than they had been fifty or sixty years ago. Edwardian mores dictated that Lord Greystoke's peers and colleagues didn't pry too closely, or ask awkward questions, when certain things didn't line up. It just wasn't done. And to be fair, Tarzan and Jane had done remarkably well at lying low and covering their tracks. Even Meriem couldn't believe that they had gotten away with the story they had spread about Korak after "the incident."

---

* See the novel *Tarzan and the Dark Heart of Time* by Philip José Farmer, now available in the Edgar Rice Burroughs Universe series.

But they had.

Now, even Korak, a natural master of subterfuge, and of blending in, whose skills in these areas had been further enhanced during his service in World War II behind enemy lines with *unité dix-neuf*, the elite special missions team run by the British Secret Intelligence Service and the free French Intelligence Service, was having difficulty maintaining the charade.

It was time to disappear.

Tarzan, not one to do things by half, had arranged for multiple new identities, fake passports, birth certificates, and other necessary papers, for all of them. If one identity failed under scrutiny, another would be available for any of them to slip into.

Tarzan had invested very wisely over the decades, never allowing their ultimate source of wealth to be discovered. He had long ago closed down the initial firm that had traded in Oparian gold, and had repeatedly moved his assets, diversifying them in investments held by shell corporations around the world. Korak, taking over the running of Easthawking Ltd., had increased the family wealth. There was no shortage of estates in Australia and India, mountain lodges in Colorado and the Swiss Alps, small-town farmhouses in rural Illinois and Cumbria, metropolitan high-rise condominiums at their disposal in Lima and San Francisco, and many more all over the world . . . just waiting for them, for whenever they decided the time was right to return from Pellucidar.

Tarzan and Jane had decided the current environment had gotten too fraught for even them to successfully pull off their faked deaths and immediately take up new identities in another part of the world. They had done all they could to live their lives under the radar and to avoid publicity, but there was something special about them: they were, or at least had been, famous. He was the English lord raised by apes in the African jungle, and she was the woman from Baltimore who had tamed him. The British tabloid media wouldn't just let the stories of their deaths go unchecked; they'd swarm all over it like African hyenas on a lion carcass.

And so, it was off to Pellucidar. They would return to the outer crust someday, when the legends of Tarzan the Ape-Man and his jungle bride Jane had long since faded into the cracked and yellowed pages of history.

Tarzan and Korak and Charlotte were ecstatic at the opportunity to live in the unspoiled inner world. No more smog, no more honking automobiles, no more corporate billing statements, no more brightly lit cityscapes drowning out the starry night sky, no more wall-to-wall humanity. Instead, they would disappear into the jungle, explore areas untouched even by David Innes' Federated Kingdoms of Pellucidar, commune with the animals, and perhaps even make friends with the Pellucidarian "monkey men" who so resembled the tailed Ho-don and Waz-don peoples of Pal-ul-don.

Jane and Meriem, no strangers to fending for themselves and holding their own in challenging environments, nonetheless would miss some of the finer things the modern world had to offer. But they were resilient, and the outer world would be there when they were ready to return. Jane—Dr. Jane Porter, as she went by her maiden surname in academic and scientific circles—would return to her archaeological work, and to her biological studies of modern and ancient fauna.* Temperatures across the world were rising uncontrollably, chlorofluorocarbons were depleting the ozone layer, species were going extinct at unbelievable rates. They would return, and battle against the world's decline, but at the moment they needed to fade away and regroup, let the world forget about the Greystokes, and come back when the time was right.

A year or so ago, in anticipation of their eventual departure, Tarzan, Jane, Charlotte, Korak, and Meriem had toured

---

* See the one-shot comic book *Jane Porter: The Primordial Peril* and the graphic novel *Jane Porter and the City of Fire*, both written by Mike Wolfer and available in the Edgar Rice Burroughs Universe Illustrated Epics series at **EdgarRiceBurroughs.com**.

Africa, one last melancholic journey around the continent they called home.

They were rendered despondent by what they saw. The highland and lowland gorilla populations had been decimated. The fields were now absent of the herds of antelope and wild bison, and of Horta the boar. Numa the lion, and Omtag the giraffe, Sheeta the panther, and Pacco the zebra were all nowhere to be found, unless one paid exorbitant prices to see them in the managed confines of a "safari park." Elephants were targeted and hunted, almost to extinction, merely for their ivory. This hit Korak particularly hard, as of all the animals of the jungle and the plains he was closest to Tantor the elephant—other than, of course, his close friend, Akut. Everywhere they turned, the forests were being razed in favor of fields of cattle.

It had all happened so fast.

Millions of years of evolution, hundreds of thousands of years of species vying for their places in the overall ecosystem, carving out their ecological niches, creating not only plains and deserts and forests and jungles, and herds and tribes and packs and gaggles and flocks, all of which were vibrantly, brilliantly *alive* . . . creating not only all of these, but also a great continent that was itself *alive*.

And now it was dying, and there was nothing that even the mighty Lord of the Jungle, King of the Apes, could do.

Though some of the stranger locales visited by Tarzan in decades past certainly had been difficult to locate and discover, as the Greystokes toured the grand continent one last time they were collectively astonished that many of these hidden cities and lands had not been exposed, given the teaming throngs of humanity swarming over the land, like red fire ants devouring everything in their path. How was it possible that the land of Pal-ul-don, and that the cities of Opar, of Cathne and Athne, of Xuja, and of Kaji and Zuli, had not yet been uncovered and devoured by man?

It was a question for the ages.

Perhaps, while they retreated to the haven of Pellucidar, mankind would destroy itself—or the dying Earth would destroy mankind in order to save Herself. Plagues were always an option. Epidemics of new diseases had wiped out ninety-five percent of the then-extant population of the New World when the Spaniards and the Portuguese arrived. Another such outbreak, to which modern man was not immune, would solve the problem, and leave the Greystokes with an empty paradise. Nature would resuscitate itself. Species on the verge of extinction would retreat from the brink. Water would flow, and reforestation would heal and restore the delicate atmospheric balance.

Korak, in particular, had been enamored of this notion, although Tarzan wholeheartedly agreed with the idea, in principle. When Meriem had reminded Korak that they, too, would be susceptible to any such pandemic, he retorted that they would be safe in the inner world. They would return when the plagues had subsided.

"Of course," Meriem had replied, "it's so simple and comforting when you explain it like that," and it was all Jane could do to conceal her amusement and stifle a rather loud guffaw.

Toward the end of their expedition, they finally found the Mangani. These were a few remaining tribes, deep in the interior rainforest, near Tarzan's original jungle home in Gabon. Thus began the project to save these last, glorious, *intelligent* creatures from extinction.

They had to do *something*.

In the intervening year, Korak and his daughter Suzanne had been working with several Mangani tribes—the very last of their kind—to gain their trust and convince them to leave their African habitats before it was too late, and move to Pellucidar. Akut helped them in this effort, almost playing the role of an ambassador between the humans and the other Mangani. As soon as the migration of the Mangani to the inner world was complete, the plan was for Korak and Meriem to immediately fake their deaths and disappear, joining Suzanne in Pellucidar. Tarzan and Jane would follow suit a few months later, under a separate set of manufactured circumstances. Korak's sister, Charlotte, and Jackie, Korak and Meriem's son, would soon follow.

"Lady. Hey, lady."

Meriem, in the cab, was jerked from her reverie and back to the here and now.

"Yes, what is it?"

"Wanted to let you know, we're about halfway there, makin' good time."

Meriem nodded. "Thank you." She leaned back on the tough faux leather of the cab's back seat and tried to relax. The streetlights cast regular shadows, alternating soft yellow light with patches of dark, as the vehicle passed under them on the freeway.

She looked up, noticed the cabbie staring at her in the rearview mirror.

"What is it?" she asked. "Would you watch the road, please?"

"Yeah, lady, sorry. It's just that, this place you got us goin' to, it's high-tech, a lotta security. And I'm lookin' at you, with your dark skin and black hair, and funny accent, and I'm thinkin' to myself, is this broad some sorta A-Rab? What's she up to, goin' ta this place, 'specially this time a 'night? We gotta lotta trouble with the A-Rabs right now, ya know what I mean?"

"Yes," Meriem said, "I know exactly what you mean. And you didn't exactly think it to yourself. I'm French, you dolt. Now, here's another twenty"—she flashed two more tens— "and it's yours, along with the first twenty, if you get me there with no more silly questions. Just drop me at the security gate and let me worry about whether or not they let me in. *Comprenez-vous?* Got it?"

The cabbie, abashed at her takedown and greedy for the sawbucks, shut his mouth and drove.

The exchange with the driver only darkened Meriem's mood.

She loved Korak dearly, but right now she was madder than hell at him. He had tested her repeatedly, and stranding her in California was merely the latest in a long string of trials.

When they had first met, in the depths of the African jungle, Korak's behavior and lack of conscience, dearth of impulse control, and desire for immediate revenge in response to the least rejection had been disturbing. Affection starved, Korak was much influenced by Meriem's favorable reactions. It was a cliché, but in this case, the truth: Meriem's love had redeemed him.

Meriem also gave Korak as much leeway as she was able, as she was well aware of the trauma and ordeals he had endured, starting at a very young age. Through no fault of Tarzan and Jane, he had been without parental guidance, essentially orphaned, at a young age. Running away to the African jungle with Akut, Korak had been beset by guilt and shame, fearing he was a great disappointment to his parents.

And there were so many qualities about him that she did truly love: his love of and natural affinity for animals; his strong bond with the ever-loyal Akut; the fact that he was unwaveringly respectful to and protective of her; and his unbridled joy at living within nature and the jungle.

At the same time, she feared what he could become in her absence. If she were dead, for instance, would the redemptive effect of her love for him dissipate as well? When they had met, in the dark jungle, Korak had been a cold-blooded murderer, several times over. She was much too young to discern and understand that then, but as they had grown up together, and after that married, he had mentioned particular incidents that had stuck with him. Meriem had figured it out.

Korak, his heart full of anger and vengeance at being rejected by the great apes, had been about to kill yet another in cold blood, when at the last minute he had realized his target was a little Arab girl, and something had stayed his hand.

Meriem never told her husband she had known she had been the almost-target of his murderous rage. And again, from that point forward, a sea change seemed to have occurred in him, for he had never faltered in his love and protection of her.

Meriem had wept when Korak had enlisted at the outbreak of the Great War, shortly after they were married, although she knew that honor dictated no other choice. His experiences in that global conflict, and especially in the last days of the war, on the Argonne Front, added to and exacerbated his existing trauma.

But he had recovered, at least as much as it was possible for anyone to recover from the horrors of war. Along with her healing love and devotion, Meriem knew that Korak relied heavily on his great ape friend Akut to help him maintain his stability and his reason—in modern parlance, to keep his cool.

Close to midnight, Meriem's yellow cab arrived at her destination in Santa Monica near the Pacific Ocean. As she paid off the cabbie and marched toward the guardhouse, for the whole facility was bounded by a tall security fence, she regretted that she had not had a chance to stop in Tarzana, as previously planned, and bid her friends there farewell.

But her daughter, Suzanne, was possibly in grave danger, and nothing would interfere with her immediate departure for Pellucidar.

Bowen Tyler met her at the guardhouse.

4
A Horib Speaks

RACING HEADLONG at the immovable cliff wall, Korak felt the beast beneath him begin to slow, for even a dumb creature such as the Gorobor, its lizard-like gray tongue lolling from its fang-filled jaws in evidence of the effort thus exerted, could see with its own eyes the looming disaster of crashing into a solid barrier of rock at this velocity.

The ape-man, still crouched on two feet on the beast's orange-and-green-striped back, poked his spear into its hide, urging it ever forward. He whipped the spear around, rotating it one hundred and eighty degrees so that the tip was now pointed upward. He waited until the last possible moment, when he knew no amount of urging would prevent the creature from braking—and when the Gorobor did so, he ran forward on its back, planted the flat end of the spear in the beast's hide, and pole-vaulted toward the cliff face.

Korak crashed into the rock wall some twenty-five feet above the floor of the canyon, and, locating finger- and toe-holds in the granite that no other could possibly utilize, save his own father and perhaps a few other members of his family, the ape-man quickly scrambled up the cliff. Attaining the precipice, he thrust himself up and over it.

Peeking his head back down over the edge of the cliff, Korak was amused to see the five Horibs milling about and looking up at him in astonishment and confusion about what had just occurred. Their prey, so recently and unequivocally within their grasp, was now far above them, out of their reach, and the reach of their lances.

Korak resisted his first inclination to play with his opponents, now that he had them where he wanted them. It might be amusing, but time was of the essence, whatever time meant in this hollow world in which there was no reliable method of measuring the passage of minutes and hours. Besides, the Horibs might grow tired of waiting and return to the canyon's mouth to take their vengeance on Akut and von Horst. Eschewing the option of toying with the snake-men, Korak approached a jumble of small to medium-sized boulders heaped near the cliff's edge. Straining, his mighty thews rippling under his tanned hide, the ape-man rolled one of the larger rocks to the ledge and sent it tumbling downward. Peering over, he saw the rock flatten a reptile-man and his Gorobor in a mass of blood and bone.

The other Horibs emitted a terrible hissing, presumably a hue and cry at the dangerous position in which they now found themselves, and reversed their mounts toward the chasm's base.

Korak smiled grimly and sent another boulder over the rim; it crashed to the canyon floor and then tumbled and rolled down the declivity, smashing into two Horibs as a bowling ball would collide with bowling pins. Two more rolling boulders accounted for the last two Horibs in the canyon, their whistling-hissing cries fading as life departed their scaly forms.

A short while later, he descended the cliff to a height of about twenty feet above the floor of the gorge. Leaping down the remaining distance due to the fact that at that point the rock wall became utterly smooth, Korak then trudged down to the canyon's mouth, passing the crushed and mangled corpses of the snake-men and their Gorobors. Blood stained the rocky floor, and cracked and smashed bones pierced the creatures' olive-green snakeskins.

Korak smiled in satisfaction.

The ape-man emerged at the mouth of the gorge to find Akut and von Horst safe, and that they had turned the tables on their Horib guard. The snake-man was their captive, tied securely to the bole of a tall evergreen-like tree.

Von Horst and Akut had tended to each other's wounds, staunching the flow of blood from the various cuts that had been inflicted upon them with the crushed herb of a plant von Horst had located nearby.

Korak approached the two and von Horst extended his hand. "I doubted you, but Akut set me straight."

"I'll bet he did," Korak said with a faint smile. "He tends to do that. Anyway, don't think anything of it. I would have thought the same thing in your position."

The ape-man turned his attention to the prisoner, who spoke the common tongue of Pellucidar spoken by all gilaks and many other denizens of the inner world. The Horib hissed and spat at them, but on pain of death he revealed that another cohort of Horibs had splintered off before their hostile en-counter with Korak, Akut, and von Horst, and was headed for the latter's village of Lo-har. Von Horst was understandably deeply disturbed by this intelligence, for he was the leader of the small village, and his mate, La-ja, had been left in charge in his absence.

Korak, whose father Tarzan had known von Horst well from their first voyage to Pellucidar, and had been told many tales of the German's courage and honor, anticipated his new friends next words. "Von, you need say nothing further. Take one of these Gorobors and go to your village and your queen. Akut and I have our voyage to Thuria well in hand."

Korak privately reflected that perhaps his latter statement was not quite true, as the journey had not gone smoothly thus far. Korak had been in Africa with the O-220 and preparing for the last in a series of expeditions to and from Pellucidar, carrying Mangani tribes and other endangered dwellers of the continent. David Innes, leader of the Federated Kingdoms of Pellucidar, had sent an urgent message to the

Gridley Wave radio apparatus installed at the Greystoke estate. The Gridley Wave, unknown to but a few, was a principle of quantum physics that allowed for instantaneous communication between Earth's outer crust and the inner world of Pellucidar. Jason Gridley, "radio bug" and inventor extraordinaire, had devised an apparatus for receiving communications via this strange "wave," which had been quite convenient, as Abner Perry, transmitting from the inner world, had unwittingly been using the same wave in his pleas for succor from the outer world. And thus had begun the revolutionary age of Gridley Wave radio transmissions, which had since expanded to include communications between Earth and Barsoom—not the dead planet Mars, but its counterpart in an adjacent angle of existence—limited to those few who could be trusted both with the technology and the knowledge of the existence of other worlds and dimensions and beings beyond our earthly plane.

The news from David Innes was not good. Korak and Meriem's daughter, Suzanne Clayton, had gone missing in the vicinity of Thuria, in the Land of Awful Shadow. Suzanne, who had been living in Pellucidar since near the end of World War II, had been playing a critical part in the Greystoke family's efforts to relocate the last of the Mangani and other endangered species to the inner world.

Korak and his daughter Suzanne had been, in particular, working with several Mangani tribes—the very last of their kind—to gain their trust and convince them to leave their African habitats before it was too late, and to move to Pellucidar. Helping them in this effort was Korak's close companion Akut, who commanded much respect among the great apes.

Several days ago—as time was measured on the outer crust, with its alternating cycle of light and dark, sunrise and sunset—Suzanne had disappeared without a trace, along with her son Rahnak and the Waziri warrior princess Kyrianji.

Korak, at the Greystoke estate in West Kenya—still bearing the name "Greystoke" although Tarzan and Jane had transferred the Uziri property to the Waziri some twenty years ago, and then leased it back—had ordered the airship O-220 to ready for departure, and to alter its travel itinerary. Now, rather than flying to California to pick up Korak's wife, Meriem, as originally planned, the zeppelin would sail directly for the north polar opening to the hollow Earth. He also instructed that a message be sent to his mate, Meriem, of the change in plan, and that he would return for her immediately upon seeing to the safety of their daughter. Upon entry into the inner world of Pellucidar, the dirigible's destination was Sari, capital of the Federated Kingdoms, where the ship would drop off Dav-An Innes, daughter of David Innes and Dian the Beautiful. This would provide Korak an opportunity to consult directly with David regarding Suzanne's disappearance before heading to Thuria.

However, an unplanned landing at Lo-har, shortly after traversing the north polar entrance to Pellucidar, had interrupted their journey, when the ship's new second engineer, Alex Ryadinsky, had called the bridge reporting a minor issue with the rudder, which was best addressed by briefly making landfall. Captain Hines had ordered the ship to land and to make fast at nearby Lo-har, and ship's helmsman Wolff Hines had made the necessary adjustments to their course while the Gridley Wave radio operator notified Lo-har of their unexpected arrival.

Korak and Akut had briefly disembarked to exchange greetings with Lo-har's leader, von Horst, while the mechanical issue was addressed. As this was to be a short diplomatic exchange with an old friend of his father's, Korak unfortunately did not come armed with his Enfield rifle or ammunition, nor his spear, rope, or bow and arrows. He had only the steel hunting knife given to him by his father, just as Tarzan carried his own father's hunting knife.

While Tarzan's son and von Horst traded greetings, Akut raised a cry. The O-220 was inexplicably quitting Lo-har without them. All attempts to raise the departing airship using the Gridley Wave set at Lo-har had ended in failure, which was extremely concerning as a radio operator constantly manned the apparatus, and had expertise in the function and mechanism of the Gridley Wave set, as well as the principles of the Gridley Wave itself.

Either the Gridley Wave set was disabled or destroyed, or the apparatus was not being manned. Either eventuality spelled disaster, both for the O-220 crew, and for Korak's mission to locate his missing daughter.

Korak and von Horst had notified Sari, via Gridley Wave, that they would attempt to pursue the dirigible, but anticipating the futility of the chase—for how could Korak and Von and Akut, astride Von's faithful mammoth, Old White, hope to overtake the aircraft?—Sari should send a sailing ship to meet Korak and Akut. Their fears were soon realized, for the O-220, at top speed, was far gone from their sight. They made for the coast of the Lural Az, where a ship captained by Ja of the Mezops was supposed to meet them and take them to Sari and thence to Thuria. Before they had reached the coast, they had been attacked by the Horibs astride their mighty Gorobors.

Now, Von regretfully bade farewell to Korak and Akut, his first duty being to protect his village and people. "Keep a steady eye upon the break in those mountain ranges," Von instructed, pointing to two ranges to their left and right, visible in Pellucidar's weirdly upcurving distance, for in the interior of the hollow globe there was no horizon. "Stay between them. Once past these chains, do your best to maintain a straight course for the coast. Do not veer to the right, that is, the north, if you are able, for there lies the Valley of the Jukans, a mad and cruel people who would as soon invite you to a feast as to kill you both for the most minor insult or infraction."

"They are to be avoided, then," Korak said, and Akut grunted in assent.

"Correct," von Horst said, without the slightest trace

of irony. "At the coast is the village of Ko-va, where the ship
from Sari is to meet you. The Ko-vans have been hostile in
the past, but they have settled down of late. They are afraid
of David and his warriors—and of me." Von smiled. "They
know I will come with my Lo-harian warriors and mete out
justice if anything happens to you and your ape friend."

Korak extended his hand. "I thank you," he said simply.
"And I wish you luck against the Horibs making for your
village."

The blond German nodded in acknowledgment, and with
but a few simple gestures to the woolly mammoth, and a
few words whispered in its shaggy ear, he set off upon Old
White, the pachyderm making a rapid pace that surprised
Korak, but gave the ape-man hope that Von would arrive
in time to help in the inevitable skirmish between the Lo-
harians and the snake-men. Korak knew that Von could
have taken a captured Gorobor and made still better time,
but the adopted Lo-harian would never abandon the mammoth, his old and loyal friend. Korak could very well understand this, and he admired von Horst's close relationship
with Old White, for among Korak's best friends—other than
his friend and mentor Akut—was the strong and loyal Tantor
the elephant, whom he knew had his own variant of jungle
language and whose intelligence approached that of dolphins
and humans.

Shortly after Von and Old White departed, a captured
Gorobor set off for the mountains to the west, laden with
Korak, Akut, and the last surviving Horib, the latter securely
bound and sandwiched between them. Korak was mildly
disgusted at the touch of the cold and clammy reptile hide
against his naked skin, but soon grew accustomed to it. He
presumed it didn't bother Akut, whose body was covered in
dark gray-brown fur, and thus was protected against the touch
of the slimy Gorobor flesh against his own skin. Not much
bothered the phlegmatic Mangani, save being roused to battle.

As they rode, Korak reviewed to himself what he knew

about the Horibs, both from his father's and Jason Gridley's experiences with them on their first journey to the inner world, as well as from other longtime denizens of Pellucidar, such as David Innes and Abner Perry. He had even heard that Christopher West—otherwise known as "Red Axe" of Pellucidar—had recently encountered the Horibs in an entirely different part of the inner world. As Korak had already seen, they were bipedal, but with weak, shapeless legs ending in three toes. From the waist up, they more resembled humans, although in form only, with two muscular arms and hands with five fingers. Their bodies were covered in scales of drab green, although the scales about their bellies, upper necks, and heads were smaller and more whitish-green. Their heads were flat, like those of snakes, and characterized by two horns mounted above the bony eye crests. Situated on either side of the horns were the nubs of ears. The eyes were the creatures' most sinister aspect, yellowish like those of reptiles, and unblinking, with vertical black pupils.

The Horibs wore tunics or aprons of some tough reptilian skin, and this served as both coverage and armor, for the undersides, or the bellies, of the snake-men were soft and white. Leather belts secured the reptile-skin aprons about the waist, from which also hung sheaths containing bone knives. All Horibs' tunics were adorned with the same design, a circle with eight equidistant arrows or prongs situated around it and pointing outward. As Korak had learned firsthand in battle, all of the snake-men carried spears with sharpened bone tips.

Korak could not fathom the evolutionary path that had resulted in this creature. He knew there were other savage beings in Pellucidar that rivaled the Horibs and had no like on the outer crust, such as the Gorbuses who had captured Von Horst, and his own daughter Suzanne, on separate occasions. Still, encountering and battling these creatures firsthand was a different matter altogether from hearing stories about them. He had a newfound respect for his daughter's decision to remain and make her home in Pellucidar. Now, the rest of the Greystoke clan would be joining her here—if he could find her. He had to get to Thuria; too much time had been wasted already.

Ruefully, he checked himself. Had time been wasted? Perhaps only an hour had passed since the O-220 had deserted him and Akut, or perhaps a year. Without the rising and the setting of a sun, without predictable, measurable daytime and nighttime, how was one to know? David Innes had once attempted to set up a universal clock; the native Pellucidarians had regarded it as a curiosity and ignored it. Tarzan, upon his first advent in the inner world, had experienced a strange disassociation, a feeling that since there was no way of measuring time, time itself did not matter, and there was no sense of urgency to complete his mission.

Korak, forewarned, had not yet fallen prey to this phenomenon, at least not that he was aware of.

The three continued on in silence atop the trotting Gorobor, making good time. The ape-man caught himself again. No time. The sun beat down relentlessly upon them. The silence of their captive was maddening.

"What are you called?" Korak asked. He wasn't sure he cared, but there was monotony to be broken, and obviously he was the one to break it. He knew Akut could travel on thus forever.

The Horib hissed in response and said nothing.

"Well, I've heard you capture people, drag them underwater, and stash them in air pockets in underground mud pits, fattening them up on eggs so you can eat them. You like human flesh? You've eaten it before?"

This elicited a reply. The Horib spoke in the common Pellucidarian tongue, in which Korak had been questioning it. The words, however, were marred by its inability, due to the configuration of its jaw and tongue, to form certain phonemes, and thus emerged in a repulsive hiss.

"What is a 'human'?"

"Ah, I used the English word," Korak answered. "A human is a gilak, like me. Have you eaten gilaks?"

The Horib went silent again.

"I wonder what Horib flesh tastes like. Don't you wonder, Akut?"

The Mangani grunted in assent.

"I've eaten snake meat before. Tastes like chicken. I wonder if this Horib tastes like chicken? Hey, Akut, do you think they have chickens in Pellucidar?"

Akut made a rude noise, the Mangani equivalent of which was, "Shut your trap, you're bothering me."

Korak chuckled. He addressed the snake-man again. "When you attacked us, and while we battled, you all were a weird bluish color, or at least your torsos were. Now you're a drab green."

"And when I eat you, gilak," the Horib said, "my skin will blaze crimson with the battle won and my hunger will be satiated."

"Aha, so you do talk, after all," Korak said. "I wonder what it was specifically about me mentioning your strange color changes that got you to speak."

The captive reptile-man resumed his silence.

Korak continued. "Since you do have a tongue, although it's forked, tell my faithful friend Akut and me about your race. Why do you want to capture gilaks and eat them? Where did you come from? What do you want from us? I am genuinely curious."

"Your questions are absurd," the snake-man replied. Although it was hard to correctly attribute emotional reactions to such a foreign being, Korak thought the other was exasperated. "We eat to live, as do all creatures. You are food. We warriors, and our females, and our little ones are bored with consuming only gyor meat and fish from our lake homes. Gilak meat is a delicacy. Besides, you said yourself that you consume and enjoy our flesh. Why should we Horibs not do the same, and eat you gilaks?"

Korak corrected him. "I said that I had eaten snake meat, not the meat of snake-*men*."

"I fail to see the difference."

Korak was momentarily dumbfounded. "You see no difference between men, people, such as ourselves, who think and talk and have societies, who ask unanswerable questions and have discussions such as the one we are having now . . . You see no difference between all that and the beasts of the jungles, and plains, and lakes, such as the fish and the gyor that you mentioned? Where I come from, gilaks do not eat the flesh of other gilaks. People do not eat people. It is forbidden, what we call a taboo to do so."

"I see no difference at all," the Horib replied. "We are all beasts, put here only to live, eat, procreate, and die. What else is there to do? Why would we expend precious energy asking questions and thinking about things we know we have no control over? How silly. And what about this one, your companion. He barely speaks. Does he think? I cannot tell. Is he a beast, such that you would eat him if the necessity arose?"

"Careful," Korak said, "watch your tongue. Akut is just as much a man, a person, as you and I are. And I have my doubts about you."

Akut, if he cared about being spoken of in the third person while he was present, evinced no reaction, though Korak, understanding his friend so well, knew the Mangani was listening intently.

"If you think we are all beasts," Korak continued, "all the same, then don't you wonder if there are any others different from you? Among my people we have myths and legends of beings more powerful than ourselves. Some factions even call them gods, and believe they are responsible for our creation. Don't you reptile-men have such legends, or do you truly only cry at birth, eat, fight, and die? Don't you ever wonder if there's more than that to your existence?"

The captive Horib whisper-hissed, and it almost seemed that he was laughing. "You gilaks truly are ridiculous creatures, worthy only of being consumed by us, if you all wonder without knowing who made you and what your purpose is. We don't have to wonder, gilak. We know exactly who we are, from whence we came, and for what we are made. We are the children of the children of Swika and exist to carry out Her will."

"I see," Korak said. "And who might Swika be?"

"Gilak," the Horib said, "you are truly stupid. Swika is the daughter of Dwak, She Who Exists Outside of Everything."

Korak shrugged, then tried a different tack. "What does the strange sign upon your tunic represent, the circle and the eight arrows pointing in different directions?"

"I tire of speaking to you, gilak," the snake-man said. "Kill me, for I will say no more."

"Come on," Korak replied, "we were just starting to become friends! Just this last question, then you can ask all you want about me and Akut."

"I wish to know nothing more of you than I already do," the Horib replied. "If it will shut you up, I will answer—one last question. The eight arrows coming from the heart emblazoned in the center represent . . ." The snake-man hissed; perhaps it was a form of laughter. "But no. Perhaps you will find out eventually," the Horib concluded.

Weary of the snake-man's evasive replies, Korak asked no further questions.

The three rode on in silence, until finally thirst and hunger pangs brought them to a halt at the foothills of the mountains von Horst had mentioned. They moved off the trail and found a hollow in a dense growth of what appeared to be Ponderosa pines, which Korak felt would provide sufficient protection from eyes of predators, man and beast alike. He knew this to be the territory of the *ryth*, the dreaded Pellucidarian cave bear, but he believed that in the event of an attack, he and Akut could easily scale the narrow boles of the tall pines, escaping to a height where a massive bear could not possibly follow. Akut kept an eye out for the Jukans and other beasts, and secured their Horib captive to the trunk of a pine, while the Korak went in search of food and drink.

The ape-man returned a short while later, having downed with his bow and arrow two small therapod dinosaurs with batlike wings. He had slaked his thirst at a nearby stream, and after he and his Mangani companion devoured the flying dinosaurs raw, Akut left to quench his own thirst.

The captive Horib eschewed all opportunities to eat and drink, and Korak determined to let him be. He couldn't, after all, force feed the snake-man.

The two visitors from the outer crust attempted to sleep, after assuring themselves once more that their prisoner was securely bound, having moved him from the tree trunk's base and then secured him once more to the bole of a pine opposite theirs at a height similar to that at which they perched. The lizard-man glared unblinkingly at them as they settled in on the upper branches. They were confident in their relative safety at this height, although attacks by *thipdars*—heavily toothed winged reptiles with forty-foot-long bodies and thirty-foot-plus wingspans—were an ever-present danger anywhere in the inner world. Of greater concern to Korak was his ability to actually sleep under the undying glare of Pellucidar's central sun, beating down on him and Akut with the inferno-like heat of the blazing coals at the center of a hellish furnace.

Finally, weariness overtook them, and Akut and Korak slept.

Korak awoke to Akut shaking his shoulder. The ape-man sprang up and crouched on his branch, fully awake and immediately scanning for danger in all directions. It was a skill, or a curse, drummed into him during his youth as he was lost and wandering for years in the African jungles, and then doubly reinforced during two World Wars—for those who did not gain this ability usually ended up dead. And those who did gain it never really lost it, going through life in a perpetual state of high alert. His father, Tarzan of the Apes, had the same ability, for better or worse.

Akut directed his attention to where a branch, near the same elevation as his, extended from the trunk of a nearby tree.

Hanging from the branch was the corpse of the Horib. He dangled by the neck, evidently having accidentally strangled himself in an attempt to slip free of his bonds.

They peered more closely. The body hung oddly, flapping in the slight breeze as if it were a child's kite caught in the tree.

Then Korak realized . . . all that remained of their captive was his scaly skin, fluttering hopelessly in the wind. The body itself—the guts and internal organs and bones and brain—was gone.

"Histah-zan," Akut breathed.

5

"YOUR MATTER TRANSMITTER AWAITS"

NEED TO GET TO PELLUCIDAR RIGHT AWAY."

Bowen Tyler nodded in support. "I agree, Meriem. But your husband . . . what I mean to say is, Captain Hines and Korak were supposed to dock the O-220 here, at Tyler Industries, and pick you up."

"And . . ." Meriem prompted.

"And . . . they didn't . . ." Tyler said. "I mean . . . you know this. They're gone. They left without you."

"Oh, I am painfully aware of that."

"Okay. And . . . the *Favonia* is off on a completely different mission."

"I am aware of that, as well."

Tyler made a helpless gesture. "Then, I don't know what you want."

"Mr. Tyler. Bowen. I know—the Greystokes know—a lot of things. We know that Drs. Moritz and Kingsley, in your employ, have discovered, or invented, a matter transmitter that can send me to Pellucidar very quickly."*

"I—I . . ."

"Of course, Dr. Moritz knew about Pellucidar, and met Tarzan, back in the mid-forties. And Abner Perry consulted

---

* See the novels *Mahars of Pellucidar* and *Red Axe of Pellucidar* by John Eric Holmes, now available in the Edgar Rice Burroughs Universe series, for the account of how Drs. Moritz and Kingsley transported Chris West to the inner world of Pellucidar.

with him in the early fifties regarding his theories concerning energy-matter transmission."*

"But—"

"We know that shortly thereafter, Dr. Moritz took a blow to the head, sustaining selective amnesia. He retained all of his scientific knowledge, but unfortunately lost all memory of Pellucidar."

"I just want to—"

"It almost seems predestined that he would rediscover Pellucidar, learning about it for the supposed 'first time' last year when he sent Christopher West there; the poor man didn't realize he had once had this secret knowledge, back in the 1940s."

"Mrs. Clayton—"

She smiled. "Please. Meriem."

"Meriem," Tyler said, "the process is entirely experimental. Do you want to know how many times we've *successfully* sent a human being through the matter-transmitter? Once. Once! Don't forget what happened to Janson Gridley back in the early fifties. He would never have come back to Pellucidar alive if Victory Harben hadn't gone to extraordinary lengths to alter his fate. We can't take the chance again, and especially not with you. In fact, the only way we'd ever risk using the matter transmitter on a live human again is if West indicates he want to come home."

Thirty-five minutes later, an adjunct escorted Meriem Clayton into a gigantic laboratory complex on the other side of Tyler Industries; the research laboratory run by Drs. Kingsley and Moritz was more hangar than office building, being a block long and eight stories in height, complete with a micro-tomic reactor.

---

* See the Edgar Rice Burroughs Universe novels *Tarzan: Battle for Pellucidar* by Win Scott Eckert and *John Carter: Gods of the Forgotten* (specifically the Quantum Interlude, "Where Angels Fear . . .") by Geary Gravel, for more information regarding these events.

Given their reputations, she wasn't surprised to find the two scientists still working, burning the post-midnight oil.

They both looked up in surprise—they worked late to avoid interruptions such as this. Moritz was small, bookish, in his fifties with a shock of unruly dark hair shot through with gray, and a gray-black beard. He pushed thick-lensed wire-rimmed glasses up on his nose, a gesture of annoyance.

"Yes, what is it?" he asked.

"This is Meriem Clayton," the assistant replied. "Orders direct from the CEO. Please extend her every courtesy, do everything she instructs, and otherwise consider yourself sworn to secrecy." The young woman turned to Meriem. "I'll get started on your travel list and should be back in about an hour."

Meriem nodded her thanks as the young lady turned on her heel and strode out. She turned back to the two scientists.

"Tiny" Kingsley, a blond gentle giant, stood there with his mouth agape.

Moritz just shook his head.

"So," Meriem said, "if I understand you correctly, all you have to do is set your earth borer to a new location terminus within Pellucidar, conduct the drilling, and use the disintegrator-reintegrator built into the borer to transmit me to Pellucidar."

"That's a very simplistic summation," Moritz said, concern mixed with irritation clouding his visage. "I need you to understand this very clearly. Your body will be destroyed, disintegrated at a subatomic level. It will not exist anymore. The composition of your entire body will be coded, stored as information. The information will then be transmitted down the laser, in a series of energy impulses, five-hundred miles, and reintegration will occur at the terminal end, drawing on atmospheric and other matter available in that location. If the transmission is successful, your body will be reconstructed, atom by atom, molecule by molecule, at the other end."

"I understand," Meriem said. "I only want to get to my

daughter. This has been successfully accomplished once, correct? With Chris West?"

"That's true," Kingsley said. "And before Chris, with mice and cats. Lately we've transmitted a plethora of complex equipment, as well, all successfully. Our only concern thus far has been the potential effects of the disassembly-reassembly on the human brain. So far, Chris seems fine, he hasn't exhibited any ill effects."

Moritz scoffed. "You call deciding to stay in those prehistoric badlands no ill effects, a sane decision?"

Tiny chuckled. "C'mon, Doc. You yourself told him you agreed with his choice, once you saw Varna."

Moritz only grumbled.

"Look," Meriem said, "I'm planning on going to the inner world for good, and I haven't even been through the transmitter yet. So, there's nothing wrong with my brain or decision-making. I'm going to find my daughter, and I accept the risks. That's it, so let's get down to it."

The two men nodded.

"Good," she said, "now, how long will it take to bore a new microtunnel to a different terminal location?"

"That's the longest part of the process," Moritz replied, "about two days."

"And," Tiny interjected, "we have to know where we're going."

"I have some thoughts about how to figure that out," Meriem said. "Pellucidar's continents and oceans are thought to be the inverse of the oceans and landmasses on the outer crust. Based on that, and with the partial maps of Pellucidar that we have, can you try to calculate the location of Thuria?"

"It's worth a try," Tiny said. "I'll get started on those calculations, Doc, if you want to prepare the borer and the data storage circuits."

Moritz nodded and they got to work.

Meriem stood in a large glass box, above which was situated the funnel-shaped disintegrator mechanism.

She was fully kitted out for an adventure in prehistoric

Pellucidar. Her expeditionary clothing included boots, tough pants, a khaki shirt, and protective headwear against Pellucidar's eternal noonday sun—a soft and pliable leather hat with a wide brim. Stacked beside her were cases of food and water.

She also had a hiker's backpack, a steel knife in belt sheath, an expandable spear (a tactical walking stick), and a Barnett wildcat crossbow with arrows in a leather quiver. She was unable to bring with her a gun or any type of explosive propulsion firearm; the ammunition would explode in the matter-transport process, killing her instantly.

She felt more than prepared for what she faced. She knew woodcraft, the Mangani language, and the art and skill of traversing the forest via branches and upper terraces. She was an eminently capable hunter. She was an accomplished horsewoman, if ever she encountered similar beasts in the inner world that she could tame and ride. She felt ready for whatever Pellucidar could throw at her.

"Meriem," Tiny said, "I can't be sure the borer we've sent through the crust, and the reintegrator at the receiving end, is at the proper location. The camera on the terminal end is showing mostly plants and trees in a shaded area, so we can't see the wider environment. I'm not even entirely certain that the theory that Pellucidar's continents and oceans are the inverse of our own is correct. And then there are the numerous differences in how the laws of physics there seem to differ from our own, which we can't explain. I just can't make any guarantees."

"I understand. Thank you, Tiny," she replied. "We're doing this. And I've already lost too much time."

"I understand, too, Meriem." Tiny gave a small, awkward smile. "Then, your matter transmitter awaits!"

She nodded to Moritz to proceed.

"Good luck, Meriem," Doc said. He left "You're going to need it" unspoken and manipulated the controls.

Meriem instantly felt like her whole nervous system was on fire. A white-hot light exploded in her brain, followed by utter darkness.

6
SHOOTOUT ON THE O-220

THE O-220 AIRSHIP, under control of the hijackers, sped toward Thuria.

The ship had made fast time with Wolff Hines at the helm. The dirigible had charted a straight-line point to point course within the hollow globe, a technique suggested by a young Dr. Stanley Moritz almost thirty years prior, traveling through Pellucidar's upper atmosphere, rather than skirting close to the surface of the inner world, which would've added a great deal of time to their journey.

Wolff would have preferred the slower course, to stall his opponents' plans, but Alex knew about Moritz's pioneering theory of airship travel within Pellucidar, and he had had no choice but to comply.

"Approaching Thuria now," Wolff reported. He, his father Captain Hines, and even Alex watched in wonder as they approached not only the Land of Awful Shadow, but the mysterious moon that hung but one mile above the inner world's surface.

They could see that the Dead World was covered in land-masses, forests, large seas, and vast plains. It was unfathomable to Wolff that such a small, orbiting body could maintain such flora. And what force acted upon the surface of the tiny pendent world such that its oceans did not rain down upon the surface of Pellucidar? Abner Perry had posited several theories, such as proposing that the counterattraction the Earth's crust on the far side of Pellucidar against the section

48

of the Earth's crust directly under the pendent moon caused the tiny world to be held in abeyance, and to hold the waters of its oceans against its surface, but to Wolff's admittedly nonscientific mind, none of these explanations made sense. Besides, Abner's theories seemed to ignore whatever effect the inner world's central sun might have, as well as the fact that Victory Harben had scientifically established that Pellucidar was actually located in an "angle"—a dimension—adjacent to that of the "Earth" from which David, Abner, Tarzan, his father, and many others originally hailed, a dimension subject to different laws of physics. Therefore, how could that "Earth" have any bearing upon the physical nature of Pellucidar?

"All right," Alex said, "enough gawking. You'll have time enough to check it all out when we're on the ground in Thuria."

"Aye, aye, 'Captain,'" Wolff replied, putting sarcastic emphasis on the rank. He tried once more to reason with her. "Alex, we were friends. Why are you doing this?"

"All that means is I and my family succeeded in fooling all of you," Alex replied. "We could have been more than friends," she added wistfully, "but there's no chance of that now. Pay attention to your console."

"Approaching Thuria for touchdown now," Wolff said.

He skillfully navigated the dirigible toward a designated landing spot. All of the villages and settlements of the Federated Kingdoms of Pellucidar had landing facilities designated for the two airships that routinely traveled the skies of Pellucidar, the O-220 and the *Favonia*.

"Hang on," Wolff said, "tipping the nose down now, and extending the forward landing cables." He manipulated several controls on the console and the ship tipped forward slightly. He activated the cables, which shot out from under the forward curvature of the ship and embedded in the ground below. Automatic clamps tightened, and the forward part of the ship was secure. The next step would be lowering the aft end, bringing the ship level again, and activating the rear cables.

"Careful, maintain enough power to rear propellers to ease us level slowly," Captain Hines said.

"Yes, sir."

Alex came forward on the bridge and leaned over Wolff's shoulder, monitoring his movements.

Wolff gave several light taps to the power levels for the rear props, and the ship began to level. He turned his head to Alex, breathing down his neck. "I've got this."

She shrugged and didn't move.

Wolff jerked the power controls in the opposite direction and the rear of the ship tipped suddenly upward. Alex was slammed forward, and her head landed on Wolff's shoulder. He head-butted her, knocking her nearly insensate.

Alex fell backward on the deck, stunned. Wolff pounced on her, and chopped at her wrist with the hard edge of his hand. The automatic fell from her nerveless fingers. He grabbed the gun, shot her in the calf for good measure—a flesh wound to disable her—and pocketed the weapon.

Captain Hines sighed. "Wolff, you know you really shouldn't discharge a weapon inside the ship. Regulations forbid it."

Wolff chuckled. "I'll try not to do it again, Dad." He looked briefly over at Alex. "I do wonder what happened with her. It's as if she's not even the same person I grew up with."

Of a sudden, the ship's intercom was buzzing with traffic, shouts and yells, and questions about what was going on. If Wolff didn't do something quickly, the other hijackers might start shooting the captive crew and passengers.

He returned to the helm and worked at the controls, quickly lowering the rear of the airship. Outside the ship, he could see the tribespeople of Thuria gathering all around, looking on in wonder at the strange antics of the airship. He released the forward cable clamps, edged the nose of the O-220 upward, and hit the controls that opened the rear hangar bay doors.

In the cargo hangar of the O-220, Bailey Mason chafed at the long confinement.

She and her fellow prisoners had been stuck in here for hours—or for whatever passed for hours in Pellucidar—without food, water, or even access to other basic needs. A good 'ole Colorado cowgirl, she had signed on to this mission out of her love for animals, and her desire to see them protected and preserved from extinction. The last thing she had thought would happen was that she'd end up in the middle of a hijacking.

The bow of the airship suddenly lurched downward, and everyone was sent tumbling toward the forward bulkhead: Mangani, crew members, animals, Waziri warriors, and hijackers alike. Some of the captors pulled their weapons in the turmoil, and started aiming them at their prisoners, including the great apes, all of whom were irritable and agitated due to the long confinement, the absence of their ambassador, Akut, and now the lurching ship.

"No, no, no!" one of the hijacker leaders cried. "No shooting in the ship! It could rupture the vacuum tanks!"

One of the Mangani, annoyed at the yelling human, slammed the man's skull against a bulkhead, killing him instantly.

Bailey ran for a nearby locker, yanked it open, and pulled out an old leather holster. She grabbed her six shooter and quickly shot two more hijackers.

The remaining seven foes, including the second-in-command of the hangar guard—now first-in-command—pulled his weapon and aimed it at Bailey. A half second later, he slumped to the deck, his neck snapped by the O-220's head of security, Isilo. The Waziri warrior grinned at her, gestured for no more shooting, and darted away in search of his next victim.

The hijackers, seeing that they were far outnumbered by an angry horde of great apes and noble African warriors, were no longer reluctant to shoot. However, action desired and action realized are two different things. Two great apes swarmed the first man to draw his weapon, each taking one of the screaming man's arms and tugging viciously, after which the victim no longer had arms attached to his body. The legs were next.

Further aft, several Waziri had reclaimed their spears and

were making short work of two opponents. Another hijacker ran toward Bailey, a giant of a man intent on revenge for her shooting down two of his comrades. Scanning quickly for nearby succor, and finding none, Bailey shrugged and, ignoring Isilo's admonition, drew her six-shooter and shot him point-blank between the eyes, blowing a hole clean through the bastard's skull.

Meanwhile, several Waziri warriors scoured the ship, taking out the captors who were guarding other crew members in the bunks, and traversing the gangways and corridors, flushing out and eliminating any remaining opponents.

On the bridge, Captain Hines and his son worked together to stabilize and secure the ship, eventually landing it properly and making it fast with the automatic cables and clamps.

When they turned their attention back to the rear of the bridge, they saw that Alex Ryadinsky was gone.

The battle over, and the O-220 reclaimed, Hines, Wolff, Dav-An Innes, and Isilo, accompanied by several other crew members, including Bailey Mason, gathered outside the ship at the rear hangar bay door.

The Mangani, still restless, had been taken in hand by the Sagoths, Tar-gash and Mok, and were being carefully intro-duced to the Mangani tribes who had already arrived on prior trips. Soon they would settle nearby, in habitats set aside es-pecially for them, where they could all have their own domains, and adapt to life within the inner world according to their own paces and temperaments.

Wolff, in the aftermath of the ordeal, had one arm protec-tively slipped around Dav-An's waist. He looked over at Bailey, who had donned her leather gun belt and secured the holster to her upper thigh with a leather strap.

"That's not exactly regulation armament, pardner," he said, smiling with amusement.

She grinned back at him. "Listen, fella, this old six-shooter was my granddad's when he was a deputy sheriff, and his own pappy used it to fight off the Pesitistas bandits just south of the border, right after Pancho Villa's incursion into New Mexico. And before that it belonged to *his* pappy, though it didn't do him no good when Dirty Cheetim had him killed and then framed the Apache for it. Anyways, this here's a family heirloom, it's seen a lot of action, and I don't go *anywhere* without it."

Wolff nodded and grinned even more broadly, then composed himself at the approach of Goork, king of Thuria, along with several of his tribesmen. They were somewhat shorter and more thickly built than some of the other Stone Age peoples of Pellucidar, such as the Amozites and the Sarians, but no less handsome.

Captain Hines stood and gave a respectful greeting.

"My apologies, Captain," Goork said. "When your ship of the air bounced up and down, we were unsure what was happening, and thus did not intervene. However," he added proudly, "once we saw two of the offenders racing from your ship, with your Waziri warriors in pursuit, we realized that they were your opponents, and I ordered two of my finest spearmen to run them clean through. I hope this meets with your approval."

Hines, with the heart of an explorer, not a warrior, regretted all the bloodshed, but knew that in this instance it had been unavoidable. "Yes, great Goork, you and your fine warriors have our deepest thanks and gratitude. May I ask, was one of those killed by your warriors a woman?"

"No, Captain, just two men."

"I see. Then, could you please show us to your Gridley Wave radio station? Our apparatus was destroyed by the hijackers."

A dark expression clouded the Thurian chief's face. "I am afraid not. There was a trail of blood leading to the hut in which we keep our Gridley Wave. When my son, Kolk, investigated, he found it smashed beyond repair."

Bailey Mason looked over at Wolff.

"On my granddaddy's six-shooter," she said, "you should've shot that one in the heart."

7
AKUT

KORAK AND AKUT STOOD AT THE BOW of the EPS *Connecticut*, breathing in deeply of the fresh, salt-tinged ocean air. They were sprayed with sea mist as the *Connecticut* crested a wave, and Akut gave what was, for him, a broad smile.

The "EPS" denoted Empire of Pellucidar Ship, a convention suggested by Abner Perry following the tradition of ship names on the outer crust, such as HMS and USS. The *Connecticut*, of an unusual two-hulled design, was a mighty sailing ship in the emperor's navy, under the command of Ja, Admiral of the Navy, who also happened to be the King of Anoroc. It was all a bit formal for David Innes—who found not a little humor in his title of "emperor"—but he had allowed Perry, who had also come up with the idea of designating tribal chieftains and chieftainesses as kings and queens, his harmless eccentricities.

Anoroc was an island in the Lural Az, a vast ocean, off the shore of the landmass on which were situated Sari, inland, and the Mountains of the Clouds, which descended down to the coastline, and Greenwich, which was further up the coast. Anoroc was the major naval shipbuilding center, although the island of Luana, home of former adversaries of the Anorocans, ran a close second. Ja and his fellow Mezop sailors spent much time in Anoroc and Luana, overseeing the construction and maintenance of naval ships to their high standards. But they were never more at home than when they were actually navigating their beloved seas and oceans.

The Mezops, a tall, handsome people with copper skin and black hair, had always been a seagoing folk. They had quickly taken to the innovations introduced by David and Abner, and were now recognized as the true masters of Pellucidar's oceans, even giving the marauding Korsars, pirates who had stumbled into Pellucidar via the north polar opening several hundred years ago, a run for their money.

The *Connecticut*, having skirted the coast northward after picking up Korak and Akut at Ko-va, had thereafter turned southward at the hairpin-shaped curve of the coastline that gave forth into the land of the Sabertooth Men. Continuing to skirt the coast, this time in a southward direction in relation to the north polar opening, the ship sailed toward Kali. Their course would then take them past Greenwich, Amoz, and the Unfriendly Islands, before turning westward toward Indiana (also known as Hooja's Island) and on toward the coast of Thuria.

Akut questioned why, if the Mezops were master sailors, the ship did not take a more direct course, rather than constantly paralleling the coast. Would they not make faster time? Korak, always amazed at the Mangani's intelligence and thoughtfulness, explained that within the hollow Earth, without any celestial bodies by which to navigate, no sun moving daily across the sky, no constellations, and no orbiting moon, there was little to do but pilot by sight, and by prior knowledge of currents, tides, and landmasses.

The sailors did have compasses, introduced by David and Abner, but the Mezops, accustomed to their long-standing methods of circumnavigation, believed it was less hazardous to stay in sight of land whenever practical. This attitude was probably further magnified by the fact that the Pellucidarians' "homing instinct"—the evolutionary adaptation to life within a world that had no rising and setting sun, and no guiding nighttime stars—did not function on the open ocean, out of sight of land. The gilaks of Pellucidar used their homing instinct to zero in on any location they had once been to, and to set course for their birthland with even more accuracy, but for the peoples of the inner world, it usually didn't work out in the middle of the ocean.

Akut nodded in understanding. Korak, taking in the sea air, and admiring the white beach sands and the lush, forested coastline to starboard, had initially chafed at the forced rest imposed by dint of being a passenger on the *Connecticut*. There was nothing for him to do, no challenges to be overcome, and it irked him. Later, after several sleeps, he began to relax. The ape-man was never one to let down his guard, but he came to accept that there was no faster way of getting to Thuria, that Ja and his sailors were experts in their field and doing everything in their power to hasten the journey, and that the best thing he could do for himself right now was to accept the circumstances, admire what the journey had to offer, and plan for next steps to be taken once they reached the Land of Awful Shadow. He admired his great ape friend's ability to slip into this state of equanimity much more easily than he himself ever could.

In some ways, Akut was a walking contradiction. At some times, a violent killer, when circumstances of self-defense demanded it, at other times, a being so at peace with himself that Korak saw him almost as a wise sage of sorts. Akut didn't lecture, nor instruct; in fact, he spoke only when necessary. Korak learned from him by trying to follow his example.

Akut had a deep intelligence, and looked into the eyes of those he loved—Korak and Meriem, and Tarzan and Jane—as if he were looking into their souls. Just as his grandfather had done before him. The ape-man couldn't be sure, but he believed that Akut's personality and demeanor were inexorably tied to the fact that he was the original Akut's grandson—and that the prior Akut's essence, his soul, if there were such a thing, lived on in the younger Mangani.

Korak did not believe this figuratively. He believed it literally. His boyhood friend and mentor, Akut, had been rein-
carnated in his grandson, in his opinion.

The Mangani was indeed special, recollecting the memories
of the original Akut, mentioning incidents and adventures
they had had together in the African jungle when Korak was
a boy. There was no one, other than his original boyhood
friend, who could have known of these things, recounted the
details with such precision: the killings of Michael Sabrov—in
reality the villain Alexis Paulvitch—and of the thief Condon
in self-defense, or in defense of young Korak; the search for
a Mangani tribe that both he and Korak could join; and the
great ape's reluctant acceptance of young Meriem after Korak
had rescued her, his attitude evolving from initial contempt
to hesitant approval as the little girl learned from them both
the laws of the jungle.

Man and great ape (and the great ape's father and grandfather) had had a special relationship over the decades, and
although they had led their own lives and had their own
various adventures, they always ended up back together,
looking out for each other.

Most of all, they were inseparable best friends. Korak owed
a great deal of who he was to old, shaggy Akut's guidance and
devotion. Although it had ultimately been Meriem's love that
had pulled him back from the brink of wanton killings in
response to rejections by African natives, and thereafter
European settlers, and then after that other great apes, it was
Akut who taught him the basics. Senses were to be relied on
in this order: scent, hearing, sight. How to avoid Numa and
Sabor. How to take joy in the challenges presented by the
jungle. How to understand and speak the language of the
great apes. The art of traversing the treetops, swinging, and
releasing from the branches. How to identify and follow different jungle spoors. How to mimic and emulate the behaviors
of many jungle animals.

Korak had wept when the first Akut had succumbed to old

age, refusing the offer of the Kavuru elixir because it would only halt the progression of his aging, not restore his lost youth. Besides, Akut had reassured the young man, they would be together again one day. Korak had not understood, nor believed it, at the time.

Now he did, and it brought him much comfort. Akut was the very definition an "old soul."

The *Connecticut* continued to skirt the coast, having successfully navigated past the Unfriendly Islands just to the south of them. They had now passed from the Lural Az into the Sojar Az, and were on a northwest course, paralleling the coast, which would eventually turn southwest and lead them to their destination, Thuria.

Korak, Akut, and Ja were conferring on the forward deck when a lookout cried out: *"Sithic! Sithic!"*

The waterborne beast was cutting a foam trail through the ocean, headed straight to the ship. The sithic was a variation on the outer crust's extinct *labyrinthodontia*, a carnivorous amphibious creature of many tons and fully twenty feet in length, with a toadlike body and impressive jaws filled with rending, gnashing teeth.

Korak looked more closely at the approaching creature as it undulated in a wavelike motion, propelling itself toward them at an alarming speed. "Ja, may I borrow your spyglass?"

The *Connecticut's* captain handed the instrument to the ape-man and moved to the forecastle deck, ordering all crewmen not performing critical ship's functions to line the port side, with spears at the ready.

As the men rushed to comply, Korak called to Ja. "Captain, that thing is a lot longer than twenty feet."

Ja leaped back down to the main deck and took the spyglass. He uttered an oath in Pellucidarian, the precise nature of which was not readily translatable into English.

"That's no sithic, it's a *rantac!*"

The monster was at least forty feet long, easily twice the

size of a sithic, with an extraordinarily long tail, which it used to propel itself toward the *Connecticut* at a phenomenal speed. It resembled a huge seagoing lizard with vestigial limbs serving as paddles, which also added to its propulsive force. Worst of all, the thing had a pointed, heavily armored needle nose-like snout, with large, scallop-shaped scales.

The monstrous sea creature attacked, ramming the ship's port side at a ninety-degree angle and knocking it off course; a few more hits like that and the hull would be breached. The Mezop sailors hurled spears at the rantac, to little or no effect given the creature's armor-like scales.

Long afterward, when the monster had been described to Abner Perry, including the beast's two gigantic, circular, dead-looking eyes, black as pools, positioned on either side of its torpedo-shaped snout, the old scientist speculated that the attacking creature was some type of *Sarabosaurus*, a type of *mosasaur*, a reptilian that had roamed the outer crust's oceans 100 million years ago.

Korak thought the thing looked like a science-fiction sub-marine straight out of a 1950s kids' movie. But this was real, and it was headed straight for them.

"That thing is going to pierce the hull, isn't it?"

"The rantac is definitely going to try to hole us," Ja replied. He shouted orders at the conn to come about on a parallel course, in an effort to deflect the impact. The rantac was much faster than they were, for the wind was low, but the helmsmen managed to bring the ship about in accordance with Ja's orders.

The rantac paralleled them for a short while, and then dove. When they caught sight of it again, it was out in the open ocean. It turned, and once again was blazing toward the port side at a ninety-degree angle, a situation that was sure to result in a pierced hull if they could not maneuver out of the way in a timely manner.

Ja, repeating his prior commands, ordered a parallel course, but as the *Connecticut* turned, the beast turned with it, and sideswiped the port hold at an angle, rocking the ship vigorously. The beast's tail thrashed across the deck, sweeping several sailors into the ocean. The remaining men who tumbled to the deck quickly regained their feet.

Ja flung orders at the spearmen: the next time they managed to parallel the monster, the spearmen were to give it everything they had.

The ocean went calm for too long, and some of the men began to think that they had successfully evaded the creature. Ja thought better, but the thing was nowhere in sight, despite his continuous scanning on all sides with the spyglass. The lookout, from his elevated vantage point, also saw nothing.

When they next encountered the rantac, it shot up vertically from beneath them, and its armored snout cut a chunk out of the hold as it thrust up into the air beside the ship and then dove back down beneath them.

The *Connecticut* began to take on water and list. The damage also inhibited the craft's maneuverability. In fact, this one tactically brilliant move on the part of the mindless monster had rendered them sitting ducks. Not that Korak knew whether or not there were ducks in Pellucidar.

The rantac came around again, this time not bothering to hide its presence deep under the ship. It raced along the surface, foam trailing in its wake, just like a World War I U-boat torpedo, coming at a helpless American transport in the middle of the Atlantic. The spearmen did their best, but the creature's angle of attack presented little surface area at which they could cast their weapons. A few of them smartly aimed for the creature's giant dead eyes, but unfortunately these cast spears missed their mark.

The beast of the seas rammed again, and the *Connecticut* shook and listed. Sailors once again tumbled to the deck, and the unfortunate lookout, high in his tower, was cast into the ocean. Ja's warriors quickly regained their feet, and took up their spears once more, struggling to maintain their footing on the slippery ocean-washed deck.

The creature came about for the kill. Once the ship was

totally destroyed, it would sink, and the rantac could pick off its meal—the helpless swimming and floating gilaks—at its leisure. The monster was not stupid.

The beast's giant tail swept the deck, the Mezops managing to avoid its deadly sweep, and then it was sucked away behind the rantac's retreating body. The tip of the tail was still above the ocean's surface, about fifteen feet to port and quickly sinking. Korak made a great leap and soared through the air, clenching the end of the tail as it sank beneath the waves.

The Mezop sailors were astonished, for none of them could have contemplated such a leap. Yet Korak, having heard the prior reports of David Innes and Abner Perry regarding the lesser gravitational effect within Pellucidar, had decided to chance it; for Korak had, since he had been in the inner world, thought he had experienced some of the same effects of greater speed and agility that David had described. Though the ape-man was a highly experienced and skilled pole-vaulter, Pellucidar's lesser gravity, and consequent lightness of step conferred upon those from the outer crust, might even have accounted for the magnificent vault Korak had made when he had been seemingly trapped by the Horibs back in the dead-end canyon.

Korak was pulled into the seawater as the rantac undulated. The massive beast skimmed the ocean's surface underwater, dragging Korak along a coral reef and tearing up his back.

Aboard the *Connecticut*, Akut stood at the railing, spear in hand, deep brown eyes searching for his friend. Worry was etched across his expressive face. The ape-man had been underwater for an alarmingly long time.

Finally, the rantac surfaced and skimmed the water's surface again, heading toward Ja's ship like a torpedo launched to make the final kill. Korak emerged from the seawater, back and arms and legs bleeding, pulling himself hand over hand up the tail and toward the thing's massive torso. He continued to clamber along the rantac's backside, the creature's tail curling around and sweeping back and forth in an effort to dislodge the tiny thing crawling upon it. Then the creature's armored skull crashed once again against the ship's hull, inflicting further damage.

As the rantac swam by the ship, Korak, now stationed near the back of the armored skull, waved and gesticulated at Akut. The Mangani took a spear and hurled it at his friend, eliciting horrified gasps from Ja and the other sailors, for it appeared the great ape was targeting his friend with the lance.

Korak deftly plucked the flung spear from the air, scrambled further up the backside of the monster's head, and repeatedly stabbed the thing in both eyes in a frenzy of blood and gore. The creature thrashed and shrieked in pain and anger, and Korak was thrown off into the sea. The blinded dinosaur was still very much a danger as it circled wildly and writhed about, sending large waves of saltwater crashing against the ruined ship.

Korak and the other sailors who had been swept overboard rapidly climbed up the sides, utilizing thick ropes tossed by their mates, while the remaining crew made haste and attempted to maneuver the wrecked ship to the beach. Others of the rantac's kind appeared in the ocean, speeding toward them, undoubtedly drawn by the lifeblood spurting from the dinosaur's ruined orbs, as well as the blood of Korak and the other gilaks.

The *Connecticut* ran aground some thirty feet from the coastline, and the men abandoned ship, diving overboard and swimming for it, bringing as many weapons and provisions as they could, which wasn't much, considering they were swimming for their lives.

8
PARADISE IN PELLUCIDAR

MERIEM MATERIALIZED IN THE JUNGLE, shaded by the deep canopy of the rainforest. The soil beneath her was rich and moist. Before her departure, the camera mounted on the end of the borer had shown a shadowed environment, dense with trees. It was impossible to discern if it had emerged in Thuria or not. Unwilling to spend another forty-eight hours retracting the borer and drilling another hole, Meriem had elected to proceed.

The pain associated with the matter-transmission had passed. She had eschewed any preventive pain medication, wanting to be fully alert when she rematerialized. Regaining her wits, Meriem explored, pushing though the dense undergrowth. Nearby, she heard what sounded like ocean waves crashing upon a reef. Thuria and the Land of Awful Shadow were bounded on one side by an ocean, the Sojar Az. Perhaps Tiny had indeed gotten the destination right!

She pushed her way through a few feet of dense foliage and emerged on a crystal-white sandy beach, the vast ocean spreading before her as far as her eyes could see. The upcurving distance of the interior of the hollow Earth was hazy, and she couldn't tell if there were faraway landmasses, or just endless ocean. The sand, bordered by thick rainforest, extended to both her left and right, curving out of her view about a mile away in both directions.

Meriem decided to explore her surroundings, to see if she could confirm that she was near Thuria. She was a bit concerned that she couldn't see the Dead World, but maybe she had arrived in a place that just wasn't close enough for it to be visible. It was, after all, a very small object in relation to the rest of Pellucidar and hung only a mile above the ground. Maybe she would able to see it if she navigated around the curves to the coastline. The leftward direction seemed as good as the right, and she chose the former.

Before setting out, she made sure that she was equipped with her knife and crossbow, and that she had sufficient water in her canteen and enough dry food packs to last for perhaps a day, in case she ventured that far. She reminded herself that she wouldn't be able to measure a day, and tried to get into the mindset of measuring the passage of time by number of sleeps. She concluded that if she got tired and slept, then she would know she had gone far enough and would return back when she awakened.

She planned to blaze her trail at regular intervals by marking the trees that grew down close to the sand. She thought about changing out of her long pants and boots into something more appropriate for the heat, but in the end decided that she had better stay outfitted as she was, in case she encountered snakes, or other reptiles; the less exposed skin the better, until she got a better handle on her environment, and what she could expect from it.

She headed off toward the left, thinking to herself that she had planned and prepared as much as possible for what was undoubtedly an unpredictable environment. Trudging through the sand in boots was not the easiest thing in the world, but it was probably better than attempting it in her bare feet, which were not hardened against the reflective heat emanating from the beach.

Meriem had blazed at least four trees by the time she reached the point that she had previously seen where the coastline had begun to curve out of her sight. She followed it around the curve, and saw that the coast still continued to arc to the left into the distance. She discerned the tinkling of rushing water up in the foliage and decided to investigate. After ten minutes of breaking an uphill trail, she arrived at a small pool. Nature had carved the small lake into the rock beneath a charming waterfall. The trees of the rainforest bloomed overhead, shading her from the intense heat. At the end of the pool opposite the waterfall, a small stream trickled its way downhill.

At first, Meriem thought she might follow the brook back down to the beach. But she decided she had better retrace her own path back down, to ensure she didn't lose track of any of the other markers she had left for herself. She opened a test kit from her pack, ran some of the stream water through it, and the results came back safe for human consumption. Rather than use up the water she had brought with her, she drank deeply of the fresh Pellucidarian pool, and thought to herself that this was a milestone, however small in her short sojourn in the inner world. She rested for a while more in the shade, and then knew she had to press on.

Back on the beach, she continued to follow the path of the sand and the curve of the ocean. The water was a deep blue and looked gorgeous and inviting, but of course she had not brought any swimwear, and if she had, she wouldn't have taken the chance of a dip in the water, knowing what she did about the monstrous and fearsome denizens of Pellucidar's oceans and seas. Nonetheless, it looked incredibly tempting, and she regretted not being able to bathe in it.

As Meriem trudged onward, following the endless curvature of the beach, with the sun hanging at zenith and beating down its heat upon her skin, a sameness, an almost miragelike drowsiness, overcame her. It was beautiful, a paradise, but everything was identical. No matter where she looked across the vast sea, there was no other land in sight; the blue water always curved up in all directions. There was no horizon. The inner world's solar orb, driving its harsh rays down upon her, always hung at noon directly above.

Not only had time, the fourth dimension, stopped, but the other three had ground to a halt as well.

Some ocean birds flew over, or perhaps they were small reptiles, but not large enough to be of a danger to her. In fact, they completely ignored her. Other than that, there was no stirring of life. Everything was still, utterly quiet; only the hypnotic tinkling of gently running water from waterfalls and streams in the rainforest above her, and the soft lapping of the ocean waves at her side, broke the overwhelming silence.

Meriem steeled herself against the repetitive, almost at this point boring, landscape and continued to trek through the sand, her legs heavy, and her eyelids even heavier.

When she finally came upon, to her left, the first tree in which she had blazed her mark, she sank into the hot sand. She crawled back up to where her supplies were stashed at the site of the borer and the transmitter-reintegrator, erected her pup tent, checked the sonic proximity alarms she had set up, and wept.

"I am on a deserted island."

"What was that? Can you repeat?" The reply via the radio transmitter was marred by a blast of static.

"Do you read me? I am on a tropical island in the middle of nowhere," Meriem said. Her frustration punctuated the last three words: Middle. Of. Nowhere. "You're going to have to transmit me back."

There was a long pause, and Meriem began to grow uncomfortable. "Are you there? Are you reading me? I am on a small island, surrounded by an endless ocean for as far as I can see in all directions, even with the upcurving nonhorizon. I am nowhere near any other land."

Tiny Kingsley's voice came through the microphone. "Copy that, Meriem, we've cleared the static. We're having a little difficulty on our end, shouldn't take too long to resolve, and then we'll transport you back."

"What sort of problem?" She asked. "Is everything okay?"

Dr. Moritz responded, "Everything should be fine, Meriem. There was a glitch in the laser transmission after your reassembly. There's something, perhaps a bit of crumbling granite in the microtunnel, that's interfering with the straight-line laser beam. We have a backup borer that we're sending down to clear the rock; I should be able to resolve this in short order."

"Is everything all right with you on your end, Meriem?" Tiny asked. "Are you safe, are there any predators about?"

Meriem replied, "The island looks completely deserted of any fauna, but I've got shelter, water, and I'll stay on the alert. Can you give me any sort of time frame for getting me out of this mess?"

"If we told you twelve hours," Moritz said, "would it make any difference to you? Would you be able to tell?"

"Well, I did bring a wristwatch . . ." Meriem said. She consulted it and saw that it had already stopped. "I guess that's not going to be of much use. I'll try to estimate the time by having some food and getting some sleep. I'll radio again when I wake up. If it's not twelve hours, so be it."

"That works," Tiny said, "but for god's sake, be careful. We know the things that Chris West has had to contend with since he's been down there. Don't let your guard down."

"Roger that," Meriem said. "I'll radio you again in a while. Signing off."

Meriem secured the perimeter of terminus point, her little base camp just inside the edge of the jungle foliage, and made sure her supplies—her food and water—were secure. She took her extendable spear to a nearby stream, and in short order had a small fire going on the beach, grilling a couple of small river-trout-like fish over the coals. If only this had been a beach at sunset, rather than the perpetual noonday sun beating down on her directly overhead, she almost would have thought it was a perfect setting, despite her uncertain circumstances.

She pondered what had gone wrong, directionally speaking. Tiny Kingsley was a brilliant mathematician. She was surprised that he had miscalculated her destination to a degree of this magnitude. She thought about Victory Harben's discovery two decades prior, that Pellucidar actually existed in a different angle, or universe, from her Earth. (To make matters more complicated, the hollow world apparently existed within a planet also known as Earth, but which had a somewhat different history from Meriem's own Earth, and from which access between it and Pellucidar did not seem to exist. It went a bit toward explaining the apparently impossible laws of physics at operation in the inner world.) When traversing between her Earth's outer crust and Pellucidar, in Abner's iron mole, or in airship or airplane via the north polar opening, or by means of the Moritz-Kingsley matter-transmitters, travelers passed through a transitional barrier between the two universes. Perhaps this had shunted her to a different geographical area than that which Kingsley had calculated. This could also explain why, decades past, David Innes had departed in the iron mole from Connecticut and had come up in Pellucidar near Sari, and then had left from the same inner world location, but had surfaced in Africa's Sahara Desert rather than Connecticut.

Meriem drank more of the fresh water she had gathered from the nearby stream, killed the fire, and lumbered back up to her little base camp just inside the jungle foliage. She examined her immediate surroundings once more to ensure there was no discernible nearby danger, and checked the matter transmitter's terminus, her other supplies just next to her pup tent, and her weapons. Then she climbed in the little shelter to nap, hunting knife gripped tightly in one hand, crossbow in the other.

9
CEREMONY FOR THE DEAD

Ja's ship, the *CONNECTICUT*, was a complete loss.

The Mezop sailors, Korak, and Akut watched from the relative safety of the beach as the grand vessel went down, some thirty feet off the coast of the Sojar Az.

To the north of them they could see the Great Peak. To the southwest, the pendent moon hung one mile above the surface of the inner world, a barely discernible black dot against the upcurving panorama in the distance.

Before the party set out for Pellucidar's interior satellite, ritual services were held for those of Ja's men whom they were able to recover from the ocean disaster. The warriors saluted Ja by touching the points of their spears to the ground directly in front of them, after which Ja spoke of the sailors' dedication and bravery, both to him as captain of the ship, and as members of the empire's navy, and most of all natives of Anoroc.

Ja's demeanor was solemn, and his black eyes showed his sorrow as he spoke of each of the dead men.

After the short ceremony, the men's bodies were placed as high as possible in nearby trees. Ja explained to Korak that the dead men would travel to the Dead World, just as their living comrades were about to travel to Thuria, but in a much different manner. Birds would come and fly away with body parts of the dead men, taking them to the pendent moon.

"So," Korak said, "Pellucidarians who live far away from the Land of Awful Shadow know about the Dead World, then, even though most have probably never seen it. The knowledge of existence of the pendent moon must have spread across vast regions of Pellucidar through . . ." Korak had been about to say, "hearsay and oral myths," but checked himself.

"Indeed," Ja replied, "it plays an important role in all of our lives and deaths—*if*, that is, our bodies are properly handled with correct placement high in the branches of the trees. With any other manner of death, in which the corpse is not appropriately dealt with, proper passage to the Dead World cannot be guaranteed. It is fortunate that we are so close to the Dead World, it is actually within our sight. Our close proximity will speed the dead men on their way."

"But what of those who are not properly prepared for passage to the Dead World?" Korak asked.

"Ah," Ja replied, "they all go to the Molop Az. You see, deep underneath the ground of Pellucidar is the Molop Az, the flaming sea. Pellucidar floats upon this sea."

"But," Korak interjected, "the surface of Pellucidar, its land and its oceans, are on the inside of a hollow globe. You know this, you can see this. How can Pellucidar float upon the Molop Az? How can there be a sea beneath us?"

"If we were to go down deep enough," Ja said, "I am told that we would reach your world, correct?

"Yes."

"Well, perhaps your world is the fiery Molop Az. I am told that those who venture very near what you call the polar opening have seen the fiery blaze of the sea beneath us."

Korak shrugged. "Go on."

"We know that those not placed in the trees go to the Molop Az, because if dead bodies are placed in the ground— we do this only to our enemies—when we come back and dig up the grave, parts or all of the corpses are already gone. Thus, they must have been borne away by the vile little men who reside underground. And the only place they could have been taken is the Molop Az."

"I see," Korak said, although of course he didn't. "Then, what exactly awaits the dead men on the pendent world?"

"I don't understand the question," Ja replied.

"Well," Korak's said, "the Molop Az sounds much like what many of the people on the outer crust refer to as Hell, Hades, the River Acheron, or the River Styx, and other names, depending on their particular religious upbringing."

"Religious?" Ja asked.

"Stories, or sets of laws, by which some men choose to live," Korak replied. "You have seen Abner Perry pray many times. He is entreating his god, according to the legends and stories by which he lives. Similar to your legend that the corpses of your buried enemies will be drawn down to the Molop Az—similar to our Hell."

"Ah," the Anorocan said, "but those are not stories. Those are the truth."

Korak smiled. "Yes. Just like the religions on the outer crust. Anyway, as I said, we have a similar concept to the Molop Az in our legends and traditions. But we also have stories and legends and myths about what happens to the dead who do not go to the Molop Az. My point is, you wish your own dead to be transported to the Dead World by putting the bodies in trees, and letting the birds take bits and pieces of flesh there. That doesn't seem to be a horrifying concept to you, but rather the desired outcome. Is that true, and if so, why?

"I see what you're asking now," Ja said. "We know much less about the Dead World than we do about the Molop Az that supports the whole world of Pellucidar upon its fiery waters, and from which little demons come to Pellucidar and carry away the bodies, piece by piece, of those who are buried in the ground, and take them back to the Molop Az. It has always been this way, that our dead should go to the Dead World. But why, I cannot explain." Ja gazed thoughtfully into the clear blue sky.

"So, then," Korak said, "by allowing the little birds to carry dead gilaks' body parts to the Dead World, you believe that there is at least some chance at a sort of life after death—

a better outcome than allowing the bodies to be spirited away to the Molop Az."

"I can speak of it no more, except to say that on that we can agree."

10
THE HATCHERY

ERIEM AWOKE TO A CACOPHONY of chirping and chittering. Her crossbow at the ready, she unzipped the flap of her tent and poked her head out, looking in all directions in case an enemy lurked above.

Perched all around her on the branches of the trees, surrounding her little makeshift rainforest clearing, were dozens upon dozens of tiny birdlike creatures. They hopped around on the tree limbs, stabbing their tiny but sharp beaks down into the cracks and crevices of the large branches and plucking out small bright red insects. The insects, being chomped upon by the hard beaks of the birdlike creatures, squirted out much like a berry crunched between one's fingers. The little pterosaurs watched Meriem with large black eyes, but otherwise went about their business of their meal, giving her no further regard.

The miniature pterosaurs, and the insects, were actually the first fauna she had encountered on the island—so it wasn't entirely deserted of other life. The creatures had batlike wings that ended in birdlike claws, with a wingspan of about nine to ten inches, and were mottled brown and orange. She thought they were adorable, with the long beaks being of a much darker brown than the rest of the body, and with large eyes in small skulls that made them resemble juveniles of the species, and perhaps they were. She resolved not to let her guard down and to keep an eye out for others in case there were adult-sized versions about.

Eventually all parties tentatively decided that neither posed a threat to the other. Meriem donned her hat against the sun and pushed through the edge of the foliage out onto the beach. The scenery appeared unchanged.

She crawled back through the dense vegetation to her clearing and opened radio contact with the scientists on the outer crust. Kingly and Moritz reassured her that they were making progress, and should be able to transport her back soon, and they agreed to check in again in one sleep.

Meriem went back out onto the beach, intending to spear a few fish for breakfast, and perhaps even bathe in the shallows, if it were safe to do so. What she saw there was entirely unexpected.

There were multitudes of baby sea turtles hatching in the sand, fighting their way out of the tiny holes in which their eggs had been buried, and struggling to reach the ocean.

At the same time, the small pterosaurs had emerged from the jungle foliage and were swooping down en masse upon the helpless baby turtles and making off with many of the hatchlings.

Meriem had read nature articles in the *National Geographic*, or maybe *Smithsonian* magazine, explaining that if one came upon sea turtles hatching, one shouldn't try to help them along to the ocean, as it could inhibit their natural abilities to acclimate to their environment and learn on their own.

Meriem was pretty sure *National Geographic* didn't have anything to say about pterosaurs with nine-inch wingspans, diving down and devouring the baby turtles as they dug their way out of the sand. So, Meriem felt confident that she was doing the right thing in trying to hit the flying creatures with her now-extended retractable walking stick. The tiny pterosaurs had no trouble avoiding her wild swings and continued to decimate the newborn turtles.

She had to think of something. Yes, the pterosaurs were adorable, or at least she had thought so a few minutes ago, but so were the turtles. She knew that Tarzan, and probably even Korak, would have thought she was behaving ridiculously, and that she should just let nature take its course. Usually she agreed with their stances, but in this case, she couldn't just stand by and watch the vicious feast. Sea turtles were already facing extinction on the outer crust; it was worth it to her to help preserve their populations in Pellucidar. (Only later did she stop to think that pterosaurs were long-extinct on the outer crust, and that there were legitimate arguments in favor of ensuring they survived and thrived here in the inner world.)

In essence, her actions were based on emotion, but that didn't make them wrong or any less valid. Besides, she remembered the stories Tarzan himself had told of engaging in many similar actions, despite his better judgment. And Korak, had he been here, would have loved her for it and pitched in.

But the swinging walking stick was not working. The pterosaurs were easily avoiding it and not in the least threatened. She had to find something else to drive them away.

Meriem darted back into her little campsite clearing and combed frantically through her backpack. Shovels—no. Matches—no. Bear spray—no. She thought about using her crossbow—she was much better than a fair shot—but really didn't want to waste all her bolts, and in any event, there were far more pterosaurs than she had arrows.

She looked around, momentarily stumped. Then she had it. She grabbed the four perimeter sonic alarm units that she had arranged around her enclave and ran back out to the beach. She kneeled down, planted the four devices in the ground by their stakes, and activated them.

Nothing happened.

She fiddled with the dials, changing the frequency and increasing the volume. She couldn't hear a thing, but she knew the four small devices were emitting sonic waves out of the range of her hearing.

Still nothing.

Meriem made some additional adjustments, increasing the frequency and volume even further.

Some of the pterosaurs started tumbling to the ground,

mid-dive; these were knocked out when they hit the sand. Others flew away in random patterns, clearly disoriented. Still others began fighting each other, agitated by the sonic disturbance. Within moments, the pterosaurs that had not been rendered unconscious had fled back into the forest.

Meriem turned off the sonic projectors and ran toward the area where the small turtles had been climbing out of the sand from their hatched shells. Once again, ignoring the advice of *National Geographic*, she helped the ones that were still alive down to the edge of the lapping sea. This was not an inconsiderable effort as there were more than a few turtles still alive, to her great relief and satisfaction.

Meriem made sure to scour the whole area several times looking for any other turtles who were attempting to break free of their hatchery. She found a few more, got them on their way, and then sat down roughly on the beach.

She assumed that the uniformly stable temperature within Pellucidar resulted in a fairly even mix of male and female hatchlings. For some species of the outer crust, such as green sea turtles, the sex of the embryo depended on the temperature of the nest. Here, she presumed that these turtles had evolved to match an environment with little or no variability in temperature. She also knew that sea turtles on the outer crust emerged from their hatcheries mainly at night; that these turtles didn't have that option and still lived was further evidence of an evolutionary adaptation.

Her feet itched and her legs did as well. Sand had gotten into her clothing and boots. This just wasn't going to work; she couldn't take it anymore. She resolved to return to her encampment and change into some khaki shorts and different footwear. After all, she hadn't seen any snakes, or other reptiles or animals, that might attack uncovered portions of her body.

Meriem stood and took another look at the shore with some pride in her handiwork. The baby turtles were floating and bobbing, and she imagined that they were happy in their new marine environment.

She was taken aback when she saw, a little bit farther out in the ocean, several extremely large and dark bobbing shapes. She retrieved her binoculars and focused in on them. They were huge leatherback turtles, beautiful creatures that were dark in coloring, with seven lighter-colored ridges, or keels, running vertically from their necks and down their leathery backs to their tails. Some were speckled with white spots, many of which were more prevalent along the ridges. Their heads were short, ending in rounded beaks, the upper and lower jaws of which came together in a "W" shape. Extraordinarily long, paddle-shaped flippers extended from just behind the necks, with shorter flippers at the rear. These turtles were made for the wide-open ocean.

She watched silently as their heads dipped up and down in the surf. The giant sea turtles were much larger than modern leatherbacks of the outer crust, which she knew were anywhere from 660 to 1,100 pounds and measured between three and six-and-a-half feet in length.

Meriem estimated these were at least twelve or even fourteen feet long!

She had the uncanny feeling they were gazing at her.

She returned to camp, changed clothes, secured her little encampment, and lay down for a short nap in her pup tent, thinking of the strange, enormous turtles. She really had had the sense of being watched, under close observation.

Could they communicate? Were they hostile?

Meriem's mind raced with questions about the sea turtles, but finally sleep overcame her.

Meriem awoke, rested; obviously she didn't know how much time had passed, but she had agreed with Moritz and Kingsley to radio again after another sleep. They had no progress to report, and she spent another restless "day" stewing about her situation.

As Meriem prepared to bed down, the branches began shaking as the wind picked up. She crawled through the foliage, back out to the edge of the beach, and a blast of gritty sand gusted in her face. She looked up and was surprised to see a massive weather formation of dark clouds, blotting out the sun. The wind whipped more severely, and she retreated into her tree-lined enclosure. Soon, the terrible gusts penetrated the densely packed tree boles and foliage, whipping at her pup tent, and she became concerned that the almost hurricane-force winds might dislodge the stakes holding the tent fast in the loamy soil.

Thinking quickly, she dismantled and rolled up the tent, and stowed the stakes in her pack, along with anything and everything else she could fit in it. She donned the backpack and tightened the straps and clasps securely about her. There was nothing she could do about the cases of water or food. They would have to stay put. And of course, the borer and the reintegrator were embedded solidly in the ground, so she had no concerns with regard to these.

Meriem scrambled up into a tree, climbing, and in some cases jumping, from branch to branch, in order to find a nestled and protected area in which she could crouch, shielding herself from flying debris, though she knew that the near-hurricane-force winds could take out the tree in which she sheltered herself by the roots. Still, she felt safer higher up in the tree than down below, where other trees could potentially fall and crush her. She thought about descending and crawling back through the thick undergrowth to try to huddle somewhere on the sandy beach, but being sandblasted was also unappealing. She opted for the environment she knew best: the middle terrace of the jungle rainforest.

Rain beat horizontally, constantly thrashing her and soaking her to the bone. She couldn't remember when she had been this cold or bedraggled. The wind lashed at her with even more strength, and she wrapped her arms around a thick branch, holding on for dear life. Her body was contorted in an awkward position, legs leveraged against an opposing branch, to try to maintain her position and not be swept away.

Eventually the winds lightened somewhat—not to a degree that it was safe to come down—but the rain persisted in showering down upon her in torrents. She curled up in her aerial nest, balancing on the tree branches as best as she was able, and continued to grip the bole tightly as she waited it out.

Later, she realized that the storm's fury had slackened off to a gentle downpour. She wasn't sure, but she thought she might have actually drifted off in the interim.

Meriem climbed down, utterly soaked, and collapsed in the mud pit of her former encampment.

Broken branches, leaves, and debris of all kinds littered the ground. She looked for the borer and the reintegrator, searching for the spot where she thought they had been located. She dug furiously, scooping the thick mud away in handfuls.

She began to panic.

Meriem grabbed a small shovel from her backpack and started frantically digging in other spots. Soon there were piles of mud everywhere, amid the detritus of the battered trees and foliage. Desperately she shoveled in various locations, searching for the equipment, but the dirt and sand collapsed back into the holes, and the cavities she excavated closer to the ocean were washed away by the rising and falling tides.

No crust borer. No matter-reintegrator terminus. No camera equipment, no radio.

The large turtles were long gone, and the small pterosaurs had understandably fled the storm.

She collapsed back in the mud and lay there, staring at the rainforest's upper terraces, wondering what the hell she was going to do now.

11
GLOOM

KORAK, AKUT, JA, AND THE REST of the Mezop sailors marched west-southwest along the coastline toward their goal. The Dead World hung a mile above the ground in the distance. Right now, it was just a black dot against the background of Pellucidar's upcurving landscape, but the ape-man could tell they were making progress toward their goal, as the outline of the little pendent world grew steadily larger in their view. He estimated that they were about one to two sleeps away from reaching Thuria.

"Korak," Akut said, "*yato-nala.*"

The great ape was pointing up at a spot in the sky, to the north of them.

"Ship of the air," Akut said.

The Mangani was right. There it was, the O-220, flying over land and miles away to their right, heading on what looked like a northerly course, which would eventually take the ship to the north polar opening if it maintained that route.

Korak clenched his teeth in frustration. He had nothing with which to signal the airship, such as a flare gun. He wondered what had happened. What were Captain Hines and the crew doing? Had they actually made it to Thuria and were now leaving? Why had they abandoned them? He couldn't imagine that Hines would have willingly left them, but why would he now be directing the ship back toward the polar opening and presumably heading to the outer crust? What was he up to?

The ape-man gripped his spear more tightly, and it began to bend under his mighty thews. A red wave of anger came over him, fueled by the frustration and helplessness at his position and the circumstances thus far. He had been stranded in the wrong area of Pellucidar. His beloved daughter was missing; it was unknown if she were alive or dead. His ship was apparently airworthy, but it was leaving them behind.

His vision blurred, and his heart raced. He was breathing hard and sweating. He saw himself sitting behind his desk at the offices of Easthawking Ltd., running the family business along with his son Jackie.

It had been a decade or so ago. Korak had just received word that Suzanne's teenage son Rahnak was missing during an exploratory expedition in Pellucidar, along with the boy's great-grandfather, Tarzan. The youngster had been raised in the inner world, and Tarzan had made many voyages to the hollow Earth, spending much time there. Korak had known no one was better equipped than Tarzan to overcome the challenges of Pellucidar, but he was still quite naturally worried about his grandson. As the hours had dragged on without any news, Korak had grown more and more frustrated at his helplessness. He needed to *do* something.

Eventually, he had attempted to contact Captain Conover of the *Favonia* to charter a rescue mission, as the O-220 was already in Pellucidar. The trip had proven unnecessary when some six hours later he had received word that both Tarzan and Rahnak had escaped from the clutches of the crew of a rogue Korsar ship, and were unharmed.

Korak *hated* being helpless. It made his skin crawl, his stomach churn. It made him want to break things.

Akut put a hand on the ape-man's shoulder. *"Dan-do. Tand tub arad."*

Korak focused and emerged from the red wave of memory. He hadn't experienced incidents such as this in decades; since his advent in the inner world, they had resumed and were increasing in frequency. He loosened his death grip on the lance, as Akut had adjured. The Mangani was right, they needed the spear and other weapons, and couldn't afford to waste anything.

The group crossed the lowlands to the south of the Great Peak, on the last leg of their journey to the Land of Awful Shadow. They saw *brontotheriidae*, giant mammals that re-sembled modern rhinoceroses, although in fact they were more closely related to horses; a *styracosaurus*, a dinosaur some eighteen feet in length, and somewhat resembling a triceratops, but with only one long horn and a longer snout; and other herbivorous giants of the plains, traveling in great herds.

These all left the traveling gilaks alone, and the gilaks did likewise.

The Dead World grew in their field of view as the weary marchers approached it, until it was a dominating, looming presence. Korak knew the tiny planet rotated; it had night-time and a daytime, the only location in Pellucidar that could boast such a claim. He could now see geographical features. Hills, valleys, forests, seas, rivers, and lakes were plainly visible. These differing topographies and environments must have been incredibly small to fit on the tiny sphere, and yet, Korak could see with clarity, they were visually quite distinctive from the other features. He knew that David Innes, Emperor of Pellucidar, upon seeing the Dead World for the first time, had speculated about equally diminutive inhabitants, which he found ridiculous. Ignoring the physical impossibility of such a notion, if there were people, where were the villages, the cities—even proportionally diminutive ones?

Coming now very close to Thuria and the Land of Awful Shadow, the soft beach sand along which they had trodden changed into hardscrabble rock, and eventually narrowed until the waters of the Sojar Az beat against sheer cliffs. Further along the cliffside, they descried what appeared to coves and inlets, with small beaches, but these were inaccessible, save for entering the water and swimming for it, a prospect no one relished, given the teeming and fearsome inhabitants of Pellucidar's oceans.

The men reversed course and retraced their steps, until the part of the beach they were on abutted a gently upsloping hill. They quitted the beach, and eventually found themselves paralleling the cliffside, but this time along the top edge rather than the base.

They crossed into the Land of Awful Shadow, and felt a perpetual half-warmth pervading the atmosphere.

Continuing to head southward along the coast toward Thuria, the tall cliffs gave way to lower and more level country. In the distance could be seen huts in a clearing near the shore, the primary village of the Thurians. Near the village, a forest of pale, scrubby ferns ran down almost to the beach. Korak recalled that David Innes, upon first sight of Thuria, had noted that it was the first "real" village he had seen, a settlement actually constructed by human hands, rather than the cave and cliff dwellings he had encountered up to that point. The village was much as David had described it, a rude rectangle walled with logs and boulders, in which resided a hundred or so thatched huts of similar construction. The natives used ladders that could be pulled up to provide or remove access over the palisade, and thus there was no gate.

Korak noticed that the Mezops exhibited some angst. The Land of Awful Shadow did not blanket Thuria with the deep, black night, such as that to which he was accustomed in the depths of the African jungle when Goro the moon did not show its face, but nonetheless the Anorocan natives were not comfortable with any darkness whatsoever. It was obvious that this twilit land, in which the formerly ever-present sun was not visible, caused considerable anxiety among Ja and his men.

Strangely, though so many of the native gilaks dreaded the murky gloom of the Land of Awful Shadow, much more than the pendent world that cast the shadow in question, Korak felt a deep sense of foreboding at the sight of the moon itself.

12
AN EPIPHANY

OVER THE NEXT SEVERAL SLEEPS, Meriem encountered several of the adult sea turtles. They had ventured back to the island after the ferocious storm, and she had the impression they were observing her. This was unsettling, but there was nothing else for her to do but go about her business: fishing, gathering fresh fruit and water, and continuing to try to figure out how to escape the island.

She was, however, close to despair. She contemplated building a raft, but in the middle of the huge ocean, under the eternal sun hanging at zenith at all times, how would she know where to go? She felt stuck, not even knowing where to start.

She had to take some sort of action. She couldn't just sit here. She rummaged through her pack again and withdrew a small axe. It was nothing compared to the large, red fire axe that Chris West had carried with him into the inner world, but it would have to do. She began pressing her way through the forest, into the foliage, cutting branches that were of a similar size, thickness, and diameter, as well as an assortment of tough vines and creepers that she could tie together.

Meriem dragged as much of this as she could in one load to the beach just on the other edge of her small rainforest encampment. She pushed her way back into the tangled forest branches and underbrush, and did it again. Cut, gather, drag, and pile. Cut, gather, drag, and pile. Within several sleeps, she had a good amount of material accumulated, and it was drying nicely under the perpetual sun.

Meriem turned her attention to the task of downing larger logs, which would be much more arduous. In fact, she was not sure she would be able to achieve it with the axe at hand, but she had no other tools upon which to rely. She chastised herself for not planning ahead well enough when she had been back in Santa Monica, as she had had two full days to consider how to equip herself. She had thought she had been careful and thoughtful about the equipment that she requested. But she had drastically underestimated the environment to which she had traveled and the necessities that she should have brought with her.

Nonetheless, she carried on, and after the passage of about ten or twelve more sleeps, she had finally pulled several cut logs to the pile of branches and vines she was accumulating on the beach, and proceeded to chop them down to complementary sizes and shapes.

Eventually some of the huge sea turtles emerged from the water and approached her, forming a loose circle around her. Meriem did not necessarily feel threatened, but Pellucidar was a hostile land, with unknown creatures of unknown intent. Over the course of several sleeps, as she labored over her raft, the gigantic leatherback turtles continued to observe her. They never took any actions that she perceived to be threatening, and eventually she relaxed in their presence, and they began to blend into the natural landscape of her life on the island.

The turtles hooted, chirped, and whistled in her presence as she labored away at the raft. It was slow going, for she was certainly no ship builder—or raft builder. She was in fine physical shape, as befitted any Clayton, and was well attuned to a life away from the modern comforts and luxuries of civilization. That was, without doubt, due to having spent her formative years as a captive in a primitive village, and thereafter in the jungle with Korak and Akut her only companions.

But raft building was never an item that she had added to her skill set.

The turtles kept her company as she worked, occasionally moving around in the sand, or trading places with some of their compatriots in the water. But now, as she was getting close to completing the raft, they never left her alone, save for the times that she crawled back into her rainforest camp to sleep in her tent.

As she cut and chopped, and whittled and tied, the turtles chirped, and did so in unison. Looking back on it, she wasn't sure when it had happened, as it had been so natural, so smooth, and almost expected. She was working in rhythm with the turtles' chants and whistles, chopping in time to their clacks, cutting in unison with their hoots. In short order, she was happily singing along with them. It took her back to a time when she had been a very young girl, alone, and imprisoned in an Arabian village, horribly mistreated and abused. Other than her tiny doll, Geeka, her only solace had been singing to herself. Even after her beloved Korak had rescued her from her captors, she continued to sing to herself as she traveled the branches and swung among the jungle's thick trees with the two friends she considered to be great apes— Korak and Akut. The singing soothed her soul, calmed her, and gave her something upon which to center her attention. She had never given it up, and in her heart of hearts believed that the power of song and music had saved her, helping her to heal from the years of trauma and abuse she had undergone.

Now, here she was again, singing to soothe herself, and singing along with turtles! There were other creatures who could make a song along with which she could sing. Her heart soared with joy, and she felt much less alone.

One "day" Meriem had an epiphany. It clicked with her. The music of the Turtle Folk, as she had begun to think of them, was a language, communication. All music had patterns, based on mathematics, but there was more to their song. There was intent and thought behind the turtles' singing.

She put aside her rudimentary woodworking and sat down cross legged on the beach, face to face with one of the large leatherbacks.

She sang, and the leatherback sang in return. She whistled, and the turtle whistled in response. After a while, she began to inject her own words into the singing. She sang to the turtle that her name was Meriem, and waited for a response. After several attempts, she understood that the turtle was responding in kind. Her name was Daali. They established a simple, but effective, form of communication.

The turtles had names. They had a society and a culture. They were singing to her, trying to talk to her through their songs. They wanted to converse, to learn more about her.

They were sentient.

13
DUEL

KORAK AND JA MET WITH THE THURIANS, while Akut reunited with the Mangani who had been just recently dropped off in the Land of Awful Shadow by the now-departed O-220.

Kolk, son of King Goork, along with Kolk's son Dek, and Dek's mate Mirina, the bird-woman, approached the newcomers. The son of Goork advised Korak and Ja that the airship had been hijacked, and that there had been a great battle when the dirigible landed in Thuria. The airship's crew had retaken the O-220, and with no hope of locating Korak and Akut—for Captain Hines and his son Wolff were smart enough to know that the ape-man and the great ape wouldn't just sit on their hands back in Lo-har, waiting for a rescue that might never come—they had proceeded directly to the north polar opening and thence to the outer crust to pick up Meriem in California, as well as the final load of Mangani and Waziri in Africa who planned to migrate to Pellucidar.

Korak was frustrated to learn that the Gridley Wave apparatus at Thuria had been destroyed in the wake of the battle. Without this, his tactical position remained the same; he could contact neither the airship nor Sari.

"What can you tell me of my daughter, Suzanne?" the ape-man asked.

"We only know she disappeared with no trace," Kolk responded, "while she was traveling to a nearby Mangani settlement to check on their progress. A follow-up party, led by her mate, Lordan of Abella, went to the settlement after Suzanne failed to return, and Tar-gash the Sagoth, who was staying with that particular band of Mangani, reported that she had never arrived.

Kolk's son, Dek, spoke up. "Thereafter, Rahnak, the son of Suzanne and Lordan, set out with the Waziri warrior Kyrianji in search of Suzanne in the Land of Awful Shadow. They expressed their intent to travel the whole of the Land, and to the far edges of the Shadow if necessary . . . perhaps even beyond the Land on the far northwestern side and to the deserted Mahar city of Kazra, for perhaps the Mahars are somehow involved in her disappearance. Lordan, upon his return from Tar-gash's settlement, learned of their intent and set out in pursuit of them. No one knows what has become of the three."

Kolk concluded his report, and as he, Korak, and Ja consulted about their subsequent course of action, King Goork emerged from a nearby hut and approached the three. Goork, of a type with most Thurians, was hirsute and muscular, although shorter and squatter than the Sarians or the Amozites. His skin was a bit lighter than that of a typical Pellucidarian gilak, due to the fact that he, like his comrades, had spent much of his life within the Land of Awful Shadow, protected from the eternal sun's tanning rays.

Korak noted that the Thurian chief was in possession of his cherished Enfield, which apparently had been recovered in the battle with the airship's hijackers.

"I see you have brought to me my rifle. Thank you." Korak held out his hand expectantly.

King Goork's face clouded. "I know not who you are, but this weapon was left here when the ship of the air departed, and was put in my safekeeping. As king of this land, I shall keep it as a prize for Thuria's part in repelling the invaders."

Dav-An Innes, princess of the Federated Kingdoms of Pellucidar, approached, having heard raised voices penetrate the hut in which she had been staying with Dek's unmarried sisters. She ignored King Goork and spoke directly to the ape-man. "Greetings Korak, son of Tarzan, Lord of the Jungle. It pleases me to see you and your comrade, Akut, safe and healthy. While the O-220 has departed for the outer crust, to retrieve your mate Meriem, and more Mangani and noble Waziri warriors, I, Dav-An, have stayed behind that I may depart for Sari and reunite with my parents, as soon as it is feasible."

Korak nodded solemnly in regard for her position, though he knew her parents, David Innes and Dian the Beautiful, did not take their positions as emperor and empress quite so seriously.

Dav-An then deigned to acknowledge Goork. "You speak thus to Korak, son of Tarzan. I know Korak, and the weapon is his. Keeping it, when our adversaries, the ones who took over the airship, did not want him to have it, is merely playing into our enemies' hands."

Korak, appreciative of the support, nonetheless felt his blood pressure rising at the chief's obdurate behavior. "Yes, King Goork," Korak added, "let us all not forget that Thuria is a member of the Federated Kingdoms of Pellucidar, pledged to mutual protection and defense, from which I understand you benefited when the Mahar War was fought in the Land of Awful Shadow. We are all allies. And allies should respect each other's property." He continued to hold out his hand for the rifle.

Korak probably did not have a future career in diplomacy. Goork, angered further at Korak's words, challenged the ape-man for possession of the weapon.

Before the offending words had left the Thurian's mouth, Korak's muscular arm shot forward like a piston, hammering a devastating punch to the mouth. He was a skilled and experienced boxer, and it showed. The ape-man's knuckles cracked with the impact, but the sound was eclipsed by the crunching of the chieftain's shattered teeth.

Goork reeled backward two steps, and Korak leaped upon

him before the gilak chief could bring his greater weight to bear. They both fell to the ground, Korak pinning Goork's shoulders, and in his escalating rage the ape-man delivered punishing roundhouse punch after punch to Goork's now-shattered jaw, preventing the Stone Age man from putting up any sort of effective defense.

Red waves of anger and violence overtook Korak, and he was transported to a time and place some forty years gone, pummeling two members of the annoyingly persistent Kriegmesser family.

They had ambushed him, thinking to trap the ape-man unawares. The two attackers and their henchmen had emerged from the melee with a variety of broken bones and internal injuries that would have been life-threatening if not treated immediately. Tellingly, Korak did not kill the men, although he always wondered if he should have. But the experience, and its wake, was cathartic, seeming to mark a turning point in Korak's overall recovery from the trauma he had experienced in the Great War. From this point forward, incidents in which he was overtaken by visions of past battles and conflicts became of much shorter duration, and he made significant progress in rebounding quickly and in being able to function in society. His wife Meriem's loving influence was also a large factor in his healing, although he still occasionally was thrust into experiences that pushed him to the furthest edges of self-control.

The red tides of violence were retreating in the ape-man's brain.

The ever-wise Akut was yelling at Korak in Mangani, warning him not to kill the Thurian king. *"Tand bundolo! Tand bundolo!"* The great ape's screams finally penetrated Korak's violent haze, and the ape-man stopped himself from killing his opponent—although it was once again impressed upon him that his self-control had not abandoned him in this manner until he had arrived in the inner world. What could it be that was affecting him thus?

The Thurians, including Goork's son Kolk, had by tradition restrained themselves from interfering in the duel. But if Korak had actually killed Goork in what had not been declared as a fight to the death, who knows how they would have reacted?

Thus, a diplomatic incident had been avoided.

Korak rose and released his adversary. Diplomacy may have won the day, but the ape-man wondered how many of the Thurians might have cheered if he had delivered a death blow to the supercilious chieftain of Thuria.

His rage having receded like the tides, and his senses having been regained, Korak reclaimed his precious Enfield rifle.

There came the sound of a buzzing in the sky, and all present, save the battered and unconscious Goork, turned their eyes to the sky in search of its author.

14

"Stupid Raft"

ERIEM AWAKENED ONE "MORNING" to discover her
partially constructed raft had been destroyed.
In fact, it had not only been destroyed, but torn
apart as if a whirlwind had gotten to it, stripping it down to
its component logs and branches and vines, and scattering it
everywhere along the beach and in the shallow water.

It appeared to be an act of great violence, and this frightened
her. She had thought the Turtle Folk, as she had dubbed them,
to be gentle and kind. If this were a ruse, then she was in deep
trouble indeed.

Meriem spent a great deal of time running through sce-
narios, trying to figure out what could have happened. Over
and over, she returned to the same conclusion: the Turtle Folk
planned to keep her trapped on the lonesome island, to help
protect their young during future hatchings.

Meriem searched out Daali and sat before the Turtle Folk
elder. She emphasized their growing relationship, and the
other friendships she was making among the Turtle Folk.

Meriem sang her concerns and her fears. Why were the
Turtle Folk trying to hurt her by destroying her raft? Did they
intend to harm her? Were they keeping her here for some
purpose? Did they intend to hold her prisoner here on this
island until the next hatching, so that she could help defend
against the preying pterosaurs? She tried to persuade Daali
that keeping her trapped on the island was unethical.

Daali was alarmed, and sang in defense of herself and the

Turtle Folk. But Meriem was angry, and once again leveled the accusation that they intended to keep her here. She sang that their actions almost made her regret her own actions. Did they have no honor?

Daali hooted, and it almost sounded to Meriem as if the tone of her response song was tinged with sadness. The leatherback protested once more that the Turtle Folk did not intend to hold her here, and that, moreover, they wanted to help her. Daali bade Meriem come with her to the water's edge.

Other Turtle Folk encouraged her to come into the ocean, which was at low tide. They too protested her accusations that they were keeping her captive. She didn't understand, and was wary of following them into the water, for they were all so much larger than she. One of them could easily crush her against the sea floor, drowning her.

Meriem stepped warily into the water, again telling Daali that she didn't know what she was supposed to see or do here in the shallows.

Daali asked her to climb on to her tough, dark carapace and the Turtle Folk elder would swim out with her a short way into the ocean, so that Meriem could better observe what Daali wanted her to see.

This was a turning point. Either trust the Turtle Folk, or sit alone on this island forever.

The little ones whom she saved, so many sleeps ago that she had lost count, swam up, chirping at her happily. They couldn't really be part of a plan to do her in. Could they? They were essentially alien creatures, in thought and form. How was she to understand their true motivations?

She decided to trust Daali for two reasons. In the first place, she didn't really have another option if she wanted to leave the island. Secondly, in her heart of hearts she couldn't really believe that Daali and the other Turtle Folk had betrayed her. But for the life of her, she couldn't imagine why she needed to go out away from the shore, atop the turtle's back.

Daali entreated Meriem once more, with several other

of the gigantic leatherbacks joining the chorus, and finally she acquiesced.

Climbing upon the turtle's back, Meriem held on while Daali gently paddled out to sea. Meriem's breath was taken away at the vastness of the ocean, and how small and alone she felt in the middle of it. There was no horizon, as the interior of the world curved upward, and the deep, blue sea turned darker and blacker in the distance, until she could see nothing but haze.

Then she was not alone.

Swimming offshore, they came upon a veritable horde of the humongous turtles, all swimming together, side by side, in what appeared to be an organized pattern.

The huge turtles had formed their floating bodies into a Brobdingnagian living raft.

Were they serious? The turtles hooted and whistled at her, conveying that they were quite serious and could help her— help her much more than the stupid raft she had been constructing out of branches, logs, and vines, which would likely only hold up for two or three of what she called "sleeps" before capsizing and casting her overboard to a watery death, or before just plain disintegrating.

Besides, the stupid raft was barely big enough to hold her, let alone the food and water she needed.

Meriem was amused at their repeated references to her "stupid raft." But they were right. It *was* stupid, and doomed to failure. It just had happened to be, up to this point, her only option for escaping the island.

She began to thoughtfully consider how to make this work.

15

"The Point!"

KORAK TURNED HIS GRAY EYES to the sky, in search of the object that was the source of the increasingly loud humming. The sound reminded him of the engine of his old RAF S.E.5, but much less smooth, with an odd clattering noise.

Akut, his eyes keener even than Korak's, pointed at a black dot in the sky, outside the border of the shadow cast on them by the Dead World. Korak gave his old friend's dark gray fur an affectionate rub in acknowledgment. The noonday sunlight glinted off the object, which grew increasingly larger in their view. The ape-man focused on it, realizing it was an aircraft, one badly in need of a muffler.

The plane approached, crossed the border of the Land of Awful Shadow, and circled for a bit, obviously seeking a flat and clear landing strip. It was a single engine biplane, a two-seater, but one such as Korak, an experienced pilot, had never before seen. The wings were too long, the rudder was too short, and the landing gear spaced too far apart.

He was astonished that the thing had taken flight.

The Thurians grew nervous, as did Korak and Akut, for none of them knew what the craft boded.

However, Dav-An spoke up, clearly pleased. "The wings are emblazoned with the colors of my father's banner. This is a plane of the Federated Kingdoms of Pellucidar!" she exclaimed. "Perhaps he has sent someone here to determine why Thuria's Gridley Wave radio has gone dark."

"If this is an example of Pellucidar's burgeoning air force," Korak murmured to himself, "we are all in deep trouble."

The plane located a suitable landing spot, clear of trees, brush, and other debris, and descended to a bumpy landing, bouncing in the air twice before finally settling on the ground. The plane turned and taxied toward the Thurian village, eventually coming to a stop several hundred yards from the northmost wall of the settlement.

Korak and the others ran to greet the plane, from which alighted David Innes and Abner Perry!

Dav-An greeted her father with an joyous hug, and old Abner with an embrace proper for a cherished uncle—which Abner was, not by blood, though he was family nonetheless.

David removed his flying goggles and doffed a fur-lined jacket. He and Korak exchanged a warm handshake. "Thanks for seeing my daughter safely back from the outer crust, Korak."

"I wish I could take credit, David, but Captain Hines and the O-220 crew are responsible for that—at least for the latter part of her journey here."

"We'd lost Gridley Wave contact with the airship," David said, "right after we received the call from Lo-har that the ship had left without you. Dian was worried sick. I guess you could say I was, as well, until we finally heard from the O-220 when we were back in Sari and learned that Dav-An was here in Thuria. But we also had lost contact with Thuria, and couldn't raise anyone here to confirm and expand on the report from Captain Hines. Can you shed any light on everything that's happened so far?"

"From what I can piece together," the ape-man replied, "the O-220 was hijacked at Lo-har. The terrorists destroyed or disabled the onboard Gridley Wave transmitter, and flew directly here, to Thuria."

"That's right, Father," Dav-An said. "We were all held prisoner on the ship, while Captain Hines was held at gunpoint, forcing Wolff to pilot the O-220 here. As we approached for landing, he was able to create a distraction. There was a big battle, and when it was all over, the Waziri security forces had retaken the ship. The whole thing was magnificent!"

"Did any of them say what they wanted?" David asked. "What was their motive?"

"It was Alex Ryadinsky," Dav-An said. "She was a new crew member, and the Hineses both knew her—or I guess they thought they did. Wolff told me he had no idea why Alex did what she did. The other hijackers were also newer crew members. Captain Hines said they had been vetted, but obviously not thoroughly enough. Maybe she paid them off to take her side."

"Well, they got paid off," Korak said. "They're all dead. And apparently one of the interlopers also managed to get to the Gridley Wave set here in Thuria and smash it. We're not sure if that person got away or is among the dead."

"So, there are no prisoners we can question," David said.

"None, unfortunately," Korak confirmed. "But the only crew member not accounted for is Alex herself. If I had to guess, I'd say she's the one who smashed Thuria's Gridley Wave set before making her escape."

"She was knocked out in the battle," Dav-An added. "Wolff shot her in the calf, hoping to prevent her from escaping."

David looked askance at his daughter.

Dav-An smiled slightly and shrugged. "Wolff doesn't fool around, I guess. Who knows what Alex would have done to us all if he hadn't, uh, intervened."

"I see." David turned back to Korak. "And what about you, my friend, and Akut?"

Korak nodded to Ja with admiration. "The captain, here, and his crew, took fine care of us after we separated from von Horst. By the way, have you heard aught from Von? When we last saw him, he was to travel back to Lo-har after receiving intelligence that the Horibs planned to attack his village. A splinter group of the Horibs who, by the way, had attacked us."

"Attacked by Horibs?" David said. "You are fortunate to have escaped."

"Yes, David," Ja interjected, "and then he fought off a rantac when all seemed lost. Though I am sorry to report the *Connecticut* is lost at sea, a victim of our battle with the rantac. And several of my crew did not survive. They have commenced their journey to the Dead World." Ja looked upward, meaningfully.

David nodded solemnly to Ja. "All respect to your lost men, and to you and your crew, Ja."

The tall Anorocan nodded gravely in acknowledgment.

Abner Perry could take the exchange of sober words and news no longer, and interrupted. "David, my boy, tell them why we are here!" The older man was a bundle of nervous energy.

"Yes, well—"

"Never mind," Abner interrupted again, "we must get to the point. The point!" The scientist turned to Korak. "We were here, young man, in the Land of Awful Shadow, when your daughter Suzanne disappeared. And may I say, you certainly look much too young to have a daughter such as her. But I forget myself . . . We were here, Suzanne was working with the Mangani, and she had gone back and forth to the other great ape settlements to confer with Tar-gash, and Mok, about how your African kin were faring." This last bit was directed to Akut.

"Well," Abner continued, "it was time for her to check on Tar-gash's 'colony,' I suppose we may term it, and she had just set out, astride her *bus-dar* companion Spy-kee, the creature's reins in one hand, her spear in the other . . . My, what a magnificent picture she painted, a valiant knight of Pellucidar, off to ensure those entrusted to her care remained safe and healthy, and were adjusting to their new lives in this strange interior world. I can assure you that, without exception, it does take anyone born on the outer crust a considerable period of adjustment before one acclimates to life under a sun that hangs eternally at zenith—just as it does take anyone born within the confines of this hollow world a not dissimilar length of time to adapt to life on the outer crust, being that there is no such thing as night and day here, and the stars! The stars, I tell you, may be the most difficult aspect for native Pellucidarians to process, for think of how difficult it is for those born on the outer crust to truly conceive of such an infinite cosmic vastness, and then put yourself in the place of a gilak who has been raised completely within a hollow sphere, which, as large as it may be, is still essentially a finite ball. You take my point?"

"Yes, but Suzanne—" Korak said.

"Case in point is Victory Harben. Now, young Victory was raised here, and went to live on the outer crust, and I understand that it was quite enlightening for her. Her complete worldview, I daresay, was altered by the experience, but—"

"Yes, Abner!" David said. "That's why we're here. Victory, remember?"

"Of course I remember, David, would you please stop interrupting, or we'll never get to explain to this young man . . ."

"Korak," the ape-man said.

"That's it! Korak. We were here when your daughter disappeared. Her bus-dar—superb creature!—came back riderless. Search parties went out, scouring for clues throughout the Land of Awful Shadow and even beyond. Her mate, Lordan, left astride his bus-dar, Mis-see, and their son Rahnak, along with Kyrianji, set out as well. Have they returned yet?

Kolk, son of Goork, spoke up. "We have seen naught of them since they departed on the search, Abner."

"Abner," David prompted, "what about Victory?"

"Ahem, Victory? Oh, yes! Well, it came to me that Suzanne's disappearance was so bizarre, so out of the ordinary—after all people just don't vanish into thin air, do they? But of course, people *do* vanish into thin air—Victory herself, and Jason Gridley had done so, though thankfully that all turned out well enough in the end.* But the point! The point, I thought to myself, was that perhaps the same thing

* See the Edgar Rice Burroughs Universe novel *Victory Harben: Fires of Halos* by Christopher Paul Carey.

had happened to Suzanne! I had some ideas, perhaps unconventional, but avenues of pursuit nonetheless, about how to possibly trace her whereabouts.

"But to test my theories, I needed some equipment back in Sari, and to consult with some Mahar scrolls that were recovered from the abandoned Mahar cities of Mintra, Phutra, and Kazra. In particular, some of the most pertinent scrolls were found in the latter, the closest deserted city to the Land of Awful Shadow. And then I refreshed my recollection regarding some historical and scientific information that Victory had once conveyed to me.

"So you see, David and I left for Sari with all due haste, and have only just returned."

Abner turned to Kolk. "May I trouble you and some of your men to bring several cases from our aeroplane and take them to a hut where I may work undisturbed?"

Kolk, of much better disposition than his father, nodded and bade his son Dek and several other warriors to do as Perry had requested.

"Korak," David said, "while we were in Sari, we received a Gridley Wave transmission from the O-220. They had managed to repair their set, a while after departing Thuria. After updating us about the hijacking, and that they had retaken the ship and left Dav-An safely with the Thurians, Captain Hines said they would prosecute a search for you and Akut. He stated he had already contacted Lo-har, and it had been reported to him that you and Akut had left just after the hijacking. Therefore, Hines said, if they did not locate you along any projected routes between Lo-har and Thuria, he would then set course for the north polar opening, the outer crust, and thereafter back to Africa, resuming the mission to take on the final load of supercargo, the last of the Mangani and Waziri who are moving here."

"Hines is a good man," Korak said. "So is his son, Wolff. He's a quick thinker." The ape-man glanced at Dav-An. The Pellucidarian princess reddened slightly.

"The Gridley Wave transmitter here at Thuria was destroyed, as I mentioned," Korak continued, "but we can use the one in your aeroplane to call the O-220 and update them. I would hate for them waste any more time searching for me and Akut when they could be getting the last load of supercargo, and picking up Meriem in California. Speaking of which, we can also call her, or at least ask Bowen Tyler to relay a message to her, and convey all that has occurred."

As Korak spoke, he noticed Abner's expression shift from surprise to a grimace, to a deep frown, until it finally settled on what could only be described as a look of chagrin.

"I, well, I regret . . ." the older man said. "Well, what I mean to say is . . . although I have succeeded in designing and building my own aeroplane . . . I, I have somehow neglected to equip it with a Gridley Wave set."

Korak suppressed his anger at this setback. Perry was only doing the best he could, and clearly meant well. He put on a smile and patted Abner on the shoulder. "Well, let's make the best of it. Can you get going on your ideas to locate Suzanne?"

Perry face lit up; it was clear he was relieved the ape-man was not upset with him.

"Right away, young man, right away!" And with that, he darted off toward the Thurian village and his equipment.

"Thank you for not being too hard on him," David said. "I know this is a tough time for you and Meriem."

"His intentions are good," Korak replied. "I hope he can validate his theories about what happened to Suzanne."

"He might take a circuitous route in getting there, but I have faith in him."

"Korak," Dav-An said, "may I steal Father away from you for a while? I have much to tell him about my experiences in the outer world. There was so much to see and do, it was hard for me to fathom."

Father and daughter walked off, arm in arm, and Korak overheard David say to his daughter, "Yes, and you must also tell me about your young man, Wolff . . ."

Korak and Akut were left alone once more, under the shadow of the pendent world that floated but a mile above their heads. A gloom overcame the ape-man, prompted by enforced inaction, and the dreariness of the murky twilight of the Land of Awful Shadow. He imagined the darkness would become even more pronounced the farther one strayed from the boundary of the Shadow. David Innes had confirmed this on a prior expedition he had taken through the area, describing it as an "endless twilight" with an odd assortment of bizarre vegetation, adding that he often observed the lidi—similar to the outer world's diplodocus, and a creature that had been tamed as a domestic beast of burden by the Thurians—stopping to graze on the flora, and to drink deeply from the rivers that flowed from the Lidi Plains on the far western side of the Shadow, all the way through the Land of Awful Shadow itself, ultimately feeding into the Sojar Az.

Korak wondered, if one stood in the exact center of the circular shadow, might one experience the perception of complete nighttime, the eternally shining central sun of Pellucidar being too far from the edges to exert any meaningful influence? As far as he knew, David's prior travels had not taken him through the precise center.

On the other hand, was the Dead World above him much too small to obscure Pellucidar's blazing sunlight, even at the center of the shadow it cast?

One would not know, unless one explored to find out. He guessed that traveling within the confines of the Shadow would be less taxing than doing so under the relentless gaze of Pellucidar's central orb.

But he must wait for Perry to test his theories and report back.

Korak turned his gaze to the Dead World itself.

It revolved on its axis in parallel to the inner world's sun and to the surface of Pellucidar, so that the small pendent moon had an actual night and day. Korak could see, as David had previously reported (for Korak had read and studied all of Mr. Burroughs' published accounts of the inner world, in preparation for making a new life there), mountains and vast forests, as well as oceans and rivers running through plains. But unlike David's prior speculations, the ape-man could not conceive of any forms of life other than flora; the tiny satellite was just too small to support anything such as David had envisioned.

Similarly, despite his admiration for Abner Perry's intellect, he was worried about relying solely on the older man's scientific prowess. For instance, the ape-man knew that Abner's prior notion that the existence of the Dead World explained the "phenomena of nutation and the precession of the equinoxes" in the outer world was incorrect, for Victory Harben had demonstrated two decades ago that Pellucidar existed in a different dimension from that in which he (Korak), and Abner and David, had been born. On the other hand, Korak was no scientist, and had no better option now than to place his trust in Abner.

Eventually, the pendent world's rotation brought into Korak's view the great lake, nestled in a distinctive mountain range, that David had reported on his prior expedition. It was a differentiating landmark, and Korak could see why the emperor had attempted to establish an observatory near Thuria, the purpose of which had been to mark the intervals of the giant lake's rotational appearances and thus to implement a timekeeping system within Pellucidar.

Korak thought that marking the rising and the falling of the tides of Pellucidar's oceans, while not necessarily comparable to those of the outer world, might be a more reliable, and easily communicated and explainable, method of timekeeping within the inner world, but in the end, it made little difference, for the native Pellucidarians had had no interest in David's aspiration to establish universal timekeeping.

In short, the gilaks just didn't care.

And unless it directly involved locating Suzanne, he didn't

care either. Exploring the Land of Awful Shadow, or speculating about life on the unexplored Dead World, or investigating the mysteries of time within Pellucidar, would have to wait.

16

CLASH OF THE SEA MONSTERS

MERIEM WAS SURROUNDED by endless blue ocean on all sides. She felt like a castaway, lost at sea.

And perhaps she was.

The ocean was a lighter blue in the immediate vicinity of her immense floating "raft" of Sea Turtle Folk, and darkened to a deep violet in the upcurving, horizonless distance. Continents and landmasses were visible, perhaps hundreds, or even thousands, of miles away—this was an advantage of being inside a hollow ball, she supposed—but she could descry no land in the vicinity and thus there was no way for her to settle on a direction to convey to her turtle rescuers.

Meriem had been at first astonished, and then wary, at the Turtle Folks' proposal that they provide a floating platform for her, and take her where she wished to go, but once they had demonstrated their ability to swim synchronously and create a stable, raftlike platform upon which she could repose as well as store her supplies, she was extremely pleased and gratified at their idea, and that they would volunteer to help her in this way.

Meriem's journey across the daunting seas of Pellucidar, riding the "raft" of synchronously swimming sentient sea turtles . . . Sing that three times fast, she thought, laughing to herself. Her journey had been long, as far as she could tell by the number of sleeps she had had, and the amount of food and water she had consumed.

She faced a threat mostly of thirst, as she had brought fruit from the island and could spear fish for protein; she had replenished her canteens with fresh spring water before departing, having exhausted the water that had been transmitted from Santa Monica with her, but would it be enough?

Meriem was also unsure she had been able to make the Turtle Folk understand where she wished to go. She knew that some turtle species of the outer crust were thought to have a magnetic homing instinct, and she wondered if the Turtle Folk relied on this or something similar, as they continually insisted to her that they knew where they were going. Daali sang to her that they could feel the correct direction based on the degree of light intensity, as the place to which they traveled was not very luminescent compared to areas directly exposed to the light of Pellucidar's sun. They explained to her, in song, that when they were away from the beachside surf, they knew, they could feel, in their minds and in their bodies, if they were traveling in a desired direction or not.

What Daali said made a certain amount of sense to Meriem. If the Sea Turtle Folk each did have an internal magnetic compass, used for navigation when out of sight of the beach, it sounded eerily similar to the homing instinct with which all native Pellucidarians were born. This could be an example of parallel evolution of similar traits in completely different species, which had been well documented by physical anthropologists on the outer crust. If Meriem ever found her way to Thuria, and by extension to Sari, she looked forward to discussing it with Gretchen von Harben, a trained anthropologist.

Meriem also observed that the marine turtles had an incredible breathing capacity. She was certainly no marine expert, but it appeared they were holding their breath and swimming underwater much longer than other turtle species of which she was aware. The Turtle Folk cheerfully sang to her that this ability allowed them to swim much deeper in the ocean to locate food or escape from predators. Of course, the hatchlings also dove straight down in order to avoid predation when birds or pterosaurs appeared overhead.

Birds!

There they were, gliding gently through the air, with re-markably long wingspans and hooked bills about half a foot long. She thought they might be some type of albatross. They were the first birds Meriem had seen since her advent in the inner world. Could land be far off? Perhaps she and the raft of turtles were indeed making progress to their destination.

One thing she had not anticipated was the difficulty in-volved in spearing fish. The ocean was churning with mon-strous creatures. When she ventured to the edge of the raft and attempted to fish for her dinner, the disturbance she created in the water invariably attracted unwanted visitors, and she made her way back to the center of the floating raft empty-handed.

This occurred several times before she was able to consult with Daali, for although the raft was extremely stable, the leatherback turtles that composed it would swim in and out of particular locations, being replaced by their comrades in maintaining a constant surface for Meriem. She did sing to the other turtles, and they sang back, but she was most com-fortable with Daali. When she next encountered the elder, the latter explained that their "raft" created so little disturbance in the water that it passed virtually unnoticed by the ocean's other denizens. Meriem's attempts at spearfishing, by com-parison, created a raging turmoil that instantly attracted sea dwellers of all types, but mostly those who wished to eat them. Daali gently suggested that Meriem refrain from any other attempts at fishing.

Disappointed, and furthermore very hungry, she now eyed the circling albatrosses with great interest.

Meriem unpacked her crossbow, a Barnett wildcat, and fitted it with a bolt. She waited until one of the oceangoing birds glided overhead; after all, she didn't want to down the bird only to have it, and the precious bolt, fall into the sea.

She took careful aim, tracking the bird, and released the bolt when it was almost directly overhead. She scored a hit, the arrow bisecting the bird's torso, and the albatross cried out in pain.

She had expected the bird to drop when she shot it.

Instead, it continued to glide in an increasing downward spiral. She watched in dismay as the bird drifted out over the sea, and then circled back over the raft, crossed out over the sea again, back over the raft, and flew once more back over the ocean before finally plummeting into the water with a loud splash.

Within moments, the sea on all sides of the floating turtle raft was churning, filled with predators prepared to devour her—and even worse, to her mind, prepared to attack and devour the gentle Turtle Folk, whom, through no fault of their own, and only by dint of her own careless impulsiveness, now found themselves the predatory objects of these ocean-dwelling hunters.

Meriem watched helplessly as the huge snakelike creatures made themselves known, surrounding the raft and swimming around it in a counterclockwise manner. They were huge, hideous creatures, with slimy snakelike bodies of a horrid mustard-yellowish color marked by algae-green blotches. The things slithered as much as swam, if that were possible in the water, and the bulging eyes, red with black pupils, were un-blinking, instilling great dread in Meriem.

As they swam around the raft, the circle they made tight-ened, relentlessly reducing the distance between them and the floating raft. The turtles sang to her to get in the middle of the large floating turtle-raft and stay there.

Meriem, however, could not in good conscience allow her newfound friends to fight on her behalf without joining in and defending the whole. She was one of them now, and would fight and die with them, if necessary. Besides, if these horrid beasts with their snapping jaws and forked tongues managed to annihilate all of the turtles, she would be next anyway. She may as well fight, and at the same time preserve her honor.

She grabbed her extendable spear in one hand and the crossbow in the other, and hopped from turtle to turtle until she crouched near the edge of the raft.

Daali was there and then entreated her to retreat back to the center, telling her that they would deal with the predators, but Meriem refused and stood her ground.

One of the serpents reared its ugly head, and Meriem saw that it had short but sturdy horns, formed from bony protuberances upon its head and snout. It snapped its jaws, showing row upon row of fanged teeth, and the forked tongue flitted in and out. The thing dove, and another one rose in its place.

The whole aspect reminded Meriem of a horrid merry-go-round, with the snakelike serpents slowly rising and falling as they circled the raft, just as the painted wooden horses rose and fell as they rotated around the amusement ride's hub. But there was nothing in the least amusing about these monsters of the deep, nor her predicament.

Meriem was later to learn that the creature she faced was the dreaded *hydrophidian*, called in the native tongue of Pellucidar the *azrib*, or sea snake.

"Sea snake" didn't begin to cover what monstrosities these things were.

The unblinking red eyes seemed to zero in on her, and she raised her spear and crossbow in defiance.

An azrib slammed into one of the huge Turtle Folk along the edge of the raft, dislodging it from its place. The turtle dove, and the azrib followed it, both disappearing deep down into the sea in a whirlpool of rushing, swirling water.

The next azrib in the dreadful circle raised its scaly head, cresting the ocean's surface, and Meriem shot it square in its red eye with a crossbow bolt. The monster screeched and writhed in pain, whipping its body in and out of the water, and creating a massive tide that rocked the raft.

The injured azrib dove, but moments later, shot up under the edge of the raft, dislodging three of the Sea Turtle Folk. The turtles regrouped, and when the thing shot up again from the water, they snapped at it with their sharp beaks, tearing at its slippery flesh, and rending it with huge, bloody gashes. The azrib screeched again, and flailed. It went headfirst below the ocean, and surfaced some ten feet away.

Meriem watched in unbridled horror as three of the monster's comrades deserted the circle around the raft and pounced on the injured creature, ripping it to bits in a frenzy of blood and snake meat and gore.

She shuddered, both at the grisly sight, and at the thought that these hideous creatures had been all around her and the turtle-raft for their whole journey, the fact of which she had been blissfully unaware.

Meriem's attention was distracted from the hideous feast taking place not three yards away by the surfacing of the first azrib, its mighty jaws clamped about the tough, leathery black-green carapace of the giant turtle it had first dislodged from the raft.

The leatherback turtle screeched, and Meriem was horrified as the azrib pulled it back beneath the surface, the seawater foaming and bubbling in its wake.

She had a little time to mourn, however, as next popped up from the roiling ocean creatures with long necks of ten or more feet, which were attached to enormous seal-like bodies, with snakelike heads teeming with teeth like razorblades. These long-necked creatures swam in a pack, and descended upon the bloody mayhem of the battle between the azribs and the Sea Turtle Folk.

Fortunately, the mouths of the seal-like creatures, which Meriem later learned were called *tandorazes*, or *tandors* of the sea, were not large enough to grasp the leathery shells of Sea Turtle Folk. The sea turtles' flippers and heads were certainly fair game for the tandorazes, but sinking their fangs into the slimy bodies of the azribs was an easier proposition, and the battle, for the most part, splintered off into a conflict between these two groups of monstrous creatures.

Not to be outdone, a pod of *azdyryths*—dreaded

ichthyosaurs—soon joined the conflict, attracted by the scent of thick blood polluting the sea. Once again, the Sea Turtle Folk were put on the defensive, as the attacking creatures had giant skulls resembling those of alligators, attached to huge whalelike bodies. The pointed snouts of the azdyryths were bristling with pointed teeth, within jaws that hinged open almost to ninety degrees, perfectly constructed for attacking the turtles, for the mouths were so huge that they could clamp down on almost the largest of the leatherbacks and pull them under the ocean to consume them at their leisure.

Meriem saw one of her sea turtle kin succumb in just this way, and upon approach by another azdyryth, she shot a crossbow bolt straight down its throat. The creature shrieked in pain and dove; it did not resurface.

Heartened, Meriem fit another bolt in her crossbow and let it loose at the next attacking creature, but unfortunately the bolt went wide when the azdyryth lunged to one side and attacked a smaller leatherback turtle about which it could easily clamp its mighty jaws.

Meriem swore in frustration, fitted another bolt, and shot it into the side of the creature's mouth, near the hinge where both mighty jaws met. The azdyryth was unable to completely clamp down upon its captive sea turtle, and bled profusely from the wound inside its gaping mouth. The leatherback struggled free, and while the azdyryth opened and clamped shut its jaws in an effort to shake the bolt loose, Meriem shot another crossbow bolt straight down its craw, piercing the interior gullet. The monster of the sea writhed in agony and sank straight down under the surface.

Meriem accounted for two more azdyryths in this manner before, by some unspoken accord, the ichthyosaurs decided in unison to abandon their attack upon the sea turtle raft, and turned their attention to the bloody battle between the tandorazes and the azribs.

The raft of interconnected sea turtles quietly floated away

from the primitive, bloody battle, and the Turtle Folk took account of their dead and wounded.

Meriem, exhausted and thirsty, crawled back to the center of the raft and collapsed on her back. She slaked her thirst with some of the remaining fresh water, doing her best to ration it, and then pulled her soft brimmed hat over her face to protect from the beating sun. She breathed hard and fell asleep.

When she awoke, Daali was there, awaiting her.

"I've brought ruination upon you and your fellows," Meriem sang. "I can't tell you how sorry I am."

Daali was silent for a while, and then sang back to Meriem. "You are one of us, although you are as like a child. Children must learn, and you have learned. We have made this journey many times, and we will make this journey many more times. Never have we made the journey in complete safety, nor without losses. All accept the cycle of life when they make the journey. All came willingly, in honor of the assistance you rendered us, without even knowing who we were or what we were about.

"All is one. We all mourn together. When one of us lives, we all live. When one of us dies, we all die.

"We approach your destination. We shall miss you, Meriem of the outer world."

17
KORAK ENDS A DEBATE

LOOK AT WHAT I HAVE DISCOVERED!" Abner cried.

"My detection equipment," the old scientist continued, "by which I hope to pinpoint Suzanne Clayton's location, is based on some conversations I once had with Victory Harben. She explained to me some of the history she had learned, or deduced, from her time among the Kjarnans. Poor girl. Got stuck on a cosmic merry-go-round and ended up halfway across the galaxy."

"Kjarnans?" Korak asked. "Who are they?"

"We would call them denizens of Mercury, although in reality, while their planet occupies the same physical space as the planet we know that orbits closest to the Sun, it actually exists within a closely adjacent 'angle,' or dimension, to the dimension in which our Earth resides."

"We all know this," the ape-man said. "Victory Harben demonstrated that Pellucidar, where we are now, is actually the hollow interior of an alternate Earth, a different 'Earth' from that where you and I and David originate."

"Precisely!" Abner said. "We are currently residing in an angle in which the laws of physics differ from those we grew up with on the outer crust.

"And it is those very laws of physics that enable Pellucidar's existence, and indeed that are responsible for the phenomenon we call the Dead World. Before we lost contact, Victory explained to me that the ancient Kjarnans fancied themselves

114

world builders, and indeed builders of entire solar systems, all artificially created and maintained by their greatest scientists and planetary engineers. But their hubris got the best of them, and an artificial world they had created, which was positioned between 'Earth'—let us call it Jasoom—and Barsoom—the planet we call, in our angle of origination, 'Mars'—inexplicably suffered complete destruction. The world exploded, hurling chunks of the small planetoid throughout the solar system, causing immeasurable damage.

"A very large and prominent remnant of the destruction of the Kjarnans' artificial world was hurled toward and collided with the third planet, Jasoom, resulting in the so-called moon that now hangs within Pellucidar. The chunk of the exploded artificial world plowed through 500 miles of Jasoom's crust undoubtedly causing immeasurable destruction as it pierced and burst from the ground comprising the inner surface. The hunk of rock doubtlessly hurled toward the interior sun before being repelled, and thence 'bounced' back and forth in the air between the sun and ground before finally entering a steady state. It was then held in abeyance, in stationary orbit within Pellucidar, between the interior surface of the hollow 'Earth' and our eternal central sun, by the Eighth Solar Ray of the inner sun and the Eighth Planetary Ray of the inner crust, and remains in that state today.

"So was created the Dead World, the pendent moon that now hangs above our heads!"

David was looking at his elderly friend with an expression of unrestrained astonishment. "Perry, we've been to Thuria several times to study the Dead World with your telescope, and you've never thought to tell me, or anyone else as far as I know, of this bit of history! When did you learn this from Victory?"

"Why, David my boy, you never asked! You never asked, now did you? As for when young Victory conveyed the Kjarnan history to me, who can say, here in timeless Pellucidar? It might have been years ago, it might have been yesterday, though who here among us can define yesterday? I really cannot say," the older man concluded, clearly miffed.

"This is fascinating," Korak said. His gritted teeth put the lie to his statement. "What does all this have to do with locating Suzanne?"

Abner shot him a look that Korak interpreted as "try to keep up," and Korak stared back at him, stone-faced.

"Ah, so. Very well," Perry said. He held up a small box in the palm of his hand. An antenna-like protrusion projected from the top, and was encircled by three concentric rings, each of which was smaller in circumference than the one below it. "This device, which is a rudimentary version of an apparatus within Victory's possession, and which I constructed under her direction, may point to Suzanne's location. I say this only because by all accounts she seemed to disappear without a trace. One moment she was there, the next she was not."

"That is so," Dek said. "When it was noticed that she was gone, once Spy-kee had returned riderless, we sent our best trackers out in all directions, but there was no spoor to trace. It is possible she was carried away by a thipdar or other large flying creature, but no one present saw any such thing in the skies, and we do keep a guarded eye out for such threats."

Abner nodded. "Just so. Therefore, it is at least possible, perhaps probable, that Suzanne was spirited away by other means."

"Go on," Korak said.

In response, Abner activated a small switch on the side of the box he held. The antenna glowed as if lit from within, and he turned the box ninety degrees so that the protrusion was parallel with the ground. "This device shares certain properties with a Gridley Wave transmitter-receiver—which, I might say, could have as easily been named the Perry Wave, since Jason Gridley and I both discovered the unusual frequency and emanations nearly simultaneously, and independently of each other."

David Innes smiled indulgently and gestured for the older man to continue.

Perry stepped away from the main grouping of people, holding the device in front of him and slowly sweeping the antenna from left to right in a 360-degree arc.

There was a violet flash in the distant atmosphere, in a direct line with the antenna, which disappeared when Abner continued to rotate the device.

Korak and the others let out a chorus of exclamations and gasps. "What was that?" the ape-man asked.

Perry stopped turning and edged the direction of the antenna back toward the spot where the skies had briefly lit up. The violet flash appeared again, blazing and swirling with an inner light. The phenomena took the form of a pillar of light, extending from the ground all the way up into the heavens.

"Dek," Abner said, "correct me if I'm wrong, but please observe where the cylinder of light touches the ground. Is that the location in which Suzanne was last seen?"

"Yes," the Thurian tribesman breathed, wonder in his voice, "it is!"

"That pillar of light, that violet energy," Abner explained, "constitutes the remnants of Suzanne's translocation aura."

"Which means what?" Korak demanded.

"It is a column of residual energy demonstrating from where your daughter was taken, and . . . where she was deposited."

The band of swirling violet energy, shooting into the sky, terminated directly above them, on the Dead World.

"Well, how do you usually get to the Dead World?" Korak asked.

"We don't!" Kolk replied. "It is forbidden!"

"And yet," David said, "Dek's own mate, Mirina the bird-woman, The One Who Fell, comes from there. If she and others like her call the Dead World their home, their ancestors must have traveled there somehow."

"What you say makes sense," Kolk replied, "yet you also know, David, that it is taboo for gilaks. And . . . with her petite stature and gossamer wings, Dek's mate Mirina is not exactly a gilak. It must not be forbidden for her people."

"Did you ever learn from her how her people got there?" David asked.

"No," Dek said. "There is still much we do not know of my mate, and much she does not know herself. When she first arrived here, Mirina could only speak with her mind to Mok, and other Sagoths, and the Mahars. She communicated with all others, including me, via sign language."

"I can recall a time when I first arrived in Pellucidar," David said, "when the Mahars could only communicate with each other via a sixth sense attuned to the fourth dimension, similar to telepathy but not quite the same. Other than that, Sagoths had to translate their wishes and commands via sign language. Then, sometime before Tarzan's and our battle against the Nazi incursion here, it appeared the Mahars had somehow gained the ability to mentally 'speak' to many other sentient species, including us gilaks and the Sagoths, rather than just among themselves."

"According to Mirina," Dek said, "the Mahars have always had this ability, but it may be that she was born after the events you describe, and therefore in her limited experience and perspective, it may seem to her that it has always been thus."

"Does she know anything about the Mahars from whom she fled on the Dead World?" David asked.

"It is Mirina's understanding," Dek said, "according to what she has been taught, that there had always been a few Mahars inhabiting the pendent moon, but that the Mahar population expanded greatly after they were driven from many of their cities in the area now encompassed by the Federated Kingdoms of Pellucidar. Mirina and her kind fear the Mahars."

"Presumably the reptilians prey upon her people just as they preyed on the gilaks of Pellucidar, before our armies drove them away," David said. "If all we have done is shift the burden of dealing with the Mahars from us to Mirina's people, I am sorry for that."

"I am sorry as well," Korak interrupted, "but I fail to see how any of this pertains to traveling to the pendent moon. Ja has already explained your ceremonial practices and taboos, but they do not apply to me."

"But they do!" Kolk exclaimed. "You are a gilak, just as we are!"

"I am a human being," Korak said, "but I am not one who has been raised here in Pellucidar, subject to your stories and myths. Your practices do not apply to me."

"Stories and myths!"

Dek intervened in the debate. "Father, just as Mirina is not a gilak like us and yet you have accepted her into our family, and thus opened your mind to the reality of accepting that there are others who differ from us, perhaps wisdom dictates acceptance of others who do not share our beliefs."

"But Dek, these are not merely beliefs, but truths!" Kolk averred.

"Father," Kolk's son replied, "you begin to sound too much like your father, Goork."

"So then," Korak said, attempting to steer the conversation back to actually traveling to the pendent moon, "that is why no one has traveled to the Dead World when we all have had access for decades to two airships, the O-220 and the *Favonia*, that could easily fly there."

The discussion among the group continued, debating the merits and deficits of an expedition to the Dead World, the prohibitions, and what that type of sortie might entail from a logistical perspective: water, food, armaments, and so on.

Korak quitted the group and strode away, followed shortly thereafter by Akut when the Mangani noted the ape-man's departure. Korak stopped at the small hut that had been assigned to him and Akut by the Thurians, where his Enfield and other weapons had been stored. The ape-man equipped himself with these and strode across the grassy plain.

The two were perhaps a hundred yards away from the grouping of men, the members of which continued to vigorously debate this or that point, when Korak looked back at them, a slight smile crossing his determined features.

"May I borrow your airplane?" he called out.

Before David or Abner could utter a reply, Korak was racing toward their primitive aircraft. Akut, taking the cue from his friend, bounded after the ape-man, quickly catching up with him.

Abner's aircraft was a traditional biplane, the body constructed and carved from a large tree trunk. There were cockpits for two passengers, the rear set higher than the front so that the pilot looked out and over his passenger. Korak leaped into this opening, while his Mangani companion spun the propeller to kick-start the engine, and then raced around and under the lower wing. Akut sprang upward, propelled by mighty great ape muscles, and landed neatly in the front lower cockpit.

The son of Tarzan took in the details of the aircraft as he heard the shouts and yells of David and Abner and the others behind him. Korak released the hand brake, and the airplane began to taxi forward. He noted that the fuselage of the plane was of a light wood, similar to the outer world's balsa. The wings were of a tough cured hide, perhaps that of a dinosaur such as a gyor, or perhaps some kind of prehistoric rhinoceros. There were several struts of a tougher wood connecting and holding stable the upper and lower wings, while the wings themselves were lashed tightly to the fuselage of the plane with long, tough leather cords. The propeller also seemed to be of the lighter balsa wood. Korak had observed as they ran toward the plane that the tires were indeed of some type of rubber, and he recalled that Abner had instituted in the inner world a limited amount of industrialization, by which the ape-man supposed that the tires were created, and the metal parts were forged for the internal combustion engine, and the fuel refined for the latter.

As the contraption wheeled forward on the grassy plains, Korak had a bad moment, thinking about whether the craft was fully fueled or not. Glancing at the makeshift dashboard, he noted with relief an indicator that seemed to reveal that the craft had remaining at least three-quarters of a tank of fuel.

The aeroplane picked up speed, and those who chased Korak and Akut on foot were quickly left behind. The ape-man glanced behind them, saw the waving and yelling pursuers, and acknowledged them with a respectful, quasi-militaristic wave. He felt badly about stealing the emperor's aircraft, but he wasn't going to wait one moment longer while Abner dithered about trying to figure out how to reach the Dead World.

He felt the wings gaining sufficient lift and pulled back on the center stick, and the one-of-a-kind plane slid gently into the air. The wind buffeted him, and he recalled that David and Abner had doffed goggles upon deplaning after they had landed.

Gray eyes scanning the cockpit's interior, he noted the goggles dangling from a hook, and pulled them up and over his head and eyes. Korak gave Abner Perry credit for his ingeniousness. The lenses were clearly those of a large dinosaur, again perhaps a gyor, which had been polished for clarity of vision. These would be much safer than glass in the event of a crash or other impact, which might permanently blind the wearer, and were connected to leather straps that wrapped around the back of the head.

The ape-man also took note of two stone axes attached by straps and hooks on the other side of the cockpit. He yelled at Akut, hoping his friend could hear him, and instructed him to look for a corresponding pair of goggles and axes in his own cockpit. The great ape pulled a pair of flight goggles over his furry head and gave Korak a sign that he was also equipped with axes.

Korak was pleased. He had his Enfield, two bandoleers of

ammunition, bow and arrows, spear, steel knife, and stone axes. His friend had two more axes, and a fine set of sharp teeth set in muscular jaws. They were ready for what may come next. He exulted at their flight, the wind whistling and whipping his dark hair. He looked upward and steered the commandeered craft toward the pendent moon.

The journey was only a mile, yet seemed to be taking longer than it should, given their air speed. Korak had little time to cogitate upon this oddity, for within moments six dark airborne specks resolved into flying creatures, which began to dive at and harry the aeroplane.

Thipdars! These were winged reptiles, an evolutionary branch of toothed Pteranodons unknown on the outer crust. Korak knew that these aggressive creatures had caused much havoc and derailed the plans of his own father, Jason Gridley, and countless others on past occasions. With wingspans of thirty to thirty-five feet, and strong beaks jam-packed with hundreds of razor-sharp teeth, they were certainly capable of downing Korak's plane, and carrying the ape-man and Akut far away in their clawed feet, to deposit them in some unscalable aerie to be kept as food for their young—or to be devoured immediately. Korak couldn't imagine that there were smaller, more friendly versions of these creatures, the bus-dars, with one of whom his daughter Suzanne had bonded, just as the people of the tribe of Abella had tamed and bonded with many other bus-dars. But he knew it was so.

In any event, Korak was determined to not allow the bus-dars' larger cousins to make a meal of him, and interfere with his mission to rescue Suzanne. It was to be a dogfight with the six ravening thipdars.

Korak banked to avoid the diving reptiles, and before he could yell instructions to Akut, the great ape anticipated him. His Mangani friend had always had a special intuition and intelligence, and this time was no exception.

Akut leaped from the forward cockpit and landed on the right lower wing, grasping in his left hand one of the struts that gave structure and strength to the whole aircraft. His other hand grasped one of the stone axes tightly in his strong fingers. The great ape's clear brown eyes searched the sky, and Korak banked the aircraft so that the plane's wings were not blocking his friend's line of sight. Accordingly, Akut got a good visual on the thipdars coming toward them.

Akut's left hand released the strut and the great ape grabbed the lower end of it with his left foot. Korak, not having eyes on his friend's prehensile feet and toes, had a bad moment as he watched his friend tie the goggles more tightly around the back of his furry head with both hands. Then the ape man realized Akut must be grabbing on with his feet.

Faster than even Korak, and perhaps even Tarzan, could have moved, Akut raced from the fuselage to the wingtip, grasped another supporting strut that spanned the lower and upper wing to curb his momentum, and hurled the stone axe at an oncoming thipdar.

The stone axe whirled through the sky, rotating end over end and, Akut's aim being true, sliced clean through the creature's neck, cleanly decapitating it. The separated head and the body, neck jetting warm red blood, tumbled to the ground below—along with the axe.

"*Kreeg-ah!*" Korak yelled. "*Tand aro!*"

In accordance with Korak's warning, Akut ran back to his forward compartment, never faltering in step despite the aeroplane's forward motion and the battering wind, grabbed the second axe as he vaulted over the cockpit, and scrambled for the end of the wing opposite that he had just quitted. He swung himself around and around the wing strut by one muscular arm, the other hand grasping the axe. Round and round he circled, until Korak was concerned the Mangani's great weight might snap the strut.

A thipdar dove too close to the plane, trying to swoop back up under the aircraft and attack it from below, and Akut's axe flashed as he was on an outswing, cleaving the flying reptile's wing in two.

The thipdar spiraled downward, joining its companion's fate below.

The four remaining monsters of the air now circled Korak's speeding plane more cautiously, avoiding the ape creature and its sharp stone weapon.

Korak held the plane's control stick securely between his knees, took the Enfield in his steady grip, aimed, and fired, blowing off another thipdar's head. Unable to reload and simultaneously fly the plane, the ape-man resecured his rifle and hoped his friend had a plan, for Abner's biplane was not equipped with modern weaponry, let alone the synchronized machine guns he had been accustomed to during the Great War and later conflicts.

One thipdar took a chance on coming closer and flew under the plane, and Akut leaped out into the open sky. The great ape angled his body, picked up airspeed, and, judging his trajectory perfectly, slammed into the top of the thipdar. He grabbed and encircled the creature's neck, so that the monster couldn't turn its head and get to the Mangani with its vicious teeth.

Akut applied the musculature of his great ape species, and clasping the creature's throat, implacably tightened his grip until the beast could take in no air. The thipdar began to plummet, and Akut eased up the tiniest amount, allowing the monster the slightest bit of air intake. The Mangani could feel the creature suck in the air, and it began to slowly revive and resume its flight.

Akut tightened his relentless grip again, and the creature shook and trembled. The great ape noticed his captive's two companions speeding toward him, and he yanked the creature's neck to the right. He let up again, allowed the creature a short breath of air, and squeezed once more. He wrenched the reptile's neck again to the right, and this time the thipdar responded by flying in a rightward direction toward one of his diving companions. The two airborne reptiles crossed each other's paths in the air, and Akut swung with his mighty axe, inflicting a deep slice to his opponent's membranous wing.

Through the repeated process of choking his mount, and alternating pulling its neck left, right, or upward, Akut was able to maintain an adequate degree of control over the captive winged beast. He directed it again toward the thipdar he had already wounded and struck a killing blow against the creature's opposing wing. Mortally wounded, the fourth thipdar fell to its death.

The fifth creature, angered beyond any instinctual control that it might have otherwise exerted over its actions, winged its way straight at Akut's beast, which it now perceived as an enemy. The two sky monsters clashed, open beak to open beak, each rending the other with row upon row of sharpened and bloodied razorlike teeth. The two flying reptiles held each other's mouths in their grasp and spiraled to the earth, heedless of the approaching death that would be dealt by impact with the ground below.

Left with no alternatives, Akut launched himself into the sky and accepted his fate with equanimity. If he died now, he would have saved his best friend, and he knew his grandson would see Korak again one day.

The Mangani spun about in the air, picking up velocity, and closed his soulful brown eyes.

The great ape landed headfirst in the forward cockpit of Korak's plane, which the ape-man had flown at a downward trajectory to match Akut's speed and angle of decent.

Akut flipped himself right side up in the cockpit, looked back at his friend, and gave what passed for a big Mangani grin.

Korak laughed, drinking in the exhilaration of victory over a formidable enemy.

The ape-man maneuvered the biplane's control stick, and the aircraft turned back toward their goal: the Dead World of Pellucidar.

At only a mile above the inner world's surface, it would be a short journey, absent any other attacks or diversions.

A short time later (at least as Korak's internal clock perceived it, for he had no objective method of timekeeping), their plane must have been closing the distance to the Dead World, but it seemed like it was growing farther away from them. Perhaps it was an optical illusion of some sort.

As they sped toward the tiny globe in Abner's airplane, Korak wondered how his daughter could possibly be on the tiny sphere. The ball of rock was floating only one mile above the ground. A mere 5,200 feet. No one had been to the Dead World before to take measurements and chart it; how big could it be? Yes, land appeared to be covered by foliage, and there appeared to be bodies of water, but none of these could be very large. He just couldn't imagine how Suzanne could be located there, but Abner seemed to know what he was talking about when he had utilized Victory's apparatus, and he didn't have any other leads as to her location.

The plane continued to approach the pendent moon, and Korak fully expected it to grow larger and larger in his field of vision. He couldn't be more than half a mile away from it at this point, given his speed and the distance he had had to cover when he had taken off a few minutes ago.

However, the pendent moon grew progressively smaller in his field of vision, the closer that he approached it.

Korak shook his head, trying to clear his vision.

He yelled back at Akut, who had crawled into the rear cockpit. "Do you see that? Am I hallucinating?"

Akut yelled back, "It gets smaller!"

Korak was stunned. Of all the tales his father had told about his various adventures and exploits, the hidden cities, the talking gorillas, the beast-men of Opar, the affair of the Dark Heart of Time, the only one he had really disbelieved as a wild, tall tale, was Tarzan's adventure in the land of the Minunians.

He had seen his father off on that particular exploit. Tarzan was to make his first solo flight after receiving instruction from his own son, and the airplane had been looked over and confirmed as airworthy by several Waziri pilots, whom Korak had personally trained.

When Tarzan hadn't promptly returned from that flight, but only returned to the Greystoke estate weeks later, telling the story of his adventure in the land of the Minunians, Korak actually thought that his father was joking with his son and the rest of his family, telling a wild story in order to distract them from their concern over him crashing and being marooned in the jungle. It seemed absurd, but it was easier to believe that Tarzan was somewhat embarrassed about wrecking and losing the plane on his first solo flight, and had made up a wild story that was frankly filled with physical impossibilities in order to entertain and distract them. Not that the Lord of the Jungle wasn't more capable than any of them at living and surviving in the jungle for an extended time, for he was more capable of that than any other living human on Earth. But they did worry nonetheless, and assumed he had made up the tale to deflect their worry.

In short, the tale Tarzan had spun was thus: he had crashed the plane, and shortly thereafter had found himself in the country of the Minunians, inside the otherwise impenetrable Great Thorn Forest. The land was inhabited by a people a quarter of his own size. These folk did not exhibit dwarfism, but rather were regularly proportioned human beings who happened to be an average of about a foot and a half tall. The Minunians inhabited elaborate city-states, which somewhat resembled ant hills, and these societies frequently warred with each other. Joining one side of the conflict, Tarzan was captured, in true fashion of Gulliver and the Lilliputians, and taken prisoner by the enemy. There, a scientist, Zoanthrohago, had subjected Tarzan to an experimental technique, and as a result had been rendered equal in proportion to the rest of the Minunians. Thereafter, as a prisoner of war, Tarzan had been made a slave. Tarzan had been four times the size of the Minunians. When shrunk to their size, he retained the strength he had at his full size, including the ability to make great leaps. The science behind his shrinking was improbable, a bizarre device that emitted a ray of some sort at a gland near the back of his head. He had finally escaped the enemy's dungeons, and, after he eventually made his way back to the Great Thorn Forest, Zoanthrohago's experimental procedure wore off, and the ape-man returned to his normal size.

Now, Korak thought, as he and Akut steadily approached the tiny moon, and as it correspondingly grew smaller and smaller in their field of vision, he was wondered if the tale that Tarzan had told was not one hundred percent accurate. He had also heard the story told by Jason Gridley, of how he had been stranded on Barsoom, and thereafter transported to the moon of Thuria—called Ladan by its natives—and how the moon was so small that he realized that somehow he had been shrunk while traveling there, so that when he landed, he was actually proportionally so tiny that the moon—the world—seemed huge. Gridley had said that the same thing had previously happened to John Carter when he had traveled to Ladan in search of his wife, the incomparable Dejah Thoris. But that was the stuff of outer space, of adventures on other planets, not right here on Earth—or *in* the Earth.

Then it struck Korak.

The Barsoomian moon called Thuria.

The land of Thuria, within the Land of Awful Shadow, directly below him now as he raced toward the Dead World.

Proportional reduction in size as one approached one moon, or the other.

He was astonished. He and Akut, and their aeroplane, *were* being proportionally shrunk down to a minuscule size as they advanced toward the exterior surface of the pendent world. The surface of the pendent moon *was* populated with vast forests, mountains, and bodies of water—oceans, and forests, and mountains, that were all incredibly small in proportion to forests and seas and mountains to be found on the inner surface of Pellucidar, or on the outer surface of Earth, for that matter.

They, like ants compared to humans, now had a much greater distance to cover in relation to their size, in order to reach their destination. They flew closer to the Dead World, and both ape-man and great ape experienced disorientation, in the darkness of the moon's shadow, as they continued to shrink.

"We have indeed gotten smaller!" Korak yelled back at his friend.

Akut grunted an obscure and nuanced Mangani word in response, indicative of his disbelief in what was happening, but also his acceptance of it.

The two travelers reached a tipping point, where it appeared that the pendent moon was above them and they were flying upward toward it, and then suddenly they were hanging in limbo. Shortly thereafter it felt as if the pendent moon were below them, but they were flying upside down, and Korak had to right the plane in order to alleviate the sensation. Then they were descending toward the vast surface of the moon—enormous, now, in comparison to their new size, and above them the inner surface of the hollow globe that was Pellucidar was more immense and more limitless than anything they could have imagined.

Finally, as their plane raced for the Dead World, the pendent moon stopped shrinking—from their perspective—and grew larger and larger. Korak presumed that he and Akut had stopped getting smaller and were now approaching the moon at an appropriate proportional size. He still couldn't fathom how it worked.

Now that they were so small, and the Dead World was so much correspondingly larger—the size of a small planet in comparison to them—how in the world were they supposed to locate Suzanne? Where were they supposed to start?

Korak noted, scanning the landscape below, that much of the landmasses were completely covered with dense vegetation and thick forests. There were also vast plains, and while these featured sporadic trees and some wandering streams cutting through the grassland, he did not observe any wildlife. There didn't seem to be any birds either. He could detect no fauna whatsoever. This seemed to be consistent with observations that had been conducted from the ground surface of Pellucidar, both with the naked eye, and with spyglass, as no one had ever detected any living creatures upon the surface of the pendent moon—not people, nor animals, nor birds. Perhaps it wouldn't be so difficult after all to locate Suzanne, if she were the only other living creature here.

He flew the plane low over a vast body of water, and both he and Akut looked out on both sides of the cockpit, seeking any sign of marine life. The water was dark, and their eyes could not penetrate deeply, but if there was aquatic life here, they couldn't detect it. Perhaps any denizens of the Dead World's oceans and seas were bottom dwellers. Or perhaps they didn't exist at all.

Korak began to worry, for if Suzanne really was here, what was she to eat? A vegetarian diet was always an option, of course, but only if there was plant life available to actually supply the necessary nutrition.

Korak turned the plane lazily back toward a coastline and flew over a dense forest.

Then the aeroplane's engine began to sputter. The engine died, and the plane began to dive toward the thick trees below.

In his mind's eye, he relived another crash. As a second lieutenant flying for the R.N.A.S. (Royal Naval Air Service) in the Great War, he and his squadron mates were returning to their airfield in northern France, having successfully completed a reconnaissance mission to identify enemy positions.

As the British fliers fled German airspace, an enemy squadron of monoplanes—the dreaded Fokker Eindecker single-seat fighter planes—was scrambled and pursued. The Fokker E.I had been the first fighter plane to be successfully equipped with a "synchronization gear," allowing the forward-mounted machine gun to fire through the whirling propeller without hitting the blades.

In addition, the Fokkers were slightly faster than the British planes, and the angle at which they pursued the reconnaissance squadron resulted in an aerial engagement. In the ensuing dogfight, Korak downed his opponent, making his third kill. However, Korak's forward gunner was shot in the head, and the Vickers F.B.5 took heavy damage to the engine, which began to sputter dangerously.

Figuratively limping through the sky, and having trouble maintaining altitude, Korak, along with the surviving escort of his squadron mates, made it to the vicinity of the French airfield before his engine coughed and completely died.

Coming in under no engine power, Korak managed to guide the plane toward the field's single runway. After somewhere between gliding and falling at an unhealthy angle of descent, his Vickers made a hard landing before ultimately upending in a wild crash.

Korak had suffered numerous broken bones and a concussion.

Here and now, in Pellucidar, tumbling toward the surface of the Dead World, Korak and Akut crashed into the vast forest canopy.

18

NO REST FOR MERIEM

A BEDRAGGLED MERIEM CLAYTON trudged through sea water that came to her knees. Dark hair hanging in salt-encrusted, tangled braids hung beneath the soft brimmed leather hat that was tightly affixed to her head. A quiver containing her remaining crossbow bolts was slung over her slender shoulder. Her boots were tied together by the laces, and hung over her other shoulder, along with an empty canteen.

The sea water was clear and crystalline blue, reminding her of the shoreline and ocean in the Bahamas. She could see sand being kicked up by her naked feet, as well as the small seashells and starfish peppering the underwater surfaces.

Meriem turned and looked back out to the ocean. Some twenty feet away, where she had disembarked from the living raft of turtles, the leatherbacks floated there peacefully. Their unblinking eyes and calm expressions were infused with a sense of confidence and calm. They had gotten her this far; now it was up to her.

She gave a small wave and hoped that Daali was there in the front row of turtles to see her. She felt sure that the turtle elder would be present to see her off. A ripple of melancholy overcame her. She had bonded with these amazing creatures, and had a closeness to them that she hadn't known was possible.

Meriem gave one last farewell wave and turned back to the shore. She waded toward the sandy beach, and the onrushing tide gave her a last gentle push. She sat heavily in the sand for a while, breathing the salty sea air and getting acclimated to solid land. Then she stood, surveyed her surroundings, and descried a fresh stream cascading in a tiny waterfall down the red rock cliff to her left. She thirstily scooped up handfuls of the fresh water, and then filled her canteen. Once her thirst was slaked, she further took in her surroundings. To the right, the coastline extended, but the pathway split in a Y, the left-hand path being composed of a rocky gravel pathway that led up the side of the cliff. There was nowhere else to go but to the left and up, and so she did.

Marching up the craggy terrain, she attained the summit of the escarpment. She scanned to her left and saw greensward spreading out before her in a low, flat valley. Not far away from her position, darkness bathed the expansive dale. She was at the edge of the Land of Awful Shadow. Above her hung the legendary Dead World, floating peacefully one mile above the surface. In front of her, then, was the land of Thuria, at the edge of the Shadow.

Meriem sat down on a large boulder and donned her boots. Out of a sense of caution, she affixed one bolt in her crossbow, and then began her short march toward her destination. She should have felt heady at coming this far, getting so close to her goal. Instead, her mood was gray and heavy, leaning toward dread.

What would she do next? Would she find Suzanne?

Was Korak here?

Meriem heard an odd noise, and she was unable to place it, although a deep part of her brain blared at her that she knew what it was, if only she would accept it. The screaming hindbrain won out, and her past on the outer crust, with its hustling and bustling cities, crosshatched with concrete and glass, and gasoline exhaust fumes, and sirens and engines buzzing in the dead of night, was stitched together with her present: eternal sunshine, the cawing of primitive birds, the roar of the ocean tides, and the singing of the Sea Turtle Folk.

What was out of place?

An engine!

Meriem looked up to the skies in wonder and spotted an aeroplane, of all things, darting up in the sky, flying toward the Dead World!

Korak!

Somehow, in her heart of hearts, she *knew* it was Korak. And once again, he was literally flying off into the unknown by himself.

Meriem threw away all caution and trotted toward the edge of the Shadow. She crested a small ridge and looked down upon what must be the village of Thuria. She was quickly noticed, and several cries went up, followed by the figures of men running toward her. Meriem kept the high ground and held her crossbow at the ready, in case the men trotting toward her were hostile.

In moments she was surrounded by the friendly faces of those she had for many years longed to meet—David Innes and his daughter Dav-An, and good old Abner Perry—and others with equally welcoming dispositions: Kolk, and Dek, and Mirina of Thuria.

Meriem, in between mouthfuls of food and gulps of fresh water, recounted her adventures in getting to Pellucidar, and then to Thuria. The others in turn brought her up to date regarding the events with Korak, Akut, and the O-220.

"Then it *was* Korak and Akut in that aeroplane!" Meriem said. "I knew it! But what awaits them on the Dead World? And how can I get there and join them in the search for my daughter?"

"We'll work on that," David said, "while you get some rest. Respectfully, you do seem a bit worse for wear," he added, smiling.

Meriem gave the slightest smile and nodded in agreement. "You're probably right. But I can't sleep too long. Every moment counts."

David agreed and turned to Dek's mate. "Mirina, would

you mind seeing Meriem to a place where she can rest, refresh, and if needed bring her more food and water?"

"Water," Meriem said, "especially water. I had thought I had brought enough fresh water on my voyage with the Sea Turtle Folk, but the journey took longer, and expended more of my supplies, than I estimated. Pellucidar is vast! And it was a small torture being surrounded by sea water and being unable to drink any of it."

"Of course," the bird-woman replied, sending her thoughts to the group, for she had not the power of physical speech. "Meriem, if you will please follow me, I will call to the guards to lower a ladder, for our villages have no gates."

The entire group withdrew to the safety of the Thurian village, and Meriem was settled in her own hut and provided with more to eat and refreshing water. Thereafter the men withdrew, and Mirina escorted Meriem to a place of privacy where she could bathe, and then back to the hut where Korak's mate could rest and recover from her arduous journey.

Meriem tried to sleep but could not quiet her brain. There was too much to be done: her daughter was still missing, had been traced to the Dead World, and Korak and Akut had absconded with Abner's aeroplane. Even taking into account all she had been through, how could she consider sleeping? She had to join her husband and Akut on the pendent moon and help with the search for Suzanne. She hadn't come all this way for nothing!

Meriem crawled out of the dark inner room that had been provided for her comfort and entered the outer room of the hut where Mirina was ensconced. A long, thick cloth hung in the hut's entrance, allowing light to leak in around the edges and providing enough diffracted light to see in the outer room. The material in the doorway was like a tapestry, with colorful and intricate repeating patterns and designs, and Meriem wondered at the flowers and plants that must grow in the Land of Awful Shadow, or at the

Shadow's edge, that supplied such vibrant colors for dyeing the fabric.

Mirina, perched on the ground near the entrance, opened her eyes. These were of a deep blue of which Meriem had never seen the like, and she found it impossible to dredge up from her vocabulary a descriptive term that matched the extraordinary shade.

"Meriem," Mirina said, sending her thoughts to the outer world woman, "what may I get for you?"

"The ability to sleep," Meriem said.

Mirina cocked her head and Meriem smiled. "Nothing, thank you, Mirina. That was a joke."

Mirina nodded. In every way, she looked like an exquisitely formed human, but on a childlike scale, being a little more than half the height of an average gilak or outer-world woman. Her skin was like the finest porcelain, and her hair was long and pure white, spilling down her back and around where two gossamer-like wings extended from between and just below her very human shoulder blades. The wings were covered in alabaster feathers; beyond this otherworldly feature—and the fact that she "spoke" in the manner of the terrible Mahars, sending and receiving thoughts via a sixth sense attenuated to the fourth dimension through which those thoughts traversed—she appeared entirely human, if diminutive.

"When I first arrived here," Mirina said, "I could speak only with Mok the Sagoth, who was also attenuated to sending and receiving mental communication though the fourth dimension. The gilaks here were concerned, as they had labeled such soundless speech as being specific to the Mahars."

Meriem looked down.

"Do not feel guilty, Meriem, for thinking it," Mirina said. "It was only that your thoughts associating my speech with the Mahars were so strong that I inadvertently received them. I assure you that I do not, and will not, willingly sense your thoughts without your acquiescence. In any case, after some time here in Thuria, and with my mate Dek, I learned to refine my speech so that I could also direct it toward the gilaks."

Mirina smiled. "Mok, I assure you, was relieved to no longer be 'tied to my hip' as my sign-language translator!"

Meriem laughed. The girl—no, the young woman—had set her at ease.

"By the way, I can hear and understand your mouth speech, in addition to your mental speech when you direct it toward me. Now, please tell me what you need," Mirina said.

"I must find a way to the Dead World," Meriem said. "I'm still so angry at Korak for taking off as he did, all alone."

"Yes," the bird-woman replied, "the world of my birth is indeed filled with many perils. As is Pellucidar, and no doubt, your own world. But did I misunderstand? We saw your mate fly away with the one called a Mangani, Akut. If Akut is with him, how is he all alone?"

"Well," Meriem said, "that's not the point."

"But Meriem," the petite woman continued, "did you not set out from your world to this one by yourself? Were you not truly all alone?"

"That," Meriem said once more, "is not the point."

But Mirina's slight smile was infectious, and within a moment Meriem was laughing at her own foibles, and Mirina was laughing along with her.

"Okay," Meriem said, "if I make it to the pendent moon—with others or alone—I'll need to know as much up front as possible. Let's start with you, Mirina. I'm very curious about you and your kind. How did you end up in Thuria?"

"It is not a long story. My people are the Vortha, and for eons, according to the history handed down by our ancients, we lived in relative peace on what you call the Dead World. There were Mahars, occasionally, and these were very frightening. There are other races, but our forest dwellings were well protected from those who might prey upon us.

"Then, more and more Mahars flew to our world. I only

learned, after falling from my world to this one, while fleeing from one of the dreadful reptiles, that these were Mahars fleeing the dominion of David Innes' Federated Kingdoms."

"I'm so sorry," Meriem said.

"It is not David's fault," the bird-woman said simply. "His people were merely trying to defend the gilaks who lived here in Pellucidar. They could not have known that some of the Mahars might flee to refuge on my home world, nor could they have known that our world was even populated. You asked how I came here to the Land of Awful Shadow. It was while fleeing from a pursuing Mahar. I flew up, up, up, and the Mahar was behind, snapping her terrible jaws at my wings. Still, I was smaller and more agile than she, and managed to evade her snapping beak. Up, further upward I flew, for I was less afraid of the *land above*—that is, the surface ground of Pellucidar, which from our perspective is above us—than of death beneath the Mahar's rending teeth. Suddenly, I was without weight, floating, and then I was falling, uncontrolled. My wings were not strong enough, then, to support me, and I plummeted into the sea. Had I crashed upon the land, I surely would have been killed instantly.

"Then," Mirina said, amused, "when Dek and the others found me, I would have already been smashed into little bits for them to put into the trees so that the birds could return me to my home."

"Mirina, you cannot say such a thing!"

The One Who Fell laughed. "But it is true! Anyway, if that had happened, I would not have met Dek—whom I saw in my dreams from the time I was a fledgling—and we would not have become mated. So, I am glad for the sea."

"Wait—you saw Dek in your dreams for your whole life, before you arrived here and met him in person?" Meriem asked.

"Yes. I cannot explain it. None of us can."

The two women were silent for a moment, and then Meriem said, "A few moments ago, you used the word 'eons.'"

"Yes. That is the best translation for the concept I sought to convey to you. Ages, long cycles of time."

"Time! That's it. You have time."

"Ah, yes, I see. Yes, the Vortha do conceptualize and mark the passage of time. The Dead World rotates and has a night and day, and its inhabitants mark those intervals. I have heard that you folk of the outer world have similar concepts . . . but that your nighttime sky is much, much darker than ours, and filled with tiny dots of light. There is still some diffuse light in our night sky, for the central orb of Pellucidar reflects sunlight from the *land above*."

"We are rapidly losing our night," Meriem said, "to the eternal artificial lights with which we carpet our cities—our very large villages. But you mentioned other races. I look up at the Dead World and I see only landmasses covered in dense forests, and grassy plains, and some ranges that could be mountains. And a great lake and some seas. The moon hangs only one mile above us; where are all these people, these races you mentioned?"

Mirina shrugged. "It is very hard to explain. The world you call a moon seems too small to me, observing it from here, that I cannot but agree with you that it seems impossible that it is home to so many races, including our own. Our ancient legends recount that the other races of the moon conceal themselves, as we do, under the vast forest canopies, which could explain why they cannot be seen from here, the surface of Pellucidar, with our naked eyes.

"But in addition, I find it hard to reconcile the extraordinarily vast world of my birth with the relatively small sphere that hangs above us. The only explanation I can countenance seems ridiculous, but . . . come with me, please."

Mirina took Meriem's hand and led her from the hut. They navigated other abodes and larger communal gathering places, and shortly came to the thatched wall that surrounded the village. Mirina asked the guards to raise the ladder for Meriem, which the tribesmen did. Mirina, meanwhile, fluttered her wings and flew over the boundary, landing lightly on her tiny feet. Meriem looked on in wonder, and then speedily clambered up the ladder, and back down the other side, to catch up with her new friend.

Mirina led Meriem a short distance across a sparsely grassed plain and stopped, still in view of the village. She pointed to a spot in the distance.

"Do you see it?" the bird-woman asked.

"No," Meriem replied. "What am I looking for?"

"Try squinting. Look at the ground where my finger points."

Meriem complied. "I don't see anything."

Mirina nodded. "Let's move closer."

They walked a short distance and Mirina stopped again. "What do you see."

Meriem narrowed her eyes. "An anthill? Maybe?"

"Maybe. Do you see any ants?"

Meriem laughed. "No, not at this distance. If that even is an anthill, the ants are much too small for me to see at this range."

The two women marched closer, until they stood next to what was indeed an anthill.

Mirina looked down. "Now do you see the ants?"

"Yes."

"Now do you understand?"

"I think I do, yes."

"I assume that the O-220," David Innes said, "has by now abandoned the search for Korak and Akut, and has headed for the north polar opening and the outer world. It's hard to know with certainty, as we have no Gridley Wave transmitter with which to contact the airship—or Sari, or the outer world, for that matter. But we do know that if Captain Hines felt that further searching for Korak would prove fruitless, he planned to head for the outer crust and pick up Tarzan, Jane, and the final load of Waziri tribespeople, as well as the last of the great apes and some other animals considered endangered species."

"David," Kolk interrupted, "look!"

David and the group to whom he had been speaking turned as one and peered in the direction Kolk pointed.

"Is it a thipdar?" Dek asked.

"Perhaps," his father, Kolk, said. "Raise your bow and arrow." These weapons were unknown before David and Perry's advent in the world at the Earth's core, but were now ubiquitous among the tribes that composed the Federated Kingdoms.

David squinted, then raised his hand quickly. "Hold!"

Kolk gave his emperor a questioning look.

"It flies my banner and colors," David explained. "It must be Lordan of Abella, returning from his search astride his bus-dar, Mis-see.

And so it was. David was correct, and Meriem was reunited with her son-in-law in short order. Lordan, one of the tribe of the bus-dar riders, had mated with Korak and Meriem's daughter Suzanne some time after the latter had made the decision to remain in Pellucidar and make a life for herself in the inner world.

Bus-dars were related to the menacing thipdars, smaller but more disposed to being ridden by gilaks. There were factions of Sagoth warriors who rode thipdars, but gilaks in general had not attempted such, for those attempts that had been made had universally ended with the consumption of the gilak-cum-trainer. The bus-dars had wingspans of twenty to twenty-five feet, while the larger thipdars sported thirty-foot-or-more wingspans and forty-foot-long bodies. Both species were a divergent, knife-toothed branch of pterosaurs, and the bus-dars had the same razor-sharp talons that protruded from clawlike feet positioned at the ends of their leathery wings.

Beyond their size differential, the bus-dars' heads also

differed from their larger counterparts. Their skulls were not quite as prolonged as those of the thipdars, and their beaks were a shade more blunted, lacking the thipdars' needle-points.

Perhaps most distinctively, the eyes positioned on opposing sides of the bus-dars' heads were a dark sea-green and highly expressive. One could tell from gazing into these creatures' eyes that they were aware and intelligent beings.

Once Meriem and her daughter's mate had exchanged familial greetings, Lordan spared no time in providing all who had gathered with tidings of his search.

"Unfortunately," the bus-dar rider said, "I have been unable to track and locate Suzanne, or my son Rahnak and the Waziri warrior Kyrianji who accompanied him in seeking the whereabouts of my mate. I elected to return to Thuria to see if there was any new information before departing again to continue the search."

Meriem and David then explained that Abner had, or at least probably had, determined that Suzanne had been somehow whisked away to the Dead World, whereupon Lordan's expression became even more glum.

"Then she is truly lost to us," the Abellan said.

"What?" Meriem said. "Not on your life! We're going after her. Korak and Akut have already attempted to reach the Dead World in Abner's aeroplane, and we're going to follow them."

"It is a fool's errand," Lordan said. "No one goes to the Dead World. It is forbidden!"

"We are *not* having this conversation over and over again," Meriem said. "I already would have taken Suzanne's bus-dar, Spy-kee, but he's been nowhere to be found since she disappeared. So, you're going to fly me there on Mis-see."

"But that is where the dead go. It is taboo—!"

"Lordan, as far as I'm concerned, its taboo to let your mate languish on a strange world when we all know she's up there somewhere."

Lordan was silent. Then: "You are correct. But what of my son Rahnak, and his companion Kyrianji? They remain missing somewhere in the Land of Awful Shadow—or perhaps beyond it, for they had stated that if their efforts within the Shadow were fruitless, they might investigate in the vicinity of the abandoned Mahar city of Kazra, thinking that Suzanne might have fallen afoul of the Mahars."

"I understand," Meriem said evenly, "but your bus-dar is our only currently available means of reaching the Dead World; the O-220 is back in the outside world now, as David stated, and the other vacuum airship, the *Favonia*, is out of contact on an undisclosed mission. Besides, Mirina has described her harrowing journey from the Dead World to Pellucidar's surface, including intense disorientation and a feeling of gravity 'flipping' its exertion upon her near a midpoint of her unplanned voyage. It's not hard to imagine the deleterious effects of such a transit upon a large airship and its crew and passengers. It's much less hazardous to risk our two lives in making the attempt, rather than one of our dirigibles.

"Besides," she concluded, "we can't just wait. I refuse to wait."

"If I take you to the Dead World astride Mis-see," Lordan said, "then others must volunteer to immediately begin the search on the ground for Rahnak and Kyrianji."

"Absolutely," David chimed in. "I will conduct the search myself."

"And I will accompany you," Dek volunteered, "for although parts of the Land of Awful Shadow remain unexplored, I am still more familiar with its terrain than you."

David nodded his appreciation to the young man, and then turned to Dek's father.

"Kolk, would you take a lidi to Sari? I will prepare an update for you to present to my mate, Dian, regarding everything that has transpired, so that the empress may in turn relay the information to the O-220 and others in the outer world: Tarzan, Jane, and Bowen Tyler."

Meriem smiled. "Yes, so that Tyler can reassure his poor scientists who stranded me here that I am alive and well."

Kolk nodded. "At once, David. I will notify my father, Chief Goork, and then be on my way."

"Father," Dav-An interjected, "should Abner and I accompany Kolk to Sari?"

"I'd rather you didn't," the emperor replied. "I want you both here, safe and sound, not traipsing across the Great Peak of the Terrible Mountains."

Dav-An frowned. "It's not as if I can't find my way to Sari; I do have the gilaks' homing instinct, you know."

"Of course," her father replied smoothly, "but as a princess of the Federated Kingdoms of Pellucidar, you must remain here in Thuria to greet the O-220 when it eventually returns with Tarzan and the others. Including Wolff Hines."

The father-daughter debate ended, and without catastrophe, the two wandered off to make their final plans.

Meriem and Lordan made to greet Mis-see, so that the bus-dar would be comfortable and acclimated to Meriem's presence when the time came for the flight to the pendent moon, but as they strode away, Mirina called out: "Stop!"

All looked back toward the small bird-woman, who cleared her throat nervously and then announced, "I will accompany Meriem and Lordan to the Dead World. It is my former home, and I am familiar with its challenges and perils."

"What?" Dek cried. "No!"

Mirina was steadfast. "Everyone in Pellucidar, and in my adopted home of Thuria, has been unfailingly kind and supportive since I arrived here and became known as The One Who Fell. Now, I must become The One Who Flies, giving back by returning to my former home to help Meriem and Lordan navigate its perils, and also to learn about what has befallen my people since I fell.

19

ON THE DEAD MOON

ABNER PERRY'S BIPLANE, engine sputtering and spinning out of control, spiraled downward toward a dense green forest. Plummeting toward the upper terrace of the trees, Korak pulled desperately at the control stick, finally managing to partially level the plane, but he and Akut were out of time.

The plane's landing gear caught on the upper branches, and the aircraft flipped and tumbled end over end, tossing the ape-man and the Mangani unceremoniously from their respective cockpits. The two managed to keep a grip on their weapons, Korak his rifle and bow, and Akut his stone ax.

The two fell through the upper terrace, and toward the middle terrace of the thickly treed forest, bouncing to and fro from branch to branch like uncontrolled pinballs. Eventually, each shot out a strong hand and managed to find and keep a grip on thick tree branches. Korak's shoulder was almost wrenched from the socket, while Akut, swinging gracefully round and round his branch like an acrobat on a trapeze, dispelled the energy of his fall until finally he perched on the branch and gathered his wits. Korak pulled himself up and rested on his own thick branch, and looked down at his friend, some ten feet below and six feet to his right. At least they were safe and relatively uninjured.

Their attention was drawn by a loud explosion, and both jerked their heads upward and to the left, where they saw a massive fireball engulfing the greenery of the upper terrace.

145

Their plane's internal combustion engine had combusted. There would be no returning to the surface of Pellucidar that way—not that the flimsy aeroplane had been in any shape to make the return trip anyway.

The two adventurers slowly made their way down through the middle terrace and to the lower levels, finally reaching the loamy soil of the Dead World. They found themselves in a closely packed forest of extremely tall trees. Here they saw that the very upper terrace from which they had descended formed a dense canopy, shielding their view above and likewise screening from view the surface of the Dead World from the inhabitants of Pellucidar.

The trees were oddly shaped, with trunks that spiraled upward rather than being cylindrical in shape. Similarly, the branches extended horizontally, for the most part, but also in an ever contracting spiral the farther they grew from the trunk. The boughs were thick with blue-green leaves, creepers, and vines, contributing to a sense that the forest was well-nigh impenetrable on all points, as well as overhead.

By silent agreement, the two marched in a random direction, and after some time had passed, Korak labeled this direction "west," for Pellucidar's primeval sun was not eternal here, and it was setting in the general direction they had set for themselves. Soon, the sun would set below the tall trees and the shadowed twilight in which they had been trooping would descend into darkness. It was not, Korak admitted to himself, a prospect he dreaded, for he had had a little trouble adjusting to the sun hanging endlessly at zenith and the sense of timelessness it engendered on Pellucidar's surface.

Presently, Korak and Akut rounded a particularly thick bole, climbing over a tangle of exposed roots, and the ape-man was brought up short, for now within their view, with her back facing them, was a human woman with jet-black hair!

"Suzanne!" Korak called out.

The woman's head turned, but before the ape-man could discern her features, a creature a quarter again the size of a

Bengal tiger launched itself from the tree limbs above them, landing squarely between the two parties. The beast resembled a tiger in many ways in addition to its size, for it had cat eyes and huge paws, the front two of which were slightly larger than the rear two. However, its ears, rather than being rounded, were tall and pointed, with elaborate tufts of white fur sticking straight up, and between these two ears were elongated antennae topped by spherical pods. The creature's fur was of a deep midnight blue, offset by stark white stripes. Although it shared the Bengal's large paws, the beast had six toes in the front paws and five in the back paws, in all of which were sheathed two rows of razor-tipped claws. The thing's tail was also longer than its earthy counterpart, and at its tip was a sharp white bony protuberance, perfectly formed for cutting and slashing.

Korak, in the half second he took to react to the creature's leap, took in the blue-white blur of the beast that otherwise evoked "tiger" in his brain; the rest of the details came later, for the creature, sizing up two beings to the left and one smaller being to the right, chose the female as its object of attack.

The beast emitted a high-pitch screech and lunged toward the human woman, who turned and leaped out of its path onto a low branch. Unless she could climb, however, she would be easy prey, for the "tiger" was obviously made for clambering among the terraced boughs, or even using its deadly claws as grappling hooks to scale straight up the trunks of the tall trees.

The monstrous catlike creature lunged, but before its hind paws left the ground, a savage fury was upon it, plunging a steel knife into its hide over and over.

"*Korak bundolo! Bundolo!*" the ape-man cried. Literally, "I, the Killer, Kill!"

The beast twisted around, snarling, its slavering jaws open for the kill, and Korak thrust his fist in its mouth, huge knife pointed upward, and jerked his hand up.

The steel knife penetrated the roof of the tiger's mouth and pierced its snout. But now the thing had clamped down on Korak's arm, but half-heartedly, for it was in immense pain, and the ape-man twisted the knife, inflicting immeasurable internal damage and causing thick, blue blood to geyser from the beast's snout and mouth. The jaws slackened, and Korak yanked out his arm and the knife. His hand, wrist, and forearm were badly cut from the creature's mighty teeth, but the damage was not permanent, and Korak was a quick healer.

The "tiger" rolled on its side and whined, pitifully. Its breathing was labored and raspy.

Korak guessed where the beast's heart was located and thrust the knife in, putting it out of its misery.

The ape-man placed one foot upon the creature and raised his arms to the now-darkened skies, emitting his signature upon a kill, an eerie, silent "cry."

Korak sank to the ground and breathed hard. He cleaned his bloody knife on the beast's furred carcass. Akut came and squatted next to him. *"Korak olo van."* Roughly: "The Killer still fights well."

Korak smiled and rested a hand upon his friend's furry shoulder. "Don't act so surprised, Akut," and the Mangani gave forth a coarse laugh.

Then Akut said, *"Kalan yud."*

Korak stood and called into the forest. "Suzanne! It is safe now!"

The leaves rustled and from the tangled branches emerged a young woman, the same woman with long, jet-black hair who had fled into the lower terrace moments before. Her face was oval and her eyes dark. Her skin was cream-colored and lightly tinged with olive. She wore leather cords about her neck, from which depended countless strings of colorful leather beads; a leather kilt covered her midsection, and she wore leather moccasins.

"Sorry. I'm not Suzanne," she said, speaking perfect English in a clear Brooklyn accent.

"Jason, it's me."

The ape-man stepped forward, stopping in a shaft of sunlight that pierced the deep forest.

"Sorry. I'm not Jason."

The woman took a step back. It was clear to Korak that she was perplexed. He sheathed his knife and raised his hands in a nonthreatening manner. "It's obvious we were both expecting other people. For my part, I'm surprised to find a human woman here who speaks English, and who is not my daughter, for I could only conceive of one such being found on this moon.

"My name is Korak, son of Tarzan."

"Tarzan!" the woman said. "Jason spoke of him. Jason Gridley, that is—that's who I was with when I left. I was right behind Jason, near his home in Sari. And then suddenly I was here."

"And you are?" Korak prompted.

"Oh, sorry. Betty. Betty Callwell. Late of Brooklyn, New York, and a bunch of other places."

"Ah," the ape-man replied. "Well, I do know Jason—"

"You do? Where is he?"

"Hold on. Can you tell me more about yourself, and then I'll tell you more about what I know of Jason."

Betty frowned. "Okay. But I was just behind him, and made the journey to the inner world with him, even if I wasn't sure I would stay, as I've finally started to make a life on Ladan."

"Tell you what," Korak said. "Let's find a place less in the open to confer. We'll make a fire, I'll cut a few flank steaks off of that whatever it is"—Korak gestured to the blue-and-white-striped tiger creature—"and then you can start from the very beginning. Deal?"

"Deal." Betty extended her hand. "Shake. That's what we do when we make a deal, where I come from."

Korak grinned and held out his hand. "I am not unfamiliar with the custom."

Betty emerged from the tangle of the forest in which she had sought to conceal herself, and looked up through the clearing. She appeared disoriented as she took in her surroundings. Korak understood the feeling: the thick forest canopy seemed to stretch off into a relatively normal horizon, but above and all around them, and rather than blue or red or yellow skies, they were surrounded by the interior of a planet. Blue oceans and green continents hung far above their heads but looked incredibly distant. Betty sat down hard, appearing to Korak to be dazed and disoriented.

"It does take a bit of getting used to," Korak said. "Take all the time you need."

Betty nodded in gratitude. After a few moments had passed, she said, "I'm okay now. It was just a bit of a stomach lurch, seeing continents and oceans above us where there should be sky. You'd think nothing would surprise me anymore."

A short while later, concealed in a small, protected clearing, and sitting around a crackling campfire, Akut grilled two steaks on branches Korak had sharpened with his knife, and the two humans sipped on fresh water the ape-man had gathered from a nearby stream. Both ape-man and Mangani attuned all their senses to threats from beyond in case their fire and smoke might draw unwanted attention.

"So," Betty said, "to really help you understand, I've got to tell you more than you probably think you want to know."

"I'm all ears," Korak said.

Betty burst out laughing.

"What? What did I say?"

"He's the one that's all ears," she said, gesturing at Akut. "They're cute, though. How come he's only grilling two steaks?"

"Akut will eat his steak raw and bloody, as it's meant to be," Korak replied. "I've asked him to grill mine lightly, so as not to offend your sensibilities as we eat together, but I do prefer mine mostly raw."

"Buddy, I've seen it all, believe me," Betty said. "You eat yours as bloody as you want. Can you ask him to make mine medium rare?"

"Of course," Korak said, and conveyed a few words in Mangani to Akut. "Now . . ."

"Sure thing. So. A long while ago I was transported to a planet called Amtor. I guess you'd call it Venus. I had no memory of my past. I didn't recall that I was really Betty Callwell of Brooklyn."

"I'm familiar with Amtor; it resides in a dimension parallel to the one containing the Earth on which I was born." Korak tore a strip of bloody meat from the steak with his strong teeth and made a noise for her to go on.

"Well, I wouldn't know anything about that. I thought Amtor was the planet Venus. Anyway . . . Who knows how long I was there, on Amtor, but finally I started to recall who I was when I encountered another stranded human from Earth. Carson was his name. While I had been transported there by means I still don't understand, Carson had traveled there in his privately constructed spacecraft."[*]

"Yes, I am also aware of Carson Napier," the ape-man said. "Your tale triggers my memory. You expected to meet Jason when first we encountered each other a few moments ago. Jason Gridley, correct?

"Yes!"

"Jason told of you, Betty," Korak said, and there was uncommon gentleness in his voice. "Jason returned from Barsoom's moon, Ladan, some two decades ago. He lauded you as a friend he had made there, who helped him get home."

Betty Callwell was silent for a few moments. Then: "Two decades, hmm? Well. I guess that *has* happened before, like when I snapped back to Amtor after briefly landing in an

---

[*] See the novel *Escape on Venus* by Edgar Rice Burroughs for the full account of Betty Callwell's first encounter with Carson Napier.

alleyway in Brooklyn. Almost a whole decade had passed. What I'm trying to say is, originally I could not control my coming and going—it just happened. Once I disappeared, leaving Carson in the lurch, I think. I awoke in an alley back in Brooklyn, stark naked, for nothing of my clothing or other accoutrements ever accompanied my bizarre and uncontrolled journeys. There I was alone and shivering in a New York alley—the same alley in which, I later learned, my dead body had been discovered some decades before!"*

Korak's eyes widened a bit, but he said nothing.

"But I thought I had a handle on this thing by now. I guess not. Two decades . . ."

"I'm sorry," Korak said. Akut made similar sympathetic noises, as the great ape had come to quite like the young woman in short order.

"So, just what year is it, anyway?" Betty asked. "On Earth," she amended.

Korak told her, and she laughed out loud. "Hey, that means I'm almost eighty years old! It's been an odd life, but look at me, young as ever."

Korak said, "Yes, and still older than me as well."

"Well, we both look pretty darn good for our ages," Betty said. "Anyway, to get to the point, as I got tossed about the cosmos, I began to be able to envision my destination and bring other objects, such as my clothing, along with me."

"That is good—if one cares about such things," Korak said.

"Yes, it is. It's been quite a relief. I'm now able to control, nine time out of ten at least, my mysterious translocations."

Korak's amusement was made evident by his expression, but Betty kept up her rapid-fire Brooklyn delivery of her story, oblivious to the ape-man's slight smile.

"This is the first time in a long while," she was saying, "that I missed my target." Betty finally saw the smile etched on Korak's face. "Wait. You're laughing at me!"

---

* See the comic book miniseries *Carson of Venus: The Flames Beyond*, written by Christopher Paul Carey.

Korak shrugged. "I don't really care about clothing. Though it would be convenient to be able to bring weapons along if one was being tossed throughout the cosmos."

"All right, jungle boy, tell me *your* story."

"You haven't finished your tale," Korak protested.

"Nope, not another word until I get the scoop from you, Mr. 'son of Tarzan.'"

Korak sighed and acquiesced, giving the short version of his background and how he had ended up in Pellucidar, searching for his daughter, with Akut chiming in here and there when his friend missed or glossed over details the Mangani thought were important and should be conveyed to Miss Callwell.

When the ape-man concluded, Betty chortled. "You're telling me your father was raised by apes, you spent years in the jungle yourself with no parenting to speak of, you and your ape friend here converse as freely in an 'ape language' as you and I currently are in English, you believe the Earth is hollow and has a vast world inside it populated by Stone Age men and women living side by side with *dinosaurs*, and you think we've been shrunk down to match the size of a miniature, one-mile-wide moon that now appears to us to be as huge as any large planet would.

"But my story of being flung across the cosmos from world to world, well, *that's* amusing!"

Korak shrugged. "Well, when you put it that way . . ."

"I do," Betty said.

"Point taken," Korak said. "I apologize. Would you please finish your story?"

Betty grinned in triumph. "Yes. So, most recently I was on Barsoom. I had looked up from the desert sands, and saw one of its moons, Thuria."

"Thuria!"

"Yes! I tried to will myself there, and thought I had succeeded, but I ended up in a strange land of perpetual twilight, which was populated by Stone Age men who rode diplodocuses!"

"The place in which you found yourself is called the Land of Awful Shadow," Korak said. "The primary village of that land is called Thuria."

"That lines up with what Jason told me, and he explained that I had actually been to Pellucidar. See, I *do* believe in your Stone Age guys and dinosaurs."

"I am not a believer in coincidence," Korak said. "There must be some relation between the two Thurias, especially as you attempted to reach one and instead arrived at the other. But tell me, how did you meet Jason Gridley?"

"I spent some time in this Land of Awful Shadow of yours, and then decided it was time to test my control over my odd travels again. I really didn't want to be whisked away once more to a land not of my choosing. So, I again concentrated on Thuria, this time focusing on the concept of 'Thuria' as a moon of Barsoom, and eventually succeeded in transporting myself there.*

"I began to build a life and settle in. And I was also able to make several trips back and forth to New York, revisiting old haunts, as it were, and satisfying my hankering for some foods you just can't find on Ladan, as the natives call it. But I kept going back to Ladan because, well, on Earth I'm dead and gone. I have no identity there, as I was declared dead long ago. And no more friends and family. I'll tell you, it's kind of unsettling to be able to go visit your own gravesite and know your actual body is buried in it."

"That *is* bizarre," Korak said. "How does that work?"

"I really don't know," Betty replied. "The best explanation I've heard is that all is mind, and therefore what you see and hear before you—me—is in reality a corporal manifestation of my mind's will."

---

* See the novella "Jason Gridley of Earth: Across the Moons of Mars" by Geary Gravel in the back pages of *Red Axe of Pellucidar* by John Eric Holmes, now available in the Edgar Rice Burroughs Universe series.

"I see," the ape-man said, although he didn't.

"I know. As I said, I'm not sure I truly understand it either. Anyway, I was back on Ladan, idling and enjoying life with my friend Umka and his fellow Masenas, when what should happen, but *another* Earthman appeared there."

"Jason," Korak said.

"Right. After several more exploits, including a side trip to Barsoom's other moon—"

"Wait. I have to ask. Is the Jason I knew dead? Is the Jason Gridley we now all know a . . . corporal manifestation?"

Betty laughed. "That's a good question. No, as far as I know, Jason was alive; that is, he had never died. And just to be clear, I am alive too, even though my body died. I feel and think and can love. It's just . . . a different sort of alive, I suppose."

"All right," Korak said. "What happened next?"

"Jason and I were in peril. He entreated me to leave, as I could control my translocations and could have made my escape. I refused, reminding him that all was mind and that he, too, could seize control of the phenomenon that had had him in its grasp for so long. He could transport himself; I helped him, for as I mentioned I had gained control over the ability to bring other physical objects with me when I traversed the void—I was sure that newfound ability also applied to other people. I was right! Together, we did it.

"The sound of the snapping cord, which reverberated through my whole body like a sonic boom, shaking my spine and my bones, came as it always does. We were thrust through the icy void together.

"And then came blessed warmth. I felt the powerful rays of a sun blazing deep into my skin and coursing through my whole body. I knew then that we had succeeded. We were in Jason's home, the inner world of Pellucidar. Like I said, I had been here once before, but only in the Shadow. The sky was a crisp blue and cloudless, and the air was humid but not overly so. We overlooked a thick forest of jungle vegetation, and in the horizonless, upward-curving distance were continents and oceans, fading into a hazy mélange of browns and blues.

"Jason saw his village, Sari, and I saw it as well. He stepped toward his home—and then I was here, on this world, crouching in the trees. I saw you, initially mistook you for Jason, and the rest you know."

Betty smiled ruefully. "That, by the way, was the highly condensed version. Someday maybe I'll write my autobiography. But," she continued brightly, "you know Jason. Can you tell me where we are, and then let's go to him. I would like him to know that I'm okay after just disappearing on him like that."

"I don't think it will be so simple as that," the ape-man replied. "I believe you have been drawn here for some reason unknown to us. Jason's goddaughter, Victory Harben, experienced a similar phenomenon, in which she was 'entangled' with certain people, places, and situations to which she was inextricably drawn by means of what she called a 'translocation aura.' I can't help but think that you are experiencing something similar, for why else should you be here, at this place and time?

Betty shrugged. "Beats me. I guess we'll find out."

Korak took another large bite of his steak, and chewed it thoughtfully. Then he continued. "I mentioned my thought that Akut and I had been proportionally shrunk when we traveled here, so that this world now appears as large to us as any other worlds, such as Earth and Pellucidar, would have previously."

"Yes," Betty said, "that is very similar to Jason's theory—or rather John Carter's theory, for Jason hadn't really believed it—about traveling to Thuria, that is, Ladan, for Carter had traveled there in a Barsoomian spacecraft long before Jason's and my advent there. Carter called it something like, if I am recalling it correctly, the theory of 'compensatory adjustment of masses' between Mars and its two moons."

"Yes," the ape-man said, "others in the cosmos have

experienced similar phenomena. We have been proportionally reduced in size so that this world, the pendent moon, so very small, seems just as large to us as the seven-thousand-mile diameter of the interior of Pellucidar had appeared to me before Akut and I traveled here. In addition, the gravitational effect upon us seems to be similar to that exerted upon the surface of Pellucidar, which in turn feels slightly less than that upon Earth's outer crust.

"Is it not strange," Korak continued, "that these two places share a name, Thuria, and other similarities, such as worlds in which one experiences a radical diminution in size in order to travel there?"

"Yes," Betty replied, "Jason Gridley raised much the same question. I'm unsure he ever answered it."

"There is more that I am pondering," Korak said, "although I cannot firmly relate it to our present circumstances. But as long as night has fallen, I may as well relate it to you in the event it later proves useful." Whereupon the son of Tarzan related his father's exploits among the hidden peoples of the Minunians, located deep in the inaccessible lands within the Great Thorn Forest in central Africa, including the most curious aspect of the tale, Tarzan's reduction to one-quarter of his normal height.

"However," Korak continued, "the diminution in size was not accompanied by a corresponding reduction in physical strength, and this aspect of his condition, in conjunction with his wits, as he put it, led him to victory in his fight for liberty. After he escaped the lands of the Minunians, the effects of the scientist's experiment wore off and he mercifully returned to his former size with no ill repercussions."

"How," Betty asked, "did the scientist with the unpronounceable name shrink your father?"

"Tarzan told me he listened carefully to Zoanthrohago's explanation to his king, in the event the knowledge would prove useful in reasserting his proper size. It had to do with a device with seven needles that projected some unknown emanation, and when placed at the back of the skull and aimed at a particular gland, caused the shrinking effect in question."*

"That seems pretty thin," Betty said.

"Agreed," Korak said. "For a long time, I thought the whole thing was a crazy story, a yarn Tarzan made up to keep us amused and distract us from worrying about his long absence. Now . . . given what you and I have experienced, as well as Jason Gridley and John Carter, I am not so quick to dismiss my father's tale. However, it remains to be seen if his experiences have some direct correlation to our circumstances or not."

Korak, Betty, and Akut spoke a bit longer as the fire died to glowing embers. The ape-man looked to the sky and discerned the grayish landscape seemingly floating far above his head—the twilit world of the Land of Awful Shadow, in reality only one mile away. Nighttime on the Dead World would never be pitch black; it was more of a gray twilight, due to the reflection of sunlight off of the concave surface of the inner world. He was unsettled at the prospect of a world with semidark night skies and yet no stars sprinkling their lights across the heavens.

Everything about this moon felt wrong to him.

Eventually, the three made their way into the branches and settled in as comfortably as they could upon the boughs. Korak and Akut agreed to alternate keeping guard, and the ape-man dozed first.

Korak had the morning watch, and yawned as the sun dappled the treetops with yellow, contrasting sharply with the dark green of the areas still shaded.

He held his breath. All around them were pairs of white, unblinking eyes. The ape-man had neither heard, seen, nor, most importantly, caught the scent of any intruders. Yet here they were.

---

* See the novel *Tarzan and the Ant Men* by Edgar Rice Burroughs, now available in the Edgar Rice Burroughs Authorized Library series, for the full account of the ape-man's adventures in Minuni.

Korak hissed at Akut, hoping to awaken the Mangani while not alerting the beings surrounding them that they had been discovered, but to no avail. The shadowy creatures darted across the connecting branches like skilled gymnasts on the balance beam.

Akut leaped from his tree to the one adjacent, grabbed the just-awakening Betty about the waist, and swung skillfully to the ground. While his friend removed Betty from harm's way, Korak raised his loaded Enfield, aimed at the largest onrushing shadow figure, and pulled the trigger.

The creature uttered a low grunt and toppled to the ground. Korak fired again and a second form tumbled downward. A third shot accounted for another attacker, and suddenly the rifle was jerked from his grasp. Korak looked up to see a dark, bony figure holding the weapon and was unable to dodge the rifle butt that slammed into his forehead.

The ape-man was knocked to the soft ground. He rolled to dissipate the impact and quickly regained his wits, forming a protective circle with Akut and Betty.

Korak always kept his quiver about his shoulders, but his bow was caught in the branches above. He whipped out two arrows and handed these to his companions, then drew his knife.

Their opponents crept from the encircling trees and brush, and Korak, Akut, and Betty could now see them clearly in the emerging daylight. They appeared to be manlike creatures, in that they walked on two legs and had two arms. They were tall, half again as tall as Korak, and gaunt almost to the point of being skeletal. All of them had thick, black eyebrows; some their pates were hairless, while others had jet-black mohawks that stretched from their foreheads to the bases of their skulls. Their pale skin was tinted bluish and appeared to be paper thin, to the point of translucence. Korak thought he could see darker blue, almost deep violet tangles of arteries and veins beneath their skin. The men grinned cruelly, showing gleaming white teeth, and this, along with their hairless blue skulls, gave them a nightmarish aspect.

The warriors—for soldiers they must be—were armored with guards of some tough white material strapped to their shins, upper legs, forearms, and upper arms. Each wore a cuirass that appeared to be of the same white substance, and Korak thought they might be formed from the bony breast-plates of some slaughtered animal. They wore tough, black footwear and each carried a long lance with a sharpened hook at the tip.

All this the ape-man absorbed in a brief moment, for the skeletal men were upon them with no further time to think or plan.

Korak rushed two oncoming warriors and leaped upward between them, utilizing the advantage that the moon's lower gravity provided and taking his attackers by surprise. His steel knife slashed, and blue blood jetted from the throat of the one on the right. At the same time, he delivered a punishing left to the other's chin, hoping to knock him unconscious. Instead, the ape-man heard the distinctive cracking of neck vertebrae, and realized he had broken the other man's neck with the force of his roundhouse.

The ape-man landed, rolled, came up on his feet, and turned right back into the melee. Betty had stabbed one of the skeletal men in the neck, the arrow he had given her piercing one side and protruding from the other. The warrior was coughing violet-blue liquid and Betty darted to avoid being showered by the dying man's lifeblood. Lacking another weapon, she darted back up into the trees.

Akut, meanwhile, had used both his stone axe and the arrow Korak had given him to good effect. He had split one opponent from groin to sternum with the axe, and then used the arrow to repeatedly stab another in the face. Korak yelled in Mangani that the creatures were fragile, and Akut took his friend's words to heart, leaping up and crunching another warrior's skull between his furry paws. Then he leaped on the back of another blue-skinned warrior and cleanly decapitated him with a swing of the axe.

Korak went low, intent on breaking the legs of the man nearest him, but the ape-man got an unpleasant surprise, for the attackers' bone leg guards held strong against his earthly strength. He warned Akut to focus on the warriors' skulls and necks, and questioned why these weren't guarded by helmets and neck braces, but he didn't stop to wonder long. His mighty thews thrust him straight upward, and his hard fist connected under his opponent's chin, once again cleanly snapping neck bones.

The ape-man landed neatly in the lower gravity, spun, and raced back into the thick of the battle. He and Akut had surprised the soldiers with their defense so thoroughly that the warriors had not even had the opportunity to bring their hooked lances to bear, for the ape-man and great ape consistently rushed in close quarters with the skeletal men, rendering their long weapons useless.

Korak gave a triumphant war whoop, and Akut responded. They each quickly dispatched two more attackers, after which the ape-man risked a quick glance away from the field of combat, to check on Betty's situation. The Earth woman was still crouched in the low boughs, out of reach of the tall warriors and their hooked lances, and Korak could tell she was also keeping on guard against attack from within the lower terrace of trees, from which the blue men had originated their morning raid. But no, all forces were focused on the ape-man and the Mangani on the ground. Betty gave him a wave signaling all was well, and he looked back to the clearing in which he and Akut waged their defense.

From all sides, at least fourfold the number of original attackers emerged from the shadowy trees and converged on the two defenders. Korak was confused when they tossed their lances aside, for the smarter strategy would have been to keep their distance and poke and prod, cut and slash, until at last the two collapsed from blood loss. The ape-man had no more time to ponder the bizarre strategy, for the blue men piled upon them, and despite their greater earthly strength, the sheer number of skeletal bodies crushing and punching and biting at them began to take its toll.

Korak screamed in fury, swinging his fists and pummeling anything in their way, breaking necks and fracturing skulls, and still the skeletal men pressed down against him, burying him in bony bodies until he almost suffocated. With another burst of energy, he thrust his muscular legs and clambered upward through the sea of hideous blue bodies, inadvertently clearing a path for his friend. Akut scrambled up, using legs, arms, and heads as steps, and surged from the top of the pile. Korak, however, was pulled back under the relentless grasping fingers and hands on his feet and legs, and felt like he would drown in the morass of blue flesh and bones.

Then Korak was seeing red, deep crimson thudding against his eyelids, and behind his eyes, and in the back of his brain. The red rage overtook him. His heart thudded uncontrollably, threatening to burst from his chest. His breathing came in short, violent pants, as it had not in decades, save the recent recurrences since his arrival in Pellucidar.

Korak was back in Pal-ul-don . . . not when he had traveled there in search of his mother and father, in the early months of 1919, but a year later. He had never told anyone of his reunion with Hans Kriegmesser, whom he had last seen at the Argonne front. It was not a pleasant occasion for either man.

A blue-skinned warrior held Korak's arms fast behind his back, while another clubbed him repeatedly on the back of the head, knocking him unconscious. The last thing he saw, his head swimming, was not Hans Kriegmesser, but Akut and Betty Callwell escaping into the middle terrace of the strangely formed trees of the Dead World.

20

THE VORTHA

MERIEM, LORDAN, AND MIRINA, astride Mis-see the bus-dar, glided over the thick forests carpeting the pendent moon.

Their journey had been disorienting, especially the mid-point where up now felt like down, and down became up. The bus-dar flew straight and true, and the three riders felt reassured that they could trust the creature to see them safely to the surface of the Dead World.

Now they looked up in wonder and saw not clear skies, but the inner shell of Pellucidar with landmasses of green and brown, and seas of blue. It was a visage to which Lordan was accustomed, having routinely flown with Mis-see at an elevation of five thousand or so feet in the past, save that now he and the trusty bus-dar were comparatively much smaller than the lands and oceans upon which they gazed. The difference in proportion changed all their perspectives, and Meriem and Lordan were momentarily struck silent at the grand sight.

Mirina adjusted the most quickly, this being her home world, and in moments she had leaped from Mis-see's back and was flying alongside them, gossamer wings aflutter. The petite bird-woman flew circles around the bus-dar, smiling with joy, and Meriem recalled that Mirina's flights had been limited by the higher gravity at the surface of the inner world, although she had made strides in increasing the strength of her wings.

"I will fly forward to scout for Mahars," the bird-woman said. "It would not do to be caught unawares by them." With that, she sped away into the sky until she was but a distant speck.

Meriem was sure that Mirina was indeed reconnoitering to ensure their safety against the hideous, intelligent reptiles who had plagued the lives of the gilaks of Pellucidar—and of the denizens of the pendent moon, apparently—but she couldn't help but think that the young woman was taking the opportunity to stretch her wings.

Mis-see glided lower, skimming ten or so feet over the tops of the oddly shaped trees, and Meriem exclaimed in alarm.

"That was a foot! A human foot lodged in that tree branch!" she said.

Lordan, in front of her astride the bus-dar, turned his head and begin to speak, but his mother-in-law cried out once more. "That's a woman's head. And an arm!"

"Meriem," Lordan said, "we have told you before of gilak funerary customs. We place the bodies of our dead in the branches of trees in Pellucidar, and the birds pick the bodies apart and bring them here piece by piece."

"I remember," Meriem said. "It's just that, hearing about it and seeing it in person are two different things, I suppose. It's somewhat horrifying."

Lordan sighed in exasperation. "That is why we call this place the Dead World. And we would find it much more horrifying to have our bodies put in the soil for the demons to come and dismember them, and take them bit by bit down to the fiery Molop Az upon which Pellucidar rests."

Meriem bit her tongue, for Lordan knew full well, having mated with a woman from the outer world, that the lands and oceans of Pellucidar were located upon the inner crust of a sphere some thousands of miles in diameter, the thickness of which was some five hundred miles, and upon the outer crust of which was located many more seas and continents— none of which evidence-based facts left room for the concept of a sea of fire underpinning the inner world.

Instead, she said, "I'm sorry, Lordan, I didn't mean to disrespect your customs and traditions."

Lordan said, "I am sorry as well. As I said, I had no wish to come here. It is forbidden. But I am here for Suzanne. If she is truly here, we must find her and go. Quickly."

Meriem squeezed his shoulder in support and acknowledgment. "We'll find her."

Mirina glided back and flew alongside them. "I think I have found the land where my people have their aeries. Much of my memory is still hazy, but the more I see of this world, the more comes back to me." She pointed off to their left. "I recognize that topography and the tree line that abuts that lake, yonder. I believe the Vortha nest-village is there, concealed from view in the upper levels of that forest."

Before anyone could utter a protest, Mirina flew off again in the direction she had indicated.

Lordan gently tugged on Mis-see's reins, and the bus-dar followed, albeit at a slower and more cautious pace.

Within moments, Mirina came back. "It is indeed the Vortha. I am home! Come!" The bird-woman sped back to the forest treetops she had indicated.

Lordan urged Mis-see on, and Meriem experienced a sense of trepidation, for they knew nothing of the Vortha, not even Mirina herself, as she had been afflicted with amnesia regarding much of her life here on the Dead World. What if her memory loss was somehow tied to trauma inflicted by the Vortha themselves?

"Have a care, Lordan," Meriem said, "for we don't know these people." Her son-in-law nodded in acknowledgment.

The bus-dar with its two human riders arrived at the destination Mirina had indicated in a gentle downward glide, descended into the upper terrace, and flapped its leathery wings toward the branch upon which the bird-woman perched among others of her kind. All around them, positioned on the larger spiraling boughs, were hutlike nests constructed of smaller branches and grasses. The nests were covered and had small openings just large enough to provide ingress and egress for the small members of the Vortha race, of a design surely intended to make the abodes defensible against assailants. The constellation of nest-huts was generally spherical, in the center of which lay a larger hut, set upon several larger crossing branches for stability, and suitable for perhaps twenty to thirty Vortha at any given time.

It was before the entrance to this larger structure, presumably a meeting and communal area for this Vortha village, that Mirina and others of her people perched. One of the larger supporting corkscrew boughs appeared more than sturdy enough to sustain Mis-see's weight, and the weight of her passengers, and it was upon this that the bus-dar settled.

As they landed, Meriem took note that all gathered were women, and all looked much like Mirina: they all had skin like fine bone china, and long white hair swept back from their foreheads and hanging down their graceful backs, from which protruded wings covered in off-white feathers.

Meriem "heard," in her head, one of other Vortha speaking to Mirina.

"Alandra, it has been too long," the woman said. Meriem could tell her tone was chilly, even with the nonaural method of communication. "Frankly, we thought you dead."

Mirina paused, cocked her head to one side. ". . . Alandra?"

"Yes," the woman said. "Your name. You were never the brightest, but—"

"I remember now," Mirina said. "There is much that is still obscured in my memory, but yes, Alandra, I recall that was my name. And . . . I remember your scorn. It hasn't changed, but thank you, Mother; it has helped me remember."

The other bird-women gathered around mentally chuckled, caught the withering glance from Mirina's mother, and suppressed their amusement.

Meriem thought this might be an opportune time to intervene; she stepped forward to introduce herself. "My name is—"

"Alandra, what manner of creature is this? It appears to be

female, but I have never seen its like, although I can hear its thoughts as its digestive orifice moves in primitive fashion."

"Mother—Phandra—this is Meriem, and her companion is Lordan," Mirina said. "They are of a race called gilaks, hailing from the *land above*. I have been living with the gilaks in a place called Thuria. I choose to go by Mirina, the name gifted to me by the people of Thuria, who were kind to me and took me in, treating me as one of their own."

Phandra scoffed. "The *land above*? No one goes there and returns save the Mahars. You had best come up with a better story, Alandra."

"I said, it's Mirina. Don't you recall, when I was younger, I always came to you upon waking, telling you of another type of being I saw in my dreams, half again as tall as us, and with kind eyes and hair growing upon its face. I asked you what it meant, but you could not tell me. I found the being in my dreams, and many more like him, in the *land above*."

"Him?" Phandra's face exhibited a mix of shock and horror.

"Yes, Mother," Mirina said, "I have mated with him. His name is Dek, of Thuria."

"That is disgusting!" Phandra said.

"And now I am starting to remember," Mirina said, sadness etched across her features, "why I fled from this village in the first place."

"You *fled*," exclaimed another Vortha woman, "because you were a *coward*!"

"Wait your turn to speak, Tendre," Phandra said. "Alandra, there is truth in Tendre's words. You ran when it was your time to meet the Mahars."

"Meet the Mahars?" Mirina was stunned.

"What does she mean, 'meet the Mahars'?" Meriem asked.

Lordan whispered to Meriem, "They are hemming us in, surrounding us."

She spoke back, "I think they can 'hear' us." She made a hand sign that only he could see, pointing upward, and Lordan nodded slowly, almost imperceptibly.

Tendre stepped forward, menace in her stance. "It was *your* turn. You had been selected. But when you flew, when you escaped, *my* daughter was selected as your replacement. *She* did her duty!"

"Tendre is correct, Alandra—"

"Mirina!"

"It does not matter. You are in violation. The Mahars have been informed. You shall be offered as a supplement to appease the Mahars and our Vortha traditions.

Lordan made hand signs to Mis-see as Tendre approached Mirina with a thick ropelike vine.

"Now," Tendre said, "we will see you to the Mahar cavern and ensure you stay there until the ritual is complete. There will be no flight to the *land above* for you this time."

Tendre attempted to slip the vine around Mirina's shoulders and bind her wings and arms, but the latter took to the air. The loop of rope caught her ankles and tightened, cutting short Mirina's flight. Tendre smiled and tugged on the vine, pulling Mirina back down as she flapped her wings furiously. Phandra and the others joined Tendre, and it was clear that Mirina's escape gambit was doomed.

Mis-see took to the air, dove toward the rope-vine, and cleanly snapped it in two with her beak. Mirina shot into the air, and the Vortha women made to pursue her, but Mis-see strafed them in a circular pass, sending them tumbling in disarray.

The bus-dar settled to the ground, Lordan and Meriem swung onto her back, and they were airborne within seconds.

Mis-see, with her larger wingspan and stronger wing flaps, quickly overtook Mirina. Behind them, the Vortha had reorganized and mounted a winged pursuit. Meriem urged Mirina to join them astride the bus-dar, for there was no guarantee the bird-woman could outfly every member of her former tribe.

Mirina saw the wisdom in Meriem's entreaty. She neatly landed on the bus-dar's back, hugging Meriem tightly about the waist. Then, with a great flapping of her wings, Mis-see sprang forward in the skies of the Dead World, leaving their Vortha pursuers far behind.

They flew until they felt safe from the Vortha, and then flew some more, for Mirina counseled that perhaps the bird-women had the advantage of endurance over speed.

They passed over several dense forests in which they could have made camp, then over grassy plains and a vast, rocky terrain cut by several deep canyons, before finally settling in the lowest level of a woodland characterized by the pendent moon's spiral-trunked trees. They agreed that after flying such a distance, it was unlikely the Vortha would locate them, and if they did, the bird-women were so tiny in comparison that it was unlikely they would triumph in head-on combat. Nonetheless, they would keep watch, for where the Vortha might fail in physical conflict, they might prevail with guile and the advantage of surprise.

Lordan went about finding suitable repast for the redoubt-able bus-dar, Mis-see. It was too bad that the multitentacled bab-ah which were so prevalent in the inner world's watering holes, and which the bus-dars found to be an unparalleled delicacy, were not to be found on the Dead World, but Lordan did manage to locate a shallow pond from which he procured several small fish of whose scales shimmered a silver-blue. All of the party, including Mis-see, partook of Lordan's find, and after they had broken their fast Meriem asked Mirina about the Mahars.

"Now that my memory has fully returned," the Vortha replied, "I can tell you that there is at least one Mahar temple on the seacoast near the Vortha village. They have a feeding pool there. I cannot tell you if there are more Mahar retreats elsewhere on the Dead World, but several tens of rotations ago, the Mahar population near my village increased dramatically. I later learned this was due to many Mahars fleeing the dominion of David Innes' Federated Kingdoms.

"It had long been Vortha custom to periodically sacrifice

one of our younglings, selected by lottery to go to the Mahars and sacrifice herself to them, for the everlasting good of the village. The demands of the hideous reptiles increased fourfold when their resident population rose as the permanency of the Federated Kingdoms became irrefutable.

"The temple is carved from the living rock, hewn straight from the cliff upon which the sea breaks. There are no ground entrances, for the Mahars come and go via openings high in the cliff face, which are connected to wide tunnels that curve down and open in the ceiling of a large, rocky amphitheater, the bottom of which is filled with seawater that flows in through various small crevices from the ocean without.

"We—the Vortha sacrifices—come by the same means of ingress, but never do we emerge. Mind you, I have not been there. I am conveying to you the description I was provided when I was instructed to go to the temple and present myself for sacrifice. The seawater pool is marked by several rocky islands, which is where we are told to land and wait for the Mahars. I was told the Mahars would fly in through the tunnels, accompanied by their thipdars. Sometimes, according to the season or to demands of the Mahars, the Vortha would be required to send several sacrifices; other times, as with my encounter, a single Vortha would be sent to await one Mahar. I was informed the Mahar would fly in slowly and eventually perch on the warm boulders situated opposite my rocky island."

"Does that mean," Meriem asked, "that the Mahars actually live elsewhere? I know that in Pellucidar, their underground cities were separate from the feeding temples."

"I think," Mirina said, "that they actually lived in caverns even higher in the seaside cliff than the temple, for I do not recall hearing of any cities or other places of Mahar habitation. I think that perhaps they used the temple—or temples—here on the Dead World before David and his armies ran them off, but did not have large population centers here. Now, they are in disarray and have only their temples to retreat to. A civilization in decline, though still deadly.

"I was told that under no circumstances was I to move from my little island of rock, or attempt to look away. Rather, my mother informed me, I was never to avert my gaze from the Mahar, for it was a great honor to be selected and I should meet my fate understanding this, and knowing that my sacrifice helped to preserve the safety and continuation not only of our Vortha village, but of the entire race.

"The Mahar arrived upon her leathery wings, as I had been warned, and it was then I lost my nerve. Her eyes were large and unblinking. Its reptilian malevolence was clear. She was large, taller than even you, Lordan, and it had sharp claws at the tips of its wings, which were mottled and of a deep purple. Worst of all was the long beak with its horrendous teeth. I knew then my fate, for this part mother had not conveyed to me.

"She dove into the water, surfaced, went under again, and surfaced once more near me, then circled the rocky formation upon which I stood, taking her time. She swam leisurely back to her rock-strewn spot opposite me, and stared at me for a long while. I felt my head swim, and underwent a loss of will. Once more she plunged into the water, staying under for a long while, as if to drive me mad as I stood there spellbound and helpless, not knowing where she was, and in the back of my mind I screamed, for these were supposedly civilized beings, but also *cruel*.

"With every shred of my inner strength, I made a soul-lurching effort to free myself from the Mahar's spell. Suddenly my will came rushing back, and I flung myself into the air. I have never flown so fast, never exerted myself to the point of utter exhaustion, and then beyond it. Up and up I flew, and then I was without weight, and then down and down I fell. As you know, this is why the Thurians call me The One Who Fell."

All were silent, respectful of what Mirina had gone through.

Meriem broke the silence after a while. "Mirina, you said earlier that a youngling Vortha is chosen by lottery to sacrifice 'herself.' Are not the male Vortha ever selected for this 'honor'?"

Mirina was surprised. "I . . . I'm sorry, it is such a matter of course to me, I didn't think to mention it. The Vortha are all female."

Meriem's and Lordan's eyes both widened in surprise.

"But then," Lordan asked, "how do you mate?"

"I'm sorry?" Mirina was affronted.

Meriem shot Lordan a warning look.

"What Lordan meant—"

"I asked what I meant to ask," the Stone Age man said.

"Quiet!" Meriem said. Then, back to the bird-woman, "What we don't understand is, how do the Vortha reproduce without males?"

Mirina shrugged. "I am tired now." She retreated to an inviting conjunction of branches in the lower-middle terrace and closed her eyes.

"Well done," Meriem said to Lordan. "There is such a thing as parthenogenesis, you know."

Lordan looked at her blankly.

Meriem sighed. The Stone Age man was not stupid. Suzanne would never have tolerated a life with someone who could not match her. He just had no background or context in what they were discussing.

As if to confirm Meriem's thought that he indeed was not stupid, Lordan said, "Mahars also reproduce without males. It is disturbing."

"I see," Meriem said. "Okay. Well then. I do agree, though, it's time for rest. I'll take the first watch. You cover the middle watch, then wake me several hours before daybreak and I will guard again until sunrise."

Lordan nodded and, choosing a comfortable spot in the boughs, closed his eyes. Mis-see nestled down in the ground;

exhausted from the day's exertions, slumber quickly overtook the valiant bus-dar.

Night fell like a grayish blanket, broken only by the chirps of evening insects, and the hoots of some distant birds.

When Lordan, Mirina, and Mis-see awoke in the morning, Meriem was gone without a trace.

21

IN THE PALACE OF THE SKETH

KORAK THE KILLER AWOKE. He was in a circular cell, the stone walls of which arched and came together in an apex some fifteen feet above his head. The gray stonework appeared to be hand-hewn and was laid in the manner of alternating bricks, the mortar in between being of high quality and not susceptible to chipping with his bare fingers. The stonework was set very smoothly and there were no readily discernible handholds. If he had had his knife, or some other implement, he might have made some headway toward destroying some mortar and loosening a brick, but even if he had, there was no way to know what lay on the other side.

The door was arched and made of a heavy wood; the bar, latch, and hinges must have been on the exterior of the door, for it was bare and smooth on his side. There was a small aperture in the door, two feet above his head, which was barricaded with three solid iron bars. By jumping up and attempting to look out the opening, the ape-man could see that the door was at least three inches thick.

Opposite the door was a twin aperture set into the stone, similarly blocked with three iron bars. Korak leaped up, grabbed hold of a bar in each bronzed hand, and pulled himself upward. Peering outside, he saw that he was in a tall cylindrical tower that rose above most of the surrounding buildings.

Below him was spread a palatial estate of which he had not seen the like. There were other towers, most not as tall as the one in which he was imprisoned, surrounded by

174

well-maintained gardens lush with flowers the colors of which spanned the rainbow; rectangular pools of crystal-clear water bordered by tall hedges, in which he observed many people of the tall, blue-skinned race he had fought lounging and swimming; amphitheaters in which more of the blue-skinned folk sat in groups playing instruments, or practiced dueling in pairs using flattened and unsharpened weapons; massive circular estate buildings adorned with turrets and balconies, the entrances to which were flanked with gigantic columns; and paved pathways leading here and there among the variety of buildings and attractions. There were high bridges connecting some adjacent towers, courtyards in which the skeletal people strolled, small foot bridges over ponds, and small trees in cultivated forested areas—small in comparison to the hugely tall trees encircling the whole settlement that composed the canopy shielding it from view.

In the center of it all, on a slightly raised hillock, was a massive, bejeweled palace that dwarfed all that surrounded it. This, Korak was to shortly learn, was the castle and the heart of the Queendom of Sketh.

The palace grounds were surrounded by a high wall, wide enough for guard patrols to march atop it, and in the distance beyond the fortification, he could see huts, larger common buildings, small ponds or lakes, and agricultural fields.

The entire area was covered by the high canopy terrace of corkscrew-trunked trees, thus shielding it from view by the inhabitants of Pellucidar.

Korak leaped down from the exterior window when came a sound at the aperture in the door. A guard was there, his blue skull-like face grinning at him through the bars. The guard tossed a set of manacles through the bars, and they landed at the ape-man's feet with a loud clank.

The proposition was clear. Put them on his wrists, or stay here in the cell. He might as well see what these people were about, and what they intended for him, so he slipped on the manacles and clicked them shut.

The door unlocked and swung open, and three of the gaunt blue guards entered, each armed with the same long lances tipped with sharp hooks that he had seen them carrying in the forest.

Korak was escorted across the grounds and into the lavish palace, his hands manacled in front of him. The ape-man strode proudly down a great hall, prodded by the soldiers who had captured him. He tried to communicate with the soldiers escorting him, asking after Akut, but they didn't understand his language. The skeletal men smiled and laughed at the strange noises he was emitting.

"Nothing had better happen to him," Korak warned his guards, "or you'll all have a death sentence hanging over you. I'll track you down and find you wherever you go. I'm holding you personally responsible, understand. If anything happens to him, you will die, in the worst possible way I can think of."

The Skethan soldiers escorting him, initially amused at his bizarre sounds, observed his expression and his demeanor, and were chilled. Korak then threatened them in the Mangani language, with its grunts and growls, and the soldiers were downright frightened. They still did not understand his words, but they knew enough to understand when they were being threatened by a wild beast, and that the beast doing the threatening might just be more than capable of carrying out its threats.

The ape-man held his head high as he was directed this way and that through tunnels, narrow curving stone stairwells, and damp underground corridors before entering another giant hall, at the end of which stood a raised dais, crowned by an elaborate throne. Blue-skinned courtiers, jesters, and hangers-on of all sorts lined the green-carpeted pathway to the throne, pointing and laughing at him, making fun of his attire and his barbaric demeanor. The people were all of a piece with the soldiers and guards he had already encountered: half again as tall as an average human, gaunt to the point of appearing cadaverous, and garbed in black kilts or tunics. They had either full heads of jet-black hair, no longer than shoulder length, or mohawks, or were completely bald, perhaps having shaved their skulls. Their eyes were dark to the point of being black.

Korak, for his own part, was unfazed by their jeers. Walking practically naked before these craven people, clad only in a leopard-skin loincloth, he cut a more imposing and dangerous figure than they ever would, and he thought that, underneath all the cheering and the laughing, they knew that. They laughed because they were afraid of him. They jeered and cackled and cawed because they thought they were safe from him, that he couldn't harm them, with his hands bound in front of him and surrounded by six guards.

How little they knew.

Korak and his escort approached the queen and halted. The guards and everyone else bowed their heads in respect for her and her station. The ape-man looked her directly in the eyes.

The queen of Sketh was a lovely woman who shared the faintly bluish skin of her subjects, but unlike them she was not tall and gaunt, but rather appeared to be a normal-sized human, in relation to Korak. Like many of her subjects, the queen was completely bald, and she was completely hairless, save for artfully arched black eyebrows. She was perhaps five foot five in relation to Korak's six feet. Interestingly, her skin, while of a blue-violet tinge, was not translucent like that of the warriors he had fought and the other Sketh, and so despite her odd skin tone she appeared less horrifying to him than the rest of her strange people. He wondered at the physical differences he observed between the queen and those she ruled, but he did not have long to ponder this disparity.

Korak sat with the queen in her outer chambers. The manacles that had bound his wrists had been removed, and a heavy guard remained present but at a respectful distance.

The ape-man had been provided an opportunity to bathe and had been presented with clean clothing: a simple black kilt and soft but tough black sandals of the same type he observed many others of the skeletal folk wearing. He was provided food and drink, of which he partook, reasoning that it was probably not poisoned, for if they wished to kill him, they could have already done so ten times over.

Queen Laina—for though there remained a language barrier, they had been able to make themselves understood enough to exchange names—sat on soft, plush pillows at a low table across from Korak. She did not partake of the food, but joined him in drink, which gave him a further degree of confidence in the safety of the refreshments.

She made Korak understand that she believed, based on the incredible strength he had displayed in defeating her soldiers, and also, of course, his very strange appearance, that he was not native to her world, but came from somewhere else, perhaps what some called the *land above*.

The queen—doing her best to overcome the linguistic differences with a combination of drawings and giving Korak a rudimentary language lesson in some simple words and concepts—explained that on her world were a variety of tribes, habitations, villages, castles, and city-states, all peopled by kings and queens, feudal governors, workers, warriors, farmers, slaves, chieftains, and tribespeople. All of these were situated under her world's thick forest canopies as a defense against attack by other denizens of their world, but also to shield them from sight by any aggressors who might live on the *land above* and wish to come to their world and attack them.

All of her world's factions were in a constant state of conflict; attacks by enemies were swift and many times unexpected. For instance, one city-state might wait years before launching an unprovoked surprise attack at another, and then pummel them repeatedly over the course of several weeks, followed by withdrawing again for years, lulling their adversaries into a state of complacency.

Queen Laina continued to explain to Korak that he had been under the observation of her warriors ever since he and his hairy companion had fallen out of the bird in the sky, followed by the bird bursting into flames and falling in many pieces. The warriors had sent reports back to her, and she had ordered them captured, not killed—especially Korak. This explained the blue-skinned warriors' failure to use their wickedly hooked lances, for these were the weapons of killing, not capturing. The queen reiterated that her soldiers conveyed to her Korak's great prowess in battle, as well as his cunning and ferocity. She believed he would be the perfect soldier to lead her personal guard in the castle, coordinating with the larger armed forces tasked with protecting the city, with the responsibility of ensuring her safety at all times.

This was all communicated with more difficulty than it took to recount it here, due to the language barrier, but eventually Korak understood her proposition. She believed the ape-man to be a great warrior. He must accept her offer to become the captain of her personal guard.

Or . . . instant death.

Korak accepted the queen's proposal, and was put in the hands of her majordomo for training, language instruction, a tour of the palace and surrounding grounds, and introduction to the palace troops soon to be under his command. Among several oddities was that the Sketh never slept upon a substance softer than a single thickness of fabric, which they either threw upon the ground, or upon wooden, stone, or marble sleeping slabs, depending upon their caste and their wealth. This was not an issue for him personally, for like his father Tarzan, Korak could sleep under many different circumstances, ranging from harsh to luxurious.

Queen Laina's majordomo, Tonzu, was diligent in carrying out his mistress' wishes that Korak be instructed in all aspects of Skethan cultural norms, the language, foods, and weapons. But the ape-man had the distinct sense that the man disliked his task and disliked Korak even more. The ape-man did not confront Tonzu on this, for if the man did his job, then what of it? The queen had not ordered her man to like Korak, only to provide the necessary instruction and information for the ape-man to be capable and proficient in his new role, and to carry out his duties in the most efficacious manner possible.

Besides, Tonzu had not done or said anything outright offensive or obnoxious to Korak. He was unfailingly polite, though distantly so. But the ape-man had learned when to rely on his gut. He would not turn his back on the major-domo. And he knew he was watched and was still very much a prisoner. He was in a probationary period, and had no illusions that even if Queen Laina did go through with her pledge to appoint him the captain of her personal guard, he would still be on probation as far as the Sketh were concerned, and would still remain a prisoner in their land.

He wondered what the queen's game was, and why she was interested in him.

After many weeks of making much progress learning the language, culture, and customs, and becoming familiar with the general layout of the citadel and surrounding estate buildings and grounds, as well as the lands outside the palace walls, Korak was brought before the queen again, and they were seated once more in her outer chambers, with guards, again, at a respectful distance but close enough if needed.

Korak tested his new skills with the Skethan language. "Before we proceed, Queen Laina," he said, "I have a question for you."

The queen nodded that he should proceed.

"What of my companion, Akut?" The ape-man was very much prepared to wring her neck and suffer the consequences of death beneath the guards' hooked lances if she answered incorrectly.

Not knowing how close she was to death, Queen Laina said, "Is that the name of your furry companion? He avoided capture when you were seized. I know not where he is, or what became of him after my soldiers brought you here. I have not ordered my soldiers to further search for him. My interest is in you," she concluded pointedly.

Korak unclenched his fists, for there was something in her answer that was believable, even though his gut warned him that the queen generally had a questionable relationship with the truth.

"Now," the queen said, after taking a deep draught of a Skethan intoxicant, "we shall speak of why I summoned you. You have made much progress, according to Tonzu. I am gratified. You are to be installed as the captain of my personal guard, as we agreed.

"Of course, you are still under a provisional period of observation. You will agree that too short of a time has passed for us to fully trust one another. That will come later," she said, smiling slightly.

"For now," Laina continued, "you must understand that there are many splintered societies and factions on my world. My army must have superior weapons for self-defense, and for a deterrent against unwarranted attacks.

"Tonzu informed me that he did ask you about the weapons and objects we confiscated when we captured you. But there is one in particular, he said, about which you were not terribly forthcoming.

"It would go a long way toward solidifying the mutual trust I spoke of, which I know we both desire for our shared safety and comfort, if you would tell me more about this thing you call a 'rifle.'"

22

SCARS

ERIEM HAD SWORN TO HERSELF that she would never
again be a captive, never again be enslaved.

Her captivity and servitude in an Arab village, in
which she had been passed off as an Arabian girl when outsiders visited, had left deep scars. The girl, though easily mistaken
for an Arabian, was in fact of French descent, with East Indian
heritage in her bloodline, and thus her skin was shaded ever-
so-slightly darker than the average Caucasian's; thus, outsiders
never questioned her presence, easily believing the story that
she was the daughter of the Sheikh, when in fact he was the
one who had kidnapped her and held her captive for years.

Not only had she been deprived of the love of a father and
mother, but the adults in the settlement actively abused her,
hurling endless insults and beating her for the slightest infraction—or for no infraction at all, but just because it pleased
them to do so.

Meriem had overcome the ordeal with an innate inner
strength, and with the help and love of her new family: Tarzan,
her father-in-law; "My Dear," Jane, who had seen in the little
waif an indomitable sunny disposition and natural charm;
and, of course, Korak, who had also greatly benefited from
the love she had reciprocated. It was a miracle that she was as
healthy and strong, both of mind and body, as she was.

Never again would she endure the depredation and inhu-
mane mistreatment to which she had been subjected as a child.

Yet here she was, held in the lower levels of the palace of

the Sketh, never to see the sunlight, and being worked as a scullery maid.

She had been in the deep forest with Lordan, Mirina, and Mis-see, and upon the sun's early rays penetrating the dense trunks and boughs, she had ventured not ten feet from the group's encampment, seeking morning sustenance and water. The Skethan soldiers had taken her before she could utter a sound.

Captured and held in the depths of the castle, she was taught the rudiments of the language and put to work under a cruel taskmaster, Zalon, the headman of the underlevels. Her work as a scullery maid kept her mostly confined to the lower levels, with only occasional assignments to deliver refreshments and repast to the upper classes and nobles who traversed the above-ground corridors and chambers of the palace.

These opportunities were rare, for her captors thought her an oddity. She had jet-black hair, similar to the Sketh, but it grew much longer than theirs, flowing down to the small of her back. Her eyebrows were black but also not as thick as those of the Sketh. Of course, she lacked their bluish trans-lucent skin and their gaunt height.

"She looks like that new captain of the queen's guard, the *aklak*," Zalon said disdainfully, using an expletive. "They're both undersized weasels with soft, pink skin."

Meriem had not yet absorbed enough of the Skethan language to comprehend everything he said.

"Leave the poor girl alone, Zalon," the kitchen headmistress said. "You may be head of the underlevels, but this is my domain, and I'll thank you to not terrorize my girls."

"Ah, just look at her," Zalon raged on, "pink skin, long hair, she barely comes up to my waist. She's got to be useless here—"

"Out," said Meriem's protector, and the nasty underboss finally wandered off.

Beledra, for that was the headmistress' appellation, turned to Meriem and said, "Don't you worry about him."

She led Meriem to a small antechamber off the main kitchen and sat her down on a four-legged stool that wobbled a bit on the uneven cobblestones.

Beledra produced a large pair of shears, and Meriem's eyes widened.

"Not to worry, dear. Let's just help you fit in a bit better." She chopped Meriem's jet-black hair to a bob, and thereafter colored her pink skin with food dye, giving the woman of the outer crust a skin tone of light blue, though lacking the Sketh's translucent skin. Hopefully this would alleviate bullying from some of the more uncouth Sketh.

Meriem touched the other woman's arm. "Thank you. I have been here weeks, and this is the first kindness anyone has shown me."

Beledra gave a toothy grin. "It's not fun down here in the hot kitchen, I'll admit, but keep your head down, I'll keep an eye on you, and you'll do fine. Now, off with you! The bread won't bake itself!"

It was some weeks after this that Meriem had been assigned to deliver refreshments to the queen, who was recovering from an illness.

She was admitted by the guard to Queen Laina's inner chambers, and quietly strode to a side table, keeping her eyes low, for she did not want to attract any attention from the ruler of the Sketh. There was another at the queen's bedside; she glanced up, and stifled a gasp—Korak!

The silver Meriem carried clattered to the marble floor, and she darted out of the lavish bedroom.

Korak had been kissing the queen.

23

THE FIRE AT THE TOP OF THE WORLD

MALDRAK!"

Mirina yelled again at Lordan. "It's a maldrak!"

The Vortha bird-woman flapped her wings and took refuge high in the branches above the small, circular clearing in which she, Lordan, and Mis-see had been ensconced.

Creeping into the clearing was a blue-and-white-striped beast that wasted no time leaping toward the Stone Age man and his bus-dar once Mirina had raised the alarm. Mis-see took flight and circled the clearing once at a low altitude, in the hope that Lordan could grab the hanging reins and she could fly him to safety, but his dodges of the roaring creature always took him away from rather than toward his bus-dar.

In some ways similar to Pellucidar's *tarag*, the saber-toothed tiger of the inner world, this beast shared Bengal-like markings, but was of a deep midnight blue, with alternating white stripes. Six toes on the front paws and five in the back sheathed lethal double rows of claws. The maldrak's tail was long and ended in a sharp, bony tip, with which Lordan did not want to be slashed. Its expression was fierce, narrowed cat eyes set under pointed ears between which long antennae ending in small pods were situated.

The thing roared furiously, for it had already been robbed of two-thirds of its anticipated breakfast, and it was obvious that it would allow nothing else to come between it and its intended meal.

The maldrak circled, Lordan circled, and the beast pounced.

With a wild Mangani cry— *"Bundolo!"*—Akut dropped from the trees onto the creature's back, tearing at its jugular with his massive fangs, blue blood gushing from the creature's wound.

The maldrak attempted to dislodge Akut and get to the great ape with its razor claws, but the Mangani hung on, riding the bucking cat like a bull rider, and chopping at it repeatedly with his stone axe.

Screeching with fury, the beast rolled over and over in the soft dirt, attempting to crush the Mangani, and still Akut hung on, the rolls becoming progressively weaker, the cries becoming ever less furious and ever more pathetic, until finally the tiger was so weak that Akut was able to snap its neck without any further resistance, putting the beast out of its misery.

Covered in the maldrak's blue blood, matting his fur and shrouding his face in a blue mask, Akut placed one great foot upon the corpse's neck and voiced the terrible victory cry of his people.

Lordan climbed down from the tree in which he had taken shelter upon Akut's advent, and stepped forward to offer his thanks, for he knew that this was his father-in-law's trusted companion. But the savage Mangani, still in the throes of his jungle fury, growled and lunged. The great ape pulled back at the last minute.

Lordan, frightened out of his wits, mustered up a few words in Mangani that Suzanne had taught him. "Suzanne *por*!" ("I am Suzanne's mate!")

Akut stared at Lordan, looking him in the eyes searchingly, and touched the Stone Age man's face. He grunted, declaring Lordan worthy, and Betty Callwell, understanding the Mangani's all-clear signal, dropped from the trees.

"Hello! I'm Betty," she said brightly.

Stories were exchanged and introductions were made, for Lordan and Mirina did not know of Betty Callwell.

"Korak was taken prisoner after being overcome by soldiers," Betty explained, "blue-skinned, and very tall and gaunt."

"We fought valiantly," Akut added in Mangani.

Betty, having spent much time alone in the forests with the great ape, had started to pick up his language. "Yes, you did," she affirmed. "We have been searching for a sign of him ever since."

"And Meriem is also gone," Lordan said, "disappeared with no trace. She was on the morning watch, and when we awoke, she was gone. I attempted to trace her spoor, without success. Like you with Korak, we have been searching for her, but have found no trace."

"What shall we do?" Betty asked.

"We could," Mirina said, "fly back to the surface of Pellucidar to regroup and seek the advice of others. David and Abner, and my mate Dek . . ."

"Mis-see," Lordan said, "could not bear the weight of all four of us."

Betty said, "I have an . . . ability, let's call it . . . I believe I can get there on my own."

"And I could fly most of the way myself," Mirina added. "I'd probably only need to ride upon Mis-see for the last part of the journey, back down to the surface of Pellucidar."

"*Tand,*" Akut said.

"What did he say?" Mirina asked.

"He said 'no,'" Betty said. "Akut, what do you mean?"

The great ape replied, *"Kor argo eho-nala goro."*

"He's saying, and pardon my translation, 'Travel fire top moon.'"

There was a sharp intake of breath from Mirina. "The Fire at the Top of the World!"

"Yes," Betty said, "that's what he's saying. He wants us to go to the 'fire,' whatever that is, that is located at the 'top' of this moon, this world."

"It is forbidden!" Mirina said.

"I have already done several forbidden things," Lordan said. "Now Korak and Meriem are lost, as well as Suzanne. We must press forward. Can you ask him how he knows this?"

Betty posed the question to Akut and translated his answer.

"As far as I can understand, this came to him in a memory or dream last night. He insists it is true and we must go. Mirina, can you tell us any more about this place? Other than it is forbidden?"

Mirina sighed. "Very well . . . It is a place located where the sun bisects the horizon but never fully rises nor sets. There is an opening in the ground there, from which the fire blazes; it cannot be seen from Thuria, for Thuria is located on the opposite side of the Land of Awful Shadow from which the fire might be seen."

"It sounds similar," Lordan said, "to the 'north polar opening,' the veil between worlds through which my mate first traveled to Pellucidar. Perhaps this 'blazing fire' is also such a veil between worlds. I have heard Abner speak of the movements of the Dead World. He has said that its 'north pole' is positioned in the direction of the Lidi Plains and the deserted Mahar city of Kazra, while the 'south pole' is pointed toward Indiana, which we also call Hooja's Island."

"I see," Betty said. "Then, the pendent world rotates on the axis defined by these poles, which is why it actually has a night and day. But why have no Pellucidarians, when making observations of the Dead World, seen this 'Fire at the Top of the World'?"

"Very few of our people," Lordan replied, "that is, the gilaks of David's Federated Kingdoms, have traveled beyond the Lidi Plains. If they had, perhaps they would have seen this 'fire' at the north pole of the pendent moon."

"Maybe," Betty replied, "or maybe not. Due to the strange proportional differences between this world and the inner surface of Pellucidar, it is possible that this opening in the ground, from which Mirina states the fire emanates, is comparatively so small that it cannot be seen from Pellucidar with the naked eye.

"Gogo, gogo," Akut said. *"Kor ara."* ("Talk, talk. We go now.")

24
INTRIGUE

QUEEN LAINA'S PRIMARY COUNSELOR, Chief Consigliere Bonshut, escorted Korak into the queen's outer chambers.

"The primitive, Your Highness," Bonshut announced.

Laina cocked an eyebrow. "Really, Bonshut, must you be so unpleasant? Korak is our guest—and as the head of my personal guard, he has accordingly been conferred a noble status. You will speak to him with respect commensurate with his station."

Bonshut lowered his eyes. "My sincere apologies, Your Highness."

"And?"

Bonshut reluctantly faced Korak. "My deepest apologies, Lord Korak. I meant no offence. It was merely a . . . joke." The man's nasty glare belied the honesty of his apology.

Korak smiled grimly. "Accepted, Lord Bonshut. I look forward to discussing with you the nuances of Skethan humor at a later time—and introducing you to how humor works among my people."

Bonshut's eyes narrowed.

"You are dismissed, Bonshut," the queen said. "Lord Korak and I have much about which to confer."

"As you wish, my Queen." The man marched out stiffly, slamming the heavy door behind him.

After Bonshut had departed, the queen gestured for Korak to approach. "Come, sit by me, we have much to discuss."

The ape-man sat upon the plush pillows arranged around

the low table, which was festooned with a dazzling array of colorful fresh fruits, meats, and breads.

"Surely you can sit closer to me than that, Lord Korak," she said, amused. She poured a goblet of mead and handed it to him, for she had dismissed her handservants.

"I believe I am sitting as close to you as is practicable, Your Highness," Korak said.

Laina shook her head and gave a small smile.

Korak was suspicious. Queen Laina's veiled romantic overtures and innuendos were unsettling.

There was something not quite right about Laina. Why would she be interested in him? He was of a much different kind than she was. Was it solely about her desire to know more about his rifle, or was there something more?

The more the ape-man pondered it, the more he challenged his own assumptions. Was the queen really so different from him? She was so much shorter than the other Sketh. Her skin was not as translucent. And she was in no way gaunt, more resembling a very well-proportioned human woman. True, her pate was bald like many Sketh, but skulls can be shaved.

Korak wondered how someone like her, who did have some marked differences from the Sketh whom she ruled, came to have power over them. Was she powerful to them *because* she was different? Usually, societies did not actively seek out people of lesser physical stature to rule, but of course this was not a universal rule. Perhaps her forceful personality, heightened by her very lack of physical stature, had swept her into power.

How had she managed to retain that power?

And again, why would Laina be interested in him, when she could have the pick of any of her own Skethan people to sit alone with her in her chambers?

Korak's ruminations were interrupted by the queen's insistent voice.

"Your mind is elsewhere, Lord Korak," she chastised, "when it should be with your queen and benefactor."

Korak nodded in silent acknowledgment.

"It is time," Laina said, "for us to speak again of the odd weapon with the metal barrel and that you called a 'rifle.' We know of your other weapons, the bow and arrows, the straight knife, and the primitive axe, of course, although the hidebound traditions of our military men prohibit the use, more often than not, of anything other than our conventional curved or hooked blades.

"But if you will share with us your knowledge and expertise so that my artisans may learn to craft your weapon of metal and wood, as well as the alchemy that powers it—oh, don't look at me that way, I know it's a weapon, there's no use denying it. I just want to know how it works."

"Queen Laina, I assure you—"

"Stop, Lord Korak. Everything else we took from you when you were captured was weaponry. You were a veritable walking armory! The long object and wood and metal, and the long leather belts holding the metal pellets, those are what I want to know more of. I'm afraid I will not take no for an answer. It is a weapon, and it must be a useful one, or you would not have been carrying it in the first place. You will instruct my craftsmen and smiths in how to reproduce more of your 'rifles,' and you will train my soldiers to use them.

"I will give you a little more time to think about it as you acclimate to this new life here. You will adjust to life as a Sketh, and then you will see the wisdom in my request, for we are, as I have mentioned, occasionally beset by enemies, and it is best to be prepared."

"But what of, Your Highness, the hidebound traditions to which your soldiers cling, preventing them from the use of anything but curved Skethan blades?"

The queen smiled. "I will handle that, I assure you. Your concern is to accept your role here and comply with my wishes."

Her expression softened. "The more we both start to trust each other, to make each other's best interests our paramount concern, the better it will be for both of us.

"Now, you may go."

Over the ensuing weeks, Korak continued to get the lay of the land, exploring the palace grounds and associated outbuildings. He was slowly granted more freedom to wander the palace grounds unattended—at least as far as he knew—but he continued to avoid the appearance of deep interest in any one thing or another, as it was certainly likely he was still being watched.

He circumnavigated the entire wall dividing the lands and residences of the nobles from the exterior lands of the farmers, workers, and craftsmen, noting the configuration of the main gate, as well as the number and stations of the guards. He was not allowed past the gate, and made no issue of it, as for the time being he sought to avoid suspicion and give the appearance of compliance with the queen's wishes.

On one such reconnaissance, Korak went by the stables, although he could not see how he could escape on a mountain beast through the palace grounds, wall gate, and across the exterior village and agriculture zone, and then past the village guard and into the forest. Nonetheless, it was worth it to the ape-man to get a complete picture of his palatial prison.

Wandering through the stables, he was surprised to see a captive winged reptile in one of the stalls. In his time on the Dead World, he had come to think that thipdars were unknown here, for he had not seen any since his and Akut's battle with the creatures as they had approached the pendent world.

He approached more closely and observed the soft saddle, reins, and the rope preventing the creature from escaping the stall.

It was a bus-dar, a smaller and more agreeable cousin of the thipdars.

Korak was familiar with the creatures as his daughter,

Suzanne, was bonded to one. He wondered how it had gotten here. The bus-dar seemed to stare at him longingly, and he was impelled to come forward and greet it. The creature opened its terrifying beak filled with sharp teeth and gently lapped out its tongue. Korak hesitantly extended a closed fist, and the beast gently licked his knuckles with the sandpaper tongue. He reached into the stall cautiously and rubbed the beast's hide. It was warm and scaly but not rough, with tough ridges that were pliable and soft to the touch. The bus-dar made a happy noise at Korak's touch.

The ape-man recalled the missing bus-dar from Thuria and things fell into place. This was Suzanne's mount, the missing Spy-kee. Korak was mightily excited, for Abner Perry must have been correct that Suzanne had been somehow translocated to the Dead World. Why else would her bus-dar, Spy-kee, have followed her here?

He spent a little more time with the animal, fed it some morsels, and promised to return.

Striding quickly through the palace grounds, he came upon the barracks of the queen's personal guard, near the door of which he observed Bonshut and Tonzu conferring. Unable to conceive a reason for their presence at the barracks, he thought to confront them, but when they saw him, they quickly turned their backs to him. Was the snub associated with their natural dislike of him—or could it be something more?

The ape-man averted his eyes and pretended not to see them. From the corner of his eye, he observed the two men enter the barracks, after which the shades in the building's windows were pulled. Korak padded lightly to the side of the building and crouched in the shade, under a window, hoping no one would see him. Despite his better-than-average hearing, he could not hear anything through the walls.

The door behind him opened; the ape-man jumped up and strode quickly away without looking backward.

Nighttime, in the queen's inner chambers, saw six Skethan

men, including Bonshut, Tonzu, and four others of the queen's personal guard, slip quietly from behind a tapestry that soundlessly receded into a narrow horizontal opening in the ceiling, which was not otherwise visible when the tapestry hung normally.

They crept toward the raised bed, almost like a throne, in which the queen reposed among plush silks, cushions, and pillows, curved knives clenched in their skeletal fists.

Korak the Killer leaped upon them from his spot of concealment, crouched upon the top of a massive and ornately carved armoire.

The first the intruders knew they had been detected was when Tonzu's bare skull flew from his neck, blue blood jetting from both ends of the clean slash that had separated the head from his shoulders. The remaining five interlopers were momentarily paralyzed with shock as Tonzu's head rolled and came to rest in a corner, lips pulled back in a permanent grin.

The first soldier to wheel about in response to the attack received the butt of a Skethan lance in the stomach. He doubled over and lost his grip on his own lance, which Korak scooped up in his other hand and wielded against a second attacker, the razor tip of the clawlike blade chopping into that unfortunate's skull and remaining embedded there.

The first attacker regained his breath and stood just in time to receive the curved blade at the tip of the ape-man's other lance under his bony chin. The last thing the Sketh saw was the point of the sharp hook poking out from the front of his own face; he died in cross-eyed shock.

The queen was not unprepared. She had been feigning sleep and was now fighting for her life. She whipped a deadly looking curved knife from beneath her pillow and disemboweled one of her attackers. Korak unconsciously noted that the knife resembled the kriegmesser knives with which Hans Kriegmesser had tortured him so cruelly decades ago. The detail lodged in the back of his brain, for he was still in the midst of battle, with one soldier and the queen's counselor, Bonshut, remaining.

The soldier turned toward the queen and knocked the knife from her hand. His hands went to her throat, but Korak, now weaponless, was unable to come to her aid as he faced off with Bonshut, who stood some twenty yards across the queen's chambers.

The Sketh scowled at the ape-man. "I know not how you were ready for us, outsider, but it means your death. Though," he added, "it would have been death for you anyway after we killed the outsider queen."

Korak grinned, and it was not one of amusement. One would not have wanted to be on the receiving end of that grin. "You could have tried, Sketh. Now, you have your opportunity sooner than you planned. And you won't just be slipping a blade into my unguarded neck from behind. You must face me now!"

Though the other man was half again as tall as his opponent, and armed with a Skethan lance while Korak had none, he blanched, for the ape-man's fearlessness in the face of such odds bewildered him. And, he had heard the stories of how Korak had fought in the forest before he was finally captured.

"You have no chance, outsider," Bonshut said, putting on a brave front. "Lower your neck to me now and I promise to make your inevitable death quick and painless."

Korak darted a glance to one side and saw the queen holding her own against her attacker, kneeing him in the groin. The soldier loosened his grasp upon her throat, and she clocked him on the chin with a right hook. To Bonshut, he said, "Perhaps you plan to talk me to death, Counselor, but that would be anything but quick and painless."

So saying, the ape-man took a running start from across the room, bent and scooped up an abandoned lance, and used it, blunt end up, as a vaulting pole to launch himself feetfirst at the other man's narrow chest. Bonshut was slammed back against the granite wall before he could bring his lance to bear. Korak felt the other man's ribs crack beneath the kick.

Bonshut tried to swing his lance, but it was too long to be effective at close quarters. The ape-man hammered a fist at the Sketh's nose, smashing it. Bonshut got both hands, with their long, skeletal fingers, around the ape-man's throat and began to squeeze. Apparently, this was a preferred mode of Skethan attack when fighting hand to hand.

Korak's sun-bronzed fists pounded at the Sketh's torso and face, but to no avail. The other man pressed his grasp even more tightly, and the ape-man began to see stars. If unconsciousness overtook him, all was lost. He recalled his battle against the soldiers in the forest, and how their Skethan bones had fared against his greater outer-world strength. He slipped his leg around the other man's lower leg, and bent his knee, hard. The Sketh's tibia snapped, and he screamed in pain, automatically loosening his death grip about Korak's neck.

Bonshut fell back against the granite wall and slid to the marble-tiled floor. Korak took the other man's head in both hands and repeatedly smashed it against the stone, crunching skull bones and pummeling cartilage until all that remained was a blue, pulpy mass of flesh and tissue.

The ape-man turned in time to see the last remaining Skethan guard knock the queen into a wall. Laina hit it headfirst and was still. Korak took a lance in hand, leaped through the air aided by the slightly lower gravity on the pendent world, and swept the man's head from its neck in a deadly scything motion.

The Skethan lances were good for some things.

Weeks passed in which Queen Laina fluttered in and out of consciousness. The head knock, Korak believed, had resulted in a concussion.

In the aftermath of the assassination attempt, Korak had taken control. After all, he was the duly appointed captain of her personal guard, and all evidence pointed to him as the queen's savior.

He asserted his right to remain in charge of her protection during her recovery, although the remaining members of her council of advisors did notify him that they would require verification from the queen of his story when she woke. If she did not confirm his account, it would be death for him. In the meantime, they would allow him to remain at his current station, but he would also be watched, and other guards would be placed around the queen.

Korak informed them that four of the dead assassins had been members of the queen's own guard, and he didn't place much stock in the others, but he would accede to their wishes, and he would be watching *them*. And so, an uneasy peace was put in place while all waited for the queen to recover and resume her rule.

Laina remained debilitated in a coma for a week. Korak felt a personal responsibility for guarding her; he had failed in his duty as the captain of her personal guard to protect her. Even though he was being held in Sketh as a virtual prisoner, he had given his word. In addition, although he did not understand all of the dynamics and politics of Sketh, he realized that not all citizens submitted to the queen's rule, and he wondered why. Was it because she was different physically, even though in many ways, she resembled them? What was it about her?

Bonshut had called her the outsider queen. Korak had resolved to remain by her side and be the first one to question her upon her awakening.

After watching over Laina for another day and a half, making sure that her handmaidens brought her water, bathed her, and least attempted to provide the unconscious woman with some nutrition, he observed a small growth of hair on her previously shorn skull.

Her hair was blonde.

Korak instructed the queen's handmaidens to bring him

a razor and hot water, for he had not shaved in days. Implement in hand, he dismissed the servants and shaved the queen's head.

Several days later, Laina finally awakened with a horrible headache. Korak was at her bedside. He ordered the handmaiden to leave, and the guards to position themselves on the other side of the room.

"How long has it been?" she asked.

"Keep your voice low; we are not alone," Korak stated. "It has been about a week and a half."

Her hand flew to her head, and she appeared shocked. She looked at the ape-man in wonder.

"Are you well enough to talk further, Your Highness?" Korak asked.

"Yes," she said, "but please being me some more water. This headache is excruciating."

That task completed, the queen thanked Korak for saving her life.

"We were wise not to bring any other of your personal guardsmen into our confidence," Korak said, "for four of the assassins were from their ranks."

"Of course," Queen Laina said, "I took an enormous risk in trusting you solely to protect me. After all, we barely knew each other."

"That remains our present state," the ape-man countered. "We still both barely know each other."

"Perhaps," she said, "you should consider responding to the trust I placed in you with trust of your own. Will you not trust me, and share the secrets of your weapon, the rifle? With that knowledge, we could rule Sketh together with no fear of attack, either from without or within."

"Who are you, really?" Korak asked. "I have seen no other Sketh with blonde hair, and you have taken pains to conceal your hair from all others."

"Never mind that," she said, clearly irritated. "We're discussing life and death, perhaps life and death for both of us, and you're going on about my hair color. You must agree to instruct my craftsmen and armorers how to make more rifles, and how to blend the powder that is in the little pellets."

"That," the ape-man replied, "is the end of your charade. How could you know that the true power of my rifle lay in the explosive powder in the bullets? Bonshut referred to you as the outsider queen."

"What? That's ludicrous!"

"I am now certain you are not a native Sketh. Tell me who you are," Korak demanded, "or I will expose you to all the other Sketh."

Laina glared at the ape-man for long minutes, saying nothing.

Then, she expelled a long breath. "I am Alexandra Ryadinsky."

"The leader of the O-220 hijackers," Korak said.

She shrugged, hardly pretending to be embarrassed at being caught in what she apparently considered to be an inconsequential fib.

"How is that possible," he asked. "Why is your skin blue?"

"I eat the same food as the natives of Sketh," Alex said. "Long time consumption of the fruits and vegetables here turns skin blue. Haven't you noticed that your skin is already slightly blue tinted? It's happening to you, too."

"But the chemicals in the Skethan food do not change hair color," he said.

"Correct. I couldn't conceal my blonde hair, so I shaved my skull to blend in with the others, and dyed my eyebrows black. It was too much to try to constantly dye my hair; the roots grew out too quickly."

"But you are obviously different in stature from the tall, gaunt Sketh."

"I lucked out," she replied. "I was wandering in the jungles and forests of the Dead World, foraging native fruits and berries, and fishing in ponds and lakes. My skin had already turned completely blue from the diet by the time I encountered the Sketh."

"Why did they not kill you on sight?" he asked. "They appear quite insular regarding outsiders."

"That's where the luck came in. They didn't see me as an outsider. Their legends stated their queen would not come from their city-state but would be an orphaned child found alone in the dense forest. I was smaller than them, and they mistook me for a youngling. I didn't speak their language, which also fit in with their myth of a feral girl living and surviving on her own in the wild. Absurd, really, but they fell for it. I was wearing a leather flying helmet when they found me, and as they were all either bald or had jet-black hair, I guessed the safer course of action would be to get rid of my blonde hair before anyone thought to remove my headgear and check. The very night that the Skethan party ran across me, while their sentry neglected his duty and fell asleep at his post, I rifled through the kit bag of a man with the most beautifully maintained mohawk and shaved my head. Been shaving it ever since.

"They brought me here, gave me high honors, and with pomp and pageantry installed me as their new queen. Who was I to say no? I knew what was in store for me if they came to think I wasn't really a Sketh."

"And yet," Korak said, "at least some have started to suspect. Or else Bonshut and Tonzu and the other conspirators came to have another reason to seek to depose your rule."

She shrugged. "That I don't know. My guess is they grew suspicious as I seemed to not grow up as they expected and still appear to be an adolescent of their race."

"Perhaps. But I don't understand. You make it sound as if you have been here among the Sketh for years. It has only been weeks, perhaps, since the hijacking of the O-220 and your disappearance from Thuria."

An expression of shock crossed her features. "I also don't understand. The passage of time is not measured here, but it feels to me that a long time, certainly years, have passed since those events."

"I understand," the ape-man said, "that due to the eternal daylight in Pellucidar, time passes strangely there. But why should it be so here on the Dead World, which has a daytime and a nighttime?"

Alex shrugged. "I have no answers."

Korak let it be for the time being and returned to the subject of Alex's role as Queen Laina. "Did you ever think to ask what had happened to the prior queen?"

Alex paused before answering. "No . . . perhaps I didn't want to know."

Korak chuckled. "Ah, you *do* need firearms, don't you?" He didn't wait for an answer. "Tell me, how did you come to the Dead World in the first place?"

"I found a reptile with wings in an enclosure in Thuria, while I was making good my escape from the forces retaking the O-220; I saw the reins and saddle, and figured I could fly away on it."

"This," Korak said, "was after you smashed Thuria's Gridley Wave transmitter."

Alex had the grace to look slightly embarrassed. "What would you have done in my place? Left it there so everyone could call for reinforcements?"

"I would not have been in your place. But we'll come back to that later. Tell me more about coming to the pendent moon."

"I couldn't control the winged beast. It had a mind of its own. It flew here to the Dead World and I couldn't guide it in any other direction, nor induce it by any means to take me anywhere else. Stupid creature. I have been trapped here ever since. A long, long time."

"And you have attempted to get the creature to help you escape from here," Korak guessed.

"Yes! The damned thing refuses! It won't even let me mount it again!"

Korak laughed and, hoping her guard was down, asked her about the wickedly curved knife that she had produced from under her pillow when the assassins had struck.

"What do you mean?" Alex asked. "All Skethan weapons are curved with this design."

"Yes, but I have only seen such curved blades attached to the ends of their lances. I had never before seen a handheld knife until you produced it."

"You have not been here long enough to see everything. I have been here a long time. Too long, surviving on my wits and manipulating these people to do my bidding. But as you've seen, time is running out. For both our sakes, you must oversee the manufacturing of more rifles and other guns, so that we can strike at our neighboring kingdoms and queendoms, as the Sketh expect—and soundly defeat them! A few solid victories will help solidify our power over the Sketh."

"From my perspective," the ape-man said, "it has only been weeks, or perhaps a month or two, since you and your fellows tried to take over the O-220. Perhaps I am not quite so ready to forgive and forget. Besides, your stunt got all of your accomplices killed. What was that all about, anyway? And why should I throw my lot in with you?"

"For my part," Alex said, moving closer to him, "I have been here years, as I said. In that time, I have grown wiser in my exile here, and am sorry for the incident on the O-220. But if I—if *we*—are to be stuck here, we had better fortify our grip on power, and make sure no one can touch us. *I* can't tell them how to make the guns—that would blow my cover as their mythical queen. Only you can do it."

Alex pulled the ape-man's head to hers, surprising him, and kissed him forcefully.

There came a riotous clatter of silver serving ware hitting the hard marble floor, and Alex turned her head to see a young servant girl, flustered and bending over to pick it up and clean up the spilled refreshments.

"Get out! Get out!" Alex screamed, and Korak turned to see the girl's back as she ran out the door.

He faced Alex once more. "My heart belongs to another. Never do that again."

"Don't forget, I am the queen here. My word is law."

"I believe," Korak said, "that like so many who come to power falsely, you have gained none of the wisdom nor empathy required of a true leader. Your 'royalty' is false. Given the assassination attempt upon your life, you may want to remember that your grip on power is not quite so tight as you wish.

"My mate, Meriem, is true royalty, French royalty, in fact, though her late father eschewed his princely title. He was also a soldier, a man of honor, and had been known as The Hawk. His true royal nature shone through in his personality when his daughter was kidnapped at a very young age. Many were involved in the search. Her father had never, not for one minute, not for years on end, given up on his daughter. That was true royalty, with honor, dedication, and love. Not this facade you coat yourself in."

"You may as well forget about Meriem," Alex said harshly. "When I realized it was you, Korak, whom my soldiers captured here on the Dead World, I ordered my men to look for and seize any others like you—of a shorter height than Sketh, but with the same pink skin and jet-black hair, and dark eyes."

Alex's eyes blazed. "They located her and did away with her."

The ape-man's face flushed red with fury. "Even if Meriem is dead and gone, I will never join you in your chambers. You had better pray you are wrong, for if Meriem is dead, you will soon be joining her."

Alex slapped him, made to slap him again, whereupon he grabbed her wrist and flung her away.

Korak stalked out of the queen's chambers, in a haze of anger mixed with deep thought. How in the world could Meriem have traveled to be here on the pendent moon? He had left her in Los Angeles!

He emerged into the high-arched corridor that led from the queen's apartments and saw movement at the far end of the long stone-paved hallway. He moved closer, squinting, for even with his exceptional eyesight, the distance made his focus unclear. He took a few more steps.

It was the scullery maid the queen had yelled at, far down the passageway.

Korak instructed the two guards stationed outside the main doors to the queen's chambers to ensure that no one entered without his permission.

The ape-man glanced back at the girl and saw that she was noticeably shorter than the other Sketh. She must be young indeed. The girl was outfitted in the garb of a handmaiden, and it did not suit her station, though he could not have explained how he knew this, only having just seen her, and at a considerable distance at that.

The girl stood there, watching him as he watched her from afar. She leaned against a pillar, and unconsciously tossed her head up and to the right, tilting up her chin.

Korak gave the young girl credit for spunk, for she should have been reporting immediately back to her station, rather than standing there staring at him.

Then . . . that tilt of the head. The tossing of the hair brushing against her chin. That chin . . .

It reminded him of Meriem!

The girl's hair was cut much shorter, and she was so far away he couldn't clearly make out her features, but that certain tilt of the head . . . He didn't know how, but it must be! He knew her!

It was Meriem!

Korak strode quickly down the hall, not too quickly so as to draw the attention of the guards back at the queen's door, and slipped into the alcove into which the handmaiden had just ducked.

The ape-man showered his mate with kisses, and she clung to him and kissed him back, for they had been parted for far too long.

Then she slapped him on the cheek. "That's for kissing that woman," she breathed.

"Two slaps in one day! Besides, she was the one who kissed me!" Korak protested. "You should have seen her face when I rejected 'Her Highness.'"

"If you say so," Meriem said. "I'm also not done being angry with you for taking off in the O-220 without so much as a 'how do you do,' but we'll save that for later."

"What?" her mate asked. "I gave orders that you be informed!"

Meriem raised a dark eyebrow and said, "Fine. You can explain it in full later."

"Agreed," Korak replied. "Alex must have intercepted the message. And I want to know everything about how you got here, but that will also have to wait. I have been waiting, biding my time for the right moment to escape, but now that I've found you here, and Alex is making her move—"

"Who is Alex?" Meriem asked.

"Alexandra Ryadinsky. She was the new second engineer on the O-220. She led a group of hijackers and took over the airship when we reached Pellucidar. Now she is here in Sketh as 'Queen Laina,' claiming to have been stranded on the Dead World for years—even though it has only been weeks. She's pressing me to instruct her people how to make firearms. So, it is time to go."

The two crept through the winding corridors of the palace, traversing lesser-used passageways. Upon reaching a sublevel, Korak showed her the location of the storeroom where his weapons were being kept. There were two guards outside the armory door.

Meriem stumbled down the hall in an apparent daze, tripped in front of the armory door, and pretended to faint. The guards stepped forward and leaned over her.

Korak came charging down the corridor. His left fist hammered at the first guard's chest, practically caving it in. He crumpled to the ground, out of the fight and perhaps mortally wounded.

The other Sketh swung his lance toward Korak, but the

ape-man leaped into the air, bending his knees so his legs were folded under him, and the soldier's lance swept through empty air. Korak landed easily, squatted, and thrust straight upward, his mighty arm extended. The ape-man's fist connected with the soldier's chin, snapping his head back, and his hairless skull slammed into the stone wall. The man slid to the floor, either unconscious or dead.

Korak entered the armory, and in moments emerged, bandoliers looped over his shoulders, along with his quiver full of arrows, rifle in one hand and bow in the other. His leather belt with stone axe and sheathed knife was secured about his waist. He had also found his leopard-skin loincloth, which he tossed in the quiver, telling Meriem he would change out of his black kilt and military sandals later.

The ape-man dragged the dead men into the room, shut the door, and bolted it.

The two departed the scene at a swift walk, but not so rapidly as to attract attention. They stuck to mostly untraveled corridors and unused, dusty rooms until sundown, and then stole slowly through the castle, their ultimate goal being the stables.

Near midnight, Korak and Meriem arrived at a main corridor crossing, the navigation of which was unavoidable if they were to attain their goal. They heard voices approaching from around the next corner—probably the night guard on their rounds—and ducked behind huge drape-like tapestries in order to conceal themselves.

After mentally orienting himself, Korak realized they were positioned behind the throne room. Korak bade Meriem to follow him, and they slipped into a little-used hallway, barely wide enough for one person, which served to bring documents, refreshments, and so forth to the queen while she sat on the throne conducting the daily royal business.

Korak and Meriem were now concealed in an alcove directly behind the queen's throne. There was an aperture in the crimson velvet curtains lining the passage that servants and counselors used to observe the daily proceedings, so they did not inadvertently interrupt any important engagements or ceremonies. Korak put his eye to the opening.

The hairless, blue-skinned woman sat alone in apparent contemplation. Korak was relieved, for if "the queen," Alex, was sitting here this quietly, then his absence had not yet been noted, and the dead men in the armory had not yet been discovered. All was not lost. Perhaps he should . . .

Meriem, in response to her mate's tensed muscles, increased the pressure on his arm, gently pulling him back from the viewport.

"Remember our time in the jungle," she whispered. "You are my protector . . . but you can go too far."

Korak remembered. When they were youths, he had returned to the well-hidden forest retreat, deep in the African jungle, in which he, Meriem, and Akut had made their home for a time. Korak had come to Meriem, bringing her the gift of a shiny bauble. She was delighted, and asked him what it was and how it worked. In response, the young great ape (for thus she considered him to be, along with Akut), had demonstrated by placing the object on her wrist. She had laughed, clearly gratified both with the gift and with Korak's thoughtfulness.

Then, her face clouding slightly, Meriem had asked where Korak had gotten it. Her young friend had refused to answer. She had removed the object, disappointed. Pretending not to understand, Korak had become upset, asking why she spurned his gift. Her words had shaken him to his core.

"If you must kill, let it be for the right reasons. In self-defense, and in the defense of others you love or who cannot defend themselves and deserve your help. Do not kill over petty offences or because you have allowed your fear to overcome you. You are better than that."

Yes, Korak remembered. He took Meriem's hand and withdrew from the hidden passage behind the queen's throne.

"I will not kill her," he whispered to Meriem. "For now."

He knew that Meriem's love had pulled him back from the brink. Would there ever come a time when her love would not be enough?

The two continued their creeping way through the maze of passageways and tunnels, finally exiting the castle on the side nearest the stables. They followed less used garden pathways, though at this time of night, with darkness hanging over the palace grounds like a gray pall, Korak hoped no one else would be about. Still, there was always the possibility of lovers' trysts, especially among the nobles, for they did not have to arise and labor with the breaking day, and kept what hours they pleased.

Korak and Meriem made their way circuitously through the manicured lawn and well-raked paths until finally they arrived at the stables. He padded silently to the large stable doors, lifted the heavy latch, and momentarily later emerged with Spy-kee, saddled with bags of supplies hanging from both sides.

Within minutes, they were taking flight in the skies of the Dead World, soaring above the jeweled palace, and the minarets and turrets of the royal edifices. The bus-dar quickly crested the upper terraces of the trees surrounding the entire Skethan settlement and flew away in a random direction.

Korak and Meriem had made good their escape.

25

IN THE REALM OF CRIMSON TWILIGHT

KORAK AND MERIEM, astride Suzanne Clayton's bus-dar, Spy-kee, sped through the skies of the Dead World.

The sun had risen, and after putting a great distance between them and the land of the Sketh, Korak had directed the beast to land near a clear pool enclosed in a small clearing of the moon's massive trees. There, they had slaked their thirst, filled their canteens, and Meriem had scrubbed off the blue dye with which the kindly Beledra had anointed her skin. Korak speared a fish with one of his arrows and prepared it for his mate, explaining that he was eschewing the berries that grew upon the bushes surrounding the huge boles of the trees, for he did not want his skin to turn blue as had Alex's.

They exchanged abbreviated versions of their tales, Korak beginning with the O-220's departure from Africa upon receiving the emergency Gridley Wave transmission informing them that Suzanne was missing, and Meriem with her final operatic performance and decision to follow Korak to Pellucidar with all due haste.

"I can't believe," Korak said, "that you took the unimaginable risk of using Moritz and Kingsley's matter transmitter. It's completely untested! I have never known you to act so recklessly, and without regard for your safety, or your family."

"It was not untested. Christopher West used it successfully," Meriem said. "More importantly, I believe you have missed the point entirely. The risk I took was imposed upon me by your desertion. You should know by now that I am, like you, unwilling to allow anything to come between me and the safety of my daughter. You took the choice out of my hands, and left me with no other options."

The two agreed to table their quarrel for the time being, for both were too overjoyed at having found each other to allow it to color their reunion. But Korak's behavior, and Meriem's reaction, would have to be addressed between them and resolved at some point. For now, the focus was back on their original mission: to find Suzanne.

Having had their fill of freshwater fish, and Spy-kee having eaten and bathed as well, they slept at sundown, Korak taking the first watch, Meriem the second, and Korak the third. They broke their fast at sunup, and soon were in the air once more, although their destination was uncertain.

They flew for days. Korak chose their route as generally to the east, for he had been taken in a westerly direction when he first had been captured by the Sketh. While they soared through the skies, the bus-dar flapping his mighty leathern wings, the two humans basked in the warmth of the sun's rays upon their flesh, for their landings in the dense forests were characterized by the shadows cast by the tall trees, through which sunlight rarely encroached unless the time was high noon and Pellucidar's orb hung directly overhead, and the cool breezes that occasionally penetrated the thick foliage.

When they were in flight, Korak's Enfield rifle was slung across Meriem's shoulder, for she had lost her crossbow long ago. He was armed with his knife and stone axe, both looped to the leather thong of his leopard-skin loincloth, as well as his bow and arrows. He had deemed a Skethan lance too unwieldy to carry long distance in flight.

Perhaps six or seven days passed thus, and the three travelers had stopped at midday to quench their thirst at a clear pond, and to assuage their hunger, when Meriem happened to turn her gaze straight upward to the circular opening at the tops of the spiral-trunked trees, far above them.

"Korak! Look!"

The ape-man directed his gaze upward.

Silhouetted against the sun was the dark shape of a winged reptile.

A thipdar?

Or, more likely, a bus-dar, for the thipdars appeared to be unknown on the Dead World, apparently avoiding the liminal barrier between Pellucidar and the upper atmosphere of the pendent moon.

Abandoning their repast, Korak and his mate quickly saddled up and took to the skies.

Beating his wings furiously, Sky-kee caught up with the other bus-dar and saw that it was indeed Mis-see, laden with Lordan, Akut, and Betty Callwell, and Mirina the Vortha flying to one side.

The two flying beasts landed on a white sand beach enclosed on three sides by tall reddish cliffs, and bordered on the fourth by the lapping ocean. The location appeared to be a safe one, though perhaps not as sheltered from view as the dense forests, but all maintained a high state of alert as they held a brief but joyous reunion.

In response to his in-laws' eager questions, Lordan explained that Mis-see had been flying them for short periods of time, but could not carry three people for long flights, and so they had been stopping and resting often. Betty sang Akut's praises for making short work of the maldrak that had attacked them, and the normally phlegmatic Mangani appeared to straighten somewhat at the recognition. Meriem and Korak recounted their adventures as prisoners of the Sketh, emphasizing that they should all be on the lookout for others of the skeletal race, for it was their understanding that there were more Skethan city-states, or kingdoms or queendoms, scattered across the Dead World, all of which were prone to unceasing conflict with each other.

"Now," Korak said, addressing Akut, "tell me more about this journey upon which you've been directing our friends, here."

The great ape repeated what he had previously told the others, that they must journey to the "Fire at the Top of the World" if they wished to locate Suzanne. Akut conveyed to his friend that he knew this because it came to him in a dream memory.

Korak, of course, was completely fluent in the Mangani language (unlike Betty and Lordan), and so he was able to dig a bit more deeply into the great ape's account. After speaking at length, the ape-man informed the rest that Akut was also conveying the concepts of "me/myself" and "five" or "fifth."

Even Korak was baffled by this and Akut was unable to clarify or explain further. But the great ape insisted they must proceed northward to attain their goal of locating Suzanne.

It was a strange assortment that raced across the gray skies of the pendent moon: three humans originally from the outer crust, two of whom had been raised in the jungle, and the third who had been flung from realm to realm, each more bizarre and dangerous than the last; a Stone Age man from the inner world clad in bear skins; a Mangani, one of the last of a race of intelligent great apes, whose sense of loyalty and honor rivaled any of the so-called higher orders; two flying reptiles who carried them all; and a tiny, pale-skinned woman with wings of gossamer, a native of this strange world, who flew alongside them.

The two bus-dars stopped often to rest, as they were not accustomed to carrying that many people for such long distances. The riders switched between three astride Spy-kee, and two on Mis-see, and the reverse, in order to conserve the reptiles' strength as much as possible.

The journey seemed to consume a couple of weeks—or rather, about fourteen day-and-night cycles, as none of the travelers had yet learned if any of the natives organized time in calendars composed of weeks, months, and years. Mirina explained that the Vortha people did not recognize any time intervals beyond days, the idea of years being entirely foreign to them.

As the travelers moved farther "north," they expected to be subject to changing climatological bands, but then realized that the temperate conditions they continued to experience were part and parcel of the generally mild atmosphere that pertained throughout the inner world, including the pendent moon. Still, as they journeyed farther and farther from the land of the Sketh, the temperature did seem to drop a few degrees, and to this they attributed the lowering of the sun on the horizon as they closed in upon the pole. At some of the landing sites, Korak took down several native animals with his bow and arrow, which the group skinned for furs, just in case the temperature might dip more severely as they essayed northward, for none of them had come equipped with cold-weather clothing, save for furry Akut, who was naturally prepared for the environment.

The dense forests of tall, spiral-trunked trees that were so ubiquitous within the equatorial band were somewhat sparser in the northern zones, and the trees attainted heights slightly less than those they had observed to the south. The travelers assumed there were still a good number of natives of the Dead World inhabiting these climes, for their cities and towns could still be concealed from view despite the somewhat shorter trees. Too, there might be roving bands of hunter-gatherers who did not establish permanent settlements, and therefore all the members of the party took pains to be on their guard whenever they landed for food, water, and rest.

As they neared the pole, the sun only skirted the horizon, and while the temperature was not so cool as to require donning the furs Korak had procured against such an eventuality, the landscape, bereft of direct overhead sunlight, had given way to a rocky zone carpeted with low-growing grasses, shrubs, and heaths.

Two more day-night cycles brought them without incident to the "Fire at the Top of the World"—a vast opening in the ground resembling an inverse volcano, funnel-shaped, that emitted a dim, deep reddish glow into the sky, dissipating far above them. The aperture appeared to lead down into the depths, so far down that none of them could descry any details such as tunnels, ledges, or a possible bottom of the cone.

As for the surrounding landscape, it was rock-strewn but otherwise barren, bereft of even hardy vegetation.

"We are here," Akut announced in Mangani. Korak asked his friend if there was anything else he could tell them about the fire—presumably the crimson glow—and the conical mouth from which it radiated. The Mangani responded in the negative; there was nothing more he could tell them.

They made camp so that the bus-dars could rejuvenate, and ate and slept, with Korak, Meriem, Betty, and Lordan splitting the watch.

When all had rested and broken their fast, Lordan said, "I woke you all up when I felt it was best. There was no 'night'—which frankly is a relief to me."

"He's right," Betty said. "The sun no longer moves in the sky; it hangs a little bit above the horizon. It's been like that ever since we arrived here."

"So, we are at one of the poles," Korak said. "The Dead World must rotate on its axis at ninety degrees, with the poles exactly, or almost exactly, perpendicular to Pellucidar's central sun. Thus, no seasons."

"But while the pendent moon rotates about an axis," Meriem said, "it does not revolve around the sun. Or it revolves around the sun, but so does the inner world, and both are revolving perfectly in sync. Either way, that explains the lack of a concept of a year here on the Dead World."

"Only days," Betty said. "Day after day, but no seasons or differing lengths of daylight to differentiate them. No weeks, no months, no years. Pretty dreary."

"Alex Ryadinsky complained that she had been here for years," Korak said.

Meriem rolled her eyes. "That woman would have said anything to get you under her thumb."

The ape-man shrugged. "I don't see how she could have taken over the Sketh in just a few weeks. Maybe the strange differences in the passage of time that have been noted in Pellucidar also have some effect here on the pendent moon, but it does appear to be a different phenomenon."

"Maybe," Meriem said. "Hopefully she feels that the past several 'weeks' since we escaped have been years. Decades even. Maybe she's already died of old age."

Korak grinned. "Maybe. But look. There is nothing here. We must take action. There is nowhere else to go except to explore this hole in the ground."

Akut grunted in assent.

Lordan said, "Korak, let us explore to a certain distance and then return. This way, we can gather knowledge and determine if all can, or should, make the journey."

"An excellent idea," the ape-man said.

"Before you go," Betty Callwell said, "I'm sorry, but I can go no further."

Korak gave her a questioning look.

"I am . . . experiencing an odd sensation. It is a feeling that is warning me off. Like I don't belong here and should go no farther. Either that, or I am more needed elsewhere."

"I—" Korak said, but she was gone.

"*That* was unsettling," Meriem said, for Betty had faded before their very eyes, leaving empty air in her wake.

"Yes," her mate replied. He stared at the empty air for a moment. Betty Callwell had been a good comrade in arms.

He and Lordan departed, climbing into the depths of the cone, and quickly disappeared from the view of the others. They returned shortly, to everyone's relief, for it seemed as if even a short reconnaissance was an opportunity for disaster to befall them.

"We reached the bottom of the funnel," Lordan said, "in which there is a tunnel entrance. We scouted a short way in, and then turned back. The tunnels are too tight for the two bus-dars to pass through. I can make them understand that they are to await us here at the entrance, for our return."

"The surrounding environment is barren," Korak said.

"They will fly to areas that are close by," Lordan replied, "to forage for food and water, but they will always return here."

"I will stay here and also watch over the bus-dars," Mirina said. "The Fire at the Top of the World is forbidden to my people, as I have said, according to the decree of lore handed down by generation upon generation. I know I volunteered to accompany you to the Dead World and help, but this . . ."

Meriem touched her on the arm. "It's quite all right. You must be true to yourself. And staying behind, you can also explain where we have gone in the event others arrive here—perhaps David and Dek, or Rahnak and Kyrianji."

Soon, Korak, Meriem, Lordan, and Akut were marching deep into a cavernous tunnel that proceeded to narrow to a rocky corridor in which each of the party could traverse only in single file. Their way was lit by the uncanny crimson glow that gave forth in front of them, and the source of which they assumed they would soon encounter, for while it was not bright, it was insistent and powerful, and it carried warmth that was strangely welcome.

After a while they attained a hollow at the end of the narrow tunnel, and it felt as though they were rolling about in the interior of the small spherical grotto. Light gravity pulled them to the other end of the pocket cavern, and then they realized that they must now look upward at the next tunnel entrance, whereas moments ago they were looking downward at it.

The explorers continued an upward climb through the next tight passageway, the ascent being not particularly difficult, as it felt to them that gravity's pull was not as strong as it had been moments before.

Perhaps one or two hours passed—it was impossible to

know with certainty—and the group emerged from the passage into a strange, rock- and crystal-strewn landscape: the unknown interior of the Dead World.

The ground had large spongy fields that alternated with enormous patches of crystal, the latter of which were slick and translucent, and through which reddish wormlike creatures could be seen wiggling and burrowing only inches below the surface. The area was peppered with twenty-foot-tall stalagmites of both rock and of the reddish crystal, around which they had to navigate as they surveyed their surroundings. Their movements were aided by the lesser gravity, which Korak estimated to be about one-third of that to which he and Meriem were accustomed on the outer crust.

The inside of the Dead World—a hollow sphere—looked to be perhaps forty or fifty miles in diameter.

"I'm not sure how that can be," Meriem said. "Have we changed size again?"

"I don't know," her mate replied, "but what draws my attention right now is that."

Directly above them was a blood-red gem floating at the dead center of the hollow globe, pulsating with brighter, and then dimmer, shades of crimson. The crystal was generally spherical but multifaceted and slightly irregular. The red jeweled core emanated a dim ruby light that faintly illuminated, and also appeared to provide warmth for, the interior surface of the Dead World. The diffuse illumination was in no way comparable to the bright light emanating from Pellucidar's central sun. Rather, the interior of the Dead World was cast in an eternal crimson dusk.

In the upcurving landscape off in the distance, the four travelers saw dots of yellow and white and blue flame, almost as if they were seated in a funhouse version of a planetarium, with stars of various colors and intensities flickering all about them in a three-hundred-and-sixty degree sphere. Were they cities? Something else? So lacking in illumination was the interior of the hollow moon that it was impossible to tell with any degree of certitude. They also observed crimson reflections, which they guessed were probably due to the large, smooth patches of crystal embedded in the ground at periodic intervals.

They wandered a little farther, Korak making sure to blaze the tunnel exit from which they had emerged, as well as stalagmites along the way, but the terrain in front of them was much the same as it was behind them.

"I haven't seen any water," Meriem said, "or anything re-sembling vegetation. There may be nothing we can eat and drink in here."

"I agree," Lordan said. "We might be wise to return to the surface of the pendent moon after we explore a little more, and gather supplies for a return trip."

"You may be right . . ." Korak trailed off.

Meriem turned back to see her mate staring up unblink-ingly at the central crimson crystal.

Korak's heart was racing. A cold sweat dampened his forehead.

He sank to his knees, still transfixed by the glowing red gem floating above him.

His companions' voices were receding into the depths of his mind . . .

"My love, what is happening to you?"

"Korak, are you all right? Can you hear us?"

"Korak, ka-yad!"

But Korak could no longer hear them.

Jack Clayton was trapped in a hellish crimson landscape. Shadowy forms, vaguely human shaped, floated above him, below him, circled around him endlessly. What did they want? He could not tell. He could never tell, but they never left him alone, never gave him any peace.

He only wanted to sleep. Why wouldn't they just let him sleep?

But they were relentless.

The crimson environment in which he floated was eternal. He could remember no beginning; he could foresee no end. There were no others like him. No one to talk to, no one with whom to laugh, or to cry.

Was he a madman? A lunatic? Had Father and Mother sent him to Bedlam? But why would they do that to him? They wouldn't do that to him. They wouldn't send him away.

Would they?

Wait!

Bedlam. Mother.

Father.

These were things not of the crimson realm. Bedlam. Mother. Father.

There was a man—*a man!*—standing among the shadowy forms.

Jack Clayton was now flying. He flew through the crimson hell, and pierced its barrier. Then he was shooting through space, and the stars rushed by. He was out in the open, no longer enclosed in the finite, crimson prison. He was free.

He flew past the Moon and rushed toward Earth.

He saw the great blue-and-green globe grow larger, with its wispy clouds and Arctic ice cap, and then he was plunging through the atmosphere. Air! Blessed air!

He fell, and fell, but was not afraid. It felt good to fall, to have the cold air rushing by, stinging his skin.

He penetrated the thick cloud cover and below him lay a great city. He rushed toward the buildings, the concrete, the granite, the streets, the carriages and motor cars, the gas lamps and new Edison lights, the houses and townhomes.

If this was the end, it was a wonderful end.

He was home.

Jack was lying in a child's bed, much too small for him, his long legs dangling off the end.

He was in his old room at the Greystoke townhome in London.

He drowsily wondered to himself why he thought of it as his "old" room. It was just . . . his room.

He heard screaming from far, far away. The yelling came closer, and he tried to shut it out.

Why wouldn't they just let him sleep?

He rubbed the sleep from his eyes and sat up.

His mother was framed in the doorway to his room, holding little blonde Charlotte's hand, screaming for Tarzan that her dear boy Jack was gone, and that some intruder was in his place.

Jack was confused and hurt.

Had she lost her mind?

Had he?

"But Mother . . . *I'm* Jack."

THE DEAD MOON SUPER-ARC
CONTINUES IN

PELLUCIDAR
LAND OF AWFUL SHADOW

EDGAR RICE BURROUGHS UNIVERSE™

PELLUCIDAR®
DAWN OF THE DEATHSLAYER™

AS RETOLD BY CHRISTOPHER PAUL CAREY

BASED ON GRIDLEY WAVE TRANSMISSIONS RECEIVED AT THE OFFICES OF
EDGAR RICE BURROUGHS, INC.,
TARZANA, CALIFORNIA

ERB
INC.™

1

DARVA THE SHADOW

I N THE STYGIAN DEPTHS of the Forest of Death, the man
stalked a prey as perilous as any he had ever hunted. Despite
this, he knew no fear. Why should he, after all? What reason
was there to be frightened by the terrifying beasts and still
more fearsome *gilaks*—that is, humans—that inhabited this
savage inner world of Pellucidar? Was that not precisely why
he had taken up his journey across two vast, sprawling continents to confront his dreaded quarry—because life now
meant so very little to him?

When he had left his home village of Sari upon his quest,
the man's heart had felt numb. He had wanted to feel again.
But none of the many hazards he had thus far encountered
roused any emotion within his breast other than frustration
at his lack of feeling. That was what happened, he thought,
when one returned from the dead; life lost its edge. At least,
that was what he told himself.

Perhaps he should have listened to his father, who had tried
to discourage his intentions to travel here, where citizens on
this far frontier of the Federated Kingdoms continued to go
missing. These were rumored to have fallen victim to hideous
creatures, ghoulish deformities that made their home in a
twisting and turning network of caverns beneath the floor of
this blighted wood. But no one really knew for sure the fate
of those who had disappeared.

The man whirled about upon hearing what sounded like
a single heavy footfall upon the spongy ground behind him.

The trees of this accursed place, bare of branches and leaves along their thick trunks, and absent of surrounding foliage, afforded little cover for any creature that might lurk in the shadows beneath the impenetrable canopy of interlocking branches high above the forest floor. And yet he saw nothing in the direction whence the sound had come.

He grinned, for though he felt no rise of emotion, the mystery whetted his curiosity, and for just a moment it had distracted him from the deadness inside his heart.

The hunter's hand fell briefly to his knife—hewn of flint and secured in the antelope-skin sheath belted to his hip—before ultimately clutching the grip of the stout bow that hung about a muscular shoulder. In a single practiced motion, he unslung the bow, withdrew a stone-tipped arrow from its quiver, nocked his deadly missile, and aimed it at the bole of the tree nearest to where he had heard the sound.

Slowly, cautiously, with every sense attuned to his primordial environment, the man advanced toward the tree. When he arrived directly before it, he began to circle its great bole with all the wariness that is honed into the nerves and muscles of any creature that hopes to survive the inner world's unending perils. If something was hiding there, it must be on the other side of—

A streak of white lightning shot from behind an adjoining tree and barreled hard into his shoulder, knocking him roughly to the forest floor. As he looked up from the bed of soft, rubbery fungi that had cushioned his fall, he caught a glimpse of a pale, hideous man-thing running away from him, heading deeper into the forest. Two blood-red pupils set within pink irises looked back at him over a hunched, ghastly white shoulder as the creature retreated, its two great fangs glistening and wet as they curved downward from its upper mouth.

The man made to rise and pursue his ghoulish quarry when a demonic fury fell upon him from above.

He grasped his assailant's wrists before the two black obsidian knives—one gripped in each of the attacker's hands—could slice him to ribbons. Fiendish gray eyes, outlined by a thick black band like a raccoon's facial markings, squinted down at him in rage, surrounded by swathes of coal-black hair, so that at first he did not know if he fought a gilak of flesh and blood or rather some infernal specter that haunted this accursed Forest of Death. But while ferocious, his opponent was smaller and slighter than he, and he used his greater weight and muscles to swing the writhing fury beneath him, pinning the two slender, dark gray arms to the ground so that the keen-edged knives could not reach him.

Then he started, realizing that the struggling form beneath him was neither demon nor man, but rather a living, breathing woman. Her heaving chest, painted with dark markings that resembled the bones of an open rib cage, panted for breath as she fought against his strong muscles. Suddenly he understood that the dusky band around her eyes was not composed of fur, as he had at first thought, but rather smudges of black charcoal streaked across her face, her arms being similarly smeared with ash.

He had only a moment to consider the situation before the woman let loose an ululating cry that made his ears ring with pain. But soon that discomfort was forgotten as a greater pain seared down his back and shoulders. He cried out and rolled away from the woman, his stone knife slashing at whatever new threat was raking his flesh from above.

A flutter of leathery wings met him as he turned, and then he knew that he faced not one, but two vicious flying-lizards, their torsos each about the length of a man's hand, with wingspans three times that measure. The tiny pterosaurs sliced and bit at him with their razor-sharp claws and teeth, the flapping of their scaled wings beating a chaotic flurry around him.

He slashed his knife back and forth to repel the fury of the pterosaurs' onslaught. The winged lizards pulled back before his defense, lashing out at him with beak and claw in the wake of each pass of his stone blade. But neither lizard nor man could find its mark and land a grave blow upon the enemy, so evenly matched was each party in evading the other's attacks. All the same, the man knew that if the ptero-saurs kept up their relentless assault, he would eventually be worn down and cut to pieces beneath their deadly talons and piercing, needlelike teeth.

Thus it was with a sigh of relief that he heard the woman again issue her ululating cry and saw the flying-lizards obey her command, relinquishing their prey and swooping back through the dim light of the forest to land upon the shoulders of their mistress.

He stood up silently, blood dripping down his back and sides from the tiny wounds inflicted by the newcomer's familiars.

"Who are you, warrior," asked the woman in the common tongue of Pellucidar, "who dares to stalk the sacred Gorbuses in the Forest of Death?"

"And who are you," the man answered back, "who defends the wretched Gorbuses of the Charnel Caves?"

"I am Darva the Shadow, Daughter of the Ul-rahn, O Nameless One." The woman sneered, but even the charcoal smearing her face could not hide the fact that she was as beautiful as any maiden he had ever encountered. "Perhaps you are ashamed of your name, as you are also ashamed of that of your own tribe. Otherwise, why would you not speak the names? Have your people cast you out?"

"I have never heard of the Ul-rahn," the man said, ignoring her questions.

Darva the Shadow smiled without the slightest trace of humor or good will. "That is because no one from outside this forest who meets the Ul-rahn lives to wag his tongue."

"And yet *I* am alive," the man said.

Again, the cold smile. "For now, O One Who Is Too Vile for a Name."

The man laughed. "My name is Janson. Janson Gridley of the tribe of Sari in the Federated Kingdoms of Pellucidar.

My village lies far away across the sea." He motioned vaguely in the direction of Sari, although he could not sense where his homeland lay by instinct as could the natives of Pellucidar, for he had been born on the outer crust.

"Are you so conceited that you need two names, Jan-son Grid-lee?" asked Darva. "A true man needs only one." She whispered something to her familiars and with nary a sound they beat their scaly wings and lifted from her shoulders, whereupon they flew off and disappeared into the dim shadows of the forest.

"Where I was born most people have *three* names."

The woman grunted with derision. "A land of show-offs, who hide behind names that carry no meaning."

"Do all the Ul-rahn meet strangers with such sharp tongues?"

Darva the Shadow fingered the sleek grips of her obsidian knives. "No," she said, "we meet them with sharp blades."

Janson Gridley smiled. "Can you tell me, Darva, why your people consider the Gorbuses to be sacred? Do not the Gorbuses prey upon the Ul-rahn?"

"Why should they?" With a toss of her head, Darva flung the great mass of her raven hair over a shoulder. "The Ul-rahn have long protected the Gorbuses. It is true that when my ancestor Dron the Deathless was but a young warrior, the Gorbuses slew my people whenever they encountered them, and the Ul-rahn in turn fled from them. But when Dron returned from his long journey"—here the woman tilted back her head and gazed up into the knotted forest canopy above as if to penetrate the veil between this world and some other beyond—"he taught them our worth as their protectors. And now that the Gorbuses are no longer swept to Pellucidar from the Dead World, the duty of the Ul-rahn is even more vital. Now the Gorbuses are but few in number, and both we and they would guard their kind against the risk of un-needed conflict."

"What do you mean by saying the Gorbuses are no longer

'swept' to Pellucidar?" Janson asked, trying to take it all in. "Is that whence you believe they come? The Dead World that hangs above the Land of Awful Shadow?"

Darva eyed Janson warily. "You are an outsider who has come to the forest to slay the Gorbuses. Already have I said too much. You would not understand."

"You might be surprised. And I am not here to slay the Gorbuses, unless I learn that they are responsible for the disappearance of the citizens from the Federated Kingdoms. *My* people."

A look of disgust twisted the woman's beautiful features and she seemed about to question Janson's statement, but just then what sounded like the blast of a distant horn carried to them through the forest.

"It is the guardians of the Charnel Caves," she said; "they have sounded the alarm." For a brief moment, she regarded the Sarian through narrowed lids, as if assessing his worth and character. "If you mean what you say, come with me and you may prove it." And then she took off running between the great boles of the towering trees.

Janson Gridley followed closely at the woman's heels. He did not know precisely why he did so, for he owed no allegiance to Darva the Shadow or her people, the Ul-rahn. But all the same, something stirred within him, and the deadness in his heart was for a moment forgotten.

For some distance, they passed along the banks of a shallow creek that wended its way through the dark woods, until eventually it ended where it flowed into an opening in the ground. They continued on, Darva flying as fleet-footed as a deer across the spongy forest floor, when suddenly there rose before them in the gloomy shadows a sheer cliff.

Before the imposing wall of rock stood an arc of five warriors and a young boy, the latter perhaps ten or twelve years of age by the standards of the outer crust. Patterns of dark charcoal streaked their faces and chests, while gray ash smeared their arms, legs, and torsos; these were clearly members of Darva's tribe. With stone-tipped spears they were thrusting at a large, dark form, sinuous and scaly, writhing on the ground before them. Janson Gridley felt his skin crawl when he realized it was a giant snake, its powerful body perhaps three feet in diameter and some forty-five feet or more in length.

"A great *slizak*!" Darva cried out as they came upon the scene. "It must have wandered out of the Korjian Swamp during the heavy rains."

One of the warriors, standing about half a dozen yards from the gargantuan reptile's triangular head, pulled back his spear arm in anticipation of impaling his weapon in the beast. But the throw never came, for that great coiling body sprang forward before the man could act. Down went the brave warrior beneath the mighty tusklike fangs of the great serpent, which, with a flick of its massive head, proceeded to fling the man's body with a sickening thud against the hard stone wall of the ascending crag. There, before a dark hole at the cliff's base, the warrior lay still and lifeless.

The youth, with a look of fierce determination, placed himself between the snake and the dark hole in the rock face. The spear he carried seemed a pitiful weapon to wield against the ophidian monstrosity that confronted him, but Janson could not argue against the boy's bravery.

"Why do they not flee?" Janson asked Darva as they inched closer. He had nocked an arrow in his bow, while his companion had again drawn her two obsidian blades.

"Koorva, son of Koorva, is not a coward," replied the woman proudly. "Nor are any warriors of the Ul-rahn. They would rather die than let the great slizak enter the abode of the Holy Ones."

Now he understood. This, then, must be the entrance to the Charnel Caves, the subterranean lair of the Gorbuses. The Ul-rahn feared the giant snake would slither into the opening to the cave system and wreak havoc on their hideous divinities.

"Well," Janson said, "coward or not, Koorva, son of Koorva, is about to meet his end."

The woman shot him a look of angry contempt, but soon fear racked her beautiful features as the monstrous snake reared its great head and prepared to strike down the puny gilak youth who stood bravely but futilely in its way.

Just as the great reptile released a horrendous hiss and spread wide its awesome jaws, Janson pulled taut his mighty bow and released its missile. The feathered shaft sang as it shot through the air. With a wet thunk the arrow sank deep into the fleshy part of the monster's palate.

Janson Gridley did not pause to take stock of his accomplishment. Instead, he ran forth until he stood directly beneath the lashing and writhing form of the titanic serpent. There, kneeling, he aimed his bow almost straight up and let loose two more arrows into the lower jaw of the terrible reptile.

Neither did the boy hesitate, for as the frightful slizak reared back from the wounds Janson had inflicted, Koorva ran forward and stabbed his spear deep into the exposed underbelly of the scaly monstrosity, groaning with great effort as he yanked out the shaft. A river of crimson gushed from where the spear had impaled the great writhing snake. For a moment the boy grinned, thinking he had dealt a mortal blow to his gargantuan foe. But then Koorva's face grew long beneath the ash that streaked it as he looked up and saw the beady eyes of the serpent locked upon him. Then, with lightning speed, the great slizak lashed down with its swordlike fangs and made to strike the defenseless youth.

But Janson had anticipated both the boy's attack and the serpent's response. And so, as the enraged slizak swung down its great triangular head to strike the brave Koorva, already was the man of Sari crouching beside the youth, his bow arched and his arrow nocked and pointing up at the monster's hideous distended maw.

Straight and true flew Janson's missile, which again sliced through the roof of the slizak's mouth. This time, however, the arrow pierced the creature's skull and emerged from the beast's left eye socket, from which a stream of blood sprayed into the air and rained down upon the two gilaks beneath it.

Half blind, the snake reared back as if to strike, but then suddenly the raised portion of its massive body relaxed and slammed down upon the hard ground before the cliffs. Instantly, the remaining warriors rushed in and began stabbing the creature at the base of its skull with the long, razor-sharp points of their spears, seeking to penetrate the reptile's tiny brain. At last it appeared they had succeeded, for soon the slizak's massive body ceased writhing and grew limp and still, its lone cold, beady eye clouded with the dullness of death.

Janson looked over at the boy to make sure he was all right, only to find Koorva's gray eyes beaming and a wide smile upon his blood-drenched face. Janson grinned back at the boy, admiring his courage and spunk amid the carnage, and soon they were laughing together as they wiped the crimson gore of their defeated foe from their eyes.

Upon seeing Darva, the boy cried out her name and ran into her arms. As the two embraced, an expression of relief, combined with that of elation, broke out on the young woman's face, and she closed her eyes tightly as if to hold back tears of joy.

Perhaps the stern and imposing Darva the Shadow had a heart after all.

"What are you doing here among the guardians?" Darva asked of the boy. "You should be back at the village, taking care of Mother and little Leena."

"I have been searching for you, Sister," replied the youth. "Why did you run away from the village and leave us? Is it because of Vrok? Do not be afraid of him. I shall kill him, and then all will be as it was before."

Darva squeezed her brother tightly to her frame but said nothing. Janson had not failed to notice the pain in the woman's eyes at the mention of the one named Vrok.

He was about to ask who exactly this Vrok fellow was when the warriors proceeded to gather up the body of their fallen comrade, laying him before the opening to the sacred caves and positioning his arms in crosswise fashion over his chest in a manner of solemn respect. Darva rose from her brother, and Janson looked on as she went about the task of gathering an assortment of wildflowers from the forest. When it seemed she had gathered all that she sought, she walked back to the others and spread the petals upon her deceased tribe member's supine remains. Then she removed a slender wand of oak from where it had lain hidden in her knee-high moccasins. This she commenced to wave about in the air above the fallen warrior while uttering a soft chant, the words of which Janson could not make out.

This was the first time he had witnessed such a unique and intricate ritual among the Stone Age peoples of Pellucidar. Certainly, he had never before seen anyone from his own village—where he had lived since age thirteen when he had immigrated to the inner world—utilize a scepter in this sort of pious ceremony. Among his own people, the Sarians, the death of a tribe member was met with the wailing of the women and the stern faces of the men, who would then proceed to place the deceased high in the branches of a tall tree, so that birds might carry the remains bit by bit to the Dead World that loomed above the Land of Awful Shadow. They did this to prevent the remains from being borne off by demons from the Molop Az, the flaming sea upon which Pellucidar was said to rest. And that, as far as Janson had known until now, was all that could be said for the beliefs of the afterlife as they pertained to his people. Perhaps here, in the Forest of Death, he was witnessing the very birth of systematized religion among the so-called primitives of Pellucidar. In any case, it was clear that Darva held a special position among the Ul-rahn, perhaps something akin to that of a priestess.

But for now, he would hold back his questions. He did not wish to offend Darva and her people, for, despite having fought beside them to slay the monster, he did not yet know whether to regard them as friends or foes.

2
LEGACY OF THE DEATHLESS ONE

AFTER THE DEATH RITUAL was concluded, the little party assembled around the corpse of the great slizak. There they were admiring their gruesome handiwork and discussing the merits of Janson's bow and arrow—a weapon wholly unknown to the Ul-rahn—when suddenly a large group of men emerged from the shadows of the forest and stepped into the clearing.

Darva whipped her obsidian knives from their snakeskin sheathes and drew back toward the cliffs, but it was too late. The newcomers, their spears drawn, swiftly encircled Darva and all of her party.

One of the men stepped forward and placed his hands on his hips. He was adorned in similar fashion to the members of both groups, wearing an animal-skin loincloth and knee-high moccasins that had been dyed a stygian black, as well as a snakeskin belt about his waist from which depended a long, wicked-looking stone knife. Gray ash and black markings stained his skin. His long, greasy black hair fell to his shoulders and surrounded a face in which was set a pair of sly coal-black eyes above a sharp nose, a thin sneering smile, and a weak chin. Unlike the others, he wore a snakeskin headband bearing a sigil at the forehead that resembled a single serpentine eye. Janson did not fail to note that the ebon designs on the skin of the man and the other newcomers resembled coiled and slithering snakes.

233

"I am pleased to see you, Darva the Shadow," said the man in an oily voice. "Have you reconsidered my offer?"

"Beware, Vrok," said Darva, "lest you end up like your cousin from the Korjian Swamp." She gestured with a proud chin to the corpse of the giant snake that lay before them.

Vrok went on, ignoring the woman's threat. "Our people have missed their Ul-vana. Do not be selfish. It is time to stop grieving your father and to do your duty for the sake of the tribe. Koorva would not approve."

Darva's gray eyes narrowed in contempt. "Do not speak my father's name, Vrok the Viper. It sounds vile on your forked tongue."

Vrok turned from the woman, a contemptuous smile upon his lips. "Who slew this unfortunate child of the Pale One Who Crawls?" he asked, addressing the guardians of the Charnel Caves.

One of the warriors who had faced off against the giant snake laid his hand on Janson's shoulder. "It was this man," he said. "If Jan-son Grid-lee had not arrived with his shooter of tiny spears, surely we would have all perished and the great serpent would have slithered into the abode of the Sacred Ones."

"Nonsense!" cried Vrok. "The Pale One sent his child to protect the entrance to the caves. This man of whom you speak has committed blasphemy with his profane weapon and slain a child of the Pale One. Seize him!"

Janson could do little in the face of such a large group of armed warriors, two of whom leaped forward at their master's order. The men quickly relieved the Sarian of his weapons and bound his hands fast behind his back with sturdy cords of leather.

"Release him!" cried Darva the Shadow. "Your Ul-vana commands it!" The men, clearly uncomfortable at defying their Ul-vana—which Janson could only imagine translated to something like high priestess—fidgeted and looked to Vrok for guidance.

"The Pale One Who Crawls rewards those loyal to his totem leader," said Vrok, "while he strikes down those cowards who waver in their duty."

The men straightened their spines and stopped fidgeting. Though the guardians of the caves looked uncomfortable, they fell in with the men under Vrok's command and offered no protest. The boy, for his part, scowled and came to stand beside his sister, making his allegiance evident to all.

"Come, Darva," crooned Vrok the Viper, clearly satisfied at having asserted his will over the warriors. "We can talk about our future together while we walk back home to Ul-nar."

Darva thrust her chin high in the air and did not answer, but when the party took up its march through the gloomy forest, she accompanied the warriors. She refused, however, to walk beside Vrok, who cursed her for her stubbornness and then proceeded to swear at two nearby warriors who murmured their dismay at seeing their Ul-vana so disrespected. Ultimately, the two men quieted, but Janson Gridley, prodded forward by the spear tips of the warriors who guarded him, took note of the divisions among the Ul-rahn. He wondered whether Darva might have enough clout to sway the inhabitants of Ul-nar against Vrok, who, based on the behavior Janson had just witnessed, seemed unlikely to let anyone live for very long who might challenge his authority.

For how long the party marched through the tenebrous woods, Janson did not know, but his stomach was growling by the time the sunlight began to filter through the trees as they approached the village of Ul-nar, which lay on the forest's edge. The location of the settlement made sense, as nothing edible grew deeper in the Forest of Death, where nary a ray of Pellucidar's fiery sun penetrated the densely intertwined canopy of the upper terrace. Here, however, the sunlight glimmering through the leaves and branches revealed berries and nuts growing aplenty amid the foliage, as well as intermittent wildlife such as antelope and hares, which sprang across the leafy floor when startled by the approaching party.

Soon came into their view a village of beehive-shaped huts. The sight might have been an ordinary one anywhere throughout the inner world save for the fact that the huts were not constructed of thatch but of dark gray stones. A sentry posted some distance from the village greeted the party and let it pass, and upon its arrival the villagers assembled in the central courtyard while Vrok mounted a little rise and stood before the assemblage. Vrok's men escorted Darva and her brother to stand before their chief at the foot of the rise, while Janson was brought to stand opposite the siblings.

"Greetings, my people!" proclaimed Vrok, addressing the crowd. "Your chief has returned with the Ul-vana, though it can hardly be said that she still deserves the title and the respect that accompanies it."

A murmur of shock and agitation ran throughout the crowd, but Vrok merely raised his voice and spoke over the stirring of dissent. "Can anyone deny but that the magic has left her? Nay, the spirits of our departed ancestors and family members now shun Darva the Shadow." He turned to an old woman standing near Darva. "Is it not true, Veela? Did you not tell me that the so-called Ul-vana took you to her sacred hovel in the woods and was unable to summon the spirit of your deceased daughter?"

The old woman first looked sadly at Darva before lifting her gaze to address Vrok upon the natural rise that served as his rostrum. "It is as you say, O Chief. Though she donned the Circlet of Dron, she could not summon my daughter. Only when I entered your own hut did my precious Deedra appear to me."

Vrok nodded, a satisfied grin spreading across the sharp features of his face. "And did your dear little Deedra sit mutely before your mind's eye, as she did when the Ul-vana was yet able to summon her spirit?"

Tears came to the old woman's eyes. "No, when she came before us in your hut she was no mute spirit, but a creature of flesh and blood as are you and I. I was able to touch her, to feel the warm tears of joy at our reunion as they flowed down her cheeks! And to speak with her, and be spoken to. After all these years, I was with my sweet Deedra again, as young and as beautiful as the day she drowned in the river." The woman cleared her throat and more tears came. "And she told me she *forgave* me." Here the woman began sobbing, and Darva placed a comforting arm around her and let her cry into her shoulder. When the woman at last quieted, she looked up at Darva and muttered, "I am sorry, Ul-vana. I speak only the truth."

Darva looked pityingly at the woman. "I believe you, Veela. I know you wouldn't lie and that you speak of only that which you saw and felt and heard." Gently, she pushed the woman away. Then any hint of compassion vanished from face of Darva the Shadow as she turned defiant eyes upon the chief.

"Indeed, your magic is powerful, Vrok," she said. "Perhaps more powerful than mine or that of my father who taught it to me. But it is also dangerous." She turned her searching eyes to the crowd until her gaze landed on the face she sought.

"Gurzo," she went on, "have you not told me how you entered Vrok's hut to visit with the spirit of your dead grandfather? And how at first he appeared to you, a man of flesh and blood, even as he was in life. But then how, in only an instant, he transformed into a towering ryth, who raked you with his claws and tore your eyes from their sockets? And only later, when you awoke, did your sight return and you discovered that you were not injured. Did you not tell me that even now, many sleeps thereafter, your grandfather comes to you in your dreams in the form of a giant cave bear who chases you into the forest so that he might devour you?"

Gurzo swallowed on a dry throat and looked down at the ground, as if ashamed. "It is true, Ul-vana," he said.

"And you, Ro-ar," Darva said, addressing a strapping young warrior who stood on the edge of the crowd. "Have you not come to me and told me how the ghost of your mother's murderer, whom you slew with your own hands, has haunted you ever since you visited Vrok's hut? How on several occasions he has leaped out at you from behind a tree, and then, when you have turned to face him, he is gone?"

Ro-ar sighed heavily and said, "You speak the truth, Ul-vana."

With the attestations of Gurzo and Ro-ar, the gathered tribe members began to whisper among themselves. Janson watched with no little pleasure to see Vrok's anxious eyes dart from person to person as he doubtless realized the mood of the crowd was swiftly turning against him. Then the man regained his composure and resumed speaking in what seemed to be his habitual tone of arrogance.

"It is no fault of your chief," he proclaimed, "that these men have offended the dead and brought misfortune upon themselves and their dearly departed family members. I warned you, Gurzo, and you as well, Ro-ar, that you must enter my hut with a pure heart or risk inflaming the anger of the inhabitants of the Dead World with whom you wished to speak. Is it not so?"

In dispirited tones, Gurzo and Ro-ar admitted that it was.

"The power has left Darva the Shadow." Vrok eyed the woman, the trace of a smirk upon his lips, before settling his gaze upon Gurzo and Ro-ar, each in turn. Then he lifted his arms like a priest of the outer world preaching to his flock and addressed his larger audience. "It is she who angered the Gorbuses, so that they have become fewer. And it is she who has failed you by being unable to call forth the spirits. No longer may she be called Ul-vana. Only I—your chief and your new Ul-volok—may serve as intermediary between the Ul-rahn and the spirits of the Dead World." Again he looked to Gurzo and Ro-ar. "And only I, your Ul-volok, may quiet the spirits of the dead so that they may forgive the insolence of the living. And so I shall do for you, Gurzo, and you, Ro-ar, and likewise for any of the Ul-rahn who, confessing and pleading redress for their impurity of heart, have angered the spirits of their departed loved ones and ancestors. And soon the Gorbuses will appear again in greater numbers, and you will have Vrok, your chief, to thank for it."

The crowd stirred at Vrok's words, and Janson saw many heads nodding as if swayed by their chief's pronouncements, but Darva the Shadow would have none of it. She strode forward to stand directly before Vrok beneath his earthen dais and let loose her fury.

"You are not the Ul-volok, Vrok the Viper. Nor will you ever be. Your vile words dishonor the legacy of Dron the Deathless. None of that which you claim comes from the tradition left to us by Dron, who, uncounted generations ago, descended into the tunnels that run up from the Molop Az and fought the winged demon who guards the entrance to Koh-ra-vor, the Land Beyond the Living. There, in the bowels of the earth, he emerged victorious and took from the demon her crown. Since the very founding of our tribe has the Circlet of Dron passed down the line from chief to chief, each of whom has imparted the secret teachings to his successor, who in turn teaches the traditions of Dron to the tribe's Ul-vana. No Ul-volok or Ul-vana has ever passed on Dron's sacred transmissions to you, Vrok. Nay, you are a pretender, a charlatan!"

All the while Darva the Shadow was making her little speech, the smirk on Vrok's face grew only more pronounced, so that by the time she was done speaking a full sneer marked his countenance. With slow deliberation, Vrok reached into a large pouch slung about his shoulder. The woven bag was embroidered with the sigil of a serpent's eye like that which adorned his snakeskin headband, and from it he removed a circlet of gleaming metal. The sight astonished Janson Gridley, who had never before seen an example of such finely wrought metalwork in the possession of the inner world's Stone Age peoples, outside of that introduced by David Innes and Abner Perry in the region of Sari. The artisanry of the specimen was exquisite, as the circlet appeared to be flawlessly contoured— a perfectly round ring of silvery metal that would have been well suited to rest regally upon the head of a king or queen of the outer world. But rather than treat this remarkable treasure with the respect for which its rarity and stunning quality called, Vrok flung it carelessly through the air to land in the dust at the feet of Darva the Shadow.

"Who is truly the charlatan?" taunted Vrok. "Who is actually the teller of empty words? Go ahead, Darva the Shadow, supposed heir to the legacy of Dron. Pick up the circlet of the Deathless One and put it upon your pretty head. Does it hum in resonance with the spirits like it did before, when it crowned the brow of your father's father? Do it! Put it upon your own brow!" Cruelty laced Vrok's laughter. "But witness—all of you, my people! She will not wear it, for she has dishonored the spirits and it is nothing but a worthless bauble now."

Darva picked up the circlet, and true to Vrok's prediction, she did not place it upon her head. Instead, she brazenly dared the Viper to follow through on his poisonous words. "Go ahead, Vrok. Bind my hands like you have done to this hero, Jan-son Grid-lee, who defended the sacred Gorbuses against the great snake of the Korjian Swamp. Imprison me and sentence me to death, for I long to haunt you as a spirit and make your life miserable."

"Perhaps I shall . . ." said Vrok; but before he could go on, a tall stalwart warrior pushed his way forward through the crowd and, standing beside Darva, looked up at Vrok.

"You will neither harm nor lay your hands upon the Ul-vana," the warrior said firmly. "You are the lawful chief of this tribe, that I admit, but that does not mean you can overturn the laws of Dron, who decreed that the Ul-vana is sacred. And though the power may have left Darva the Shadow, she is still the Ul-vana of the Ul-rahn. There is not a member of our tribe who has not benefited from her wisdom and compassion. We all know it, Vrok the Viper, all seemingly but you. And do not think that we have not all wondered why it is that Koorva, the chief before you, never returned after going on the hunt with you. You say he was eaten by a tarag so that no one ever saw his corpse, but everyone knows that even a tarag leaves bones behind after his meal. No, you will leave the Ul-vana alone, if you know what is good for the tribe . . . and for its new chief."

Vrok clenched his fists, and Janson thought he could see color creep through beneath the pale ash that smeared the man's face. "Do you threaten your chief, Kakar the Bold One?" countered Vrok.

"Of course not," said Kakar. "I merely give him advice that he might continue to live through many sleeps."

Upon the utterance of Kakar's reply, a group of about a dozen warriors stepped forward and stood behind the Bold One. In response, a similar number of Vrok's guards—positioned on either side of their chief—grabbed their spears and pointed them down menacingly at Kakar and his braves.

Vrok raised a hand and smiled broadly. "We are all friends here," he said, "among our Ul-rahn brothers and sisters. Of course I shall not imprison Darva the Shadow, whose past deeds, once upon a time, proved their worth. She is a daughter of the Ul-rahn, and so shall she be treated. But this man"— he pointed at Janson Gridley—"is a foreigner who has blasphemed by slaying a child of the Pale One Who Crawls. Lock him up and prepare what is needed for the ceremony, for after the next sleep he is to be sacrificed upon the altar stone of the Pale One!"

3
THE CIRCLET OF DRON

J ANSON GRIDLEY'S MIND WHIRLED as he leaned against the post to which he was tied in the prison hut of the Ul-rahn. Never before had he either heard of or encountered a tribe such as this in all of Pellucidar, whose Stone Age inhabitants had little time to spare for superstitious ritual, engaged as they were in the life-and-death struggle for survival in a world thriving with ferocious beasts and savage gilaks. And yet somehow the Ul-rahn had managed to develop a unique and seemingly advanced religion centered on worship of an ancient ancestor, a forbear who had emerged victorious from a battle with a demon reputed to guard the gateway to the afterlife itself. Moreover, the Ul-rahn had also developed a religious caste system, overseen by a high priest and a high priestess. Nowhere in the Federated Kingdoms—nor in the regions with which he was familiar that lay beyond the empire's borders—did there exist any such sophisticated belief systems, with the sole exception of the religion of the Xexots, a Bronze Age people who lived on the far side of the Nameless Strait in relation to Sari. But there could be no connection between the Xexots and the Ul-rahn, who were separated by vast distances and whose faiths did not resemble one another in the least. He did not count the religion of the Jukans, for though they had priests and lived not far from the Forest of Death, they were idol worshippers, and their mad, simplistic creed bore no similarity to the refined and very specific mythology that lay behind the beliefs of Darva's people. Nor did

242

he count the spiritual practices of the Krataklaks, for the crab folk were not even gilaks. No, the Ul-rahn were unique, and he wondered why. There was something he was missing; he could feel it in his bones.

Then there was the mystery of the crown of glimmering silver metal. Where had the Ul-rahn come by it? Janson could scarcely credit the folktale that it had been taken from the head of a demon. Though he had not been able to examine the circlet closely, what he saw of it reminded him of polished Harbenite, that rare, ultradurable lightweight metal mined on the outer crust in the Wiramwazi Mountains of central Africa. But as far as he knew, the first time Harbenite had entered the inner world was when the O-220 airship had flown through the north polar opening some two decades earlier. Yet, according to the tale Darva had recounted, the Circlet of Dron had been in the possession of the Ul-rahn for uncounted generations.

But soon these unsolved mysteries and any other thoughts he might have would matter nothing to Janson Gridley. After the next sleep, he would be placed upon a sacrificial altar, and thereafter all would go dark and he would have no more questions or contemplations.

Or would he? Had he not survived death once and returned to tell the tale? He was not foolish enough to believe he would be so fortunate again. However, for one thing he was glad. Only a short time ago, he had not cared whether he lived or died. Now, though the hollowness still remained in his heart, he was not so sure. Something subtle had changed within him, even if he did not know exactly what it was, or what had prompted the change.

It was with this mix of both intriguing and gloomy thoughts that Janson was preoccupied when he heard a disturbance on the other side of the thag-skin curtain that served as the door to his prison. He thought he heard a muffled cry, and the next moment a slender ashen gray hand pushed through the curtain and swept it aside. In strode Darva the Shadow, who swiftly went about the task of cutting his bonds with one of her obsidian knives.

When he was made free, Janson stood up, flexing his prickling hands, but before he could speak Darva put a finger to her ash-stained lips and shushed him. He followed her outside into the perpetual daylight, where he found Kakar and two other warriors standing over the prone and unmoving form of the guard who had been stationed outside the hut.

Darva clasped arms with Kakar. "I shall not forget this," she whispered. "I owe you a great debt."

The tall warrior replied in hushed tones. "There is no debt, Ul-vana. Goran, Flug, and I have seen nothing." He smiled. "In fact, we are all asleep in our huts beside our women right now."

"Sleep well then, Kakar the Bold," said Darva. "Once again you have earned your name, even if it was while you slumbered."

With those parting words, Darva grasped Janson's hand and led him swiftly into the woods, away from the village and the forest's edge.

After they had gotten out of eyeshot and earshot of the village, Janson asked his guide where she was taking him.

"Save your breath for our journey, Jan-son Grid-lee," she replied. "We must move swiftly. Vrok's men will soon be at our heels."

And so they continued on, deeper into the Forest of Death, for how long neither the man nor the woman knew, for time passes strangely in a world without a sun that rises and sets.

They stopped briefly only once to eat from the nuts and fruits that Darva had brought in her antelope-skin pouch. But soon they were again on the move, the woman being so fleet of foot that even Janson, who was in excellent shape, taxed his stamina in his effort to keep up with her.

At last they came to a stone hovel nestled in a shallow vale, almost imperceptible in the murky illumination of the dark woods. They entered the structure through a low, narrow opening in its side, and Janson squatted in the darkness while Darva proceeded to light a fire with the kit she carried in her pouch. Once the kindling had caught, the fire the woman had lit in the hearth revealed a neat little room whose walls were lined with wicker shelves holding numerous supplies, including what appeared to be an array of medicinal herbs and provisions, as well as gourds full of unknown liquids. These, Janson guessed, were the tools of trade for the Ul-vana, who, from what he had gathered, acted as a sort of medicine woman for her people. When Janson asked about the latter, Darva confirmed his suspicions, saying that her father, as the Ul-volok, had taught her what plants to gather in the forest and how to grow and cultivate others herself.

While she was talking, she began rifling through the shelves and gathering up several bundles of herbs, and even a small gourd that presumably contained a potion or emollient of some kind. These she proceeded to place in her antelope-skin pouch. Janson asked her what she was doing.

"I do not know when I shall be able to return here, if ever," she replied. "Vrok may come here and destroy my supplies, for he does not wish me to retain any influence over my people, or for them to hold any good will toward me. But more importantly, I needed this." She removed the small gourd she had placed in her bag and held it up in the firelight. "Rub this on our bodies and, if we are stealthy, it will allow us to move undetected by the Gorbuses in the Charnel Caves."

"Why should we wish to enter the caves?"

"To solve once and for all the mystery of why the Gorbuses are becoming fewer," replied Darva the Shadow. "Once, for a brief while in my grandfather's time, it seemed as if the Gorbuses were increasing in number. But now it is just the opposite. It was not long after the Gorbuses ceased to multiply, at the time of the great earthquake, that the Circlet of Dron stopped summoning the spirits. I do not believe that to be chance. And if I can solve the mystery, then perhaps I can regain the trust of my people."

Janson smiled and regarded Darva with admiration. She was a smart woman. He had been wondering exactly that: What was the connection between the Gorbuses and the Circlet of Dron? Darva was perceptive enough to realize that if there was indeed a correlation, it might be the leverage she needed to discredit Vrok and regain her status as Ul-vana.

"Darva," said Janson. "Why do you not simply ask Kakar to lead his warriors against Vrok and his men. Kakar is loyal to you, and he appears to be a respected and powerful figure among your tribe."

"Do you not understand what it means to be the Ul-vana?" she asked. "Of course you do not. You are a foreigner. You would never understand the oath that I have taken. I would never harm the Ul-rahn. To do as you suggest would be to tear my people apart."

"I do understand," Janson replied. "You are a good leader, Darva. You are the Ul-vana."

The woman regarded him for a moment with her intense gray eyes. Then she resumed her task of foraging through the hovel's supplies.

As Darva proceeded thus, Janson noticed a stone tablet leaning up against a wall beneath one of the wicker shelves.

"What is this?" Janson got down on his knees and pulled out the heavy tablet, brushing off accumulated dust with his hand. "These are Mahar hieroglyphs. Where did you get this?"

"It is said that the father of my father's father communed with Dron the Deathless himself, who told him to retrieve it from Dron's tomb deep in the bowels of the Charnel Caves."

The word "tomb" did not exist as such in the common tongue of Pellucidar, but Janson understood well enough the meaning of the portmanteau term that Darva used for it.

"Wait. Your ancestors *buried* Dron the Deathless? But what about the proscription against burying the dead? Were your ancestors not afraid that demons would arise from beneath the ground and carry Dron's remains down to the Molop Az, the fiery sea upon which Pellucidar floats?"

"Foolish man. Do you not know that the Charnel Caves are protected from the demons of the Molop Az? No demon would dare show its face there."

"Why not?"

"They are afraid of the Mistress Who Sleeps, a hideous monster that lairs deep within the caves near Dron's tomb, a place that even the Gorbuses avoid. No demon would dare go near it. It is said that a single glance from the Mistress, should she awake, will turn one's flesh to stone as cold and hard as the pointed rocks that hang down from above throughout the Charnel Caves. That is why Dron's bones lie undisturbed."

"What about the father of your father's father? Was he not afraid to enter the caves?"

"Like Dron, he was a Vakrahn, a Deathslayer. He feared nothing, neither gilak nor Gorbus, demon nor spirit. But even he stepped quietly when he entered the tomb, so as not to awake the Mistress. But even had the Mistress awakened, he would not have been afraid. Alas. A Deathslayer comes only once in a thousand generations. Would that we had one now."

"Have you ever seen any other tablets like this one?"

"My father said that his father's father saw many such tablets in the tomb of Dron the Deathless."

Janson's heart beat faster as he pored over the glyphs on the tablet and began translating the strange characters. When he had finished, his thoughts were unreeling almost faster than he could keep up with them. Suddenly he knew the answer to what he had felt in his bones about the Ul-rahn but had not been able to understand.

"Darva, listen to me," he said. "I need you to tell me where in the Charnel Caves lies Dron's tomb. This is very important."

Once more Darva peered at him with those intense gray eyes, as if assessing his soul and judging whether it was worthy of a reply. Finally, she must have come to the conclusion that she was already in such deep waters with this stranger from

Sari that to tell him more mattered little, for she said, "The tomb lies hidden in the heart of the caves. I have never been there myself, but my father made me memorize the route. The way is too difficult to explain, but I can take you there. But you must first explain why I should, for one does not tread lightly upon the path to Dron's resting place."

"I have been thinking," Janson said. "My friend von Horst, a great chief who lives not far from here in the village of Lo-har, has told me that he has found no evidence that the Mahars occupied this area in any great numbers for countless generations. Little is left of them in the region but their ancient, abandoned ruins and a few weak and scattered flocks. Haven't you ever wondered why the Mahars never enslaved your people or the other gilaks living near the Forest of Death?"

"There is no need to wonder. They avoid the Forest of Death like everyone in Pellucidar. They fear the Gorbuses."

"Perhaps that is it. But I haven't known the Mahars to fear much. They are powerful. Moreover, they're not a superstitious people. They're . . ." Janson struggled to find the word for *scientists* in the tongue of Pellucidar before finally settling on the closest equivalent. "They're *inventors*. Makers of things. Darva, do you have the Circlet of Dron in your possession? May I see it?" The woman hesitated, but finally she reached into her pouch and withdrew the circlet, which she held out to him. He grasped the ring of shining metal and weighed it in his hand. It was cool to the touch and extremely lightweight, and yet seemed to be as unyielding as steel.

Darva, watching Janson examine the circlet, said, "There is nothing like it in all of Pellucidar. That is why Vrok once coveted it." Her pale face now grew long with sadness. "But now it is worthless. The spirits have departed the circlet and entered Vrok. I am no longer the Ul-vana."

"Darva, I have to tell you a story. You will not believe it, even if you understand my words, as I hardly can do either myself. But it is a story that you must hear, for it bears upon the fate of both you and your people.

"I once gave my heart to a young woman," he began, "but she got in over her head and ended up lost . . . very, very lost in a faraway place. I tried to find her and bring her back home, but in the attempt, I died. Yes, you heard me right. I died; I lost my life."

Darva's gray eyes grew wide in the flickering light of the hearth.

"After I died," Janson continued, "I found myself in a very strange place, overseen by beings who kept me imprisoned there."

"Koh-ra-vor," Darva intoned with awed reverence. "The Land Beyond the Living."

"There, in that strange place, I awaited something worse than death. The masters of my captors intended to consume my soul, the essence that makes up who I am. But before they could, the young woman I had attempted to save came to rescue me. She brought me back to the world of the living, while she herself went on to confront the masters of . . . Koh-ra-vor, to put an end once and forever to their scheme to prey upon the souls of the departed."

Darva's mouth hung agape. "I should like to meet your mate. She must be a very powerful Ul-vana."

"Oh, she's got smarts, all right. But she is not my mate." Janson frowned, and a little pang broke through the familiar numbness that had haunted him since returning to the land of the living. "She did not return my affections."

Darva placed her hand on Janson's own. "Sometimes," she said solemnly, "one destined to walk the path of the Vakrahn must do so alone."

Janson paused, looking down at Darva's hand. He had felt a little tingle run through his frame at her touch. What did she mean by comparing him to Dron?

Darva withdrew her hand and said, "Continue with your story, Jan-son Grid-lee."

"Very well," said Janson, mentally shaking off his ruminations. "My friend did put an end to the scheme of the masters

of what you call Koh-ra-vor. That, I believe, is why the
Gorbuses are . . . as you told me . . . 'no longer swept to
Pellucidar from the Dead World.' And if I'm correct, it's
also why you and your father ceased being able to commune
with the spirits for your departed kin. It's not that you have
lost your special talent." Janson weighed the circlet in his
hands. "It's that the connection has been cut off on the
other end."

Darva the Shadow furrowed her brow as if struggling to
understand Janson's words. "But why, then, is Vrok able to
peer through the veil behind life and commune with the
spirits?"

"I have a theory about that, too," replied Janson. "But for
now, there are more important matters we must attend to.
Now we must fly as swiftly as possible to the tomb of Dron
in the Charnel Caves."

A grave look came over Darva's face. "If I am to trust you,
there is more you must explain. Why did the defeat of the
masters of Koh-ra-vor cause the Gorbuses to cease being
swept to Pellucidar from the Dead World?"

"I have also been thinking about that. It is my belief that
the masters of Koh-ra-vor meant to bring their evil scheme
to Pellucidar. I hate to shatter all that you have been taught
about the Gorbuses, Darva, but they are not sacred beings.
I believe that the masters of Koh-ra-vor created the Gorbuses
as vessels to hold the souls of the deceased, all for the purpose
of creating a sort of advance foothold in Pellucidar. How
shall I put it? Just as your father taught you to grow certain
plants and to harvest them after they had matured, so too
did the masters of Koh-ra-vor cultivate gilaks, reaping them
when they had matured and their souls had become tastier
and more satisfying to their otherworldly palates. If they
had succeeded in their scheme, the Gorbuses would have
become numerous, and eventually they would have . . . well,
changed into beings that looked and acted like gilaks—gilaks

for which the masters hungered, for their spirits would be very nutritious, like fine thag steaks to them.

"But the masters were thwarted during a war they had fought with the Mahars uncounted generations ago. I believe that war was fought in a subterranean city called Mintra that lies not far from here, and that after that city was destroyed during the final battle with the masters of Koh-ra-vor, Dron descended into the ruins and recovered this apparatus"— he held up the Circlet of Dron—"which the Mahars used to open the gateway to the Land Beyond the Living and communicate with its masters. In that dim and distant past, the Mahars, after their costly battle with the masters, were able to close the gateway to Koh-ra-vor. And yet, for some reason, the Gorbuses continued to multiply, though clearly at a slower pace than before. Perhaps the gateway was still open a crack, but not so wide that the masters of the other world could get through. And when the gateway opened fully once again about a generation ago, the Gorbuses began to multiply at a faster rate, as you have told me they did when your father was a youth. But then, only just recently, my friend closed the gateway, this time for good. Now the Gorbuses are dying out, and the circlet found by Dron in Mintra, and used by you and your father to commune with your deceased kin, no longer does so. My friend closed the doorway for good this time, and defeated the masters of Koh-ra-vor. Thus, the Gorbuses will soon grow extinct, and the circlet will never again function."

At this, a sad look overcame Darva's beautiful features. "Then I am truly no longer the Ul-vana. Vrok will win the hearts of my people, for his magic allows him to open the doorway to Koh-ra-vor."

Janson was about the reply when suddenly they heard voices approaching from deeper in the forest.

"It is Vrok and his men," said Darva. "They have come to slay us!"

4
THE GORBUS GRAFT

SWIFTLY, DARVA THE SHADOW took the Circlet of Dron from Janson's grasp, placed it in her bag, and threw dirt on the fire to extinguish it. Then Janson was following her through the low, narrow opening and emerging from the hovel into the murky illumination of the forest. For a moment they paused and listened. Again they heard the sounds of distant voices, perhaps a few hundred yards distant but getting closer fast.

"Come," said Darva. "I know of a secret entrance to the caves not far from here. If we move quickly and carefully, we can make it there without Vrok and his men discovering us."

Not far from Darva's hovel they picked up a trail upon which many bare feet had trodden.

"Gorbuses?" asked Janson.

Darva nodded. "They use this trail when they wish to leave the Forest of Death."

"You mean when they seek victims from the nearby villages." Janson frowned. "Victims they wish to bring back to the Charnel Caves to devour. Does that not bother you, Darva?" A cold shiver ran down his spine to think that his companion and her people considered the predatory Gorbuses to be sacred beings who must be protected.

"We must all eat," was Darva's only reply.

Eventually the trail down which they passed met a little stream, along which it ran for some distance before Darva stopped. On the opposite bank rose a steep rocky slope that ascended to an even steeper forested hill, far to the left of which he could see the bare walls of precipitous cliffs.

"This way," commanded Darva. "Do exactly as I do and our pursuers will be unable to follow our spoor."

Carefully, the high priestess of the Ul-rahn stepped from the trail and out onto the adjoining rocks. There she sat down and brushed off the dirt and detritus from the soles of her moccasins into the adjacent stream. Then she stood and waited on an adjoining rock while Janson brushed off his own feet. They proceeded to walk along the rocks that ran beside the stream, the bed of which began to curve to the left while descending rather steeply into a shaded nook that was devoid of almost all light. Here Darva took Janson's hand, and together they stepped from the rocks into the bitter cold water.

Janson could see virtually nothing, but Darva seemed to know the way, and before long they had crossed the stream and were climbing up onto a shallow bank. Darva told Janson to stand still, and presently he felt her warm hands rubbing an ointment over his chest, back, arms, and legs.

"To us it has little smell," she said, "but to the Gorbuses it obscures the scent spoor of gilaks. Now apply the ointment to myself."

"Don't worry," said Janson, accepting the gourd that was offered him, "I shall be the perfect gentleman," and then in the darkness he proceeded to do as she bade.

"What is a 'gentleman,' Jan-son Grid-lee?" she asked.

He thought for a moment. "Do you know Vrok?"

"Of course I do."

"Well, I imagine it's the opposite of him in this same situation."

"I think I understand." Darva paused. "Is every man of Sari a 'perfect gentleman'?"

Janson laughed. "I would never claim that. But on the whole we are a good people. As for me, let's just say my mother and father raised me right."

"I should like to meet your mother and father."

The man grinned. "Don't you think that's a little too soon, Darva? Why, we only just met."

Invisible in the murk of the little hollow in which they stood, a tiny fist struck Janson hard in the arm.

"Hey, what was *that* for?" Janson exclaimed, rubbing his sore arm.

"A 'perfect gentleman' does not mock the Ul-vana," pronounced Darva in a severe tone, but a glint of soft light reflecting from the rippling stream revealed the trace of a smile on the woman's lips. "You have used up all the ointment. Give me the gourd and let us go."

Again Darva took Janson's hand and led him through the darkness. Soon the sounds of their footfalls and breaths echoed hollowly around them, and Janson knew they had entered an opening in the wall of the steep rocky bank and passed into a closely confining tunnel.

"I can see nothing," whispered Janson.

"Quiet. My father taught me the route, but it was long ago and I must concentrate."

By sense of touch alone, Darva led them down the twists and turns of the stygian passageway as it ran deeper into the labyrinth of the Charnel Caves. As they passed deeper and deeper into the maze of suffocating tunnels, Janson began to feel disconnected from reality, as if he had passed into a timeless, unending nightmare. As the feeling intensified, so too did his respect for his guide, who evidenced no sign of fear or hesitation, at least that he could detect as they walked blindly on into the unknown. Soon he began to feel that he might go mad, so that he was relieved, even knowing what it portended, when a flickering yellow light refracted along the irregular granite walls of a cross passage.

As they moved forward through the intersection of shafts, Janson caught a brief glimpse down the way of three ghoulish, pale-skinned figures sitting around a fire and tearing meat with their large fangs from what might have been human shin bones. Darva quickened her pace, and soon they left the ghastly trio far behind as they probed deeper still into the spectral warren.

Once they caught sight of a lone hunchbacked figure moving away from them down a narrow shaft. Eerily, a dull radiance surrounded the creature's form. After they had passed beyond earshot of the creature, Janson stopped his guide and asked, "Was that a Gorbus?"

"Yes," replied Darva the Shadow. "Occasionally, the rare Gorbus bears such a cloud of light. Such a Gorbus is less dangerous than the others. Never has one been known to kill a gilak. Such Gorbuses survive by catching and eating rats and small reptiles, but they are very uncommon."

"I wonder . . ."

"What is it?"

"My friend who confronted the masters of Koh-ra-vor . . . She said the masters, as part of their evil scheme, had created a caste system in the afterlife. Each caste glowed more radiant than the next as they became more good-hearted. And the purest of heart . . . well . . ."

"What?"

"Well, the masters found them more palatable and nutritious, and consumed them to gain more power. I fear that I may actually have guessed correctly. It seems the Gorbuses were indeed an attempt by the masters of Koh-ra-vor to enact their hideous scheme in Pellucidar, to establish a foothold in our world. But the masters have been defeated. Now the remaining Gorbuses are on their own." Janson paused, considering the spiritual upheaval his words must be causing in the heart and mind of the high priestess of the Ul-rahn. "Darva, I'm sorry. I don't mean to shatter your faith. But the truth is always better than a lie. The Gorbuses are not sacred beings. They were but unfortunate pawns in the defunct machinations of a hideous race that preyed upon mortals like us. Now that the masters have been defeated, the Gorbuses have no purpose. They are but vestiges of the masters' erstwhile scheme."

When the woman did not reply, he said, "Darva, tell me what you are thinking."

"What would you have me say, Jan-son Grid-lee? That I am happy to discover that everything I have been taught is a lie."

Instantly, Janson regretted having said anything. What had he been thinking, to thus destroy the worldview of this proud Stone Age priestess?

"I take it all back," he said. "It was just an idea. I am probably wrong."

"No. You cannot take it back. The Ul-vana does not look away from the truth merely because it is difficult or uncomfortable. You have given me much to think about, Jan-son Grid-lee. Now let us go."

They had traveled not much farther when they saw the flickering of torchlight ahead.

"Is there another way?" he whispered in the darkness.

"No, we must travel forward to reach the tomb of Dron."

"Let me go first then."

When he stepped ahead of the woman, she placed her hand on his shoulder. "Take this." She handed him one of her obsidian knives, which glistened in the faint torchlight from ahead. Darva drew her remaining blade and they padded forward down the stone corridor as stealthily as they were able.

Before long there came into view the source of the light. A male Gorbus, his back turned to them, was crouching in a natural recess nestled in one side of the passageway. In one hand he held a torch, and with the other he appeared to be foraging a species of bluish fungus growing on the surface of the rock. This he was collecting in a woven bag embroidered with the sigil of a serpent's eye.

Darva clutched Janson's arm and pointed at the bag. He turned back and nodded to her, for he recognized it as well: it was the satchel of Vrok the Viper. Something was rotten in the state of Denmark, he thought—very, very rotten.

He pantomimed to the woman what he planned to do,

and she nodded and held up her knife to indicate that she understood. Janson returned the blade he had been given to Darva, for he did not anticipate needing the weapon for what he intended to do, nor did he want it snatched from his belt and turned against him when he did it.

They proceeded to inch forward, getting as close as they could to the oblivious Gorbus without alerting him. Then Janson pounced on his target.

The Gorbus let loose a piteous screech when a steely, crooked arm shot out and wrapped itself around his neck and secured him in a headlock. The hideous, misshapen thing writhed and thrashed, dropping his torch as he attempted to squirm out of Janson's viselike grip, but he ceased struggling when he eyed the sharp point of Darva's gleaming blade thrust up against his belly. Janson thrust the abhorrent creature, which reeked of an array of malodorous effluvia the sources of which were better not to imagine, up against the rocky wall of the tunnel, while Darva made short work of tying the Gorbus' arms behind his back with leather cords she kept in her medicinal pouch.

Done with their task, they commenced the interrogation of their prisoner.

"Where did you get this, Gorbus?" Darva held up the bag the creature had been carrying before its hideous pink-irised eyes. In the fury of her anger, she no longer seemed to hold the Gorbus and its kind in reverence. "Tell me what you were doing with it!" she cried. In her other hand she held her glittering blade up to the creature's throat.

"It was given to me!" pleaded the Gorbus. "I did not steal it. I swear!"

"Who gave it to you?"

"The one called Vrok. He wished me to gather the blue fungus."

"Why did he want the fungus?" asked Darva the Shadow.

"Because it makes one dream a waking dream if eaten . . . or if mixed into what one drinks."

Janson pulled the woman gently back from their prisoner. "Well, now we know the source of Vrok's power. It is nothing but a trick. He has no power. He simply poisons the bodies and minds of his subjects with this fungus so that in their delirium they see what they wish to see, or what they fear to see most. You were right all along, Darva. Vrok is nothing but a charlatan."

He turned back to the Gorbus. "Tell me . . . Wait, what is your name, by the way?"

"I am Plog."

"Well, Plog, tell me. What does Vrok give you in return for bringing him the fungus? If you answer truthfully and you do not attempt to escape or attack us, I swear we shall not harm you."

"He made me promise never to say. He said he would kill me if I did."

Here Darva made a little gasp, for though she was clearly seeing the light as regarded the base nature of the Gorbuses, old habits die hard. Some part of her must have still regarded the creatures as sacred, untouchable beings and been shocked that even one of her tribe as corrupt as Vrok would consider threatening a Gorbus with death.

"Would you rather that you died now? Or would you instead like to answer my question?" Janson did not intend to murder the Gorbus, for he could never bring himself to kill a sentient being—no matter how vile—in cold blood, but it would not burn his conscience too severely if Plog happened to misconstrue his hypothetical questions as a threat.

Plog thought for a moment, and then the floodgates opened. "It is not my fault!" cried the pitiful creature. "Do not kill me! I am but a hungry Gorbus, and I and my kind must eat! Eating is all that distracts our minds from the horrible things we did in that other life. Can you blame us? The memories from that other place torment us! Vrok has been sending out his men to the villages and bringing us the gilaks they capture in exchange for the blue fungus. Please do not kill me! Please!"

Darva's beautiful features twisted in disgust and revulsion at hearing a sacred Gorbus, a member of a race she had considered divine beings for her entire life, confess to such degraded crimes for the most debased of motivations. Then her expression softened as reason took hold of her once again and she realized the implications of what the creature was saying.

"Are they still alive?" she asked. "Have you slain and consumed all the captives Vrok has brought to you?"

"Some have already been eaten," admitted Plog, "for you cannot blame us for being hungry. But many are still alive. We have gathered them in a chamber near the lower entrance to the caves, to eat as we feel hungry."

"We must rescue them, Darva," said Janson. "And in doing so, we shall expose Vrok's crimes to your people, who will welcome back their Ul-vana with open arms."

The gray eyes of Darva the Shadow sparkled with hope in the torchlight, but also in them was a look of fierce determination. She picked up the torch from where it had lain burning upon the cavern floor.

"Yes," she said. "But there is something else we must do first."

5

THE VAKRAHN'S TOMB

DARVA, WHAT ARE THESE?" Janson Gridley had stopped
to examine a number of dried-up spherical husks lying
in a wide crevice that opened along one side of the corridor down which they trod. When he prodded one of the
things with his toe, it rolled over and he saw what looked like
a tiny flattened arm and five-fingered hand wrapped around
the facing surface of the little ball.

"It is a *grokas*," she said. "Though I have never before seen
one. Do not touch it."

"A grokas?"

"My father said they appear out of the thin air in a little
ripple of light, but only here in the caves. They are the larvae
of the Gorbuses."

"Well, I'll be!" exclaimed Janson. "I've been wondering
how they reproduced."

"No longer do the grokases come," said Plog. "It has been
many, many sleeps since I have seen one drop out of the air.
The ones here are dead. They will never grow into Gorbuses."

"It is because of your friend," said Darva, "that the grokases
have ceased to appear, is it not?"

"I believe so." Janson whistled. "I guess when she pulled
the plug on the masters of Koh-ra-vor, the whole apparatus
of their machinery just broke down. It all just came to a dead
stop. Including the influx of the Gorbuses to Pellucidar."

"I do not understand all of your words, Jan-son Grid-lee,"

said the high priestess of the Ul-rahn, "but I do understand the essence of what you say."

"The Ul-vana is wise," said Janson. And then, to make sure she understood he was not mocking her, he added, truthfully, "And in many ways wiser than I shall ever be."

"Perhaps," said Darva. "But perhaps not. We shall soon see if your legacy will be greater than mine. Let us continue."

Janson still had no idea what the woman had in mind. She had refused to answer his questions as to her plans, saying only that he would soon understand.

They left behind the grokases and continued on. Presently the tunnel opened into a large chamber, in the back wall of which grinned a great serpent's skull formed out of a clever arrangement of sizable rocks. Darva led Janson to stand directly before the serpent's gaping maw.

"The tomb of Dron the Deathless," she announced solemnly.

"Darva," said Janson, "why was Dron called the Deathless if here lie his mortal remains?"

"He was the first Vakrahn. The first gilak to travel to Koh-ra-vor, the Land Beyond the Living, and to return to live again in Pellucidar. Rare is it to become a Vakrahn. Only one in a thousand generations crosses the barrier to Koh-ra-vor and returns to tell the tale. Only one such as you, Jan-son Grid-lee."

Suddenly understanding blossomed in Janson's mind. After all, the term Vakrahn translated loosely to Deathslayer. One Who Slays Death. "You think I am a Vakrahn, because I returned from the dead."

"No," said Darva. "You are not a Vakrahn. After the time of Dron, the ala-oh of a Vakrahn comes only after surviving the test."

"I do not know of what test you speak," said Janson, "nor am I familiar with the meaning of the word 'ala-oh.'"

The woman wedged the butt of her burning torch into a

pile of rocks leaning against the cavern wall, then reached into her pouch and removed the Circlet of Dron. "Once," she said, "when the magic still lay upon it, I placed the circlet upon my head while alone in my hut and fell into a deep sleep. It was then that I had a dream. A dream that felt as real as I feel now speaking with you, and perhaps even more real. I was flying like a thipdar in a darkened sky. I felt as if I might actually have *been* a thipdar, or perhaps some smaller winged creature. My body did not feel like that of a gilak's. In any case, I flew on and on through that darkened sky, until at last the sky began to lighten. Slowly there formed before me the very edge of the world, although it was not curved like the land with which we are familiar when we see it in the distance." She formed a concave arc with her hands. "No, it was curved like this." Now she made a convex arc with her hands. "Then came a sight that will forever be seared upon my inner eye, for the burning orb of Pellucidar's sun crested the edge of the world and shone upon me in all its glory. This is what is meant by ala-oh." Her eyes had grown moist as she spoke and she wiped away the forming tears. "It was then that I realized I was flying above the Dead World, looking down upon Pellucidar below, although truly it was as if Pellucidar was in the sky, and the Dead World was below me. I had never before, and have never since, seen such a sight. It was there the dream ended and I awoke once again in my hut."

Janson stood there in the cavern, astounded, his mouth agape. How could this savage priestess of the Ul-rahn—who knew nothing of the science of astrometry, who had never before flown in an aircraft or traveled to the outer crust, or even gone beyond the Forest of Death, let alone to the faraway Land of Awful Shadow above which hung Pellucidar's pendent moon—how could she describe in such exquisite detail the experience of the dawning of the sun above a celestial sphere?

"Anyway," said Darva, "that is what I meant when I compared the coming of a Deathslayer to the ala-oh. It is like the coming of the sun to a world shrouded in darkness: that is the coming of the Vakrahn."

"And what of the test, Darva?"

"That is for you to decide. Those who travel to Koh-ra-vor do not truly come back to the living unless they undergo the test. I have sensed it in you, Jan-son Grid-lee. You are like this gourd." She pulled the vessel that had contained the ointment from her pouch, uncorked its stem, and held it upside down. "Empty. There is nothing inside. If you wish to fill the vessel that is your spirit, you must enter the tomb of the Deathless One and face the Mistress Who Sleeps. If you survive the test and emerge alive, you will be the Vakrahn."

Janson gazed into the Cimmerian maw of the great rock serpent that marked the entrance to Dron's tomb. "The Mistress Who Sleeps. You mean the monster whose gaze turns you to stone?"

"You do not have to undertake the test," said the high priestess of the Ul-rahn. "But then I shall mourn for you, for you will never be at peace, and . . . " A veil of deep sadness fell over Darva's face. "And like the Ul-vana, you will forever be alone."

"Well, we can't have that," said Janson. "Would you loan me one of your knives again? I have a feeling I might need it."

Darva bent down and picked up a stick from a pile of unlit torches stacked to one side of the tomb. This she lit with the torch she had taken from Plog and handed it to Janson. "You may bring this so that you may see, but you must not bring a weapon. All else that you need you will find within yourself and inside the tomb."

"I had a feeling you'd say something of the sort, but I had to ask, right?" Janson eyed their Gorbus captive. "Will you be able to handle him?"

For reply, she fingered the hilts of her obsidian blades in their snakeskin sheaths.

"Well, there's no point in putting this off," said Janson.

He turned to crawl down into the mouth of the stone serpent but stopped when he felt a tiny hand on his shoulder.

He half turned, and Darva stood up on her tiptoes and kissed his cheek.

"For courage, Jan-son Grid-lee," said Darva the Shadow. Then she stepped back and rested her hands on the hilts of her knives as if to stand vigil over the tomb.

Janson crouched down and crawled over the stone fangs into the dark maw of the serpent.

Once inside the mouth of stone, he found himself hunched upon the surface of a sharply sloping shaft. For a moment he rested there, his knees bent, his feet and one outstretched arm the only things keeping him from sliding down the sheer incline to whatever awaited him below.

He experienced the unsettling sensation that he had been swallowed by the monstrous stone snake and was about to pass down its gullet, on his way to being slowly digested.

Well, he thought, I am committed at this point; there is nothing for it but to go all the way down. And so he released his hold upon the smooth stone surface and felt the cool clammy air of the shaft rush past him as he slid rapidly downward on his hindquarters.

It seemed as if he fell a long time, but then suddenly he was tumbling head over heels onto a hard stone floor. Flung forward by momentum, he dropped the torch—which had somehow remained lit during his wild ride down the shaft—and he saw it go flying. When he finally stopped, he stood up and brushed himself off, checking for injuries but finding only minor bruises and scrapes. Without further delay, he picked up the torch and began examining his surroundings.

He was in a large chamber some dozen yards across, so cavernous in height that its ceiling was lost somewhere in the shadows far above. An elongated mound of carefully stacked rocks lay before the center of the wall that rose before him.

Upon a large flat stone on top of the mound rested a massive axe hewn out of a single hunk of polished black obsidian. Alongside the axe was a large vicious-looking serrated knife with a long triangular blade made of the same dark volcanic glass. He could only be looking upon the final resting place of Dron the Deathless.

To his right he spied a series of recesses in the rocky face of the wall, a tumble of debris piled on the floor beneath a larger niche nested in the center of the others. Standing upright in the majority of the niches were what appeared to be rows of large stone tablets like the one he had seen in Darva's hovel. A wide crack in the floor ran across the chamber and up the wall to the base of the central recess, as if some great geological upheaval had once shaken the chamber and ruptured the rocky floor, tearing out part of the wall and collapsing the bottom of the largest niche.

Something shiny lay partially hidden beneath the pile of rubble on the ground, glinting in the torchlight. Janson crossed the chamber and kneeled beside the mass of broken rock, whereupon he began casting off debris with his free hand, while he held the torch in the other, to uncover whatever was reflecting underneath. Soon his efforts were rewarded when a boxlike form began to take shape. His pulse quickening with excitement at his discovery, he wedged the torch between two stone tablets in one of the niches so that he could excavate with both hands. Before long he had cleared the rubble completely away to reveal a perfect metallic cube, seemingly made of the same silvery material as that of the Circlet of Dron. The cube lay akilter on the rubble, as if it had fallen from where it had once rested in the larger niche and been buried by the collapsing rock.

He wrapped his arms around the box, expecting his burden to be heavy, but to his surprise he lifted up the cube easily, as if it were made of cardboard instead of gleaming metal. Now that the box was clear of the debris, he could see that one side bore what appeared to be several switches, each in the form of an oblong metal loop attached to a short digit affixed to a joint embedded in the face of the cube.

He set down the box on a clean, level area of the floor and examined it. Three of the switches were flipped up where he had noted that a rock had lain under them, as if forced into that position when the box had fallen from the shelf above. Now that he looked closer, he could see several tiny Mahar hieroglyphs running vertically under each of the switches. Well versed in the language of the former reptilian overlords of Pellucidar, having studied under Abner Perry and even undertaken a solitary expedition to plumb the archives at the Mahar city of Thotra, he recognized the glyphs as numbers.

He stood up and pulled from the wall niches first one tablet, and then another and yet another. Etched upon each tablet were column after column of the hieroglyphic symbols of the Mahars. Then it dawned on him that a looped switch, such as each of those found on the box, would be a perfect fit for a Maharan claw. Of course, the Mahars, having foreclaws positioned at the anterior bends of their wings, would have great difficulty in operating machinery of any kind. But that they had indeed occasionally built certain types of machines and other apparatus was evidenced in the excavations at the abandoned Mahar cities of Phutra and Kazra, which had been carried out under Abner Perry's supervision after he and David Innes had led the great gilak revolt against their reptilian masters in the region surrounding Sari.

The marvel, of course, was that flying reptiles could build any machines at all, but then again, for eons untold they had exercised total dominion over the region's gilaks and Sagoths—the latter being an intelligent species of gorilloids—both being primates whose dexterous hands and fingers were quite useful for such purposes. What need was there for the Mahars to dirty their claws at manual labor while their slaves could do it for them? The Mahars could concentrate their vast intellects on science and invention while they simply exerted their will over these "inferior" species to build what they wanted, an act facilitated by the fact that the intelligent reptiles could communicate via sign language with their Sagoth servants, though there was debate over whether the Mahars truly considered gilaks to be mindless chattel, as they had claimed, for had they not held an uneasy truce with the Mezop gilaks for countless generations? And if the Mahars had held a truce and communicated with the Mezops, it followed that they must have known the gilaks were sentient beings capable of intelligent thought.

Looking down at the strange apparatus sitting where he had placed it beside the pile of rubble, and then at the great crack in the cavern's floor, Janson recalled something Darva had told him. She had said that the Circlet of Dron had stopped summoning the spirits at the time of a great earthquake. Again, his heart beat faster, and his mind raced.

What if he had been wrong? What if it was not the defeat of the "masters of Koh-ra-vor," as he had put it to Darva, that had caused the circlet to stop "summoning the spirits," but instead it was the earthquake that had struck the area of the Forest of Death at around approximately the same time? Was there a correlation between the apparatus and the Circlet of Dron? Were they both two parts of the same machinery?

He kneeled beside the apparatus and took a deep breath. Then he flipped down the three switches whose position had presumably been altered when the box had fallen from the niche upon which it had once rested.

Instantly the box began to hum with a low but discernible frequency. The machine was operable! And apparently it *had* been switched off when it had fallen from its shelf during the earthquake!

Suddenly the cavern grew dim as the torch began to gutter.

Janson rose slowly to his feet. He had felt a waft of cool air blow over the nape of his neck. At the same time, an unnerving, spine-tingling feeling, as if someone or some*thing* was watching him from behind, shivered though his entire frame.

Slowly, ever so slowly, he turned. As he did so, he mentally cursed himself. He had become so overcome with excitement over his discovery of the apparatus that, despite Darva's dire warnings about the Mistress Who Sleeps, he had not taken the time to fully examine the cavern.

When his gaze at last fully turned, he saw a dark, hulking form crouching in a shadowy hollow set within the far cave wall. Two large reptilian eyes peered out from the darkened area, glowing orange in the torchlight. Janson tried to turn his gaze from those terrible mesmerizing orbs, but they seemed to penetrate his very soul and hold him fast.

The long, dark triangular patch of blackness surrounding those awful, captivating eyes—which he could only surmise was the thing's head—commenced to move slowly back and forth. He began to forget even who he was. What was his name? Why had he come here? All that mattered were those eyes. Those terrible, beautiful reptilian eyes.

He hardly noticed when he took his first step forward. Again he stepped. As the eyes grew larger, closer, they grew more powerful, more entrancing.

The hum of the machine behind him only made him feel more somnolent.

The machine . . . it was important for some reason. No . . . it was important to . . . to some*one*. Darva . . . Darva the Shadow . . . He knew her from a dreamworld . . . from some other place that was not those eyes . . . those irresistible eyes . . . It was Darva who had warned him . . . warned him of . . . the Mistress Who Sleeps . . . who would turn him to stone . . .

It was a *Mahar* . . . he was in the trance of a Mahar queen! A very ancient one . . . a Mahar who had doubtless resided in the cavern for eons . . . hibernating . . . preying on the stray Gorbus when it needed sustenance . . . watching over the machine that had let the masters of the afterworld penetrate the world of Pellucidar . . . waiting for . . . for what?

It did not matter. He was about to die beneath the monster's razor-sharp teeth!

With the greatest effort of his life, he commanded himself to look away . . . to turn his gaze from those hypnotic eyes . . .

He could not! Again he stepped forward and the eyes became yet more powerful . . . more hideous . . . more beautiful . . .

He forced himself to reach out with his right hand. It touched something . . . something cold and smooth like glass. His fingers wrapped around it—it was the haft of the axe of Dron!

The realization stirred something deep inside him, something far deeper in his soul than those terrible eyes could ever penetrate. He had defeated death once before . . . and in the name of Dron he would slay death again!

He lashed out with the axe, swinging it with terrific fury. A horrendous screeching filled his ears. Again he swung, and again. No longer was he Janson Gridley. No longer the man from Sari or the man from the outer world.

The frightful screeching continued, accompanied by the frantic flapping of great wings. He felt a cold wetness splatter his face, and yet still he swung on with the axe, fighting, ever fighting against she who sought to petrify his soul. Even after the screeching had ceased, and the whooshing of the great wings grew silent, he continued to swing his axe.

She could not win . . . she would never defeat him . . . for he was the Vakrahn—the Deathslayer.

6
THE VIPER'S REWARD

WHEN JANSON GRIDLEY and Darva the Shadow emerged from the lower cliffside entrance to the Charnel Caves, their captive Plog in tow, they found Vrok the Viper and his men waiting to confront them.

"There they are!" cried Vrok. "See it with your own eyes. They have desecrated the sacred caves and are abusing this poor Gorbus! They must die instantly!"

It was then that Janson noticed that Vrok and his men were not alone. Behind them stood Kakar the Bold along with a large group of his loyal warriors. When Vrok raised his spear, ready to hurl it at Janson's breast, Kakar struck it down with his own spear.

The chief shook in anger and indignation. "How dare you? You will die for that, Kakar, along with these two blasphemers!"

"It seems to me, Vrok," said Kakar, "that you are too eager to kill these two before we have had a chance to speak with them." Then he turned to Darva as she and Janson approached, and said, "I am thinking you have a story to tell, Ul-vana."

"Right you are, Kakar," said Darva the Shadow. "Or, I should say, Plog has a story for you, as well as for all those present who can hear his words. Speak, Plog, and ensure that you tell the truth." She fingered the hilts of her obsidian blades, and the Gorbus proceeded to confess all that he knew of Vrok's nefarious scheme.

"Lies!" exclaimed Vrok. "To think that I would round up

270

gilaks from the local villages and feed them to the sacred Gorbuses. It is absurd. You can prove nothing, for it is all lies!"

"Is this not your bag?" Darva tossed the satchel of fungus at Vrok's feet. "Does it not bear your sigil and contain the fungus that you have used to poison our people's minds and deceive them?"

Vrok folded his arms over his chest in a gesture of defiance. "Anyone can weave a sigil onto a bag. It does not belong to me."

Janson crossed the distance that stood between him and Kakar the Bold, and proceeded to whisper into the warrior's ear. Kakar nodded and then called over his fiercest brave, instructing him to ensure that Vrok would not move from the spot until he returned. Then he ordered half of his band of men to accompany him into the Charnel Caves.

A short time later, Kakar and his warriors emerged from the caves, followed by a large group of men, women, and children. The latter were all smiling and laughing in their exuberance, stretching out their arms after their long confinement and soaking up the brilliant light of Pellucidar's eternal noonday sun where it shone down through the rare opening in the forest along the cliff face.

"I—I—I can explain," sputtered Vrok the Viper as Kakar strode up to him. "Kakar, my old friend, I have a great reward waiting for you back at the village. Beyond anything you can imagine. You will be rich, rich and powerful, and all in the village will bow down to you and—"

"That is my reward for you, Vrok the Viper," said Kakar the Bold as he pulled out the spear he had just thrust into the chest of the dying man. The false chief collapsed at the feet of the warrior, and that was the last act in the life of Vrok.

Vrok's men, who had been standing nearby their leader, looked at one another sheepishly, and then dispersed and melted into the large group of warriors under Kakar's command.

While all this was transpiring, the group of prisoners who had been freed from the Charnel Caves approached and began mingling among the gathering of the Ul-rahn. Most of them were from nearby villages and had never before encountered the tribe of their liberators, for few villagers ever dare to visit the Forest of Death, and hence few have even heard of the Ul-rahn. Now, however, the newly freed were eager to express their gratitude and make friends with their saviors, for only moments before they had all believed their lives had been about to end torturously beneath the cruel fangs of the dreaded Gorbuses.

Suddenly Darva let loose a squeal of joy and ran forward into the crowd, where she proceeded to embrace a tall, ruggedly handsome bearded warrior. A few moments later, she brought the warrior over to Janson and made introductions.

"Jan-son Grid-lee, this is Koorva, my father!" she exclaimed. "He was not eaten by a tarag, after all, nor was he slain by Vrok, although he did intend for my father to die. He gave him to the Gorbuses, along with those his men had abducted from the other villages." Darva took hold of Janson's hand. "Father, this is Jan-son Grid-lee. He is the Vakrahn."

For a moment, Koorva, chief and Ul-volok of the Ul-rahn, regarded Janson gravely. But then his grim countenance disappeared as a hearty smile broke out upon his face. He embraced Janson warmly, thanking him for saving his life and standing by his daughter when all had turned against her. From now on, Koorva said, the new Vakrahn would always be a welcome member of the Ul-rahn.

They spoke for some time before at last Koorva left to join his warriors and learn of all that had transpired in the village while he had been absent.

When they were alone, Darva reached into the pouch at her side and withdrew the Circlet of Dron.

"Once more it hums in resonance with the spirits," she said. "It began doing so while you were in the tomb of Dron. And yet . . ."

"And yet what?" asked Janson.

"I am not sure I am ready to use it again. There is much I do not understand."

For a long moment the woman grew silent. Then she said, "Will you leave now? Now that you have found your missing people?"

Janson smiled. "You once told me that no one from outside this forest who meets the Ul-rahn lives to wag his tongue."

"Hmmm." The Ul-vana rubbed her chin, her gray eyes searching the forest canopy high above, as if contemplating her options. "Perhaps, if you stayed, I would not have to cut out your tongue." Then Darva the Shadow leaned up on her tiptoes and kissed him on the cheek.

He watched, smiling, as the high priestess of the Ul-rahn walked away, her shapely figure swaying in the distance, and went to be with her father.

For a great while he stood there in the dark wood, staring up into the soaring trees as he contemplated the future. Then he turned to rejoin the others.

ABOUT THE AUTHORS

KORAK™
AT THE EARTH'S CORE™

A lifelong Edgar Rice Burroughs reader, WIN SCOTT ECKERT is the author of the ERB Universe novel *Tarzan: Battle for Pellucidar*. He is also the authorized legacy author of science fiction Grand Master Philip José Farmer's Patricia Wildman series (*The Evil in Pemberley House, The Scarlet Jaguar*), as well as the coauthor with Farmer of the fourth volume in the Secrets of the Nine series, the Doc Caliban novel *The Monster on Hold*. His other professional credits include authorized tales of Zorro, the Phantom, Honey West, the Avenger, the Lone Ranger, and the Green Hornet, as well as numerous other stories featuring Phileas Fogg, the Scarlet Pimpernel, the Domino Lady, and Sherlock Holmes, among others. He lives in Colorado with his wife and a bevy of four-legged family members.

PELLUCIDAR®
DAWN OF THE DEATHSLAYER™

CHRISTOPHER PAUL CAREY is the author of several books, including the ERB Universe novel *Victory Harben: Fires of Halos*; *Swords Against the Moon Men*, an authorized sequel to Edgar Rice Burroughs' *The Moon Maid*; *Exiles of Kho*; *The Song of Kwasin* (with Philip José Farmer); *Hadon, King of Opar*; and *Blood of Ancient Opar*. He has also written comic books featuring Burroughs' characters such as Tarzan, Dejah Thoris, Carson of Venus, Jason Gridley, and Gretchen von Harben. Carey is Vice President of Publishing and creative director of the ERB Universe at Edgar Rice Burroughs, Inc., the company founded by Mr. Burroughs in 1923. He lives in Southern California.

Edgar Rice Burroughs: Master of Adventure

The creator of the immortal characters Tarzan of the Apes and John Carter of Mars, EDGAR RICE BURROUGHS is one of the world's most popular authors. Mr. Burroughs' timeless tales of heroes and heroines transport readers from the jungles of Africa and the dead sea bottoms of Barsoom to the miles-high forests of Amtor and the savage inner world of Pellucidar, and even to alien civilizations beyond the farthest star. Mr. Burroughs' books are estimated to have sold hundreds of millions of copies, and they have spawned 60 films and 250 television episodes.

About Edgar Rice Burroughs, Inc.

Founded in 1923 by Edgar Rice Burroughs, one of the first authors to incorporate himself, EDGAR RICE BURROUGHS, INC., holds numerous trademarks and the rights to all literary works of the author still protected by copyright, including stories of Tarzan of the Apes and John Carter of Mars. The company oversees authorized adaptations of his literary works in film, television, radio, publishing, theatrical stage productions, licensing, and merchandising. Edgar Rice Burroughs, Inc., continues to manage and license the vast archive of Mr. Burroughs' literary works, fictional characters, and corresponding artworks that has grown for over a century. The company is still owned by the Burroughs family and remains headquartered in Tarzana, California, the town named after the Tarzana Ranch Mr. Burroughs purchased there in 1919 that led to the town's future development.

In 2015, under the leadership of President James Sullos, the company relaunched its publishing division, which was founded by Mr. Burroughs in 1931. With the publication of new authorized editions of Mr. Burroughs' works and brand-new novels and stories by today's talented authors, the company continues its long tradition of bringing tales of wonder and imagination featuring the Master of Adventure's many iconic characters and exotic worlds to an eager reading public.

Visit **EdgarRiceBurroughs.com** for more information.

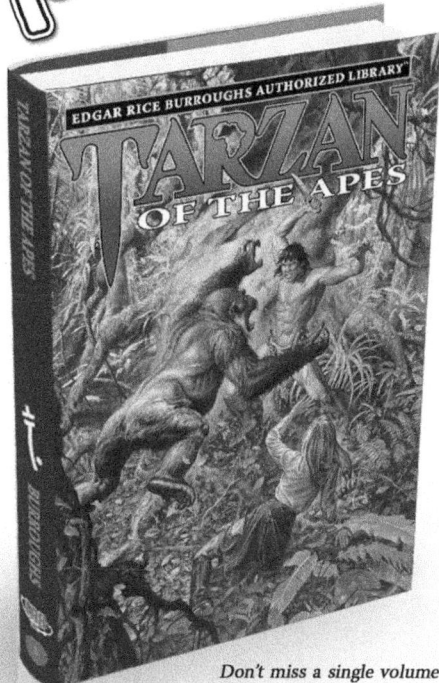

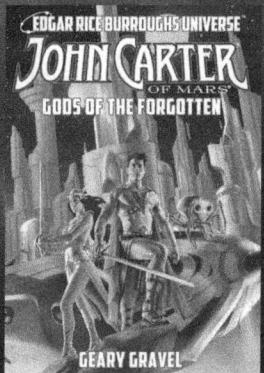

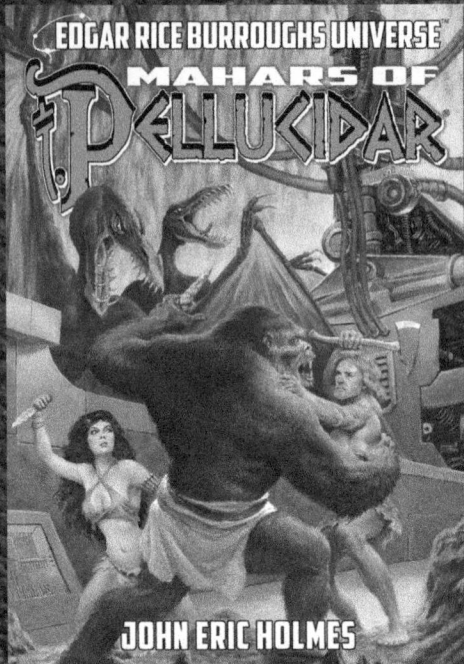

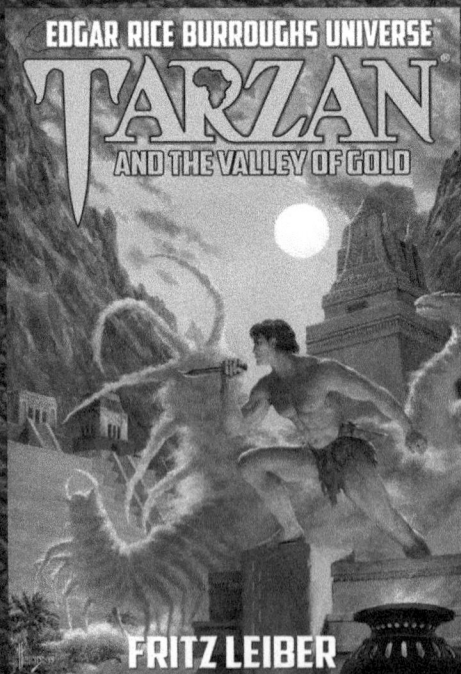

Edgar Rice Burroughs, Inc.

A whole universe of ERB collectibles, including books, T-shirts, DVDs, statues, puzzles, playing cards, dust jackets, art prints, and MORE!

Your one-stop destination for all things ERB!

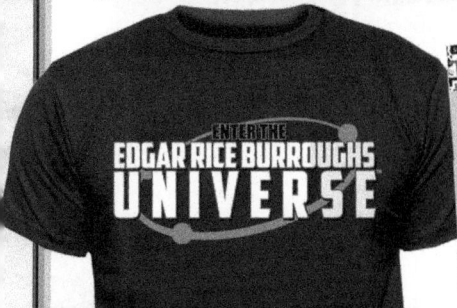

ERB INC.

VISIT US ONLINE AT ERBurroughs.com

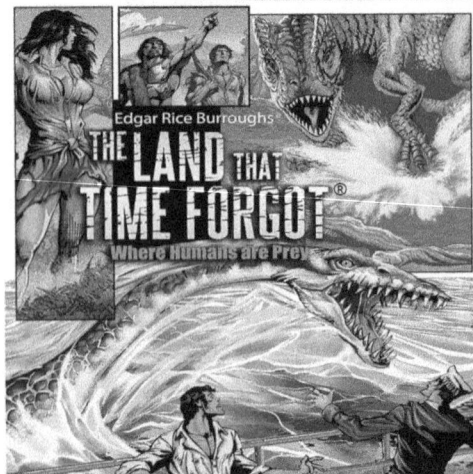